*He offered to give her
a few lessons in passion....*

Praise for the
Princess Brides Romances

Her Highness and the Highlander

"Warren continues her impeccably written Princess Brides trilogy with a thrillingly romantic, intrigue-infused tale of a blue-blooded royal who discovers both her one true love and the inner resources she never imagined she possessed while taking a walk on the wilder side of life."   —*Booklist*

"The second installment in this delightful series has just as much charm and joy as every other one of Warren's novels. A bit of *It Happened One Night* mixed with Scottish atmosphere and engaging characters (including an adorable dog) make this read irresistible."   —*Romantic Times*

"Tracy Anne Warren dazzled me once again. . . . She knows what romance readers enjoy."   —Romance Junkies

The Princess and the Peer

"The charm of the plotline, innocence of the heroine, and pride of the hero are all classic elements of the genre, and Warren uses them to her advantage."   —*Romantic Times*

"A fairy-tale-like story with characters full of personality, depth, and humanlike qualities . . . a fun adventure for all types of romantics."   —Once Upon a Romance

continued . . .

The Princess Brides Romances

The Princess and the Peer
Her Highness and the Highlander

TRACY ANNE WARREN

The Trouble with Princesses

A Princess Brides
Romance

A SIGNET SELECT BOOK

SIGNET SELECT
Published by the Penguin Group
Penguin Group (USA) LLC, 375 Hudson Street,
New York, New York 10014

USA | Canada | UK | Ireland | Australia | New Zealand | India | South Africa | China
penguin.com
A Penguin Random House Company

First published by Signet Select, an imprint of New American Library,
a division of Penguin Group (USA) LLC

First Printing, November 2013

ISBN 978-0-451-23971-6

Printed in the United States of America
10 9 8 7 6 5 4 3 2 1

For my little Christofur
Love you forever

ACKNOWLEDGMENTS

Sincerest thanks to my wonderful editor, Wendy McCurdy, for all her support and also to the team at Penguin and my publishers, Leslie Gelbman, Kara Welsh, and Clare Zion. Deepest appreciation to Helen Breitwieser for our years together and her unwavering belief in my writing and all that the future may hold. And finally to Les, who keeps me going even on the toughest days.

Chapter One

London, England
May 1820

Princess Ariadne of Nordenbourg—a nation that now existed only in memory and history books—took a sip of lemonade as she surveyed the crowded ballroom. Couples whirled past on the dance floor, the waltz being all the rage, especially since it had earned the approval of the powerful Almack's patronesses half a decade earlier.

But Ariadne wasn't interested in dancing—at least not unless it furthered her objectives. She had far more important matters on her mind. She was on the hunt, but not for the usual matrimonial prize that most unmarried young ladies pursued during the Season. No, Princess Ariadne prided herself on being anything but ordinary, and for her, the usual social expectations and restrictions held little sway.

After six fruitless Seasons she had decided to give up the notion of searching for a husband. What she sought now was a lover.

Since he would be her first, she needed to be selective. But not just any man would do. And thus, the reason for her hunt.

She remembered her friend Emma's reaction when she had confided her plans.

Her Highness, Archduchess Emmaline of Wiessenschloss, née Princess Emmaline of Rosewald, had tossed back her head on a rippling laugh, grinning at Ariadne from her place on the sofa in the Lyndhurst House family drawing room. "Arie, you say the most outrageous things. You must lie awake at night trying to dream up ways to surpass your last bon mot."

But when Ariadne did not join in the laughter, Emma's smile began to fade. "You are jesting, surely?"

Ariadne calmly gazed at her friend. "No. I am completely serious."

Emma's mouth fell open briefly before she snapped it closed again. She laid a hand against her bosom, still ample since the birth of her second child three months earlier. "But you cannot take a lover! You aren't even married."

"Nor do I plan to be."

"*Arie—*"

"Oh, don't act so shocked. It's not as if I've made a secret of my opinions on marriage and men over the years. I am four-and-twenty and only a few months from coming into my full inheritance. I've decided it's high time I enjoyed myself and found a suitable *cher ami*."

"Arie, as much as I sympathize with you about the freedom and rights of women, you cannot pursue this insanity. You will be ruined, utterly and forever. There will be no going back. The scandal alone will rock the very foundations of Society. You will end up becoming notorious."

"I should certainly hope so," she told her friend as she studied her elegantly manicured nails with a nonchalant air. "I not only plan to be notorious but the *most* notorious woman in all of the modern world. Madame de Pompadour will become but a mere cipher when compared to me."

"Madame de Pompadour was a common harlot who wormed her way into a king's bed and thus into a position of power. She wasn't royal. She was not born a princess like you."

Ariadne waved a dismissive hand. "Have you not yet learned, Emma, that it is not who we are born, but what we make of ourselves that matters most? Everyone remembers and admires Madame de Pompadour, regardless of her origins. I plan to be remembered as well."

Remembered as my family is now forgotten. Valued for who I am as an individual and not for what I can provide as yet one more lonely pawn in men's eternal games for wealth and power.

Emma frowned and leaned forward, reaching out a hand. "I do not mean to seem a prude nor a slave to social convention. I understand that you are an intelligent, strong-willed woman who does not wish to be forced into an unwanted relationship. It is only that I do not wish to see you hurt. I know you will find someone to love if only you will keep trying—a man who will respect and cherish you, someone you will want to marry."

Ariadne met her friend's blue-eyed gaze and resisted the urge to roll her eyes. They had been over this subject innumerable times before. But after so many fruitless years of waiting for her soul mate to arrive, Ariadne was done looking. Her perfect mate simply did not exist.

Of course, Ariadne knew that Emma had only the best of intentions, as did her other joyfully wedded friend Mercedes. The pair of them were forever extolling the virtues of wedded bliss. But they were the exceptions rather than the rule, and she had come to accept that a happy marriage was just not in the cards for her.

From what she had seen of the world, a happy marriage wasn't in the cards for most people. For every successful union there were dozens more that were nothing short of ritualized torment, miserable traps designed to enslave women and turn reasonable men into callous brutes.

She'd spent her entire childhood knowing precisely how bad marriage could be, as she witnessed her parents' constant fights and manipulations, each of them wounding the other to the quick with their never-ending schemes and myriad infidelities.

When she'd been sent to school in Scotland in her teen years, it had been a relief to be away from her family. Little did she know that she would never see her parents again, that war and death would put an end to their acrimony and bitterness once and for all.

As for her cousin Teodor, well, she had stopped dwelling on his betrayal long ago.

Emma wanted her to be sensible and continue trying to make a good match. But the only match she had any interest in making was the kind that promised heated passions and the illicit pleasures of the flesh.

And why should she not indulge? Just because she had given up on marriage didn't mean she couldn't enjoy men.

Soon she would be a young woman of independent means, free to go where she pleased and to dally with whomever took her fancy. All she needed to do was choose the man, then take care to be discreet.

She sipped more lemonade from her glass and resumed her perusal of the current selection of prospects scattered throughout the ballroom.

Which gentleman, she mused, *shall I invite to my bed?*

Just then a large, masculine shoulder garbed in stark black impeded her view of the dance floor. She looked up into a pair of piercing midnight blue eyes.

Vexingly familiar eyes.

Devil take it, what does he want?

She repressed a sigh.

Most women would have been quivering with delight to find themselves singled out by none other than Rupert Karl Octavian Whyte, Prince Regent of Rosewald, but Ariadne wasn't among them. High titles didn't impress her—not even kingly ones.

As for the man himself, she could not deny that he was physically appealing. He had the chiseled features, tall, leanly muscled body, and golden-haired countenance of a sun god—and the born arrogance to match. His entrance into a room alone had been known to induce swoons in young ladies, who would stare as if blinded by Apollo himself before falling into a dead faint at his feet.

For his part, he hardly seemed to notice them. He gave even the daughters of dukes and marquesses no more thought than he would a fly that had buzzed through a window and needed shooing.

But his aloof demeanor did nothing to discourage his admirers—quite the opposite, in fact. He was a monarch, after all, and monarchs were supposed to be beyond the reach of ordinary mortals. That, combined with his keen intellect, easy sophistication, and natural charisma, made Prince Rupert the most sought-after man in London. His mere presence inspired whispered speculation about which royal princess he would eventually take to wife and who his next mistress might be.

Rumor had it that George IV, newly ascended to England's throne after the death of his father in January, had been rather put out by all the attention lavished on "The Bachelor Prince," as Rupert was sometimes called.

Emma had relayed to her that a private meeting had been arranged between the two rulers, and although Emma had not been privy to all the details, Ariadne gathered that Rupert had thoroughly charmed King George. The two men had parted on the most amiable of terms, with firm promises of mutual support and alliance—and an invitation from George for Rupert to hunt on any royal lands to which he might take a fancy.

But as affable as Rupert could be when he chose, Ariadne knew him as Emma's arrogant, dictatorial, prideful older brother, who never seemed to tire of needling her.

He'd been even worse since Emma's marriage to Dominic Gregory, Earl of Lyndhurst, now the Archduke of Wiessenschloss. Ariadne had championed the match, going so far as to secretly conspire to thwart Rupert's plans to make a dynastic marriage for Emma. In this matter, Rupert had not prevailed, and he had laid all the blame squarely at Ariadne's door, where it had stayed ever since.

Really, it wasn't fair at all considering that Mercedes had been in on the plan as well, not to mention Nick and Emma herself.

But that was another one of the many annoying things about Rupert Whyte—he had a mind as sharp as a steel trap—he never forgot anything.

And he knew how to hold a grudge.

Then again, so did she.

"Princess Ariadne," Rupert said in a mellow baritone that was as golden as his hair. "Not dancing, I see."

"No. I decided to catch my breath for a set. My next partner will be along shortly."

Any second, if God has mercy.

Although for the life of her she couldn't remember whom she had agreed to partner, and she wasn't about to peek at her dance card to find out, not with Rupert looking on.

She sipped more lemonade. "And what brings you here to

the ballroom? I assumed you would be tucked away with our host, elbow-deep in billiards and brandy by now. Either that or debating politics and military strategies and deciding Rosewald's next move on the great global chessboard."

"I prefer to leave such weighty matters for the daylight hours. Evening ought to be devoted to more pleasurable pursuits. This is a party, after all."

"Well, only fancy, you are right. I had no idea you took notice of such trifling occasions as parties, Your Royal Highness."

His lips twitched slightly, but he didn't rise to her bait. Instead, his eyes narrowed with one of his serious looks. "Oh, you will find that I notice a great many things, Princess."

Then without warning, he smiled, his eyes crinkling at the corners in a way that would have caused more than one tittering debutante to reach for her smelling salts.

Despite her immunity to such provocation, an odd little shiver chased over Ariadne's skin.

She looked away.

"Actually," he continued, "I was looking for Emma. Do you know where she might have gone?"

"The last I saw she was dancing with Nick. Since they do not appear to be in the ballroom any longer, I presume they've wandered off somewhere together."

Rupert frowned.

As Ariadne well knew, Rupert might have come to accept the fact that his younger sister was now the married mother of two, but he never liked anything that reminded him how such a circumstance had come to pass. His mouth tightened whenever Nick and Emma were openly affectionate with each other, especially in public, and he positively loathed any comment that emphasized the fact that his sister and her English husband not only shared a bed but put it to active use.

For her part, Ariadne found Rupert's reactions highly amusing.

"They're probably outside in the garden, passionately embracing behind some well-placed shrubbery," she said. "The doctor stopped by the town house yesterday to check on Emma and baby Peter. He pronounced her in excellent health and said she can resume marital relations anytime she likes now."

Rupert frowned.

"I'm sure she'll be along soon," Ariadne said, "but if it's anything important, you might want to wait until morning when she'll be less—how should I say?—distracted."

Rupert's frown turned into a scowl. "And what would you know about such matters?"

"Not a great deal firsthand, at least not when it comes to garden trysts," she admitted, "but I do keep my ears and eyes open. Plus, I love to read. It's amazing the things a person can learn from a book."

"Yes, I know all about your unsuitable reading habits," he said in a severe tone. "Were it up to me you would be forbidden to open half the books you somehow manage to get your hands on. Such works do nothing but give you dangerous ideas."

"Oh, I come up with plenty of dangerous ideas all on my own. I don't need books for that."

His eyes flashed blue fire, then narrowed again. "On that point, we are agreed."

She hid a smile. "So what is it you wished to speak to Emma about? Last-minute details concerning your return home to Rosewald next week?"

Raising her glass, she took an idle sip.

"Actually, I was going to tell her that I've decided to stay in London a while longer, through the Season at least."

Ariadne choked on her lemonade. Her eyes streamed as a series of wracking coughs squeezed her lungs.

"Are you all right?" Reaching over, he laid a hand against her back and gave her a pair of bracing thumps.

She gasped again but nodded to signal that she would recover, even as she continued gasping for breath.

He offered her a silk handkerchief from his coat pocket. She accepted it gratefully and let him take the drink from her hand and set it aside.

She mopped her eyes and fought to collect herself, even as Rupert took hold of her elbow and steered her gently toward a private spot behind a nearby pillar.

"Better?" he inquired after a minute.

"Yes," she whispered, finally able to find her voice again.

A slow smile curved his mouth. "That is a relief. I would hate to have to inform my sister that one of her dearest friends had expired, and that I was at least in part to blame. Had I known the news of my continued residence in the city would elicit such a dramatic response I would have made certain to keep all beverages well out of reach."

"You caught me off guard is all. I breathed in when I ought to have swallowed."

"Again, I shall have to take better care in future."

She became aware of his hand on her arm, his fingers warm against the narrow area of exposed skin between her long gloves and her sleeve. She met his eyes, which were so deeply blue, and felt her pulse quicken.

A reaction to nearly choking to death, of course. She drew her arm away.

So, he is remaining in London for the next several weeks.

But what did such news really matter to her? Emma's brother he might be, but that did not mean she need spend a great deal of time in his company. She would find ways to make sure she did not. Her little project would ensure that she was otherwise occupied.

The music had stopped and guests now stood in small groups, talking while they waited for the next dance to begin. No one was looking at her and Rupert; her small incident had apparently gone unnoticed.

A tall man with coal black hair and a long, narrow face appeared at her side. He sketched a bow, then inclined his head toward Rupert before turning back to her. "Your Highness, the next dance is mine, I believe."

Ariadne smiled as she appraised him, racking her brain to remember his title. She was sure she would recall if he was a duke, considering how few of them there were, so "my lord" ought to suffice for the time being.

"Of course, my lord," she said brightly. "I have been awaiting your arrival these many minutes past."

He smiled, displaying a set of even, white teeth, a twinkle in his cool gray eyes. "I am flattered by your kind attention, Princess."

She studied him anew, finding him not unattractive. In fact, he was rather appealing in a very dark, English sort of way. Perhaps she ought to take the time to actually learn the man's name. If she decided to add him to her list of prospective lovers, she would need to know what to call him, after all.

Smiling more broadly, she accepted the arm he offered. Only then did she turn to Rupert. "If you will excuse us, Your Royal Highness?"

"But of course." Rupert took a step back, his eyes meeting hers once more.

Her pulse raced in the most perplexing way. She was anticipating the dance to come and the man in whose arms she would enjoy it, she told herself. Perhaps, if all went well, she would eventually enjoy a great deal more than just dancing with him.

Angling her head closer, the better to hear what he had to say, she let him lead her toward the dance floor.

Chapter Two

Prince Rupert was bored.

There were no two ways about it. Try as he might, he was finding little pleasure in the social game the *Ton* called the London Season.

I should never have let Emma persuade me to stay in England longer than I'd originally planned, he mused as he drained the last of the champagne from his glass.

Duties awaited him back in Rosewald, responsibilities that required his personal attention as regent. Arrangements had been made for his ministers to handle the day-to-day details of running the kingdom, with orders that an emissary be dispatched immediately should any business of an urgent or extremely delicate nature arise. But none had. At the moment, however, he wished an emissary would rush into the ballroom with an emergency that required him to leave. At least then he wouldn't be put to the bother of pretending to listen to the Belgian ambassador as he droned on about the continued need for road repair in his country nearly five years after Napoleon's ouster at Waterloo.

Rupert tried hard to look interested, even as he accepted another glass of champagne from a passing footman. For as tedious as his visit was proving, it was still better than the infernal nagging that awaited him back at court.

Before his departure from Rosewald, his ministers had been quietly but persistently pressing him about the necessity of taking a wife. Not only had they enlisted the support of his ailing father, who bellowed at him about grandchildren from his sickbed, but they had gone to the lengths of slipping a list of eligible princesses into his official correspondence.

He'd been so annoyed at the time that he'd threatened to dismiss the entire lot of them over the incident, forbidding them to mention the topic again.

But at four-and-thirty years of age, even he knew the time was drawing near. Soon, he would have to pick a suitable bride, a young woman of royal blood who would not only provide him with heirs but whose alliance would strengthen his place on the throne.

Not yet, however.

Not now.

From across the room, Princess Ariadne caught his eye as she floated across the dance floor on graceful slippered feet.

Her name, he recalled, had been omitted from the list of eligible royal brides. She was a princess, true, but one without a country. An alliance with her would provide nothing in terms of wealth, position, or political gain. As for her inheritance, he knew she had more than sufficient to be comfortable for the entirety of her life, but nothing remarkable enough to tempt another royal into offering marriage. Any number of nobles would be happy to wed her, of course, but from the comments he'd heard her make to Emma, she had no interest in agreeing to a sensible marriage of convenience.

Holding out for love or some such sentimental nonsense.

Across the room she tossed her head back on a laugh, bestowing a flirtatious smile upon her partner, one that the man returned with rapt intensity. Rupert followed her movements, aware of how she stood out like a swan amid a flock of geese.

She had beautiful, creamy, milk-pale skin, a straight patrician nose, and bow-shaped lips that changed easily with her mood. Her body was long and slender, but graced with feminine curves that invited a man's touch. If she weren't so infuriatingly headstrong, he would have found her quite attractive.

Then there was her hair—a glorious red-blond that always came as a bit of a surprise. Considering her Nordic heritage, she ought to have had extremely fair coloring with pale, perhaps even near white hair. Instead, it was as if she had been lit from within, her tresses a vibrant gold that gleamed as if warmed by a fire. Apparently nature had seen fit to expose her true passion in the color of her hair.

And she was passionate, throwing herself fully into any endeavor she pursued.

She danced with passion as well, he noticed, the skirts of her vivid green dress billowing in a lively flourish around her trim ankles.

He gave an imperceptible shake of his head, a smile playing across his mouth. Only she would be brazen enough to wear such a shade when she was yet unwed. Unmarried young women—even ones with numerous Seasons to their credit—confined themselves to white and a few light, muted shades.

But not Ariadne.

She defied the rules of propriety at every turn. He thought she sometimes did things for the express purpose of flouting social convention, as if she were daring Society to find fault and kick her out of its exalted ranks. If she wasn't careful, and pushed the boundaries too far, he feared she might get her wish one of these days.

The music ended, the dancers drawing to a halt. He expected her partner to escort her across the ballroom to where Emma sat chatting with a group of young matrons. Instead, as Rupert watched, Ariadne rose up on her toes to whisper something into the man's ear. He gave her a nod and a smile, then turned away.

Ariadne moved into the throng exiting the dance floor, half disappearing into the crowd. But Rupert's height allowed him to keep track of her, especially given her green dress and the red-gold hair that set her off like a beacon.

He followed her progress across the room to the main doorway that was packed elbow to ankle with a mad crush of party guests. Then suddenly she was gone, vanished somewhere into the house beyond.

For a moment he considered trailing after her to see what sort of mischief she might be up to—since Ariadne was always up to her pretty ears in one kind of trouble or another—but then he decided it was none of his business. He and Ariadne managed to live in his sister's house in just the same manner, by a judicious and carefully honed talent for mutual avoidance.

Yet her escape had given him an idea.

Why not follow her lead and escape the party for a brief while?

"This has been fascinating, Ambassador," he said, interrupting the man in midsentence, "but if you will excuse me, I really must be going."

The man's white eyebrows flew high as a pair of flags on his lined forehead. "Oh, o-of course, Your Highness. M-my pleasure as always."

Rupert didn't remain long enough to acknowledge the other man's bow as he strode away.

He managed to make it halfway across the ballroom before he was stopped again.

And again.

And yet again.

It took him more than fifteen minutes to extricate himself from everyone who urgently craved his attention.

Finally, he made it into the refreshingly cool atmosphere in the rear of the house, not sure where each corridor led and not really caring so long as he found some peace and quiet. The noise from the party grew more and more distant as he moved away from the ballroom. Occasionally he passed other guests who had also wandered away from the festivities, but none of them sought to stop him, as they were too preoccupied with their own interests to wonder about his.

He turned into a dimly lit hallway and approached a door that stood partially open. To his pleasure, he discovered it was the study. He moved into the darkened chamber, where a cozy fire burned in the grate.

He was halfway across the room, his goal a comfortable-looking armchair, when he realized he was not alone. A couple stood huddled in one corner, locked in a passionate embrace.

He shifted on his heel, aware that he should leave, when he noticed a telltale glint of familiar reddish-blond hair.

Softly he cleared his throat.

The pair sprang apart and he looked directly into Ariadne's luminous green eyes. He expected to see chagrin or passion or perhaps even annoyance.

What he saw instead was relief.

Ariadne gazed at Prince Rupert across the darkened study, silently grateful for the intrusion. Not that she had any intention of letting Rupert know that, but his unexpected entrance was exactly the excuse she needed to put an end to a tryst that had not gone at all as planned.

In the two weeks since she had actively begun looking for a lover, the search had proven a great deal more difficult than she had imagined—and a lot more bothersome.

As part of her effort to choose her first paramour, she had decided to kiss a few of the top contenders. As important as mutual interests and like-mindedness might be, physical compatibility was essential as well. How else was she to know if she wanted a man in her bed if she hadn't so much as kissed him first?

So far, though, her kissing trials, as she thought of them, weren't proving nearly as satisfactory as she'd hoped. Still, she'd held out high expectations for Mr. Knightbridge when she'd agreed to a tryst with him here in the study.

He was strong, handsome, and athletic, a Corinthian who moved across the dance floor like a dream. She'd been sure he would be the one to set her senses afire with his kisses. But almost as soon as their lips met, she'd known he was not the one for her.

Not that his kisses weren't acceptable—she was sure some women found his technique quite enthralling—and at least he didn't grope at her like a couple of her other gentlemen prospects had tried to do.

But, sadly, she found herself detached from the whole exercise, more aware of the overly spicy scent of his hair pomade, the soft weave of his superfine coat under her fingertips, and the quiet pops of the logs burning in the grate than she was of his kiss.

Never one to shrink from a challenge, though, she had determined to give their embrace more of a chance. Closing her eyes, she'd thrown herself into the enterprise with gusto. But after another long two minutes, she'd known it was just no good. Kissing him was about as exciting as drinking a cup of tepid tea. She needed far, far more from the man to whom she would gift her innocence.

Apparently he'd enjoyed their embrace a great deal more than she and had interpreted her response for genuine enthusiasm. Which was why she'd found it far from easy to end their kiss.

For the first time in her life, she could genuinely say she was thrilled to see Prince Rupert.

Taking advantage of the interruption, she stepped sideways, putting space between herself and Knightbridge.

For his part, Knightbridge looked startled and not a little annoyed. He was plainly not happy to see Rupert.

"Your Royal Highness," he said in a clipped tone.

Rupert, arrogant as few men could be, spared him barely a glance before turning his sights on her.

"Princess Ariadne."

"Prince Rupert. What brings you here, so far from the party?"

Rupert raised a sardonic brow. "I could easily ask you the same, although it seems rather unnecessary given the circumstances in which we find ourselves."

Deciding that Shakespeare was right and discretion really was the better part of valor on certain occasions, she linked her hands in front of her and did not reply.

He turned suddenly toward Knightbridge. "You may return to the party. You will, of course, say nothing of this to anyone. I presume I make my meaning plain?"

Knightbridge, who was every inch as tall and muscular as Rupert, flushed like a schoolboy at the reprimand, the ruddy color staining his cheeks visible even in the low light. "Of course not, Your Highness. I would never think of besmirching the princess's good name. She and I . . . well, we were . . . That is—"

"Whatever you *were*, pray spare me the details. I do not wish to know," Rupert said, cutting the other man off in midstammer.

Knightbridge closed his mouth. He frowned, his gaze moving uncertainly between Ariadne and Rupert.

But he did not leave.

"Have we been speaking English?" Rupert demanded with cool impatience when Knightbridge continued to hover.

The other man's frown turned to confusion. "Y-yes, Your Highness, we have."

"Then why are you still here?"

Knightbridge's face flushed again, and he gave a pair of jerky bows. After a last look at Ariadne, he exited the room.

She waited until Knightbridge was out of earshot. "That was cruel. There was no need to mock him."

"If he doesn't wish to be treated like a fool, then he ought not act like one. Whatever do you see in him?" He paused, then held up a hand. "No, do not answer that. Again, it is more than I wish to know."

"Well," she said, smoothing a hand over a wrinkle in her skirt, "that being the case, I believe I will take my leave too."

But she managed only three steps before his words drew her to a halt again.

"Not so quick, Your Highness. There is the little matter of your behavior tonight."

She drew a calming breath and turned. "Yes? And what of it?"

"You and that cloth-headed pretty boy were kissing when I came in."

"He is pretty, isn't he?" she interjected, knowing the remark would annoy him. "But I thought you weren't interested in details."

Rupert's jaw tightened. "I am not. But as the brother of your best friend, I think it my duty to advise you—"

"You overstep yourself, Your Royal Highness. You have no duties where I am concerned and I require no advice." The gratitude she'd felt at his earlier timely interference had melted away.

"And you underestimate the amount of influence and good-will you enjoy among the English *Ton*. They are a fickle lot and turn on each other like hungry dogs fighting for prey. You would do well to be careful."

She fisted her hands at her sides. "Having cut my eyeteeth among those at my father's court, I am quite familiar with fickle people and their deceitful ways. Your concern is unnecessary."

She glared at him, her pulse beating hard, and he glared back.

"The man you were with tonight may be a fool, Ariadne, but you are not. What if it had been someone other than I who caught the pair of you together? Unless there is something you are not telling me and you have a happy announcement to make."

She stared for a moment as his meaning sank in. "Heavens no. There is no understanding between Knightbridge and me. We are most definitely not engaged."

"Then it really is a good thing I happened by or you might even now be making plans for your wedding."

Slowly she shook her head. "But I would not. Being compelled to marry for the sake of my reputation supposes that I care what Society thinks of me. I do not."

He scowled. "Even if I believed that, which I am not sure I do, what of the scandal that would surely ensue?"

She shrugged. "What of it? People will talk or not as they like. It would be no concern of mine."

"Then what of Emma? As your close friend, she would naturally suffer from any rash actions you might take—or have you no care for her feelings?"

"Of course I care about Emma. She is like a sister to me, as you well know. Which is the reason I am doing everything

I can to be discreet in my efforts. Even so, I cannot live my life solely for the sake of others. What use is there in protecting my good name and reputation when they do nothing but stifle me? You are right that I would be sorry to hurt or embarrass Emma and Dominic. Very sorry indeed. But I must do what I must do, you see."

Rupert crossed his arms over his chest. "Oh? And what is that?"

Should she tell him? Never in a million years would she have imagined she might consider the idea. But the notion of telling him, of seeing his expression, made it somehow all worthwhile. And really, would it matter if Rupert knew her secret? He wasn't her guardian, and she would be coming into her majority and her inheritance soon anyway. There would be nothing he could do to stop her, even if he decided to try.

"Well," Rupert repeated imperiously, "what is this grand scheme that is so important you care nothing for the scandal it may cause?"

She hesitated for a moment, then plunged ahead. "I have decided to take control of my independence and pursue my own goals, aspirations, and desires. Rather than suffer the misery of a loveless marriage that I do not want, I have decided instead to take a lover."

Chapter Three

R upert stared at her for several long moments, then tossed his head back on a hearty laugh. "A lover?" he repeated between guffaws. "*Ach, liebchen*, you have a better sense of humor than I ever realized. How amusing."

Ariadne's mouth tightened. "It is not meant to be amusing. I fail to understand why you and Emma both find the idea so preposterous." She crossed her arms over her breasts. "And I am not your *liebchen*!"

He laughed again, but as his merriment began to subside, her words started to sink in. What did she mean that she wasn't trying to be funny? Surely she wasn't serious?

His laughter ceased abruptly. "What is this about Emma? You have told her this as well?"

"Yes. And she laughed at first too. Until she realized that I am in dead earnest."

"But you are unwed."

"She said the same thing. I've never thought the two of you had much in common as siblings, but now I see that I was mistaken."

"What else did Emma tell you? Surely she did not encourage this insanity."

"No, she tried to talk me out of it, but my mind is made up."

"You really are insane."

"I am nothing of the sort. Women take lovers all the time."

"Yes. Experienced, *married* women who know what they are getting themselves into and all the things that may happen, good or bad."

"No one can know all the things that may happen in a relationship," she countered dismissively. "At least I will not be committing adultery through my actions."

"No, you will just land yourself in the boughs and ruin any chance you may ever have of making an acceptable marriage."

"I told you how I feel about that. I have decided to live my life as a woman of independence without need of a husband."

"I've always known you were a willful, headstrong creature, but this . . . well, this is just absurd." He paced a couple of steps before a new thought occurred to him. "Don't tell me that is why you and what's-his-name, the pretty boy, were in here together tonight. Surely the two of you aren't actually . . ." He twirled a pair of fingers through the air to finish his sentence.

"No, we are not," she said. "And his name is Mr. Knightbridge. I met with him this evening so I could find out if we are compatible."

"Compatible how?"

"I wanted to know if he has any talent at kissing."

He glowered. "And does he?"

She linked her fingers in front of her again. "He's reasonably skilled. Much better than the others."

"*Others?* What others? Just how many would-be lovers have you wandered off into secluded corners with lately?"

"Three or four," she said with a casual shrug, as if such behavior were a commonplace thing. "I had to have some means of comparison, after all, since I am conducting kissing trials."

Rupert stopped dead. He had assumed she couldn't surprise him any further, but apparently Ariadne had more alarming details up her sleeve than even he could have predicted.

Kissing trials? Good God.

He dragged his fingers through his hair. "Did it never occur to you that word might get out? That one of your gentlemen . . . friends . . . for want of a better term, might mention your new penchant for secret assignations?"

"Well, I cannot see why. None of them has reason to expose our tryst, and it isn't as if I've revealed my intentions to them. As far as each man is aware, he is the only one I've let kiss me and our little rendezvous is nothing but a harmless flirtation."

"Believe me," he said on a low growl, "there is nothing harmless about you, Princess. And though you may have no care for your reputation, you ought to have a care for your safety. You're playing a dangerous game, Ariadne. A very dangerous game, one that may well get you hurt."

"Oh, I'm not worried. They've all been lambs," she said with complete unconcern. "I am perfectly safe."

He moved closer. "And what if you aren't? What if you choose a wolf next time and he isn't as pliable and obedient as the others?"

"I have everything well in hand. All the men in my circle are gentlemen."

"Even among gentlemen, predators exist. As far as I can see, you've been lucky up till now. Take heed and put an end to this ridiculous pursuit of yours."

"It is not ridiculous and I shall not stop. I crave passion

and adventure, and that is what I am going to have whether you approve or not."

He took another step closer, narrowing the space between them so that she was only a few inches away. "So you like living life as if you were balanced on a cliff's edge, do you? Perhaps you need someone to show you just how risky such choices can really be."

She set her hands at her hips. "Oh, and I suppose you're the one to do it? Preparing to read me another lecture, are you, Your Highness?"

"No," he said with soft menace. "No lectures. I think in your case a more direct form of instruction seems appropriate."

Reaching out, he caught hold of her wrists and pulled her arms behind her back, imprisoning her against him. "Prepare to be taught a lesson, Your Highness."

Ariadne stiffened beneath his touch. Clearly Rupert had taken leave of his senses. What did he think he was doing, manhandling her like this when she had never so much as given him permission to touch her hand?

"What do you think you're about? Release me," she demanded.

"Not until you've been made to understand a few important points at least."

"And exactly what points might those be?"

His face was stern, his dark blue eyes nearly black in the low light. "First, that it was a simple matter for me to take hold of you like this, and second, that it will be an easy matter to keep you here. I am far stronger than you, Ariadne, so there's no use struggling. You're not going anywhere until I allow you to."

Is that right? she thought, as a hot burst of fury spread through her veins. Determined to prove him wrong, she bucked and struggled, fighting to be free. But rather than loosening his hold, he only reinforced it by shifting her captured wrists to one hand and walking her backward until she was pressed against the wall.

"Now you're even more under my control," he murmured in a voice that flowed over her like warmed brandy. "You have no choice but to surrender."

In answer, she brought her foot down hard on his, her goal being to cause him pain—enough that he would instinctively release her. But her thin silk evening slippers were no match for his fine leather shoes and glanced off with barely any impact.

Drawing her foot back next, she tried to kick him. But he stepped aside at the last second, having clearly guessed her intent.

"Ah, ah," he cautioned. "None of that now. I ought to have known how feisty you would be. I see I shall have to resort to further tactics to subdue your resistance."

Pressing his body fully against hers, he leaned in so that she became aware of every inch of his long, muscled strength. He increased their intimacy by moving his legs so they were on either side of hers. Slowly, he edged them inward until they enclosed her own, leaving her neatly trapped between.

Yet even trussed as tight as a Christmas goose, she wasn't ready to admit defeat. Jaw clenched, she struggled anew.

And couldn't budge him an inch.

"Only imagine if this wasn't me but some other man," he said. "A man who cares only for his own pleasure and none for yours. Someone who would ruin you and think nothing of the consequences afterward. Is that what you want, Ariadne? You need to put aside this ridiculous fantasy you've spun and realize that you can't simply take a lover."

"But I can. That is why I am being careful in my selection. That is why I am conducting a few tests first, to make certain of the character of the man I invite into my life."

"Ah yes, the kissing trials. Don't think I've forgotten about those. That's one of my other points in this perilous game you're playing."

"I have everything under control."

"Really?" He lifted his free hand and cupped the side of her face. "Like you do at the moment?"

"This"—she shifted against him again, unable to move, much to her frustration—"isn't something that will happen. You're just being nasty."

"Is that what I'm being? What if one of your trial subjects decides to be nasty too? What if you meet him for an assignation and he doesn't want to end your embrace? The pretty boy didn't look too pleased to be interrupted. What if I hadn't come in when I did?"

"Knightbridge would have stopped."

But even as she said the words, she wasn't entirely sure. Rupert was right. Knightbridge hadn't been ready to take no for an answer. But she would have managed him, just as she'd managed the others. Rupert was just trying to scare her and she wasn't going to let him.

"Fine. You've had your say," she told him. "Now let's have done with this charade."

"Not quite yet. There is one more point on which I believe you require some additional education."

And before she had time to consider what he meant, he angled his head and pressed his mouth to hers.

Ariadne gasped silently and held very still—not that she had much choice, given Rupert's grip on her. But maybe if she did not react to his kiss, he would grow tired of this game he was playing and let her go.

Yet even as she tried to go limp and feel nothing, she couldn't help but notice the tendrils of pleasure that began creeping to life inside her body as his lips moved over hers.

Her pulse throbbed in her veins, beating a crazy tattoo that made no sense. At the same time, the air grew thin in her lungs in a way she'd never experienced before, making her strangely desperate to catch her next breath.

More alarming still was the fact that she wasn't repulsed by the bold, nearly overbearing intrusion of his hold upon her—rather the opposite, if she were being truthful with herself.

In the past, she had barely touched Rupert—maybe once or twice when he'd offered his hand or arm to help her from a carriage. Yet here she now stood literally surrounded by him, his long, hard length pressed against her from breast to calf with a stunning intimacy that would have caused a lesser woman to swoon. His arms seemed as strong as tree limbs as they held her, his hand twined around her wrists like an unbreakable vine. Against her cheek and temple, his fingers played to clever purpose, stroking her face so that it felt as if her skin was stretched too tight, hot as if it might turn to flame.

"Open your mouth," he whispered against her lips without breaking their kiss. "Let me in."

She shouldn't. She knew it was a mistake and yet something inside her urged her to comply.

From the instant he'd touched her, it was as though she'd lost all control, possessed by needs and longings she hadn't known she could feel and couldn't seem to resist. She'd been kissed before, but never like this. His touch turned the memory of those other experiences to ash.

Dizzy with sensation, she did as he asked, parted her lips as he demanded. His tongue swept inside and she was lost.

Giving herself over to the pleasure, she breathed him in, his clean, masculine scent a dark, delicious spice in her nose.

And his taste.

God, his taste was divine, like an intoxicating liquor that went straight to her head and left her wanting more.

She shivered as he drew her deeper. Down, down, until she couldn't remember why she shouldn't be doing this with him, and why she hadn't done it sooner.

Dully, with some last spark of functioning brainpower, she realized she was free, that he'd let go of her hands so they were no longer confined at her back.

She could push him away.

She could stop this insanity, for that is exactly what it was. Insane, brilliant pleasure the likes of which she had never conceived.

Still, he'd forced this on her, literally trapped her by means of his superior masculine strength.

She ought to turn the tables and put an end to his manhandling.

She ought to teach him a lesson.

But even as she reached up to do that very thing, her hands instead slid caressingly over the fine, soft wool of his coat, then up into the thick bright gold of his hair.

He shuddered at her touch and kissed her harder, demanding more of her than she truly knew how to give.

But she could try.

Resolved to do exactly that, she arched deeper into his embrace, savoring the heat of him, the power, the bliss.

Somewhere in the distance, a clock began to chime, each stroke ringing in the hour.

Ten.

Eleven.

Midnight.

Then came a giggle—a girlish giggle—accompanied by the deeper laugh of a man. And pattering footsteps.

Where were they? Running past outside in the hall? Or were they coming inside?

Rupert obviously heard as well, since he broke their kiss and glanced toward the door, which they had quite foolishly left standing wide open. Turning, he concealed her body, keeping her in the deepest shadows while he surveyed the room.

But no one entered.

They were safe.

They were alone.

After several more long moments, he turned back.

Their gazes met, his eyes blazing with an intense light, and his hair was tousled out of its usual neat arrangement.

I did that, she thought with a kind of wonder, her fingers tingling along with a great many other body parts.

Then reality set in. Suddenly aghast, she knew she had to leave.

She pushed at him this time, using the flat of her hands against his chest.

And he let her, stepping back to give her room, to allow her an escape.

Then, for the first time in her life, she ran away.

Chapter Four

Ariadne smothered a yawn as she helped herself to eggs and toast from the buffet the following morning. Crossing to the breakfast table in the Lyndhurst House morning room, she sank into a chair to the left of Emma.

To her immense relief, Rupert hadn't joined them. But then he rarely did, preferring to rise early and take breakfast in his rooms before departing for a morning ride.

As for Nick, he'd eaten and been on his way out of the morning room when she had been coming in. They'd exchanged a friendly greeting in passing.

Emma had still been eating her meal, so she had remained, offering a few remarks about how much she'd enjoyed last night's ball.

If only I could say the same.

She scowled and held her hand over her mouth again to conceal another yawn. She was horribly tired, having barely slept last night. But then how could she have been expected to sleep, considering what had happened between her and Rupert? Even now the interlude didn't quite seem real.

Had Rupert actually kissed her?

Worse, had she actually liked it?

To block out the answer that whispered back in silent mockery, she bit unthinkingly into a slice of toast. Immediately she wished she hadn't, the bite sticking in her throat like a cruel scold.

She coughed and reached for her tea, sipping it gratefully until she was able to swallow normally again.

Emma gave her a questioning look. "Are you all right?"

"Yes."

"Is something wrong?"

"No? Why would it be?"

She eyed her friend under her lashes. What did Emma know? Surely Rupert hadn't told her what had happened between them and about the kisses they had shared.

Kisses that were better by far than any she had known before.

But to him they had been nothing more than a lesson, a punishment. Only imagine if he kissed her with something of a more pleasurable nature in mind?

Her heart thumped hard and she reached again for her tea.

Emma glanced toward Ariadne's plate. "It is just that you seem frazzled this morning. Usually you take butter and jam on your toast."

Looking down, Ariadne realized Emma was right. She had forgotten to dress her toast.

"Just a little tired," she said, and she reached for the butter.

"Well, it was a late night."

"Indeed."

She could have said more. Emma was one of her two best friends in all the world, and generally she confided everything to her.

Or nearly everything.

She'd kept her kissing trials to herself. Emma disapproved

of the whole project, so she had thought it wise not to share in this instance. But what about Rupert? She could only imagine how that conversation might go.

"Oh, by the way, your brother caught me kissing Knightbridge last night."

"What!"

"Yes, and then after reading me a lecture and trying to convince me I'm putting myself at serious risk, he kissed me himself."

No, best friends or not, that just wasn't a conversation she could have with Emma. And certainly not about her brother.

"But you don't even like him!" she could hear Emma saying.

And she didn't.

But galling as it might be to admit, she had liked his kisses. She could see now why women lined up to hop into his bed in spite of his unpleasant demeanor.

Fighting down an uncharacteristic blush, she busied herself by spooning strawberry preserves onto her toast. Rather than eat it, though, she took up her fork and moved a few rapidly cooling scrambled egg curds around on her china plate.

One of the footmen provided some much-needed distraction by approaching to refill her cup of hot tea before moving on to do the same for Emma.

A quiet knock came at the door and the butler entered, bearing a letter on a silver salver.

"This just arrived for you, Your Highness," he said, stopping next to Emma.

She picked up the missive. "Thank you, Symms."

He bowed and withdrew.

Emma studied the letter and smiled. "It is from Mercedes."

Ariadne smiled back, not only because she was eager to

hear news of her other best friend—which she was—but because it would help get her mind off Rupert.

"Well, how is Mercedes? What does she have to say? Will she and Daniel be coming down for the Season?"

Emma shook her head, which was still bent over the pages. "No, but for good cause. It seems she has happy news to share."

"Oh?"

"She's in the family way again." Her smile grew even wider before it disappeared again. "But poor thing isn't feeling up to the journey. She says she, and I quote, 'cannot see much point in coming all the way to London just so I can sleep, swoon, and be too sick to keep down my breakfast every morning.'"

Ariadne chuckled and drank some tea.

"Apparently Daniel has forbidden her to travel," Emma said as she continued scanning the letter. "You know how protective he is."

"Well, that's a Scotsman for you," Ariadne observed. "Although as I recall you had quite a time talking Nick into letting you make the trip from Lynd Park after little Peter's birth."

"Nick was only concerned for my well-being. Luckily I had an easy pregnancy, easier by far than I did with Friedrich. Nick could hardly insist I remain in the country when I was out of bed and accepting congratulatory calls from half the county scarcely a week after my lying-in. As I told him a hundred times, I felt splendid."

Pausing, she set the letter aside. "Besides, I couldn't have sent you off for the Season on your own. You've no relations other than a few distant cousins on the Continent, and I wouldn't hear of you being compelled to stay with some older woman willing to act as your sponsor, however socially acceptable she might be."

"You are very good to me, you and Dominic both."

Emma gave a small shake of her head, as if it were of no moment.

But Ariadne forestalled her with a light touch of her hand. "No, truly," she said. "I'm not entirely sure what I would have done these past few years if not for you and Nick, and Mercedes and Daniel too. The four of you have all been so generous, opening your homes and your lives to me when I had no real right to intrude."

Emma made a tsking sound under her breath. "You are *not* intruding and don't let me ever hear you say such a thing again. You are as dear to me as a sister—dearer, actually, considering how Sigrid can be sometimes. We love having you with us and this is your home for as long as you like. You may grow quite old and gray here if you prefer."

Ariadne smiled slightly, turning over the spoon on her saucer. "But still, it must grow tiresome having a permanent houseguest. Or semi-permanent, since I spend part of each year with Mercedes and Daniel."

"We've dozens of rooms, so I cannot see how it is an issue. There's plenty of space for us all. Anyway, who would persuade Friedrich to go to bed if not for his dear aunt Ariadne? He refuses to fall asleep if he hasn't had a story from you, you know."

She smiled again. "Oh, I'm sure you'd find a way to manage. He loves his mama best. And his papa. I know that for certain."

For in spite of her great affection for the boy, she wasn't really Friedrich's aunt, however much she might wish she were. Neither was this her home, despite the undeniable warmth and love she felt in her friends' company. They were all too kind for their own good as well as hers. But in only a few more months, on her twenty-fifth birthday, she would come into her inheritance and her independence. However easy and comforting it would be to continue living with her friends, she knew she could not. She needed to make her own way in the world on her own terms.

"So," she said with forced brightness, "that will be three babies for Mercedes with this new one. You and Nick had better get busy catching up," she teased.

Emma's cheeks flushed a light pink and she laughed. "Arie, the things you say. It's one of the reasons I love you so."

"Well, just remember that the next time I say something that embarrasses you."

Emma laughed again and sipped her tea.

Deciding that she really ought to eat something after all, Ariadne applied herself to her eggs and toast. As she did, her thoughts turned to the conversation she'd just had with Emma and the subject of babies.

If there was one thing that gave her pause about her plan to take a lover, it was the fear that she might find herself with child. An out-of-wedlock pregnancy would be a serious complication indeed, but from what she'd read and gleaned from a few carefully worded questions to Emma and Mercedes, there were methods that could be used to minimize the risk— herbal concoctions and timing and such. Not that either of her friends bothered with such precautions, since they were far too happily married and didn't mind the prospect of increasing the size of their families. But for her, a baby would equal the complete destruction of her reputation—not that she particularly cared about preserving it. Still, while there might be hope of hiding an illicit affair, there would be no concealing a pregnancy and the addition of a child into her life.

Some might recommend going into seclusion during the pregnancy, then giving the child away to a worthy couple once it arrived. But she would never do that. She understood what it meant to be without the security of family; any child of hers would know its mother and the warmth of her love.

Of course, if all went as planned, there would be no baby—at least not until she decided it was time. Just as she had decided not to cut herself off from the pleasure of being with a man, she didn't see why she had to cut herself off from the joy of being a mother. Clearly, it would be better if she were wed, but plenty of women had illegitimate children, including royal ones. Society was teeming with royal and aristocratic bastards; what would one more matter? Her child would have a good life—she would see to that—and no one would dare make him feel ashamed because of his parentage.

She would see to that as well.

But for this first time, with this first lover, she wanted it to be just the two of them. And so she would be careful. Her lover would naturally wish to do so as well.

Whoever he might turn out to be.

Thoughts of Rupert flashed through her mind and her mouth throbbed ever so faintly at the memory of his kisses.

The tea, she told herself. It was just that the tea was too hot. She was making far too much of last night's encounter.

Undoubtedly, Rupert kissed well, giving credence to all the rumors of his prowess in the bedchamber. But she was sure there were other men who were equally as talented in such matters. She hadn't found one yet, true, but she would. A man even more skilled than Prince Rupert.

Surely it couldn't be that difficult. Could it?

She just needed to continue her search. The right lover for her was out there; it was only a matter of patience.

As for Rupert's warning that she was putting herself in harm's way by conducting her little project, he was simply overreacting. None of her gentlemen prospects had overstepped the bounds of proper conduct—well, not much anyway.

As she'd said, she could handle them.

Perhaps she would put her kissing tests on hold for a while, though. As Rupert had suggested, it wouldn't do for her would-be lovers to start comparing notes and find out she was conducting trials.

"I thought we might visit the shops this afternoon," Emma remarked, breaking into her reverie. "The guest bedrooms could all do with new linens and I should value your opinion."

"Oh, I'm sorry, Emma, I meant to tell you, but Lord Twyford has offered to show me his family's art collection. They have two van Ruisdaels and a Rembrandt. He's arranged everything, including nuncheon afterward in the garden. Or perhaps I should say his mother has made all the arrangements, but he will be conducting the tour of the galleries. You're more than welcome to join us."

The only son of a duke, Twyford was on her list of prospective lovers, but just barely. He was a nice man, and they shared a lively mutual interest in poetry and art, but he could be almost painfully shy at times. She honestly couldn't imagine even broaching the idea of sharing a clandestine kiss, let alone getting to the point of them becoming lovers.

"No," Emma said with a hint of irony in her voice, "you go ahead without me. The artwork is tempting, but Lady Twyford is a bit of an acquired taste. I believe I shall content myself with my shopping."

Ariadne laughed. "She is an awful harridan, isn't she? But nuncheon seems a small price to pay for a chance to see the duke's collection."

"I suppose. Still, I wouldn't count on anything coming to fruition from that quarter."

Emma, of course, meant marriage—a goal she still had not abandoned when it came to Ariadne. But Ariadne had long since learned to hold her tongue on the subject, since discussion of her taking a lover always made Emma scowl and grow cross with worry, a trait she apparently shared with her elder brother.

"From what I understand about Lord Twyford," Emma continued, "his mother arranges most things in his life. But he's a nice boy for all that."

"Boy?" Ariadne laughed. "He's older than either of us."

"Perhaps so, but I suspect his mother doesn't plan to let him grow up anytime before his fiftieth birthday, and maybe not even then."

Considering, Ariadne feared her friend was right.

Mentally, she marked off another prospect and concealed a sigh in her tea.

Two days later, Rupert descended the staircase of Lyndhurst House. Voluble noise burst from the main-floor drawing room, laughter and voices—deep male voices—punctuated by a single lilting feminine strain.

Ariadne was receiving callers again.

He hadn't seen much of her since the night of the ball— actually no more than a glimpse as she came and went from the town house. He could have sought her out, but what was there to say? He thought he'd made his point pretty clear. More than clear, actually.

What had he been thinking, taking hold of her like that? Kissing her the way he had? He'd meant to shock her, shake her out of her foolish complacency and make her see how ridiculous she was being.

Take a lover, indeed.

He'd never heard of anything so idiotic and foolhardy in his life. She was inexperienced and idealistic and had no idea that it wasn't just her reputation she was putting at risk but herself as well.

As for her "kissing trials," he'd never heard the like. He

was well aware that on occasion young unmarried men and women stole a chaste kiss or two behind a garden bush, but to deliberately court the attentions of random men in order to find out how well or ill they kissed . . .

His hands turned to fists at his sides at the very thought.

Not that he was jealous, not in the least, he assured himself. As he'd told her, she was his sister's friend and he didn't want to see her hurt. That and that alone was the extent of his interest.

Obviously, he'd always known that Ariadne was headstrong and impulsive, but he'd never thought her lacking in basic common sense. When he'd heard her ludicrous plan, he really had thought she was jesting. He could only imagine how his face must have looked when he'd realized she was not.

When he'd grabbed hold of her, he really had meant to do nothing more than teach her a well-deserved lesson. So how had it ended up going so wrong?

Or perhaps the correct term was *so right*?

At some point not long after he'd started kissing her, he'd forgotten all about teaching lessons and lost himself in their kiss.

Unlike Ariadne, he couldn't use inexperience as an excuse. He'd been kissing women since he was a boy of fourteen, when one of the royal housemaids decided he needed more than the sheets on his bed tended to. Not that he'd ever minded. He enjoyed women, found them soft and inviting and pleasurable to be with both in bed and out.

But Princess Ariadne?

She'd always been his young sister's friend, a bit of an annoyance but easily enough dismissed. Lovely as she might be, he'd never really seen her in a sexual light before.

With one kiss, all that had changed.

In fact, since that night he hadn't been able to get her out of his mind. He'd even dreamed about her, awakening with an arousal as strong as the one she'd left him with when she'd fled the study. To his consternation, he'd had to stay behind in that blasted study for an additional fifteen minutes before he'd felt presentable enough to return to the festivities.

Yet whatever may have happened between them two nights ago, it made no difference. They would continue on as before, their indiscretion forgotten and buried in the past where it belonged.

All that remained now was to hope that Ariadne had actually learned something from their encounter and had decided to put an end to her ill-conceived scheme to take a lover.

Yet here she was, entertaining again.

Perhaps they were just ordinary suitors come to call. Certainly, in spite of her declaration that she did not plan to wed, she had never lacked for suitors or marriage proposals over the course of her many London Seasons.

At last count, he believed she had turned down seven—or was it eight?—perfectly reasonable offers of marriage. Although to be honest, only one had been from a fellow royal—a man so boorish and lacking in intellect that Rupert would have advised her to refuse him even if he'd been her last hope to be a wife and mother.

The round, mellow tones of her laughter drifted once more from the room, followed by a chorus of enthusiastic male replies.

He supposed he ought to continue on to the library, where he had planned to relax with a glass of wine and a good book. But even as he headed off in that direction, he couldn't resist the temptation to find out exactly who was in the room with her and what she was doing.

Striding along the corridor, he took a detour into the drawing room.

There she sat, holding court like a queen, with a retinue of courtiers scattered around her. Emma, he noted, was nowhere to be seen; likely she had gone up to the nursery to visit the boys. Instead, an older lady's maid sat in one corner with her head bent over some needlework, there to maintain some semblance of propriety.

Ariadne smiled at a remark made by one of the gentlemen, her green eyes alight, while the other men sought new ways to draw her attention.

Abruptly the laughter and talk halted, heads turning as one in his direction. The men rose to their feet and bowed. "Your Royal Highness," several of them said in greeting.

He nodded, then gestured for them to resume their seats. "Carry on," he said as he moved deeper into the room. "I merely stopped by for a sandwich and a libation. Please, pay me no mind."

Ariadne's smile disappeared, her gaze meeting his for a brief but significant moment. "Why, Your Highness, good afternoon. You have no need to trouble yourself making a plate here. I am sure Symms would be more than happy to send down to the kitchen for whatever you wish."

Her voice, he noticed, was so sweet that bees could have sated themselves on its honeyed tones. "Why do I not ring for him now and he can bring you something. In the archduke's study perhaps?"

He nearly laughed at her thinly veiled attempt to shoo him out of the room. "My thanks, Princess, but I am more than content to sample the fare I see before me."

And truthfully, he was a bit peckish, having eaten only a late breakfast and no nuncheon that day.

He crossed to the tea tray and began to prepare a selection for himself. As he did so, he took a moment to note the identities of the other men in the room. Among them were a duke's heir apparent, a marquess who at thirty was already losing his hair, and a distant—very distant—cousin of King

George who had teeth like a horse and who ranked no higher than an ordinary mister.

As for the rest, five more in all, he was not familiar with their names, although he believed he'd seen them at various *Ton* functions. One in particular that he did remember was the dark-haired gentleman who had interrupted his conversation with Ariadne that night at the ball in order to claim a dance. He focused on the man for a long moment, knowing he'd seen him somewhere else as well.

Then it came to him. It had been at a gaming hell, an establishment he had visited strictly as a favor to a friend. As he recalled, the dark-haired lord hadn't looked terribly happy at the time, seeing as he had been in the process of losing a rather substantial sum of money.

So what was he doing sniffing around Ariadne?

He didn't like any of the answers that came to mind.

Letting none of this show on his face, he filled his plate with an array of small sandwiches and biscuits, then took a seat in one of the few open spaces remaining—on the sofa next to Ariadne.

Out of deference to her rank, none of the gentlemen had seated themselves beside her, leaving the sofa unoccupied except for herself. But he outranked everyone in the room, including her, which meant he could sit anywhere he liked.

He hid another smile as he sank down beside her, noticing the way her lips thinned with barely concealed annoyance. Gracefully, she shifted a couple of inches away to put more space between them.

He laid a napkin across his knee and began to eat.

He watched her silent struggle as she decided whether to offer him tea, but a lifetime of training could not be ignored, not even by Ariadne.

"Would you care for tea, Your Royal Highness?" she inquired, reaching toward the silver urn.

"Nein," he answered in his native Rosewaldian dialect. "A small beer would be appreciated, however."

Her gaze met his, her lips parting as if she longed to make some retort. Instead, she nodded toward a footman who waited in a far corner.

"*A beer* for His Royal Highness," she informed the servant.

The man gave a smart bow, then departed.

She turned back to her retinue of admirers, smiling widely at them even as she strove to ignore Rupert. "So, gentlemen," she said, "if I remember correctly, Lord Norling was just about to tell us about the most amusing wagers currently being laid at the clubs. Pray do continue, my lord."

Norling, the marquess, cleared his throat, looking uncomfortably at Rupert before speaking. "Yes, well, I seem to recall one about Viscount Hertsly. He bet his friend that he could shovel . . ." He frowned, his words trailing away as if reconsidering. "Well, no, maybe not that one."

He paused, running a hand over his thinning pate. "There's another tale, highly droll . . . It concerns eels, but—" He broke off again, shooting another unsettled glance at Rupert.

Rupert said nothing. He just sat calmly eating his snack.

"Yes, well, again, not really suitable for ladies, Princess."

"Oh, pray do share, my lord," she entreated. "You have us all most intrigued, myself in particular."

Norling stuck a finger inside his cravat as if it had suddenly decided to strangle him.

"Yes, Norling," Rupert drawled. "By all means, regale us with your tales that are, by your own admission, wholly unsuitable for the ears of ladies."

The marquess's face paled and he shot to his feet. "A-another time perhaps. I am dreadfully sorry, but I just recalled that I am promised at my solicitor's office in fifteen minutes. I shall have to hurry to make it across Town." He bowed awkwardly. "A pleasure as always, Your Highness. Prince."

And then he was gone.

Several other of the gentlemen suddenly remembered appointments of their own and began making their excuses as well. A veritable exodus ensued as they hurried out the door.

Rupert's beer arrived. He sipped it as he watched the by-play, finding Ariadne's gentlemen callers as entertaining as a production on Drury Lane.

Ten minutes later, only two remained—the king's horse-toothed cousin, who sat cramming his mouth full of biscuits, and the dark-haired lord. The latter looked amused and relaxed, one arm draped over the back of his chair. With leisurely ease, he rose to his feet and strolled forward.

"Princess," he said, "I too ought to depart. As one of the first to pay you a call, I have no wish to overstay my welcome."

"Not at all, Lord Selkirk. You may stay and visit as long as you wish."

Selkirk smiled. "You make a tempting offer, but I really must go. What time shall I come for you tomorrow? Does nine o'clock sound agreeable?"

Ariadne extended a hand. "Most agreeable. I look forward to the occasion."

Selkirk made her an elegant bow. Then he turned. "Come along, Bartsby," he told the king's cousin. "I believe you have made deep enough inroads into the tea tray for one afternoon."

Bartsby made a huffing noise that couldn't be understood past the food in his mouth. Hastily he swallowed; then he too rose to his feet.

"Your Highness," Selkirk said to Ariadne. "Your Royal Highness," he added to Rupert.

Rupert lifted a brow and drank more beer.

Bartsby made a pair of darting bows, then followed the other man from the room.

Sudden quiet descended.

Ariadne glanced over at the lady's maid, who sat with her head bent inconspicuously over her sewing. "Jones," she said.

The woman looked up.

"I believe it is past time for your tea. Why do you not go ahead and take it now while you have no pressing duties?"

The lady's maid hesitated briefly, then secured her needle into her sewing. "Yes, Your Highness. As you wish." She cast a quick glance between Ariadne and Rupert, then gathered her belongings and left the room.

The moment they were alone, Ariadne rounded on him. "What exactly do you think you're about, coming in here like that?"

"Like what?"

"Oh, don't act so innocent. You know exactly what. You deliberately decided to disrupt my afternoon."

"That is an awful lot of *d*'s for one sentence. Perhaps you ought to rephrase."

Her green eyes flashed fire. "Don't be flippant. You came in here specifically to chase away my gentlemen callers and you know it."

"Is that what I was doing?" he drawled. "As I recollect, I stopped in for a sandwich. They're quite good, by the way. Would you care for one?"

Her lips grew tight. "No, I would not care for one. *Ooh*, you can be insufferable sometimes. I don't know how Emma abides you."

"She's my sister. She doesn't have a choice."

Ariadne glared at him and he gazed steadily back. Abruptly, she blew out a breath and rolled her eyes skyward, her lips twitching ever so slightly, as if she were fighting the urge to laugh.

He remembered how they'd felt, those lips, and wondered what she would do if he leaned over and kissed her now. But such passion, however pleasurable, was not to be repeated, he reminded himself. There would be no more lessons of that sort, since hopefully she had learned hers that night in the study. As for himself . . .

Far more dispirited by the realization than he had any right to be, he consoled himself in his beer.

"In regard to your accusation that I came to shoo away your gentlemen callers," he continued, "I would remind you that if said gentlemen possessed any steel in their spines, they would not have been so easily scattered."

"Mayhap not, but then, you are unfairly intimidating when you wish to be. You are a future king, you know."

"True." He took another swallow of beer, then set the glass aside. "So why is it that my supposed powers of intimidation never seem to work on you?"

A little smile played at the corners of her mouth. "Ah well, that comes from my being of royal blood and knowing that underneath that formidable exterior of yours you are still just a man. An extraordinary one, but a man just the same."

"Extraordinary, *hmm*?" Leaning back, he played his fingers slowly over the silk on the back of the sofa. "I believe that is the first compliment I have ever had from you."

Her eyes turned intensely green; then she looked away, busying herself with the tea tray. "Yes, well, do not get used to it. You have already made your opinion clear on the subject of my private life. I will thank you not to interfere in it any further."

So she didn't like his interference, did she? Well, he would stop when he decided he was done and not a minute before. "I would have no cause to intercede in your affairs were it not for the lack of wisdom you have so recently displayed."

"Lack of wisdom?" She held up a hand. "We are finished with this conversation, Your Royal Highness. You may leave."

He chuckled and reached for another sandwich; the chicken and watercress was especially delicious.

"Fine," she declared after a moment. "*I* shall depart."

"Sit," he commanded. Reaching over, he caught hold of her wrist to keep her where she was.

She arched a reproachful brow. "Manhandling me again?"

"No," he said, making no effort to release her. "Just keeping you in your place, that's all."

"As I said before, you are insufferable."

He laughed and finished his sandwich. Only then did he let her go.

"Stay," he warned, not certain she wouldn't bolt off the sofa.

"I am not one of your trained spaniels."

"No. They are much better behaved. Now, before you fly into the boughs completely, ease my mind and tell me that you have put aside this nonsensical notion of yours and that today's gentlemen callers were suitors vying for your hand in marriage."

"I could tell you that, but then I would have to lie. I don't like to lie."

"Ariadne," he said on a growl, "I thought surely after the other night—"

"That you would scare me off? Not a bit, Your Royal Highness. You will find that I am made of far sterner stuff than that."

"Stuff is right, since your head is full of stuff and nonsense on this subject."

"Now you are insulting me. I really must leave before I say something I will forever regret."

"Oh, don't hold back on my account. We are better friends than that, I should think."

"Is that what we are? I have to confess I had never thought of us as such."

He tipped his head to concede her point. "Then as my sister's friend, pray continue."

"What is the use? We shall never agree. Just let me be, Rupert. I ask nothing more."

And that is exactly what I should do, he realized. *It is her life to ruin or not as she chooses.*

"So you and that man, the one who mentioned an outing tomorrow. Where is he taking you?"

She frowned, clearly suspicious. "Lord Selkirk. We are going riding in the park. And no, I haven't decided to take him as my lover, if that is what you are wondering."

"Good God, I should hope not. I trust you are taking a groom? It is far too early to be out alone with such a man."

"There are plenty of people in the park at that hour, so I shall be perfectly safe." She paused. "What do you mean by *such a man*?"

"Perhaps you are not aware, but Selkirk has something of an unsavory reputation."

"Oh? In what way?"

"He gambles, for one."

"Yes, well, many gentlemen like to test lady luck. That is nothing out of the norm."

"Except that when he does it, he cannot afford to lose."

"You are saying he is penniless?"

"Scraping by."

He watched as she took in that information. "I thank you for letting me know, but since I am not considering marriage to him, I can see no reason why his lack of wealth should trouble me. If I should decide on him, I have more than ample funds to keep both of us amused."

"Ariadne, don't do this. You will only end up getting hurt."

Something in her expression softened. "I have been hurt

before. Should I be again, I am sure I shall recover in due course."

He considered that for a moment. Someone had hurt her. He wondered when that had happened and who had done the damage.

He glanced down, surprised to find that his hands were fisted. Deliberately, he forced his fingers open again.

"Now, if you will please excuse me, Your Highness," she said, taking refuge in formality. "I really must go to my rooms. I am promised at the theater tonight and wish to rest."

He could have argued further; words crowded like pebbles in his mouth that he longed to spit out. But as she said, what was the use? Her ears were closed to his exhortations.

If only he were in Rosewald. He could have her locked in the dungeons until this insanity of hers wore off. But he was in England, where everything was so annoyingly civilized—at least on the surface.

No, he would have to think of another way to keep her from bringing ruin down upon her head. Until then, he would let her believe she had won.

He could wait.

He was good at waiting.

And at winning.

Chapter Five

A light breeze blew warm and pleasant against Ariadne's cheeks the next morning as she rode through Hyde Park. Although there were a number of other people scattered throughout the park, the grounds were not crowded, certainly not the way they would be later in the day when the *Ton* emerged from their homes to promenade there like flocks of preening, brightly colored birds.

Having endured such scenes on more than one occasion, she much preferred this quieter alternative, where she could actually ride her horse rather than be confined to a tedious, stop-and-start walk.

At her side rode Lord Selkirk, his roan gelding an excellent match for her spirited bay mare, Persephone. The two horses were enjoying the carefree outing just as much as their owners.

She looked over at him, and he smiled at her, his teeth very white in his darkly handsome face. Grinning back, she kicked her mount into a full-blown canter, leaving Selkirk to give chase. He did, catching up easily, his skills as a horseman quite admirable. They were both laughing by the time they slowed their horses to a sedate walk.

The vigorous ride had tugged more than one pin loose from her hair. Inhaling deeply to catch her breath, she tucked an errant curl behind her ear. "Oh, I've missed that. In the country I ride nearly every day."

"Then the city must feel sadly confining to such an excellent horsewoman as yourself."

"Well, my skills are no more than adequate, particularly given this sidesaddle and riding habit, but I thank you nonetheless. As for London, it has advantages the country lacks. I find I cannot complain."

Ariadne took a moment to tuck another stray wisp of hair underneath the edge of her tall riding hat. "I must remember this stretch of park grounds in future."

"Yes, at this hour it allows for a very tolerable bit of exercise."

"Indeed."

Silence fell between them, but one that was not uncomfortable.

Ariadne stole a sideways glance at Selkirk, contemplating the attractive lines of his profile. Rupert had warned her against him, but rather than taking heed, she had left her groom behind and gone out with Selkirk alone.

And she had been right to do so. In the past half hour, nothing untoward had happened. She and Selkirk were enjoying what anyone would agree was a very pleasant excursion to a very public park. Once again Rupert was exaggerating the risks.

He really ought to learn to mind his own business.

What had he imagined he was up to yesterday, chasing off all her suitors?

Except that he had not chased away Selkirk. He had left on his own terms without falling victim to Rupert's domineering presence.

Good for Lord Selkirk.

But why was she thinking of Rupert at all? Even here the dratted man found a way to plague her. Determined to banish him from her mind completely, she turned and showered Selkirk with a brilliant smile.

He seemed surprised, his dark eyes agleam with some hidden thoughts. Then he too smiled. "I was wondering, Princess, if you might allow me the opportunity to take you up in my new high perch phaeton. I recently had the pleasure of acquiring the vehicle in a game of cards."

"How lucky for you," she said, suppressing a frown.

Rupert had told her Selkirk was a gamester. But as she had decided before, what of it? Besides, in this instance, Selkirk had won, had he not?

"Yes, dame fortune was on my side. So what say you? Shall we take to the roads together?"

She opened her mouth, on the verge of replying, when a new rider cantered into view. She recognized the huge black stallion at once, just as she recognized the man—tall and golden-haired and unmistakably Rupert.

She bit back a curse.

What is he doing here?

But of course she knew exactly what he was doing here.

The wretch.

She wondered how long he'd been riding around in the park, searching for them.

And clearly their presence had not gone unobserved by him either, she realized, watching as he turned his horse with a silent command and steered the great stallion in their direction. The thoroughbred's hooves ate up the distance between them as if it were nothing.

Soon, Rupert was drawing to an easy halt, while she and Selkirk did the same.

"Hello, Princess," he said. "I trust you are well this morning." He paused, his gaze flicking quickly over to the other man. "Snelbert."

Ariadne caught the tiny gasp that rose in her throat, somehow managing to stay silent.

"*Selkirk*, Your Royal Highness," Selkirk corrected with calm politeness. "And good morning."

Rupert paused for a scant second, making no effort to acknowledge his mistake—assuming it had been a mistake—before returning his attention to her. "They said at the house you'd gone riding. I wondered if you might head this way."

So he wasn't even going to pretend that he hadn't come looking for her. Well, at least he wasn't adding liar to his list of infractions.

"Yes. Lord Selkirk kindly invited me to enjoy the park with him. It is usually quite pleasant at this hour of the morning. So few unanticipated interruptions from passing acquaintances, you see."

Rupert's lips twitched, clearly registering the hit. But he in no other way acknowledged any understanding of her remark.

"So true," he replied. "I take pains to avoid the place in the afternoons. Morning is the only time one can enjoy a decent ride here. I confess that I greatly miss the forest trails in Rosewald. They are so peaceful."

She could almost see them in her imagination. Emma had told her so much about her home country over the years that she felt as if she knew the place too, with its deep pine forests, flower-strewn valleys, and snow-covered mountaintops.

But this was not the time to lose sight of Rupert's infraction; she wasn't about to let him escape so easily.

"*Hmm*," she mused aloud, returning the conversation to its original topic. "And here I should have thought you would revel in the *Ton*'s afternoon promenade, given all the opportunities it presents to see and be seen."

She waited to find out if he would take offense. Instead, his eyes twinkled with amusement. "Ah, but I can do that anytime I like. I have merely to set foot onto any London street and let the circus begin."

And for him, she supposed, it was a circus. She'd seen the kind of response he elicited through no conceit of his own. Much as she might be loath to admit, Rupert never invited people's fawning. It came quite naturally to those who sought his attention and patronage.

Her brows drew tight. How had he managed to turn the conversation to his own advantage when he was the one at fault?

He shifted his gaze to Selkirk. "So, you're a horseman, are you?"

"I do my best," Selkirk stated, "though clearly I am not as adept as yourself, Prince."

She might have thought Selkirk was trying to be falsely ingratiating if it weren't for the fact that Rupert was indeed an exceptional equestrian. One had only to see him ride to know that.

"May I take the opportunity to remark upon your horse?" Selkirk continued. "He's a real beauty."

"Yes, he's my pride," Rupert said with a smile, as he reached down to pat the animal's neck. "I raised Odin from a newborn foal. I suppose I ought to have left him back home in Rosewald, but he grows fractious if I'm away too long. In other words, he starts biting the grooms."

Clearly aware that he was the center of attention, Odin huffed out a quivering breath through his nostrils and tossed his head, his equine muscles rippling with barely harnessed strength beneath his glossy coat. Rupert controlled the spirited steed with an easy hand on the reins, not the least bit intimidated.

Odin, she realized for the first time, was rather like his

master—strong-willed, powerful, and dangerous when he chose to be—although to her knowledge, Rupert had never tried to bite anyone.

The stallion sauntered a few inches closer to Selkirk's gelding and aggressively showed his teeth, causing Selkirk's horse to step hastily back. Rupert responded by moving Odin nearer to Ariadne's horse, Persephone, in a way that separated the two of them from the other man.

She shot Rupert a glance out of the corner of her eye, wondering if the maneuver had been deliberate on his part. But he gave no sign of anything other than polite concern over his horse's less than friendly behavior.

"You can see what I mean about him," Rupert said. "But he is a full-blooded stallion and used to having his own way."

Selkirk moved his gelding another foot back, putting him well out of harm's way. "You must have trouble finding staff who are willing to work with him."

"It takes a skilled touch, I admit. I find with lively beasts that one wants to use enough control to keep them in line but not so much as to break their spirit. It's the spirit that makes it all worth the effort."

Ariadne scowled, wondering why she suddenly had the feeling he wasn't talking solely about horses anymore. From the look on Selkirk's face, she thought he might be wondering the same thing.

Her lips tightened, along with her gloved hands on the reins. "It's been a pleasure running into you like this, Your Highness. Now, if you will excuse us, Lord Selkirk and I must continue on our way."

"Yes," Selkirk said. "I told the archduchess, your sister, that I would have the princess back in time for a late breakfast."

Rupert regarded them, his eyes alight with sudden intrigue. "Well, if such is the case, there's no need for you to trouble yourself riding all the way back to Lyndhurst House. I am going there myself and shall be pleased to escort Princess Ariadne home."

Selkirk's jaw stiffened with clear displeasure, his eyes moving to trade a look with Ariadne.

She spared him barely a glance before she set her sights on Rupert once more. "There's no need for you to cut your ride short, Your Highness. I am sure Lord Selkirk doesn't mind the brief journey back to Grosvenor Square."

"No, not at all," Selkirk said. "Lyndhurst House is on my way."

Rupert smiled, showing his teeth in a way that reminded her of Odin. "Actually I was finished with my ride, so why do we not all return together?"

He had them cornered and he knew it. Short of being unpardonably rude, there was no choice but to agree to his plan.

She met his unrepentant gaze, then turned her horse toward home.

Chapter Six

Two weeks later, Ariadne walked out of Lyndhurst House, fuming as she stepped into the waiting coach.

Blasted man! He's driving me mad!

She took a seat and leaned back against the comfortably upholstered cushions, smoothing a stray crease from the skirts of her periwinkle blue day dress. Idly she gazed out the window at the residential Mayfair street and up into the nearly cloudless sky above. Moments later, the coach jerked and they were off.

How lovely to be alone.

Or perhaps she ought to amend that sentiment.

How lovely to be without Rupert.

Lately, it seemed that everywhere she went, he was there as well. Balls, soirees, musicales, garden parties, afternoon fetes, even carriage rides and strolls around the city with one prospective gentleman or another—somehow he managed to appear at them all.

She couldn't prove that he was following her, but she knew very well that he would never have bothered to accept a fraction of the invitations that arrived daily in his correspondence were it not for his sudden interest in tormenting her.

In fact, he was making the social hostesses of London swoon with delight, leaving more than one of them to speculate excitedly that perhaps his unprecedented socializing meant that he was considering taking an English bride, an aristocratic girl from outside the usual royal circles.

But Ariadne knew better. She knew his real game was to thwart her plan to take a lover.

What an idiot she'd been to share such a confidence with an unreasonable tyrant like him. He'd caught her in an unguarded moment, when her defenses had been down. To say nothing of the fact that his kisses had been directly responsible for muddling her brain at the time.

Since then he had not tried to repeat their embrace. He hadn't so much as touched her except to share a single quadrille one evening at a ball.

Not that she wanted him to touch her; she most certainly did not. It was mortifying enough that she was still awakening some mornings with the memory of his kisses on her lips. All she wanted was for him to respect her wishes and let her live her life as she chose.

If only he would stop trying to interfere! Honestly, she didn't know why he was being so overbearing. It wasn't as if she was a part of his family.

But Emma was.

And therein lay the crux of the problem. What should have been her reputation to ruin, or not, as she chose, had gotten all muddled up with Emma's reputation and, by extension, Rupert's own.

As prince regent and future king of Rosewald, he had standards to maintain, rules that must not be broken, in his regal estimation. Since she was so set on breaking them, he was now set on stopping her.

He claimed he cared about her safety, and perhaps in some respects he did. Still she suspected his motives went deeper and were bound up not just in Emma's reputation, but in an annoying determination to exert his power over her.

If only he had gone home when he'd originally planned, her life would now be heaven. Instead, he'd turned her world into one frustration after another, interrupting her at the most inconvenient times, intimidating all but her most persistent suitors.

Honestly, he was worse than a Spanish duenna.

If she didn't get rid of him soon, the Season would be over and so would her chance to secure a lover.

Which was precisely what he wanted.

But Rupert sadly underestimated her if he thought she would be so easily discouraged. She would find a way around him. She just had to come up with a plan.

For today, though, she was simply hoping for a respite, an activity designed strictly for her own enjoyment and edification. Over the past few weeks, she had missed several intriguing lectures given by the literary and intellectual club to which she belonged. When she had received the invitation to hear a talk on the natural rights of women and the tyranny of traditional marriage, she realized it would be the perfect way to spend a free afternoon.

A *Rupert*-free afternoon!

For surely even he would not wish to listen to a lengthy discussion of modernist notions about the role and place of women.

A short while later, the coach rolled to a stop in front of a small but well-kept town house in Bloomsbury. This section of London was decidedly middle class and not at all the usual kind of neighborhood a member of the *Ton* would visit, especially a princess. But she prided herself on her open mind about such petty distinctions, relishing the sense of independence she always experienced when she came to one of the lectures in this part of the city. Here she could be among like-minded individuals, who valued others for the sharpness of their minds rather than for the weight of their pocketbooks or the fashionable quality of their attire.

Once inside, she greeted a few acquaintances, accepted a cup of hot, sweet tea, then took a seat in the back of the drawing room, as was her habit. This afternoon's speaker was a female writer and lecturer who had traveled extensively throughout Europe seeking to understand the status of women in various cultures and find universal themes and solutions for their intellectual and economic enslavement.

Ariadne opened her blue silk reticule and took out a pencil and paper. She listened attentively as the lecture began, making notes now and then on her pad.

Nearly an hour later, her tea was long gone and her pad and pencil lay idle in her lap. She repressed the need to yawn, opening her eyes wider and wishing the room weren't quite so warm.

She sensed someone slipping into one of the seats in the row of chairs behind her. She did not turn, but forced herself to sit up straighter and refocus on the speaker as the woman launched into a detailed comparison of the educational levels of females in southern versus northern European regions.

"Are these things always this dull?" mused a rich masculine voice near her ear, "or is this one just particularly deadly?"

She stiffened and whipped her head around to find Rupert leaning forward in his seat, his arms folded casually atop the back of the chair beside her.

Her lethargy disappeared. "What are you doing here?" she said under her breath.

Devil take it. Was there nowhere she could be safe from him?

He shrugged. "I had a spare hour. I thought I'd see what was so interesting that you would come halfway across Town for it. From what I've heard, you would have had more fun staying home and taking a nap."

"This is an intellectual discussion. Just because the subject is not to your liking does not make it unworthy." As for its excitement level, she refused to comment. Not everyone could be counted upon to be a scintillating speaker.

"It still sounds like a great load of trifle to me."

"Then why do you not go away?" she shot back, careful to keep her voice down.

"And miss an opportunity to watch you try to keep your eyes open? I've rarely been so entertained."

Just how long had he been here watching her? she wondered in outrage.

"Besides," he said quietly, "I wished to speak with you."

She glared at him. "You *are* speaking with me."

"Privately. Why do we not go somewhere less crowded?"

She bit back the first retort that sprang to mind, which was to tell him that he could go to Hades for all she cared. Yet loath though she was to admit it, Rupert was right: the speaker was exceedingly dull, however worthy her philosophy might be.

"Very well," she agreed with a barely veiled sigh.

Careful not to be any more disruptive than necessary, she secured her pencil and pad inside her reticule and rose to her feet. She ignored the few stray glances that came her way, including a chastening frown from the lecturess herself, and followed Rupert from the room.

The town house had one other small parlor, on the opposite side of the hallway. She led him there, grateful there were no servants in sight. "Now, what is so colossally important that you felt the need to disrupt my afternoon?"

"I'd hardly say that was a disruption. More like a rescue, in my estimation."

Pikes Peak Library District

Sand Creek Library
1821 S Academy Blvd
PPLD.ORG

Borrowed Items 11/15/2017 at 11:07
XXXXX6217

Item Title	Due Date
Tempted to touch	12/6/2017
The princess and the peer	12/6/2017
Her highness and the highlander : a princess brides romance	12/6/2017
The trouble with princesses	12/6/2017

She crossed her arms. "What do you want, Rupert? Or have you come merely to give me another lecture on the evil of my ways?"

He arched a golden brow. "If I thought a repetition of the sentiments I expressed during our last private encounter would have any effect on you, then yes, I would recite my warnings afresh."

Strolling toward the window, he gazed out on a narrow side garden before turning back toward her. "But from what I have observed over the past couple of weeks, you do not seem to have taken my words to heart."

"If you mean that I refuse to see villains around every corner, then you are right. The men with whom I choose to be acquainted are gentlemen, who treat me with care and respect. I have no need to fear them any more than I fear you. I shall not allow you to frighten me out of my decision to take a lover, Your Royal Highness, simply to appease your sense of propriety."

"Is that what I'm doing? You think it is the potential loss of your virtue and reputation that concerns me?"

"In the main, yes."

"Then you would be mistaken, although those are assuredly considerations that are difficult to overlook."

She opened her mouth to argue, but he held up a hand to forestall her. "However," he said, "I can see that continuing to debate the point is of no use."

"Absolutely none. I am quite determined, you see."

His brow furrowed. "Yes, I believe I do. Which is why I have been giving your . . . wishes on this matter a great deal of thought."

"Oh really? Have you been devising new ways to harass and vex me? Plotting new schemes designed to thwart my every attempt at enjoyment? You may think that by popping up at every ball and party I attend you will deter me, but it only makes me more persistent, more determined to have my way."

"So I can see, though I can hardly be held to account for receiving invitations to the same social functions as you, considering that we both move in the same social circles."

"Perhaps not, but you can be held to account for accepting those invitations. I'm sure you would have refused half of them were it not for your sudden, and unwanted, interest in my affairs."

He shrugged, making no effort to refute her charge. The clear amusement in his gaze made her blood boil.

"I am a fully grown woman," she stated. "I have no need of your protection."

"Maybe you do not, but you would be wise to take it. Which leads me back to the reason I wished to speak with you. I have a proposition I would like to make."

"Really?" she said skeptically. "And what, pray tell, might that be?"

"Why do we not be more comfortable and take a seat?" He gestured toward the nearby sofa.

She stood, unmoving. "I am perfectly comfortable as I am."

"Very well. As I said, I have been doing a great deal of thinking, and although I believe you would be best served by putting aside this radical notion of yours, I can see that you are indeed as determined as you say."

"I am."

"Knowing you as I do and given your sheer propensity for courting trouble—"

"I do not *court* trouble."

"Maybe not, but it finds you nonetheless. Which means that if you continue on your present course you will most surely land yourself in a great deal of difficulty. Rather than invite such calamity to rain down upon you, I suggest you take measures to minimize the risks."

"What sort of measures?"

"By taking a lover who will have a care for your reputation and your safety. A man who will see to it that no great harm comes to you in the course of this madness that you voluntarily seek."

"But that is precisely what I have been attempting to do in my search of eligible gentlemen!" she exclaimed.

"Yet you risk exposure by the very nature of your search. You need a man you can trust implicitly," he said smoothly. "A man who would never have cause to reveal your secrets."

"Oh? And just who might this paragon be that you have in mind?"

The blue in his eyes darkened, gleaming with a light she had seen only once before. "Why, myself, of course."

Chapter Seven

Rupert watched as Ariadne's arms dropped to her sides, her lips parting on a quick inhalation. Her eyes widened, her pupils dilating so that the black nearly swallowed up the green of her irises.

"Clearly you are surprised," he observed. "Perhaps you might like to take that seat now?"

She nodded, making no objection when he took her elbow and steered her to the sofa. She sank down onto the cushions. He believed it was the first time he had ever seen her speechless.

"Would you care for a glass of sherry?" he asked.

She shook her head.

After a moment she lifted her gaze to his. "Why are you making this offer . . . ?"

"I believe I have given you my primary reasons. I don't want you left damaged without so much as a shred of your reputation remaining."

"I told you I don't care about my reputation," she murmured.

"Then you are shortsighted and foolish."

Hot color flooded her cheeks, her mouth drawing into a tight line.

"Now before you get your ribbons in a knot, hear me out," he said.

"Why should I?"

"Because," he began, as he took a seat on the couch next to her, "I can give you exactly what you want without your having to take any undue risks. In other words, you can, as the saying goes, have your cake and eat it too."

A frown creased her strawberry blond brows. "I thought you were opposed to my taking a lover."

"I was, but at heart I am a pragmatist. Short of locking you up, which sadly I have not the means to do here in England, there is nothing I can really do to stop you."

"Though you have certainly given it a good try these past two weeks."

He chuckled. "I have. You are right. But my efforts grow wearisome for us both, I think. Upon reflection, I realized that you would simply persist in this notion of yours until you found some way to succeed, to your everlasting detriment."

"You don't know that."

"I know the character of the men you have been considering, and none of them are worthy of the great trust you would be placing in their hands by taking them to your bed."

Her frown deepened.

"So, it seemed to me that a compromise was in order."

"Meaning that this arrangement would simply be a way to keep me from causing an embarrassing scandal?" she shot back, regaining some of her natural fire. "It sounds rather cold-blooded to me."

"Oh, an affair with me will be anything but cold-blooded. I promise you that."

Reaching out, he stroked his knuckles over the side of her face from temple to chin. Though she tried to conceal it, he felt her response, a faint quiver beneath her skin that gave her away.

He smiled and leaned forward. "You can't pretend we aren't compatible, not after that night in the study. You must think of it sometimes."

"You are wrong. I don't," she said.

But he could tell she was lying by the way her gaze refused to meet his own.

He caught her chin between his fingers. "Then maybe you need a reminder. A little something to convince you I'm right."

Bending low, he crushed his lips to hers, using just enough pressure, just enough skill and persuasion to hold her in his thrall. For a second she tried to pull away, but then she quivered again, her mouth trembling as a ragged sigh escaped.

And he knew he had her.

He deepened their kiss, not giving her the chance to do anything but feel. Her eyelids drifted closed, her lips softening as they grew warm and pliable against his own. Using the very tip of his tongue, he drew a damp line across the plump curve of her lower lip and felt her quake.

He smiled and stroked again, the honeyed taste of her, the lush texture of her soft skin, sizzling through his veins like wildfire. How easy it would be to give himself over to the sensations.

The temptations.

But for now, he needed to keep his head. Needed to make her see the wisdom of choosing him as her lover. There would be time enough later to sate himself on her loveliness. Not that he intended to go quite as far as she thought or wished, but he would give her the pleasure she craved. He would see to it that she had nothing to regret.

Slowly, reluctantly, he drew away.

She sat unmoving, eyes still closed. She looked a bit like she was floating.

He skimmed his fingers over her cheek. "See how good we are together? Tell me you will be my lover, Ariadne."

Her eyes opened, a misty passion lingering in their depths. As he watched, she worked to push it away. "I–I don't know. I need to think."

"Very well. But do not think too long. I'll want an answer soon."

She nodded.

Later that evening Ariadne stood in a crowded ballroom, her mind still awhirl with thoughts of Rupert and his startling suggestion.

Be my lover, he had said.

She shivered again just remembering his words and his kiss.

Of all the men she had considered as potential lovers, she had never thought of him—well, not seriously.

Naturally, she'd thought of his kisses from that night in the study, despite the denial she had offered when he'd questioned her this afternoon. She'd even dreamed of being in his arms again, reliving the raw passion and heady delight of his touch.

But in the cool light of day, any notions of pursuing a more intimate relationship with him had seemed laughable at best. They were longtime adversaries, for one, the pair of them mixing together about as well as two cats in a basket. He needled her and she needled him back. That's the way it had been since their very first meeting years ago.

So how could she now be expected to think of him in such a radically different manner? How could she contemplate taking him into her bed and letting him be the one to introduce her to all the pleasurable mysteries of physical love?

Yet the idea sent hot and cold tingles coursing over her skin, made her stomach clench and the most delicate parts of her body ache with a longing she had never felt before.

He would teach her—or so he said.

This could all be nothing more than a ruse designed to keep her from making a connection with a likely gentleman. Yet in all their dealings, Rupert had never lied to her, and she did not think he was lying now. He'd offered to be her lover and he meant it. He'd told her he would keep her safe and he meant that as well.

But did he truly desire her?

Did he really want to be her lover?

Her first?

If it had been anyone else, she would have discussed the whole situation with Emma. Asked for her advice on how to proceed. But how could she when Rupert was Emma's brother, and her older brother to boot?

Ordinarily she was too brazen for her own good, and not easily embarrassed. Yet part of her cringed to think of revealing the details of her amorous encounters with Rupert. Even as close as she and Emma were, she just couldn't imagine confiding the truth, not even to her dearest friend.

Besides, she sensed that Rupert would be far from pleased if she shared what she imagined he considered a private matter between the two of them. If she agreed to this affair, she realized that he meant them to keep it in the strictest of confidence—from everyone, even from his sister.

So, was she really thinking of accepting him?

There would certainly be benefits to the arrangement, over and above the excellent points he had already made. He was right when he said she could trust him. Out of all the gentlemen she was considering, he was the only one who truly had no reason to reveal their affair. He had nothing to gain, no pride to stoke, no financial agenda to seek. With him she wouldn't have to worry for her reputation, which would be nice to keep if she could, she realized. She also knew him, knew the kind of man he was, so there would be no surprises there.

Plus, from a purely practical standpoint, an affair between them would be easy to conduct. After all, they lived in the same house, with his rooms only just down the hall. It would make meeting at night no more difficult than maneuvering through the house unobserved.

Except for the servants, of course. There were always the servants to consider.

But her maid was loyal; Ariadne knew she wouldn't say a word, even if she found out. And his servants were scrupulously tight-lipped, especially his valet. She had met his valet and could tell that the man would rather have been put to death than reveal Rupert's private dealings.

So as long as she and Rupert were careful, an affair between them might be the very best of all worlds.

Have I decided, then? Shall I tell Rupert yes?

She was contemplating the question yet again when her dance partner presented himself.

Lord Selkirk bowed low, then straightened with a smile on his face. "Princess Ariadne, a pleasure as always. May I say that you are looking particularly lovely this evening."

"Why, thank you, my lord." She smoothed a gloved palm over the skirt of her bronze silk gown with its rounded half-sleeves, sheer white gauze overskirt, and wide flounce embroidered with small blue and gold birds in midflight. It was one of her favorite dresses. She had worn it tonight specifically to soothe her unsettled thoughts and give her a little extra confidence.

"And may I say the same of you," she replied.

Selkirk's eyes widened momentarily; then he laughed with clear good humor.

She smiled and accepted his arm so he could escort her onto the dance floor. As they strolled deeper into the ballroom, she glanced around in search of Rupert. But for the first time in the past two weeks, he was nowhere to be seen.

Was he even there? He hadn't accompanied her, Emma, and Nick in the family coach tonight. And rather than join them for dinner, he'd sent word through his valet that he had a prior engagement and would see them later.

How much later? And what was he doing?

Odd as it might seem, she wondered if he was giving her some private time to make her decision. Although tonight's ball was hardly private, surrounded as she was by a crush of people who were all wildly determined to make merry.

But she'd had no more chance to consider what she would tell Rupert when she saw him, as Selkirk drew her into the dance. And maybe that was Rupert's ultimate goal. To lull her into a false complacency where she imagined she still had a choice.

What worried her most was wondering if she really wanted one.

Selkirk was an excellent dancer and soon her mind was pleasantly preoccupied. By the end of the set, she was slightly out of breath from the lively movements of a contra dance, her cheeks flushed and moist with an invisible sheen of perspiration.

"Warm?" he inquired, as they left the floor, arm in arm.

"A bit." She opened her silk fan and waved it over her heated skin.

"I supposed I should return you to your friends, but perhaps you would enjoy a few minutes in the garden first?"

His offer did sound lovely, the cool night air and open spaces beckoning just beyond the glass doors of the ballroom.

A glance across the room showed her that Emma and

Nick were standing together, his head bent attentively over hers as they talked and laughed. Many frowned on the pair's unfashionable habit of living in each other's pockets—including Rupert, who thought displays of affection should be private.

But Ariadne found her friends' devotion charming. More couples should be so obviously in love.

"Yes," she told Selkirk, meeting his dark gaze. "A breath of fresh air would be most welcome."

The night was warm, yet still felt cooler than the packed ballroom. She drew in a deep lungful of air, relishing the subtle fragrance of jasmine and roses dancing on the slight breeze. A few crickets sang a happy tune, while fireflies winked in little bursts of light that briefly illuminated the dark garden beyond.

She let Selkirk lead her a few yards along the wide stone terrace, the noise from the party growing dimmer with each step they took. Just as she was about to call a halt to their wandering, he stopped.

"It's a lovely night," she said, gazing at a white marble statue that stood out like a pale ghost in the darkness.

"It is," he agreed in a soft voice. "But nowhere near as lovely as you."

Yesterday she would have been glad to find herself alone and in a secluded location with Lord Selkirk. He was handsome and interesting and sophisticated, everything she could want in a potential lover. Yet now that she was with him, here in this spot where it would be so easy to let him kiss her, all she could think about was Rupert.

Rupert's voice.

Rupert's mouth brushing against hers.

Rupert asking to share her bed.

"We should be returning," she said abruptly, starting to go back the way they had come.

Before she could do so, Selkirk took her hand, holding her in place.

"Not yet," he said, his voice deep and lyrical, yet containing none of the whiskied rhythm of his rival's.

And then he was kissing her, his touch practiced and urbane with none of the hesitation from which some of her other kissing partners had suffered. He was an excellent kisser, his skills in that area as impressive as his skills on the dance floor.

Suddenly curious to know if she would experience the same dizzying rush of pleasure that she had felt earlier that afternoon in Rupert's arms, she gave herself over to the moment. She waited, part of her wanting, even wishing, that she would lose herself within his embrace and forget all about Rupert Whyte.

But the rush didn't come. Pleasure didn't burst in her veins and leave her breathless and giddy for more. Instead, she found the kiss sadly hollow, her mind disappointingly her own, her senses those of an observer rather than an eager participant.

Reaching up, she laid her palms against his chest and gave a little push.

Selkirk hesitated, then broke the kiss. "Forgive me," he said in a husky voice. "You're so beautiful. I couldn't help myself."

"No, no, it's quite all right. But we really should be getting back now."

She was willing to court scandal, but not for this. Not for him.

"Wait. There is something I must ask you," he said.

"Yes?"

Without warning, he squeezed her hand and dropped to one knee. "Princess Ariadne, I know I am but a lowly baron, nothing to compare to you in rank or wealth. But I find that I must have you. You are all I think about these days. All I want. Say you will set me free from my misery and agree to be my wife."

She stared.

His wife?

Good God.

She gazed into his dark eyes, which were shining with hope and anticipation. She'd had suitors propose before, and refusing them never got any easier. It was worse when she actually liked the man, as she did Selkirk. But liking and loving were two very different emotions and she would not be persuaded to accept a pale substitute for the real thing.

"My lord, you have quite taken me by surprise," she began, searching for some easy way to let him down. "I was not expecting a declaration from you."

"No, I suppose not, but you have one before you nevertheless."

"Indeed. Oh, pray stand up. I cannot have you kneeling on this hard stone."

"I would willingly continue to do so if you would but relieve my anxiety with an answer. But it shall be as you wish, Your Highness."

Smoothly, Selkirk gained his feet and straightened. He waited in patient silence for her reply.

"My lord, I—," she began, then stopped when she heard the scrape of a footfall and sensed they were no longer alone. She gazed out into the darkness and saw the shadowed outline of a tall man with broad shoulders and golden hair.

She scowled and suppressed an oath.

Of all the times for Rupert to finally make an appearance, he could not have chosen a worse one. He must have arrived and come looking for her. Just how long had he been watching them? And listening?

Slowly, obviously aware that she had noticed his presence, he strolled forward.

As he did, she drew her hand out of Selkirk's grasp, then looked up again to meet Rupert's gaze across the dimly lit terrace. "Your Royal Highness."

"Princess. Selkirk. Don't let me disturb you," he told them. "Do carry on."

She cringed, hearing the underlying displeasure in his words. Though what right did he have to be angry? She'd made him no promises.

Not yet.

Still, an uncomfortable sense of guilt slid through her, leaving her short-tempered and on edge. "Well, Lord Selkirk and I were having a private discussion, but I suppose we can continue it later."

Now it was Selkirk's turn to scowl. "I would rather we continue it now, Your Highness, if you do not mind."

Blast it. She'd hoped to at least have a reprieve, maybe even be able to give her refusal in a letter. But turning down a man's proposal of marriage in a note was a cowardly thing to do and Lord Selkirk deserved better.

"Yes, of course, my lord. You are right." She met Rupert's gaze again. "Some privacy, Prince Rupert, if you would be so good."

He raised a sardonic brow. "Of course. I would not wish to intrude any further on your tête-à-tête."

With a curt bow, he strode off.

She repressed a sigh, deciding she would find a way to handle Rupert once she was done handling Selkirk. Although handling Rupert was always a tricky matter at best. But she would deal with that particular bit of bother later.

"Now, my lord, where were we?" She forced a smile.

Selkirk looked very solemn. "I had just asked you to marry me and you were about to give your reply."

"Yes, I was." She threaded her fingers together. "You do me a great honor, my lord, with your proposal, but as much as I enjoy your company and friendship, I am afraid—"

"That you cannot accept," he finished in a flat tone. "Yes, you needn't continue. I understand your sentiments completely."

"My lord, please do not be angry. I have no wish to hurt you. Truly, I like you very much. I just do not believe we would suit, at least not as husband and wife."

His eyes were cold. "He'll never marry you, you know."

She blinked but otherwise did not react. "What's that? I do not know to whom you refer."

"Of course you do. You may be as royal as he, but the prince has too much ambition to settle for an empty legacy. You would bring him nothing in terms of alliances or wealth. He may want you in his bed, but he'll never offer you a ring."

She stiffened, angling her chin at an arrogant tilt. "You mistake the matter, my lord," she said coldly. "His Royal Highness is my friend's brother, nothing more. I have no interest in marriage to him."

"Keep telling yourself that, Princess. It will make the future disappointment easier to abide." He bowed sharply. "I bid you good night."

"Yes, my lord. Good night."

But she knew for them it was good-bye.

As for his assertions about Rupert, he was wrong. She and Rupert could barely be in the same room for five minutes without quarreling. Marriage between them would be absurd. Insane. As for Rupert wanting her? Was Selkirk right about that? Did Rupert desire her for reasons that went far beyond his wish to keep her out of trouble? Remembering his kiss this afternoon, she thought he must.

And how did she feel?

She shivered again, gooseflesh rising on her skin despite the warm evening air.

"You really shouldn't be out here alone, you know," said a deep, smooth voice from behind her.

She spun around and found Rupert standing in the shadows.

Her pulse slowed, but not much.

Slowly, he walked forward. "Selkirk ought to have escorted you back inside, even if the two of you did have words."

"How do you know we had words? Were you listening?" she added, aghast.

"I didn't need to. The way he stalked off spoke volumes. He looked sorely disappointed."

"So you were watching?"

He shrugged. "I agreed to give you privacy—I didn't say how much. Don't worry, I only returned in time to see the last. Neither of you looked terribly cozy."

She linked her hands together again. "We weren't, not that it is any of your business."

"Oh, I think it is very much my business, particularly given what happened between us this afternoon. I presume you refused his suit."

"So you *were* listening," she accused.

"No. I just know that if he'd made you an improper proposal, rather than a marriage proposal, he would not have looked so bitter. He would just have taken it in his stride and tried importuning you again later."

"Oh, you're impossible."

"But I am right, am I not?"

Her silence was her answer.

"You aren't sorry, are you?" he asked after a moment.

"About what?"

"Turning him down. It was the correct decision. You can do far better than a lowly baron with an impoverished estate."

"I didn't refuse him because of those things. Material considerations do not matter to me."

"If they do not, then you are even more foolish than I imagined."

She fixed him with a hard look. "It is not foolish to wish for affection in a marital relationship. Love ought to have something to do with such things."

"Perhaps, but it so rarely does."

"Your sister married for love and is blissfully happy. And our friend Mercedes—she adores her Scotsman, even if they do live in the hinterlands. Love is not an impossible thing."

"If you believe that, then why have you given up on finding it?"

"Who says I have given up?"

"If you had not," he said darkly, "you wouldn't be seeking a lover."

Reaching out, he pulled one of her hands free and enfolded it inside his. "So, are you still seeking a man to take to your bed, or have you had second thoughts and changed your mind?"

She met his gaze, his eyes blue even in the dim light. "No, I have not changed my mind."

Why did her voice sound so husky?

"Then have you decided about us?" He lifted her hand and pressed a kiss against her palm that sent a few hundred butterflies fluttering through her stomach. "Will you be my lover?"

Would she? She knew the time had come to choose. And yet something inside her still wasn't certain.

"Why are you doing this?" she asked. "Is it just to keep me out of trouble or is there something else?"

Her heart thudded in her chest, afraid to hear his answer, knowing he would not lie.

"You are a handful, no doubt about it." He curved his arm around her waist and pulled her nearer. "But it is more. Far, far more. I want you, Ariadne. And I want you to want me too. Say yes."

She trembled and arched up on her toes to meet his kiss. "Yes."

Chapter Eight

Ariadne closed her eyes and let herself fall, tumbling down into the dark, sensual depths of his kiss. She breathed him in—starch and spice and clean, healthy male. He tasted like wine and sin, his lips firm but smooth, almost silken. And warm, deliciously so.

"Open up," he whispered against her trembling mouth.

She slid her arms around his neck and obeyed, parting her lips to let him claim her more deeply, ready to let him teach her all the forbidden things she so desperately longed to learn.

Her heart pounded, thrumming in her chest and even, it seemed, in her ears. She shivered with pleasure, her body arching instinctively closer to his. He gathered her nearer, pressing her against the hard planes of his silk-covered chest.

She had never really noticed how tall he was until now. As she stood in his arms, her head reached barely past his shoulders. He settled her more securely inside his powerful embrace and kissed her harder, bending so he could ravish her mouth with a thoroughness that left her dizzy.

She gasped as he caressed the length of her spine with a slow, tantalizing glide, then gasped again when he reached the curve of her buttocks and cupped her there. She shuddered, wild heat and raw chills chasing over her skin. Mercy, if he could make her feel like this fully clothed on a terrace, just imagine the wonders he would surely be able to perform in the privacy of a bedchamber.

The thought had her quivering inside.

He kissed her neck, inviting her to arch back over his arm so he could have freer access. Utterly lost, she allowed the intimacy, a soft purr reverberating low in her throat.

She felt him smile before he kissed his way up to her earlobe and caught the nub between his teeth. He gave a tiny nip.

Her eyes popped open and she moaned.

But instead of kissing her again, he straightened up.

She blinked, disappointed, and then reached to pull him back down again.

Gently, he resisted. "I think we've gone far enough tonight. It wouldn't do to let matters get out of hand and be caught here together."

No, she supposed it would not. Still, she would have liked another kiss or two. But she nodded anyway and let him ease away.

"What's next, then?" she asked with a breathless hitch to her voice. "Will I see you later tonight? Will you . . . come to my room?"

His eyes widened momentarily; then he smiled. "You are eager, aren't you?"

Her pulse picked up speed again as she waited for his answer.

He skimmed his thumb lightly over the crest of her cheekbone, leaving a trail of fire in its wake. "I can see that having an affair with you is going to be anything but ordinary. But no, I will not come to you tonight."

Her shoulders sank a little, revealing her disappointment.

He chuckled. "Don't worry, we'll begin soon. I find it's wise not to rush into these things too quickly. Anticipation, after all," he added in a velvet voice, "only enlivens the game."

Warm tingles spread through her chest and down low into her belly. Now that the decision was made to take him as her lover, she wanted to begin, especially after his kisses this afternoon and here now this evening. But in this matter, even she had to admit that Rupert was the experienced one. The teacher, if you will.

Then again, that didn't mean she had lost her independent streak or her determination. She was still in charge of her own decisions, her own destiny.

"If you insist, Your Highness. Just don't delay too long," she challenged, "else I grow bored."

His eyes narrowed. "Oh, you won't be bored. You have my word on that."

Another shiver raced through her because when Rupert gave his word, he never broke it.

"Allow me to escort you back inside," he said, offering his arm. "It won't do for you to be missed."

Laying her hand on his sleeve, she let him lead her back into the noise and bright candlelight of the party.

"Will there be anything further this evening, Your Royal Highness?"

Rupert glanced across the dressing room to where his valet waited with polite attentiveness. "No, that will be all, thank you, Becker."

"Good night, sir."

"Yes, good night."

The servant let himself out, the door closing almost soundlessly at his back.

Tightening the tie on his dark blue silk dressing gown, Rupert strode through the connecting door that led to a sitting room and his bedchamber beyond. He stopped next to a small table where a cut-crystal decanter filled with brandy and a pair of glasses were arranged on a silver tray.

Unstoppering the decanter, he poured an inch of brandy into a snifter, then carried the drink across to a comfortable armchair that was positioned at an angle near the unlighted fireplace. A leather-bound book waited on a narrow side table, left there from his reading the previous evening.

Setting his drink down on the table, he took a seat, then picked up his book. He opened it to the marked page and began to read, taking an idle swallow of brandy as he did. But after only two paragraphs, his thoughts began to wander.

Will you come to my room tonight?

Ariadne's words, spoken in her melodious contralto, echoed through his mind and whispered like satin over his senses. His fingers tightened against the edges of the book, a slow, warm arousal heating his blood. It would be easy, too easy, to go down the hall to her room. A little stealth, a quiet knock, and she would let him in; he knew that much without hesitation.

But now was not the right time, however much his body might assure him otherwise. This affair that he'd agreed to begin needed to be handled with care. She craved passion, but even more, he knew, what she needed most was to be seduced. Well and thoroughly seduced so that her usual defenses gave way beneath the force of her desire.

Ariadne was a strong-willed woman. Actually she was one of the strongest-willed people—man or woman—that he had ever met. Despite her stubborn insistence that she wanted to explore the sexual side of her nature, she had no true notion of what would bring her real pleasure. Had she chosen some other man to take to her bed, she would surely have ended up disappointed. He said that not out of hubris on his part, but because he knew her too well. She wouldn't let her guard down easily, no matter how much she might believe otherwise. She trusted few people, and trust was an essential ingredient to pleasure.

That and surrender.

She would have to learn to surrender, and he had to admit that he relished the opportunity to be the one who was there to watch her let go.

He groaned and tossed back a healthy swallow of brandy.

Honestly, he was mad. He should never have agreed to this folly. Hell, he'd been the one to suggest it.

But she was determined to ruin herself, so he'd talked himself into believing it was the wisest choice.

And it was.

Anyone else would have used her, then cast her cruelly aside, leaving her abandoned and likely humiliated. She thought those things couldn't happen to her, that she could weather such storms, that she could be infamous and live without feeling shame. But she had a softer heart than she let on. Headstrong as she might be, she did not deserve to be crushed and embittered.

He would see to it that she enjoyed their affair and came out unscathed at its inevitable end.

Really, when he thought about it in such terms, he was doing a noble thing.

Hah!

What a fraud he was.

Just admit it.

You want her.

He drank more brandy and tried not to think about Ariadne in her bedroom only just down the corridor. Forced himself not to imagine her lying against the sheets, her fiery hair spread like a molten river over her pillows, her night-gown bunched against her milky white thighs.

Groaning under his breath, he resumed his reading.

But it was a long time before any of the words actually made sense.

Chapter Nine

Ariadne covered a yawn with a hand as she walked into the breakfast room the following morning. Thanks to Rupert she hadn't slept well—again. She'd spent the night tossing and turning beneath the sheets, her dreams filled with memories of their kisses and his promise of more to come. Part of her had waited all night, dosing off and on, in hopes that he would change his mind and come to her bedroom after all.

She'd awakened a few hours later, as morning light crept around the velvet curtains, surprised to realize she'd slept at all. Tired and irritable, she'd flung aside the bedclothes and padded barefoot into the adjoining bathing chamber.

After she took a warm bath and drank the cup of hot tea her maid brought, her spirits improved greatly, even though her weariness lingered on.

Attired now in a morning dress of spotted green muslin, with her hair pinned in a simple knot at the nape of her neck, she stepped into the breakfast room, only to stop short.

Emma and Dominic were seated at opposite ends of the

breakfast table as usual, talking quietly. But this morning there was one other individual who almost never joined them. In fact, she could count on the fingers of one hand the number of times he had.

Her pulse gave an annoying little stutter as she looked across at Rupert's bold patrician features, his hair gleaming the color of ripe wheat in the morning sunshine. He lifted his coffee cup just then and took a sip, his midnight blue eyes moving to meet hers over the rim.

"Oh, good morning," Emma chimed in a cheery voice, taking notice of her.

Ariadne entered the room. "Good morning."

Nick greeted her as well, but Rupert just drank more coffee, then set his china cup into its saucer.

"Look who decided to join us this morning," Emma continued, casting a speaking glance at her brother.

Ariadne met Rupert's gaze again, careful to keep her own expression impassive. "*Hmm*, so I see."

Emma stirred her tea. "You could have knocked me over with a feather when he came in. How long has it been since you joined us for anything other than dinner, Rupert?"

He leaned back, taking a moment to consider. "Truly, I cannot recall. Yet somehow this morning seemed like an excellent opportunity to correct my errant behavior."

A half smile curved his lips, his eyes gleaming in a way that reminded Ariadne of the night just past. Warmth crept over her skin and she turned away abruptly. It wouldn't do to let Emma notice anything amiss—or at least anything *more* than she'd already noticed was amiss. Keeping this from Emma was going to be harder than she'd imagined, particularly if Rupert continued acting out of character.

Honestly, what does he think he is doing? He was the one, after all, who was so emphatic about keeping their affair a secret. Obviously he didn't have a proper sense of caution. Then again, maybe he'd taken a blow to the head last night, sometime between leaving the party and arriving at the breakfast table? she speculated with a bit of wry humor.

Deciding that keeping herself occupied was the best strategy for now, she crossed to the buffet and took a plate out of the warmer. She lifted the lid off the first silver chafing dish, only to quickly put it back.

Steak and kidney pie.

She wrinkled her nose in distaste. She detested offal of any kind—heart, liver, kidneys, pancreas—organ meats always sent her appetite scurrying away. She didn't understand why anyone wanted to eat such things. Although she had to admit that in her youth, she'd been subjected to worse fare, such as pickled fish served in a variety of brines and sauces.

It was bad enough being subjected to such ghastly dishes in the evening, but for breakfast . . .

She gave another inward grimace.

"The blood sausage is quite delicious," said a smooth, deep voice beside her. "May I offer you a serving?"

She startled. How had Rupert crept up on her without her being aware? She hadn't even heard him approach.

She shot him a withering look. "No. You know I detest such fare."

"Kippers, then?" he inquired blithely, even though she could see the evil glint in his eyes. "I am certain you'll want two or three at the very least."

"I don't want any," she said quietly, "as well you know. Are you deliberately trying to annoy me this morning?"

"I am only trying to shake you out of your nerves. You're tense as a fox in a ring full of hounds. If you keep this up, my sister will be interrogating you until you break."

She resisted the urge to turn around and see if Emma was indeed watching them. "Well, she's bound to wonder regardless, since you suddenly decided to grace us with your presence this morning. What *were* you thinking?"

"Actually, I decided it would be easier in future if we are openly seen to have laid aside the old gauntlet between us. A better rapport seems wise under the circumstances, particularly since we will be spending a great deal more time in each other's company."

Her brows drew close and she lowered her voice to barely above a whisper. "I cannot see why that should be necessary. Nothing has to change between us except . . . well, you know."

His lips twisted sardonically. "Ah, so you just want me to sneak into your room at night, have my way with you, and then leave, *hmm*?"

She held back a gasp. "Well, not precisely, but something close. We hardly need to live in each other's pockets, I should think."

"I've found that taking a lover is far more enjoyable when it's about more than sex. Which I would be happy to teach you if you would but follow my direction."

Before she could open her mouth to debate the point, he lifted the lid off another chafing dish. "The ham is very good," he said in a carrying voice. "Allow me to cut you a slice."

Aware that they had been whispering together far too long, she held out her plate and waited for him to carve.

"And a scone as well," he suggested, indicating a cloth-covered basket nearby.

Resigned, she took a scone.

"Eggs?" he inquired, after he had laid the ham on her plate.

Her lips tightened since she knew she would never be able to eat half the food he was insisting she take.

He laughed and spooned a generous helping of golden scrambled eggs next to the rest of her meal.

"What are the two of you talking about over there?" Emma called. "Something interesting, I hope."

Ariadne sent him a stare from under her lashes that clearly said, *Yes, what is it we are discussing, oh great teacher?*

But the look he returned was easy and unconcerned.

Replacing a last lid, his own plate replenished, he turned and strolled back to the table. "I was just agreeing to give Ariadne some instruction."

Only long practice enabled her to hide her shock. What on earth was he saying? Surely he wasn't about to reveal their affair to Emma and Nick?

But he resumed his seat at the table as if his remark was nothing out of the ordinary. Biting the inside of her lip, she slid into the chair across from him.

"Instruction?" Emma asked. "And whatever might you be planning to teach our Ariadne?"

"Yes," Nick said, joining the conversation. "I find I'm most intrigued to hear as well."

Rupert's gaze met Ariadne's as he calmly chewed, then swallowed, a forkful of eggs and blood sausage. He wiped his mouth on his napkin, clearly in no hurry to answer.

She frowned as subtly as she could and gave a nearly imperceptible shake of her head, warning him to remain silent.

He smiled serenely back. "She told me she's been dying to learn to drive a carriage, so I've decided to give her a few lessons."

Driving lessons? Was that supposed to be the big secret?

If her foot could have reached, she would have kicked him underneath the table for putting her through so much unnecessary anxiety. But as far as stories went, she had to admit, he'd thought of a good one.

Emma turned to her. "I didn't realize you were interested in learning to drive. Why did you never mention it before?"

And why, said Emma's look, *did you decide to mention it to Rupert, of all people?*

"Oh, it's a recent development," she said in a breezy tone. Picking up the scone on her plate, she broke it in two, delaying. "You remember when Mr. Elliston took me for a spin in his high perch phaeton. I had a magnificent time and have been toying ever since with the idea of learning to take up the ribbons myself."

Emma smiled. "Well, that does sound like something that would appeal to your sense of daring and adventure."

"Yes," Ariadne agreed, warming to the theme. "I shall cut quite a dashing figure driving my own equipage, do you not agree?"

"Indeed." Emma turned toward her brother. "But how did you come to be involved in this undertaking, Rupert?"

"Yes, Your Royal Highness, do tell Emma and Nick all the details," Ariadne urged.

Rupert pinned her with a look that promised retribution at some later date.

Now who wanted to kick the other person underneath the table?

He raised his cup to his mouth and took a long, deep swallow. "It's quite simple. I chanced upon Ariadne at a party where she was discussing the idea with a few of her suitors. She was debating which gentleman to accept, despite her obvious lack of knowledge as to whether the gentlemen in question were nothing but a bunch of ham-fisted dolts."

Quietly, he replaced his cup on its saucer. "Ordinarily I would have left matters as they were, but I feared she would choose unwisely and land herself on the scandal pages. Rather than letting the situation get out of hand, which it was sure to do with Ariadne involved, I offered to provide her instruction. She quite wisely said yes."

Ariadne's eyes narrowed. "Although it's not too late to change my mind."

"But you won't," he said confidently. "You want this too badly."

Her pulse kicked into a faster rhythm.

Fearing that she might give herself away, she looked down at her plate.

"Well, I for one think it an excellent notion that you learn to drive, Ariadne," Nick stated from his end of the table. "More women ought to have at least a rudimentary understanding of how to handle a carriage. Who knows when an emergency might arise and leave a lady in need of such an ability?"

Ariadne looked up, surprised, and a bit chagrined, to have Nick's support.

"Really?" Emma piped. "You've never said so before. Does this mean, then, that you would teach me, should I wish to learn?"

Nick smiled indulgently across at his wife. "Of course. It would be my distinct pleasure."

Emma clapped her hands together. "Oh, what a grand idea. And all thanks to Arie." She sent a beaming smile Ariadne's way.

She could do nothing but smile back.

How on earth had this all become so complicated? She supposed now she really would have to take driving lessons from Rupert. Although the more she thought about it, the more she liked the idea. It would be lovely to have her own carriage and to be able to handle the ribbons with as much skill and confidence as any man. Perhaps she would even buy herself a high perch phaeton, just as she'd claimed.

"So when is your first lesson?" Emma asked, looking from Ariadne to Rupert.

Rupert finished the last of his meal, then laid his fork and knife neatly across his plate. "This afternoon. I see no point in delaying."

Ariadne fidgeted. Was it really driving lessons they would be undertaking or the start of the other lessons he'd promised to give her? Now that they'd told Nick and Emma she was having driving lessons, though, they would have to leave the house.

So driving lessons it was.

For today anyway.

As for tonight . . .

A delicious little shiver chased through her.

"You've barely touched your plate," Rupert remarked, nodding toward her untouched meal. "Eat. It won't do for you to take to the roads hungry."

She opened her mouth to tell him that she would eat or not as she chose. She didn't like taking orders from anyone, particularly Rupert. But she had willingly agreed to this clandestine affair of theirs, so she guessed she would have to get used to his dictatorial ways.

For a while anyway.

"I suppose I will need my strength," she said, picking up her fork. "If for no other reason than to deal with you."

She waited for a scowl to crease his golden brows.

Instead, he laughed. "More coffee," he called to a waiting footman. "I can tell I am going to need my strength too."

"Arie," Emma said nearly half an hour later when it was just the two of them left at the table. "I just wanted to say how pleased I am that you and Rupert are getting along better. You've always been so much at odds. I never imagined a day when the two of you would be voluntarily participating in an activity together."

Ariadne kept her face impassive. If only Emma knew the real activity in which she and her brother were planning to participate.

Should I tell her after all?

But much as she hated keeping secrets from Emma, she knew this was one thing she could not possibly share with her.

She forced a wry smile and rolled her eyes with exaggerated derision. "Well, I wouldn't get too excited about my truce with Rupert. I suspect it will be of a temporary duration at best."

Emma shook her head. "No, I suppose a permanent truce would be asking too much, wouldn't it? I am just glad the two of you are finding a way to be more than politely civil. Who knows, maybe you'll surprise yourselves and end up friends."

Friends? With Rupert? Now that would be something.

But friendship with Rupert was no more likely than the chance that their affair would last longer than a few fleeting weeks.

Once she'd satisfied her sexual curiosity and he felt reasonably assured she wouldn't do anything too extreme to disgrace herself or his family, they would go their separate ways. Naturally, Rupert would need to return to Rosewald to resume his official duties, while she would leave for Scotland to spend time with Mercedes and Daniel before the winter closed in. Whether she and Rupert parted as friends, who could predict?

But until then, she had the rest of the Season in which to explore and enjoy.

And, oh, do I plan to enjoy.

She blinked, only then realizing that she'd fallen silent and that Emma was gazing at her with a speculative expression on her face.

"Is there anything else I should know about this new . . . peace accord—for want of a better term—between you and Rupert?" Emma asked.

Oh, bother it all. If she weren't more careful, Emma would figure out what was going on without Ariadne saying a single word. Emma was an intelligent woman and if she became suspicious, well, she would make it her mission to learn the truth.

Ariadne gave a nonchalant shrug. "What else could there be? Other than the fact that he will likely irritate me to the point of violence within five minutes of our first driving lesson. I shall have to take care to leave my dress pins and penknife at home."

A laugh rippled from Emma's lips. "No, please do not wound him—at least not much. You know how men fuss when they are unwell."

"Indeed, even royal ones. Or maybe I should say, especially a royal one."

They both chuckled again, in complete agreement.

Ariadne breathed a sigh of relief.

Chapter Ten

Later that afternoon, Rupert stood on the pavement outside Lyndhurst House and watched Ariadne descend the front steps. She looked lovely in an afternoon dress of striped yellow and white muslin, a wide-brimmed bonnet on her soft, shining hair that appeared more red than gold in the sunlight. Rather than slippers, she'd worn a pair of sensible half boots of supple brown leather and on her hands a pair of thin driving gloves in an outrageously bold shade of cerise.

She drew to a halt, her eyes fixing on the waiting curricle. "Oh, is that what we're taking?"

"Yes," he said, walking forward to assist her up into the vehicle. "What did you imagine we would be driving?"

"Well, there was talk of a high perch phaeton this morning at breakfast."

He shook his head with wry amusement as he got her settled in the seat. "That was *your* talk, not mine. Only a fool would let a beginner try to learn on a high perch phaeton. The first time you drew up short, we'd both be tossed over the horses' heads and break our necks."

She was unusually quiet as he leapt into the curricle and took a seat beside her. Gathering the reins in his hands, he checked for traffic, then set the horses in motion.

"So, are you really going to teach me to drive?" she asked after a long moment, "or did you just tell Emma and Nick that so you could get us conveniently alone?"

"Both, actually. As I said this morning, we need a plausible reason to be in each other's company more often."

"And I told you I don't see why. You could come to my room at night and we can continue on as we've always done the rest of the time."

"Trust me," he said, not surprised by her stubbornness. "This will be the better arrangement." He maneuvered past a heavy, slow-moving coach and four. "Do you not want to learn to drive? Somehow I thought it might appeal to you, particularly given the freedom it would afford you."

She shot him a glance from under her eyelashes. "I hadn't really given serious consideration to the idea before, but yes, you're right. It does have a distinct appeal, I must confess."

Her blush-pink lips curved upward as if she were savoring the notion, her jewel-bright eyes sparkling. She let out a sultry little laugh, a sound that went straight to his groin.

His hands tightened on the reins and he shifted on the seat. He forced himself to keep his eyes on the road rather than giving in to the impulse to stare at her.

There would be time later for that and more.

A great deal more.

But first he had driving lessons to give.

"When do we begin, then?" she asked. "Can we start now? Here, pass me the reins."

He gave a short laugh. "Are you mad? I would like to live through the rest of the afternoon, if you don't mind."

"I wouldn't be that bad."

"No, you would be worse."

She crossed her arms. "If you think my driving will be so very dreadful, then why are you bothering to teach me at all?"

"I believe we've already established the reason. But you mistake the matter. I don't think you'll be dreadful, not once you have a bit of instruction. Until then, however, I'm not about to set you loose on a street full of unsuspecting passersby."

"Fine," she bit out. "You don't have to be so cross about it, you know."

His brows rose. "Who is being cross?"

"You are. But then what else should I have expected? Perhaps I ought to have you take us back to Lyndhurst House. I knew if I was with you for any appreciable amount of time, we were bound to start a row."

"Is that what we're doing? I can't say I mind arguing with you these days. Not when it leads to such interesting consequences."

When she remained silent, he turned his head to look at her, trying to decide if she was really angry or not. "Do you truly want me to turn around? It seems a shame, seeing we're nearly to Green Park. I thought it would be a nice quiet place where you can practice without fear of encountering a great many other vehicles. Assuming you still want to learn to drive, that is."

She lowered her arms to her sides and said, "I do. But only if you curb that nasty tongue of yours."

"As you wish. But be careful, Ariadne. You might find you like it if my tongue is a bit nasty every now and again."

Her gaze flew to his, her green eyes wide as she digested the implications of his remark.

He grinned back, suddenly realizing that he was going to enjoy this affair of theirs even more than their sparring.

A few minutes later they arrived at the park. He drove to

one of the less-used lanes, then brought the team to an easy stop. The meadow stretched around them, the grass rippling slightly in the light breeze.

"Here we are," he announced. "Time to begin. Let me show you how to take the reins."

"Oh, I can take then now, can I?" she said mockingly.

"Only because you're in no danger of killing anyone here."

She made a face.

"Don't pout. It's very unbecoming, even if it does put me in mind to kiss you."

Her brows arched. "Does it?"

"Indeed. But only because of the way your lips look and not because of what is coming out of them."

"You're treading on very thin ice today, Your Royal Highness," she warned teasingly. "Very thin."

But rather than rise to her bait, he laughed.

After a moment, she laughed too. "So, how do I hold the reins?"

Half an hour later, Ariadne slowed the powerful team of horses from a gentle trot to a controlled walk, her arms aching slightly from the unaccustomed strain as she guided the carriage along the park lane.

"Splendid, Ariadne," Rupert said encouragingly. "Really splendid. If I didn't know this was your first time driving, I wouldn't have believed it. You're clearly a natural."

She smiled, but kept her eyes fixed on the road ahead, not confident enough yet to look away, despite Rupert's approval. She had to admit that in the past she'd never thought driving looked terribly difficult, but now she realized just how mistaken she'd been. There were an astonishing number of factors involved, every one of which needed to work in harmony in order for the carriage to be driven safely forward.

Most important of all, however, was her ability to communicate well with the horses. The animals were keenly aware of her every movement and gesture, able to sense even the slightest uncertainty or hesitation in her actions. The team had been wonderful, though, tolerating the worst of her novice errors with a benevolent patience that many other creatures would not have displayed.

It had taken a few attempts before everything had fallen into place. One minute she'd been struggling to remember the myriad tips and instructions Rupert had given her, the next she'd been maneuvering the carriage smoothly around a turn, everything suddenly making perfect sense.

She directed the team carefully to the left side of the lane, then brought the carriage to a halt. Only then did she give herself permission to celebrate, a wide smile on her face as she turned to Rupert.

"Well done," he told her again. "Excellent."

She beamed, suddenly becoming aware of the way her heart was thundering in her chest. "Thank you, Your Highness. That was quite . . . exhilarating."

"Did you enjoy yourself?" he asked, raising an inquiring brow.

"Yes," she answered, surprising even herself. "Or at least I did once I figured out how to keep from driving us off the path. You were right not to let me drive in traffic. I would have murdered us all."

He met her gaze. "If you would be so good, please say that again."

"That I would have murdered us all?" she asked, confused.

"No, the part about me being right. I cannot recall ever hearing those words come out of your mouth before."

She shot him a look. "And you likely won't ever again, so enjoy the moment, Your Highness."

Rupert tossed his head back and let loose a deep, throaty laugh, his eyes a vibrant blue in the sunlight.

She relaxed, marveling that she felt so at ease in his company. Strange, when they'd never gotten along in the past. Yet to her great surprise, she now knew it to be the truth. She was comfortable with him in a way she could be with only a handful of people. And soon she would be even closer, allowing him the liberty of both her virtue and her trust.

How had that happened?

Was Emma right? Was it possible she and Rupert might actually end up friends?

"If you are sufficiently recovered," she said, her words brusque with unexpected emotion, "where shall we go next? Or are we returning home?"

"No, not unless it is your desire to return to Lyndhurst House." He gave her an inquiring look. "I had rather thought we might venture out into Town instead. There is a place I thought we would visit."

"Oh? What place is that?"

A slight smile flickered over his mouth. "I would prefer to keep it a surprise for now."

She thought that over for a moment. "I rather like surprises, so long as they are good ones. Very well, then, Your Highness, you have my leave to surprise me."

"Rupert," he reminded her gently.

Taking her hand, he raised it to his mouth and placed a kiss against the bare skin of her wrist just under the edge of her glove. "When we are alone, Ariadne, let us enjoy the intimacy of using our given names."

She swallowed, hoping he couldn't feel the wild beating of her pulse. "Very well, then, *Rupert*, please do surprise me."

His smile deepened with a look that made her pulse speed

even faster. "Would you care to drive? You've done so ably today; I think you could handle some actual Town driving."

She shook her head. "I thank you for the compliment, but I would rather save the Town driving for our next outing. For now, I shall happily entrust the ribbons to you."

"Perhaps you are right," he said, taking up the reins. "There's no need to do everything in one lesson."

She peeked up at him from under her lashes.

He flicked the reins and set the horses in motion, heading toward the gates.

Twenty minutes later, Rupert brought the carriage to a halt inside the mews at the rear of a great stone house. In that time, he had driven them steadily west into the less-populated area surrounding London, where there were great expanses of open land and quaint, tidy villages.

"Whose home is this? Are we visiting someone?" Ariadne asked.

He turned his head and read the curiosity and interest in her luminous green eyes. "The estate belongs to a friend of mine, who said I might avail myself of its use whenever I like. Presently, he is away."

"Oh," she said, her eyes widening fractionally.

"There is minimal staff," he went on. "Only a caretaker who lives in a small cottage on the property. Otherwise, we are quite alone."

She linked her fingers together in her lap and glanced down.

He put a knuckle under her chin and forced her to look at him. "Where is my bold Ariadne? Surely you are not nervous?"

"Of course not," she declared. "I was just not expecting this today. Here, in the afternoon."

"Ah, but daylight is the best time. It makes everything so much easier to see."

He laughed at her expression. For all her brazen talk, she was still such an innocent.

And I have sworn to corrupt her.

He swallowed a sigh and wondered if he shouldn't just turn the carriage around and drive her home. But if he did, and they did not proceed with the affair as planned, he knew she was stubborn enough to look elsewhere. Foolish enough to seek out another man, who might use and discard her without a second thought for either her well-being or her reputation.

Then there were his own personal motivations and the fact that the more time he spent in her company, the more he wanted to proceed with their mad arrangement.

The more he wanted her.

"You may relax," he said. "I did not bring you here just to seduce you. I had a picnic luncheon packed and stored in the boot. I thought we might begin with that."

"Oh, yes," she said, with a breathless quality to her voice. "That sounds lovely."

He nearly laughed again. Only imagine if he'd taken her up on her offer to come to her room last night—how nervous she would have been if he'd really put her resolve to the test.

He was smiling as he sprang from the carriage. He reached up to lift her down, fitting both hands around her trim waist. As he lowered her to the ground, he couldn't look away. Even shaded by the wide brim of her hat, her eyes were more vividly green than the ripe June grass that swayed gently on the lawn around them, her skin as soft and fragrant as the roses that grew in the gardens nearby.

It would be easy to kiss her, easy not to wait. But here in the stableyard wasn't the place.

Reluctantly, he let her go.

With no grooms in attendance, it was up to him to see to the horses. Despite the fact that he had been born a prince, he'd learned young how to care for a variety of animals. He'd never felt that seeing to their needs was beneath him; in fact, he'd always enjoyed working with animals. They were honest and open; they either liked you or they didn't. One never had to wonder about any ulterior motives when it came to creatures of the non-human variety.

Ironically, he could say the same of Ariadne, although she might take some slight offense at being compared to a horse or a dog or a cat. But she wasn't one to suffer fools lightly, and she made little effort to conceal the truth of her views from anyone, no matter the consequences. Wasn't that one of the reasons they were here today? Because she acted on her wishes and beliefs in a straightforward manner without regard to the dictates of Society's rules? As for liking or disliking people, she was generally honest in that regard as well.

So how did she feel about him these days? A month ago he'd known he was in the *Dislike* column, but now he wasn't entirely sure.

After the horses were watered and secured in a shaded area next to the stables where they could stay cool and clip grass at their own leisurely pace, he retrieved the picnic hamper from the carriage and hooked it over one arm. Striding across to Ariadne, he took her hand without a word and led her toward the house.

But rather than escorting her inside, he went around to a plain wooden door set in a tall stone wall. He flipped open the latch and led her into the intimate garden beyond.

"Oh, how beautiful," she said. "Just smell the flowers. *Hmm*, it's like breathing honey." Pulling her hand free, she moved deeper among the verdant cultivars, stopping here and there to inspect a bloom, rather like a butterfly collecting nectar.

He watched, enchanted.

After taking a moment to make sure the garden door was securely latched, he scanned the grounds for a choice spot for their picnic.

While she wandered deeper into the well-tended foliage, he spread a large blanket over a patch of thick, springy grass. Nearby stood a great tree, its heavy branches stretched above like a pair of sheltering arms to provide protection from the sun and afternoon heat. Sunlight filtered through the leaves, creating dappled patterns on the blanket that shifted with the light breeze.

He opened the hamper and began laying out the food.

"Oh, that looks delectable," she said, appearing suddenly at his side.

"Yes, Emma's cook appears to have outdone herself," he agreed, motioning to a selection that included a cloth-covered ramekin of pâté, a plate of lobster-and-watercress sandwiches, deviled quail eggs, fresh strawberries, and a wedge of ripe golden cheese. "And there are still a few more things I've yet to unpack."

"Gracious. She clearly wanted to give us a variety. Here, let me help," she offered, kneeling down. Her skirts billowed around her in a riot of color, putting him in mind of the flowers she had just been admiring.

He reached into the hamper again.

She reached in too. Their hands touched, skin sliding against skin in the shallow depths of the basket.

Their gazes lifted and locked. He could see the faint beating of her pulse at the base of her throat beneath her fair, nearly translucent skin. He caught hold of her hand and threaded his fingers through hers. With his thumb, he drew a slow circle against the tender flesh of her palm.

Her lips parted and he thought he detected an increase in her pulse.

He smiled. "Which shall it be? Bread or wine?"

"I beg your pardon?" she said, breathless.

"Bread?" He circled his thumb again and felt an answering quiver of her hand. "Or wine? I believe those are two of the items left in the basket. Which one would you like?"

She blinked. "Bread. Or the wine. I-it doesn't matter."

He nearly tugged her forward, images filling his mind of pushing the hamper out of the way and forgetting all about their meal. How easy it would be to tumble her back across the blanket, how simple to jump directly to the best part of their outing.

But they should eat first. There would be time to play later.

He moved his hand away. "In that case, I'll take the wine—that way I can open it. The bread I leave to you."

She gazed into the hamper, giving her head the tiniest of shakes as if trying to clear out the lingering haze.

He smiled to himself, pleased to know he had the power to unsteady the nerves of the brash, seemingly fearless Princess Ariadne. He looked forward to unsteadying her a great deal more.

While he opened the bottle with a few deft twists of a corkscrew, she laid out the loaf of crusty, freshly baked bread together with china plates, silverware, and glasses.

"Here," he said, pouring a glass of golden wine and offering it to her. "Tell me what you think."

She accepted and first raised the glass to her nose to test the bouquet, then took a sip. "*Hmm*, it's delightful." She drank again. "Fruity but not overly sweet. It should be excellent with our meal."

"I am glad you approve." He poured himself a draught. "It's one of mine. That is to say, the vintage was produced on one of the royal farms in Rosewald. It's an experimental variety I've been working on, crossing native grapes with a few cuttings from France and Spain."

"Really? I didn't realize you took an interest in wine cultivation."

"In other words, you thought I just liked to drink."

She chuckled. "Well, you must admit that as regent you have a great many duties. I didn't imagine vintner might be one of them."

"Everyone needs an occasional distraction, even us royals."

She nodded in agreement and took another sip of wine.

"My father enjoyed farming before his health began to fail," he told her. "Potatoes were one of his favorite plants to grow. He said they were a worthy challenge. I remember him when I was a boy, carrying a pitchfork and shovel out to a field behind the palace and digging up the mounds himself. The servants, of course, carried the tools and the baskets full of muddy potatoes back to the kitchens."

He paused to drink his wine.

"My mother thought he was insane," he continued. "Some of the court did as well. He became known as King Kartoffel, although no one ever dared call him that to his face. But he was happy when he was out in his fields. I think if he hadn't been born a prince, he would have been a farmer. I suppose you could say I inherited the trait, although potatoes are of little interest to me except when they appear on my plate."

"What a wonderful story. I'm surprised Emma never told me anything about it."

"She was too young to remember much of it. Papa had already begun to slow down by the time she was out of leading strings, and after our mother's death, he gave his gardening up entirely. Actually, I haven't thought of him like that in years. He's so frail now; I'd nearly forgotten how strong he used to be. As big and stalwart as an ox. He used to toss me in the air and carry me around on his shoulders."

He drank more wine, remembering.

He didn't realize she'd moved until he felt her hand covering his where it lay on the blanket. "I am sorry. Such things are very difficult."

He met her eyes. "Yes, but then, you understand. My troubles must seem slight compared to your own. You do not speak of them often, but I know you miss your family."

Seeing the shadow that passed over her face, he wished immediately that he had not brought it up. She was very stoic about her loss, about the murders that had stolen her parents and siblings from her. He wondered if that was why she let so few people past her guard. Why she kept almost everyone in her life at arm's length, sometimes even her best friends, Emma and Mercedes.

"I miss them terribly," she answered, pulling her hand away. "But dwelling on the loss will not bring them back. One must look to the future rather than staying locked in the past. They would not wish me to mourn endlessly or to be perpetually sad. I know that, so I am resolved to live my life with pleasure."

She drew a deep breath. "Speaking of which, we are letting all this excellent food go to waste. Shall we eat?"

He surveyed the picnic meal laid out before them. "Most definitely yes. Here, have some more wine." He refilled her glass.

She picked up a plate. "Lobster sandwiches first?"

He smiled. "And some of that pâté, if you please."

Their conversation moved on to less personal topics as they ate.

He didn't honestly know why he'd told her all of those

things. Usually he was careful not to mention anything to do with his worries about his father, or his past. But Ariadne was surprisingly easy to talk to, especially now that they weren't trading barbs with each other every other second.

Determined to set their outing back on a more lighthearted path, he regaled her with amusing stories about some of the flamboyant characters in both his own court and those he had encountered on his visits to England.

She contributed more of her own.

Soon they both were laughing.

"More wine?" he asked, taking up the bottle again and angling it so that the sun shone through the colored glass to reveal a last liquid inch. "There isn't even a full glass remaining. No point letting it go to waste."

"Oh, I shouldn't," she said with a shake of her head. "Then again, why not?"

Her eyes twinkled audaciously as she held out her glass.

Obligingly, he poured.

She took a long, appreciative swallow, her head tipped back to expose the swanlike grace of her throat. Watching her was a revelation; she enjoyed everything with such carefree panache, especially now that she was full of wine and good food.

She straightened, nearly all of the wine in her glass gone, then hiccuped loudly. Giggling, she laid a guilty hand over her mouth. "Oops."

Maybe I shouldn't have opened that second bottle, he mused. He'd drunk the majority of both bottles, so she could hardly have consumed enough to get tipsy. On the other hand, he really didn't know her tolerance for alcohol. He'd seen her sip wine at balls and dinner parties but he couldn't say he'd ever paid attention to the actual amount she was drinking. Perhaps she didn't carry her wine well.

For his part, he was simply feeling pleasantly relaxed. He

had a hard head for liquor, though; it took a great deal to get him drunk.

Hopefully Ariadne's head would clear quickly and he wouldn't have to concoct an excuse for bringing her home inebriated. With luck, Emma and Nick would still be at the estate auction in Hampstead that they'd agreed to attend with Nick's aunt that afternoon, and for which he and Ariadne had made their excuses. Considering that Emma and Nick would most likely stop for an early dinner on the way back, he and Ariadne should still have plenty of time before their absence would be noticed at the town house.

Unless Ariadne really was seriously tipsy. In which case he should just drive her home and save their first lesson for another time.

He didn't believe in taking advantage of women—well, at least not *unfair* advantage, he amended.

She giggled again—something she never did—and drained the last drops of the wine from her glass with a flourish.

He shook his head with a regretful sigh and began packing the remains of their meal back into the hamper.

"What are you doing?" she demanded. "I haven't had any strawberries yet." Leaning dramatically forward, she reached for the dish and plucked out a ripe red berry.

She popped it straight into her mouth, sliding her tongue around the fruit before sinking her teeth in up to the small green hull.

He couldn't tear his eyes away as she ate the strawberry, which left her lips moist and pink and looking extraordinarily kissable.

"*Mmm*, delicious!" she pronounced. "You have one."

"Thank you, but I have had sufficient." He forced himself to continue packing up the hamper.

"*I have had sufficient,*" she repeated, lowering her voice

in a mocking impression of him. "Don't be so stuffy, Rupert."

He gave her a half smile. "You, my dear, have had too
much to drink."

"I have not. But even if it were true, whose fault would it
be? After all, you're the one who's been plying me with alcohol all afternoon."

"How was I to know you have no tolerance for liquor?"

She reached for another strawberry. "Here. Have one."

"Thank you, no."

"I insist," she said, jumping up onto her knees and moving
toward him, holding out the berry. "Eat it."

He turned his head away and closed the lid on the hamper.

She waved the fragrant fruit in front of his lips. "As a
royal princess, I command you to eat this strawberry!"

"Command me, do you?" he asked, amused. "Perhaps you
forget to whom you speak."

"And perhaps you have forgotten your promise. We're
here, alone, and yet you haven't so much as kissed me. And
now you won't accept my offering. Have you decided you
don't want to be my lover, after all, Your Royal Highness?
Shall we return home and pretend we really were only out for
a driving lesson? I can always begin my search for a lover
again if you find you have changed your mind."

Desire surged within him, along with other, darker emotions. He knew it was the wine speaking, but her taunt enraged him.

Take another lover? He would show her exactly what he
thought of that idea.

Reaching out, he caught her around the waist and pulled
her flush against him, all his earlier good intentions drifting
away as if caught on the breeze.

"If you ever mention seeking out someone else again," he
said warningly, "I won't be responsible for my actions." He

grasped one of the ribbons tied under her chin and yanked it free.

She gasped, the strawberry falling unheeded to the ground.

"There won't be any other lovers, Ariadne." He pulled off her bonnet and tossed it aside. "Only me."

Bending his head, he crushed her mouth to his.

Chapter Eleven

Ariadne's head swam, but not from the surfeit of wine she'd drunk. It was Rupert's kiss that made her dizzy. Rupert's touch that left her intoxicated. She trembled and closed her eyes, pressing herself closer and putting everything she had into their kiss.

She wasn't really drunk—not like he thought—just loosened up enough to be bold, or rather bolder than she usually was. She sighed and followed his lead, opening her mouth so that he could slide his tongue inside.

He had a wicked, wonderful tongue.

Gifted, actually.

He could do things that she'd never dreamed a man might do, silken, seductive things that made her heart stutter in her chest and her breath come in quick, ragged puffs.

She knew this was a reaction she experienced only with him. During her kissing trials, she'd had one or two of her suitors try putting their tongues in her mouth, much to her great distaste.

But there was no distaste with Rupert; quite the opposite.

She liked this kind of kissing with Rupert—loved it, in fact.

She moaned softly as he traced her lips, then tangled their tongues together in a dance that sent her senses spinning like a whirlwind.

If she didn't take care, she might soon find herself craving his touch like a drug, needing more from him than even she would be wise to take.

She didn't resist when he tumbled her backward and she found herself suddenly lying against the blanket. The sun that shone through the trees in dappled splotches lay warm against her eyelids and cheeks, but she barely noticed, too caught up in the luxurious bliss of Rupert's kiss.

His lips roamed over her face—forehead, temples, eyelids, cheeks, nose, chin—before traveling the length of her throat. He paused at the base and buried his face there for a moment, his thick golden hair brushing like silk against the underside of her jaw.

Then he opened his mouth and drew against the flesh of her neck with a gentle, yet insistent pressure that tingled all the way to her toes. She shivered and angled her head so he could repeat the process on the other side.

"It seems to me," he murmured a small while later, "that you are far too buttoned up in that gown. Let's remedy that, shall we?"

Her eyes fluttered open, her lids heavy, as if drugged. "But we're outside. P-perhaps we should go in the house."

Yet even as she made the suggestion, she had no great desire to go anywhere. She was much too relaxed, her insides as smooth and pliable as warm butter. Honestly, she wasn't even sure she would be able to walk.

"We're completely alone out here," he said, kissing a spot beneath her ear that she'd never before realized was sensitive. "The caretaker knows not to bother us."

"Does he?" she said on a husky sigh. "How convenient."

Rupert chuckled.

His fingers slipped beneath her shoulders and sought out the row of buttons on the back of her gown. She offered no complaint as he deftly unfastened the first few, then pushed the short sleeves halfway down her arms.

The tops of her breasts quivered where they swelled above her white silk chemise and stays. He lowered his head to brush his lips over the first plump curve in a tantalizing caress. He made a thorough exploration before moving on to her other breast to repeat the kiss in a way that was akin to slow torture, and yet utterly divine. His breath whispered over her skin, and she thought he was going to kiss her again. Instead he retraced his earlier path, only this time with his tongue.

She gasped and burned hotter still, her eyelids falling closed against the exquisite pleasure as he laved a trail across the upper curve of both of her breasts, just above the edge of her undergarments. Then, without warning, he slid his fingers beneath her chemise and popped one breast free. Instinctively, she tried to raise her hands to shield herself, but found her arms trapped by her sleeves. He had her, she realized, utterly at his mercy.

She forced herself to relax. After all, this is what she wanted—to be his lover—to explore this unknown, carnal side of her nature. She'd always been fearless, even on those occasions when she'd secretly quailed inside.

Be fearless now. Give yourself over to the moment.

And so she did, watching boldly as he studied her with the leisurely appreciation of a connoisseur admiring a piece of fine art. His eyes were extraordinarily blue and blazed with a heavy-lidded expression that she realized was desire. It was a curious sensation, being so openly regarded, exposed to both the elements and a man's gaze—Rupert's gaze.

"Beautiful," he said. "All soft pink and creamy white, just as I knew you would be."

"You thought about this? About me, like this?"

His eyes flashed. "Of course. And a great deal more. This, my sweet, is only the beginning."

He stroked the edge of one thumb over her nipple, sending a ripple of sensation through her. The flesh of her breast tightened in pleasured agony, drawing into a hard nub that reddened as if it were blushing.

Smiling, he flicked her nipple again . . . back and forth, then back and forth again before circling it so the tip puckered even more.

She groaned, a deep ache lodging low between her thighs, the sensation growing more intense with each stroke.

His fingers slid around to cup the underside of her breast, holding her as if testing its weight and shape. He had large hands, so she didn't overflow his palm, yet he seemed well satisfied, rubbing his thumb over her sensitized bud again and smiling when she shuddered.

Then he bent and took her into his mouth, savoring her as if their picnic were still taking place and she was the dessert. Her back arched, pressing her breast harder against his eager mouth as if begging for more. Clearly he was not loath to comply, drawing on her with a sweet suction that was all but her undoing.

She shifted restlessly, trying to lift her arms again, suddenly desperate to touch him. She longed to bury her fingers in his hair, to stroke his face as he pleasured her. But she was trapped and despite her faint struggles, he seemed in no mood to release her.

"*Shh,*" he hushed her, his breath warm against her moist flesh. "Just let yourself feel, Ariadne."

"B-but I want . . . I want . . . *Ahh*—" She couldn't speak, her words forgotten as he raked his teeth over her tender nipple.

"Good. Wanting is exactly how you should be. Now let's see what else you may like."

He slid her other breast free of her chemise and stays and began working his dark magic on her again, his tongue warm and wet against her aching flesh. Her body responded more forcefully to his new ministrations, as if it had already learned what pleasure to expect and could not wait to enjoy more. He suckled harder, wringing a long cry from her throat, while he kneaded her abandoned breast with gentle, rhythmic strokes.

She ached, her entire body aflame.

"Do you like this, Ariadne?" he demanded, his tongue moving to press her nipple briefly against his teeth before suckling her again in a way that drove her half mad.

"Y-yes."

"Do you want more?"

She nodded.

"Say it."

"Oh, yes, p-please," she cried.

"Please what?"

"Please. More."

He laughed softly. "I rather like hearing you beg. Let's see if I can make you beg some more."

Is that what I'm doing? Begging?

The idea ought to have outraged her. In fact, she knew that under any other circumstance, she would be throwing such words back in his face. But at the moment she couldn't seem to muster the will to do anything but feel. She needed him, wondered if she might die if he didn't continue. No matter the consequences to her dignity later on, she couldn't conceal that knowledge from herself or from him.

He lifted his head from her breasts and moved to capture her mouth, taking her with an ardor that was a ravishment of sorts. Wildly, she kissed him back, frustrated again at her inability to free her arms and touch him. He forced her mouth open wider, their tongues tangling in a frenzied mating that made her breath come in quick, ragged pants.

He wasn't immune to the power of their kiss either, his own breathing rapid and unsteady. Without breaking the kiss, he slid his palm in a slow glide over her body.

Across her bare breasts. Along the flat plane of her stomach. Over the curve of her hip and thigh, all of which were still demurely clothed.

He stopped when he reached her knee. Lost in a haze of passion, she was only half aware of his movements as he began pulling up the material of her skirt, gradually exposing her ankle and stocking-clad calf.

Then his hand disappeared beneath.

"And what do we have here?" he murmured against her mouth as he boldly explored. "Are you wearing drawers, Your Highness?" His fingers plucked at the thin silk, the undergarments secured by nothing more than a simple tie at her waist.

She nodded, her heart racing madly. "They're all the f-fashion these d-days."

"And yet many still consider them fast. I confess that I can see why." His hand stole around to the open placket in the center of the garment to stroke the bare skin of one thigh.

She trembled and bit her lip.

"I suppose," he mused as he continued his daring survey, "that I shouldn't be surprised to find you wearing something so brazen, even if they are not ordinarily meant to be seen."

He glided his fingers along her right leg from knee to inner thigh, then back down again. She began shaking, suddenly unable to speak.

"I find myself wondering, however . . ."

Wondering what? she thought, letting the pleasure radiate through her body.

". . . what they look like," he finished, as if she had spoken aloud.

He reached down and tugged her skirt higher, flipping it and her thin summer petticoats up so they pooled at the top of her thighs.

She stiffened, then twisted up to cover herself. But it was impossible, trapped as she was by her damnable sleeves. Her bare breasts jiggled with her efforts, drawing his gaze there for a long, heated moment before he looked lower once more.

Instinctively, she drew her legs closed, her most private areas covered now by nothing more than a few wisps of cloth.

He chuckled and kissed her mouth before moving to whisper in her ear. "Where's my bold girl? Surely you aren't afraid to let me see?"

Her gaze locked with his, his eyes the color of a twilight sky.

Is he right?

Am I afraid?

She'd never been a coward, had thought herself ready to delve into this new, unexplored world of physical craving. Yet it would appear that she was still fettered by some natural inhibitions. But he was her lover now—of that there could be no more doubt—which meant that she had given him a certain claim upon her body. Of course he expected not only to touch her and kiss her but also to look upon her naked form—no matter how unnerving that might seem to her at the moment.

Perhaps her unexpected shyness stemmed from the fact that she was lying practically naked while he was still fully clothed—he didn't have so much as a wrinkle in his cravat! Then too there was the fact that they were outside in a garden, leaving her exposed in ways she had never imagined she might ever be.

Merciful heavens, what have I gotten myself into?

She plucked futilely at the side of her bunched-up skirt, trying to push it down. It barely moved. "Are you sure we are absolutely alone?"

"Of course. You know I would never do anything to put you at risk."

And she did know that. She could trust him, remembering again why she had decided that he, above all other men, should be her first lover.

With that thought, she gave in and lay back again. She considered closing her eyes, but realized that she wanted to watch him as he looked at her.

Will he like what he sees?

He kissed her again with a fervor that set her atremble. She moaned, relishing the dark bliss of his mouth as it moved against hers. Then he was inching her skirts even higher, exposing her completely to his gaze. A breeze rose just then, sliding over her skin like a caress.

He leaned up on one elbow. "*Hmm*, I do like these drawers of yours." He smiled and ran one finger under the tie at her waist. "They're quite . . . evocative."

She shivered, her breath coming faster again.

His eyelids grew heavier, his expression rapt with hunger and masculine approval. "You're every bit as lovely here," he said, moving a palm over one quivering thigh, "as you are here." Bending down, he nuzzled her breasts again, kissing them both before playfully taking one nipple between his teeth and giving it a light nip.

She arched and cried out, pleasure raking through her like a violent storm.

His hand roved onward, exploring again at his leisure, as if he had all the time in the world, his eyes following the progress of his hand. Up one thigh he went, then down the other, stroking her in a tantalizing dance that set her teeth on edge. He caressed her stomach too, teasing her, before he began the tortuous pattern again.

She ached deep in her core, becoming uncomfortably aware of the moisture gathering at the juncture of her thighs. Squeezing her legs tighter, she fought the sweet agony.

Yet, as if he knew exactly what she was feeling, he stopped his roaming and lifted his palm, only to lay it directly atop the triangle of pale curls that grew between her legs.

"Spread your thighs," he commanded, his fingers playing lightly on her.

A jolt shot through her, the traitorous wetness between her thighs turning into a slow weeping. But as much as her body urged her to obey, she hesitated.

"If there's anything you don't like, I promise to stop," he said.

But that was the problem. She wasn't afraid she wouldn't like it. She feared she would—too much. She was already on the verge of losing what little control she had left. If he touched her as she suspected he was about to touch her, she would have no free will left at all.

"Let me, Ariadne," he whispered. "Let me in."

Her whole body trembled, her pulse racing as if her heart might burst. Then she did as he asked, forcing her muscles to unwind, her thighs to edge apart.

His fingers slid down, parting her before delving into her slick heat. She gasped, her eyelids fluttering as he eased a single finger in up to his knuckle. But she didn't close her eyes. Instead, she watched him as he watched her.

Slowly, gently, he began to stroke with a deep inner massage that heightened the ache rather than alleviated it.

"You're so wet," he said, sliding deeper.

She groaned. "I-is that b-bad?"

He gave a quiet laugh. "Not at all. It only means you're passionate. But then, we knew that already."

He stroked faster, in and out, then in and out again.

She bit her lip and dug her nails into the blanket, her breath coming in rapid little pants.

"That's it," he said encouragingly. "Give in. Just let yourself feel."

She ought to have been embarrassed, but she wasn't, his touch doing things to her that she had never thought possible, not even in her wildest imaginings. Her eyelids drifted down, her sight glazing over from a surfeit of unbridled pleasure.

He used his thumb to some devilish new purpose, flicking it over a highly sensitive nub of flesh that sharpened the ache to a knife's edge. She moaned and opened her legs wider, inviting him to go deeper. He did, quickening his strokes, making her gasp and moan and burn.

Need built higher, a craving that she didn't understand but sought desperately to relieve. He held her quite literally in his palm, her whole world poised on the brink.

Then he pressed a little harder, moved a little faster, and sent her flying over the precipice. A keening cry sang out from between her lips, the sound drifting away on the breeze. She shook as rapture exploded within her like a sunburst, golden and glorious, warming her inside and out.

She collapsed, the earth spinning wildly around her even though she'd never left the ground.

With a giddy smile on her face, she let herself float.

Chapter Twelve

Rupert watched her, relishing the play of emotion that flickered over her face, savoring the dusky pink flush on her cheeks that had nothing to do with the sun shining through the trees above. She looked stunned, but blissfully so, as though the world had been tilted off its axis and she was trying to set it right again.

Her body lay warm and wet against his hand, her tender inner flesh clamped around his finger with a sweet suction. Her muscles twitched sporadically in the aftermath of lingering bliss.

He knew he ought to break the connection, but he stayed where he was. He wasn't entirely sure that he trusted himself, with his shaft hard and begging for relief. It would be far too easy to unfasten the buttons on his falls and take her. She wouldn't resist; he knew that much as well. But he'd promised himself he would leave her a virgin—or at least enough of one to still have an intact maidenhead for her future husband to claim should she ever change her mind about marrying.

By damn was he tempted, though, her luscious feminine flesh spread before him like some decadent feast ready to be sampled. But even if he couldn't indulge in a full meal, there were still ways to satisfy himself.

And truly he was enjoying himself in spite of the savage ache in his balls. Watching her take her pleasure for the very first time had been a satisfaction all its own. He could think of few experiences he'd ever found more beautiful, or more memorable.

Her inner muscles flexed lightly against his finger again, reminding him exactly how vulnerable and at his mercy she still was.

Should I? he wondered, a slow, wicked smile curving his mouth.

She opened her eyes, her expression dreamy and replete, but returning to rationality.

Suddenly he didn't want her to return. He wanted to keep her in his thrall, to drive her mad with desire.

Sliding his finger out, he added a second and pushed them back in, careful but insistent. Her eyes widened, her body stretching to accommodate this new intrusion. She was already wet, but she grew suddenly wetter, her channel slick and clearly anxious for this second round of pleasure.

"R-Rupert, what are you—I can't," she protested softly.

"Of course you can." He stroked her deeply, deeper than before. "You will."

Her hips arched against his touch, her movements forcing him even farther inside. She groaned and shuddered, her eyelids falling closed again.

Bending down without slowing the movement of his fingers, he resumed his earlier attention to her breasts. She had beautiful breasts, plump and round without being overly large. They filled his palms as if made for just that purpose.

He played on her, teasing her erect nipples that had ripened to the color of raspberries. Then he leaned closer and took them once more into his mouth, rolling the turgid nubs against his tongue. She tasted sweet, like lilacs and honey. He suckled harder.

She went wild, one leg bending upward at the knee so that he could sink his fingers in as deeply as they would go—a service he was more than happy to provide. He bit one nipple gently, then the other before flicking her little spot below, over and around and around again.

Long moments later, he pressed hard on the spot with his thumb and felt her begin to crest. Rising up on his elbow, he watched as she climaxed, her whole body shaking with the force of her bliss.

Smiling, he slid his hand behind her head and claimed her mouth with a rapacious kiss, thrusting his tongue inside the way he wished he could thrust his shaft inside her. He'd nearly climaxed just from watching her take her pleasure. And this was only their first time together. He could hardly wait for the next.

At length, he released her, knowing they needed to be on their way home. His fingers glistened with her fragrant juices. Rather than immediately wiping them dry on his handkerchief, he held her gaze and put one in his mouth, enjoying the shock in her eyes as he sampled her flavor like a candy stick.

"*Hmm,*" he said, slowly withdrawing the digit. "Delicious. I have to say, Ariadne, that I like picnicking with you. We must be sure to do this again."

Later that afternoon, Ariadne luxuriated in a tub of steaming water, letting the heat seep into her muscles and bones.

She'd sent her maid away, needing to be alone. Her body was still too alive with remembered sensation, her mind still too full of everything she'd experienced in Rupert's arms to abide the idea of company.

In fact, she had been distinctly relieved when she'd arrived at the town house and discovered that Emma and Nick had not yet returned from their excursion. Honestly, had they been home, she was sure that Emma would have taken one look at her and known something new was in the wind.

How could she not have? One look at herself in the mirror had confirmed her worst suspicions—her eyes were too bright, her skin was too flushed, and most condemning of all was the naughty little grin she couldn't quite keep off her mouth.

Saints above, Rupert is dangerous—his touch is absolutely combustive.

As much as she might tell herself, it wasn't the heat of her bath that was making her heart race right now; instead it was the memories of their afternoon together.

Oh, but it had been divine.

She'd craved pleasure, and that's exactly what he'd given her. So when, she wondered, would she be alone with him again?

He'd been quiet on the drive back, wisely taking the reins. Despite the earlier success of her driving lesson, she wouldn't have been capable of keeping her mind on the task long enough not to send them into a ditch. She supposed she'd been quiet as well. After all, what did one say to one's new lover after being so thoroughly and exquisitely satisfied?

Yet as she considered it now, she realized that he had not taken the same ease. Was that why he'd seemed distant? Because he had enjoyed no release of his own? She would have been quite willing to let him, to see to his needs as well. He had only to instruct her on the best ways to do so.

Next time, she promised herself, she wouldn't lose control so completely. Next time she would take care not to be so centered on her own needs and think nothing of his.

She let out a little laugh and leaned her head back against the rim of the bathtub.

How quickly things changed. If someone had asked her even a week ago if she would be lying here concerned for Rupert's pleasure, she would have scoffed and told them they were a fool. But strangely enough, she did care.

And she shouldn't.

Then again, such impulses meant nothing. She liked what he did to her body and only wanted to be fair. He was her lover now, after all. He had a right to enjoy their affair as much as she now knew she was going to.

Sighing, she reached for the soap, her muscles reminding her again of exactly how she'd spent the afternoon. Perhaps when she rinsed off, she would use the pitcher of cold water, just to make sure she had her emotions under strict control for dinner and tonight's entertainment later on.

"Heavens, what a crush," Emma declared that evening, as she unfurled a painted silk fan and waved it back and forth in front of her face.

Ariadne enjoyed the slight residual breeze that drifted off her friend's fan where the two of them had found seats in a relatively quiet corner of the ballroom.

Emma was right, though. It was far too warm, and far too crowded, but then their hostess was well known for inviting more people than her house could comfortably hold. The Society pages loved to remark on her overflowing entertainments, and she loved reading about them. From what Ariadne had heard, the woman actually pressed the clippings in a book.

"I'm surprised you aren't still dancing," Emma remarked. "You've scarcely been without a partner all evening."

Emma was right again. Ariadne had been popular tonight, dancing with one gentleman after another—every man, it seemed, but Rupert.

She frowned at the thought, but knowing that Emma was

watching, she forced herself to smile instead. "Yes, I've all but worn a hole in my slippers. It's a relief to sit down for a few minutes."

"I feel exactly the same. In fact, I'm tempted to take my slippers off, but I suppose if I do I'll get caught. Maybe at supper. Nick is taking me in and he won't tattle."

Emma sent her an impish grin, which she returned.

"He and I got in so late this afternoon," Emma continued, "that I never did have a chance to ask. How was the driving lesson? Did you and Rupert have fun?"

Ariadne blinked, then lowered her gaze, using the excuse of opening her fan to conceal her reaction. She hid behind its silk-covered staves for a long moment while she worked to slow the rapid pounding of her pulse.

"Yes, it was quite entertaining," she said, striving for a casual air, "though a great deal more effort than one might imagine. The horses do tug at one's arms. Once I started getting the gist of it, though, it was rather exhilarating."

And it had been. She might even have given the adventure some thought tonight had it not been for everything that had followed afterward. Truth be known, she'd completely forgotten about that first part of the day.

"So where did he take you? Where did the two of you do it?"

She stared at Emma, alarm racing through her. Could Emma have possibly guessed that she and Rupert had spent the afternoon alone in a secluded garden? That she'd lain nearly naked and utterly at his mercy while he did the most intimate, exquisite things to her body? Things of which the mere memory made her burn?

"He . . . um . . . took me to the park. Green Park. It's far less crowded at that time of day, so I was in no danger of getting in anyone's way while I practiced."

Emma's pale eyebrows crinkled. "Did anything else happen? You seem . . . discomposed. Not at all like your usual self."

"No, of course not," she replied quickly.

Emma's crinkles turned into a scowl. "Is there something you're not telling me? You and Rupert didn't get into a fight, did you?"

"No. Well, we may have had a few words." And quite a few kisses and caresses and loud moans of delight.

"Oh, Arie, I'm sorry. I had hoped this truce between the two of you would last longer than one day. Though I must say I am not surprised."

"We're going out again," she blurted. "He's promised to keep teaching me." Although she wasn't sure how much actual carriage driving would be involved. But it wouldn't do for Emma to believe that she and Rupert were on the outs, not after they had gone to so much trouble to create a good excuse to be together.

"You know how Rupert and I like to snipe," she went on. "It's nothing."

"Oh." Emma gave her another considering look. Then her expression cleared. "Oh, well, I suppose you're both used to it. If you don't mind being at each other's throats, then why should I?"

Ariadne laughed, hoping Emma didn't catch the slightly maniacal edge to the sound. She fanned herself again, suddenly glad for the uncomfortable warmth of the room, which provided an excuse for her flushed cheeks—propensity to blush or no.

"Don't look now," Emma said, "but I believe my brother is coming this way. He must have realized we were talking about him."

"Well, you know what they say about the devil."

Emma shot her a glance and laughed, not the least bit offended.

He came to a halt and made them an elegant bow. "Emma. Princess Ariadne."

She regarded him over the edge of her fan, struck by what a fine figure of a man he was.

In a word, he was beautiful. There was no other way to describe him. His golden hair lay neatly brushed back from his patrician forehead, his simple black coat and evening breeches a perfect foil for his smooth ivory skin. His eyes gleamed a vivid blue, as deep and unfathomable as gemstones.

She waited for him to acknowledge her further, perhaps give her a smile, a small something that she would know was meant only for her.

Instead he turned back to Emma, with no hint of the afternoon they'd shared anywhere in his gaze.

She frowned.

"So, this is where you've hidden yourself, is it?" he said, addressing his sister. "Taking refuge among the matrons and the wallflowers."

Emma laughed. "Ariadne and I are hardly hidden, seated so near the dance floor. If you consider the crowd, though, I suppose it does offer some measure of concealment."

He glanced around at the guests, many crammed shoulder to shoulder along the room's periphery. The only real space was on the dance floor itself. "A deuced annoyance, this party. I don't know why I let you talk me into attending."

"I had nothing to do with it," Emma stated. "As I recall, you agreed only because the Swiss ambassador is here tonight and you wanted to have a word."

"I should have made him attend me at Lyndhurst House, but I know how you hate it when diplomats and functionaries start congregating in your hallways."

"You're here visiting family, not conducting affairs of state. You'll have plenty of time for all of that once you're back in Rosewald."

A mocking glint showed in his eye. "The work of a nation doesn't cease simply because its ruler is out of the country, you know."

"True," Emma admitted, "but with the assistance of your ministers, your private secretary, your military guard, and that bulging satchel of correspondence that arrives each morning, you appear to be managing quite well."

His lips twitched. "I am kept satisfactorily informed. I would have the heads of everyone in the palace and the parliament were I not."

"Yes, well, for the time being, why do you not attempt to enjoy the festivities, however crowded it may be in here? There is dancing, for instance. I am sure there are any number of ladies who would be more than delighted to accompany you for the next set."

His gaze slid over to Ariadne.

Her pulse picked up speed as she waited. Surely now he would speak to her and ask her to dance so they could go in to supper together afterward, as etiquette prescribed. Actually, she had saved the next dance specifically for him, refusing several offers from other gentlemen who were only too eager to share her company. But she didn't want to spend the supper hour with any of those men. She wanted to be with Rupert.

Her heart kicked and she held her breath.

Then he glanced away. "As it happens, I am already promised for the next dance to Lady Sudcliffe."

Ariadne's heart stopped—or at least that was how it felt.

Lady Sudcliffe! He was promised to that notorious, overly endowed widow with her limpet blue eyes and her caramel brown lashes that she fluttered invitingly at every male who passed within twenty feet? The brazen temptress with her low drawl and throaty laugh that men apparently found irresistible? Ariadne had scarcely paid her any heed in the past; the woman was too ill-bred to warrant her consideration.

Now Rupert was dancing with the creature, was he? Sharing supper as well? Apparently being lovers with her meant nothing. *And why should it?* she reminded herself. After all, her arrangement with him required no emotional connection; it was an affair driven by mutual desire, no more, no less.

She smiled, seemingly unconcerned. If he could pretend there was nothing between them, then so could she. Of course, now she would be put to the bother of finding another gentleman to take her in to supper. Surely not all of the ones she'd refused had found other partners. A bit of light flirting should give her the information she required.

She snapped her fan closed. "Since you mention it, Emma, I believe I see my next partner. I think I'll go over and surprise him." She stood, refusing to look at Rupert. "If you will both excuse me."

Emma's crinkly frown returned. "Of course. There's nothing amiss, is there, Arie? You seem . . . uneasy of a sudden."

"Not at all. It's only this heat. Our hostess ought to open a window or two—or doesn't she know it is summer?"

"I believe she thinks it adds atmosphere to the crush."

"If you like perspiring men and swooning women. Good thing I am not given to such unbecoming weaknesses." She paused, unable to resist turning to Rupert. "You might want to check to make sure Lady Jane has her hartshorn, Your Royal Highness. I hear she has been known to drop at the slightest provocation. The bark of a tiny dog in the park apparently shocked her unconscious only last week."

"I shall bear that in mind," he replied in a grave tone, not rising to her provocation in any way. "Ladies." He bowed, then turned away, disappearing quickly into the milling crowd.

Inwardly, she sighed, weary all at once and not at all in the mood for the party. If only she could go home.

She was buoying up her smile when Emma straightened abruptly in her seat.

"Only look," Emma said. "Here comes Nick."

They both watched as he approached, love brimming like a beacon in Emma's eyes; it was an expression that was unmistakably returned by Nick.

What must it be like to be so truly loved?

"My dance partner must be stranded somewhere," she murmured, after taking a moment to greet Nick. "I shall go rescue him. See you both after a while."

"Yes, dear," Emma said, her arm already linked through her husband's. "Have fun."

Ariadne nodded and moved away, knowing that the only kind of fun she had tonight would be for show.

Chapter Thirteen

Ariadne rearranged the mound of feather pillows behind her, then snuggled back against them, smoothing the sheets neatly at her waist. Picking up her book, she opened it to the marked page and began to read by way of a small branch of candles on her bedside table. The house stood quiet around her, everyone retired for the night.

After returning from the ball, she'd found her maid waiting. The sleepy girl had stayed long enough to help her out of her ball gown before seeking her own bed, with orders to sleep later in the morning.

Wide awake despite the late hour, she'd decided to read, hoping it would lull her into a state of relaxation. But the printed words held little sway, her mind returning again and again to the disappointing evening just past.

But I am not going to think about it. Just as I am not going to think about Rupert.

A low sound of displeasure rumbled under her breath. Her jaw tight, she returned to her book.

Ten minutes later she closed the volume with a snap and

tossed it aside, deciding that the exercise was useless. She might as well try going to sleep. Maybe if she snuffed out the candles the darkness would be able to do what the book had not.

Leaning over, she reached out to extinguish the small flames. As she did, she heard a light scrape at the door, so faint that for a moment she wondered if she had imagined it.

She froze, listening.

Then the doorknob turned and Rupert walked in, closing and locking the door silently at his back.

He was attired in a dark blue robe, belted at the waist, the royal crest of Rosewald embroidered in gold on the breast. He wore slippers, but the feet inside them were bare, as were his muscled calves. His hair was damp but neatly combed, and his cheeks recently shaven, if she wasn't mistaken.

He strolled toward her as if he were in the habit of doing so every night, his quiet arrogance remarkable to behold.

Briefly, her lips parted on a stunned inhalation before she recovered herself. "And just what do you think you're doing here?"

He continued forward, stopping only when he reached the bed. "The answer to that should be obvious. I thought we would enjoy another lesson."

After ignoring me all evening? Hah!

She crossed her arms. "Well, you thought wrong. I was about to go to bed."

His lips curved, showing his teeth to devastating effect. "But you are already in bed. Why have you braided your hair?"

"I always braid my hair to sleep."

"You'll have to stop. I want it left loose from now on."

"I really don't care what you want. I am tired and wish to sleep. Go away, Your Royal Highness."

She made a shooing motion with her hand.

He ignored her and reached for the tie on his robe. With a smooth, economical shrug, he removed it and went to drape the garment over a nearby chair.

She stared, unable to look away from the magnificence of his wide shoulders, sculpted chest, long arms, and flat stomach—every inch of which was bare. She'd never seen a man's naked torso before—although she'd spent plenty of time studying them in paintings and sculptures. The real thing was by far superior to the facsimile.

Saliva pooled in her mouth and she swallowed hard, her breath hitching as her eyes moved lower.

A pair of fine cotton men's drawers rode low on his narrow hips, clinging in a way that only enhanced his bold sexuality. A light sheen of golden hair dusted his chest and extremities, giving him a burnished quality in the mellow candlelight. He was, as always, nothing short of beautiful.

He caught her arrested expression and smiled. "Since you showed me your drawers earlier, I thought it only fair to return the favor. You're not still wearing yours, are you?" he added hopefully.

Heat spread into her cheeks.

It's just anger, she told herself. *Simple irritation at his effrontery.*

"No," she said as coldly as she could manage. "Now put your robe back on and leave. I am not in the mood."

"Are you sure about that?" His gaze dropped to the bodice of her nightgown. "Your nipples don't seem to agree."

Only sheer willpower kept her from folding her arms over her traitorous breasts. She donned her haughtiest expression. "I'm cold."

He tossed his head back on a laugh. "You're delightful, is what you are, Ariadne. I don't know why I didn't realize that sooner."

"Oh, so I'm delightful now, am I?" she said sarcastically.

"You certainly didn't seem to think so earlier this evening at the ball."

"Is that what has you miffed? Because I didn't ask you to dance?"

"Hardly," she scoffed untruthfully. "If you're in the mood to play tonight, why don't you see if Lady Sudcliffe will accommodate you?"

He regarded her for a long moment. "So you don't mind if I seek out other women while we're"—he waggled a pair of fingers meaningfully—"involved?"

She didn't pretend to misunderstand. "Why should I care if you keep a mistress so long as you fulfill your bargain with me? It's only sex, after all."

A brief silence fell. "You're very understanding. Most women wouldn't be."

She shrugged and gazed down at the sheets. "I am nothing if not practical." A terrible exhaustion settled over her of a sudden. "I really am tired, Your Highness. Perhaps we could resume this tomorrow?"

She plucked distractedly at the sheets, waiting for him to leave.

Instead he came forward and sat on the bed next to her. Reaching out, he gathered her long braid into his hands and slid off the bow. Laying the ribbon aside, he began freeing her hair, the skeins falling loose in a fiery mantle.

"Jane Sudcliffe means nothing to me," he told her softly.

"So she's *Jane*, is she? I suppose the two of you had a cozy chat over supper tonight."

They'd certainly looked cozy. She'd been unable to keep herself from watching them surreptitiously from where she and her partner had sat across the room.

"We talked. Well, actually she did. She's the sort who likes to hear the sound of her own voice. Sadly, much of what she says is nonsense. She has a great deal to say on the subject of clothes."

"Oh. I'd heard rumors that she has quite a clever tongue. Or is that only in bed?"

He laughed. "Leave it to you to be aware of something like that."

Angry again, she tried tugging her hair out of his grasp, but he wouldn't let go. Tears stung her eyes. Realizing there was no point in resisting, she dropped her hands into her lap again.

He resumed his unbraiding, sliding his fingers through the heavy mass from scalp to the ends once the tresses were completely free.

She shivered, wishing she didn't like the way his touch felt.

"She is not my mistress, Ariadne. I have never been, nor do have I any interest in being, intimate with her."

"Oh?"

"Yes, *oh*."

"Then why would you not dance with me tonight? Why were you so distant?"

"Because, my foolish girl, I didn't want to give the game away to everyone in the room. If I start paying special attention to you, there is bound to be speculation, or worse. It seemed prudent to go on as we've always done. You might recall that I've never been much in the habit of dancing with you, let alone taking you in to supper."

When he put it that way, she had to admit that he was right. In the past, they never had spent much time together at balls and entertainments. Were they suddenly to be seen spending far more time together than usual, the rumor mill would begin churning as if its blades were caught in a windstorm. People were always looking for secret trysts and budding scandals. He was wise not to want to give the gossip mavens extra fodder.

"I thought," he mused as he combed his fingers through her loose mass of hair, "that escorting a notorious widow like Jane Sudcliffe in to supper might throw people off the scent. Apparently it worked rather better than I might have wished, since it deceived you as well."

"So you want Society to think she is your mistress?"

He shrugged. "Or someone like her. It will keep them busy guessing, and I had rather their speculation not be about you."

She took a moment to consider his words. "Is that what I am now, then? Your mistress?"

"That's an interesting question." His thumb glided softly across her lower lip. "I'm not sure what I ought to call you."

She trembled, tendrils of pleasure stealing through her.

"I suppose we'd do well to stick with lover, since it serves better than anything else at present."

He cradled her cheek with his wide palm and bent to kiss her temple.

"So, do you?" she ventured at length.

"Do I what?" He brushed his lips over her throat.

"Have a mistress? A real one?"

Do I really want to know that? And if he does, will it matter? Suddenly, she very much feared that it might.

Pausing, he leaned away so he could look into her eyes. "I ought to be flattered that you think me capable of servicing more than one woman at a time, particularly given the logistics of visiting another house across Town, managing to maintain my usual schedule, and still finding time to eat and sleep in between."

Looking at him, feeling his heat and his strength, seeing his magnificent body, she knew he was more than capable. She steeled herself, waiting for his answer.

"But even if I could manage it, I wouldn't want to," he told her with grave sincerity. "You are all the woman I want right now. All the woman I need. There is no one but you, Ariadne."

She exhaled a pent-up breath that she hadn't even known she'd been holding, more relieved and, yes, happier, than she had any business being.

"Actually," he continued, his fingers moving to the buttons on her thin lawn nightgown, "I can tell that you're going to be a real handful. I'm certain you'll be monopolizing all of my time with our lessons."

Peeling the material from her shoulders, he cupped one of her breasts in his hand. "But enough talk. Let's continue what we started this afternoon."

She laughed and looped her arms around his neck. "Yes, let's."

Then his mouth was on hers, her fingers burrowing into his hair to caress him as she'd longed to do earlier that day. He kissed her slowly at first, with a leisurely thoroughness that set her whole body aflame. Eager to test out her nascent skills, she slid her tongue into his mouth and traced the silky contours she discovered there. He growled his approval and kissed her harder, his next kiss more ardent than the one before. She lost herself to the pleasure, her thoughts turning hot and hazy.

She slid her hand along the back of his neck, tracing the warm skin and tensile strength that she discovered there before moving on to the corded muscles on his shoulders and back.

He quaked beneath her untutored hands, his own hands busy fondling her breasts, which grew heavy and aching with need. Her nipples budded into taut points that seemed even more sensitive than the first time he'd touched them, as if they now knew what to expect and wanted more.

She cried out when he bent to take her in his mouth, her fingers sliding over the smooth skin on his back, seeking purchase. Closing her eyes, she gave herself over to the rush of sensations, basking in the sweet suction of his lips and tongue as they moved over her.

Suddenly, without quite knowing how, she found herself on her back, her nightgown pushed to her waist. Then it disappeared altogether, tossed haphazardly aside. She lay completely naked, vulnerable and absolutely at his mercy.

He leaned above her, large and imposing, but she wasn't the least bit afraid. Rather than trying to hide herself from his gaze, she stretched against the sheets with sinuous pleasure, enjoying the flash of liquid heat that ignited in his eyes. A slow grin spread over his face; clearly he was appreciative of her daring response.

Her body throbbed deep within, her nipples beading even tighter under his attentive examination. Reaching out, he laid his palm against her throat, then stroked downward, across her breastbone and over the flat plane of her stomach. He paused, then slipped a finger into the dip of her belly button.

She sucked in a ragged breath, her stomach muscles flexing under his hand. Biting her lip, she waited for him to continue his exploration as he had earlier that afternoon.

Instead, he leaned over and took her mouth, kissing her with a dark intensity that plumbed the depths of her own yearning. She ran her hands over him, wanting to learn the shape and temperature and texture of his body.

But he was a big man and she couldn't reach as far as she might have liked. She contented herself with his chest, threading her fingers in and out of the thatch of curling hair that grew across its firm surface. And then around to trace the smooth contours of his back, and down the long limber curve of his spine.

Her mind muddled with pleasure, she kissed him wildly,

unable to get enough, each new kiss a revelation, every touch as sweet as a prayer.

He seemed to feel the same, urging her to follow where he led, to give in to the raging desire that threatened to turn her blood to smoke. She strove to match him, moaning as she rose to meet his increasing demands. The sound that came from her was low and raw, filled with the strength of her ardor.

"*Shh,*" he cautioned softly. "We don't want anyone to hear us."

She struggled to make sense of his words, her brain distinctly fuzzy. "E-everyone is asleep," she panted, trying to keep her voice low. "Th-the room next door is empty. No one will hear."

He kissed her again, hard and long. "Still, if you think you might scream, use one of the pillows."

Scream?

Why on earth would she do that?

But then she had no more time to think, as he began touching her again, his palms ranging over her in long, devastating sweeps that began at her shoulders, then moved on to her arms and breasts, and down across her stomach to her hips and thighs and calves. When he reached her ankles, he wrapped his hands around them and pulled her legs apart.

Kneeling between them, he began kissing her, slowly making his way up one leg, then down the other. As he went, he licked her, tasting her in a way that left behind small damp patches that tingled, shockingly sensitive to each faint movement of the air.

He kissed and laved her everywhere, so that she felt as if there was no inch of skin left untouched. But then he showed her that he'd only just begun.

Her eyes flew open when his mouth touched her in a place where she hadn't imagined she would ever be kissed.

She ought to be mortified, she supposed. Maybe even repulsed.

Instead, her body gave a deep, all-over tremor, as a violent need rose up inside her that was almost frightening. Giving in, she spread her legs wider, then reached down to sink her fingers into his hair to urge him on.

He gave a growl of satisfaction that reverberated through her most tender parts. Then he deepened his intimate kiss, using his tongue to lap at her slick heat.

A whimper slid from her throat, then a moan. Another followed, longer and louder.

Suddenly she remembered his words about the pillow and understood. If he kept this up, she was going to need to silence herself.

Then he was driving her higher, doing things with his tongue that surely had to be illegal in certain parts of the world, if not here in England. She rolled her head, her fingers clutching desperately at the sheets, her hips arching as if they had a will of their own. He grasped her and held her still, forcing her to accept an even deeper caress.

She shook, fearing she was going to break apart and splinter into a thousand pieces. With her last ounce of rational thought, she grabbed the pillow and covered her mouth with it.

Then he slid his fingers into her and sucked against her harder.

She screamed, exactly as he'd warned she might, the sound muffled against the mound of feathers and cloth pressed tightly to her lips. Rapture spread through her like a molten river, so fierce it threatened to melt her very bones. She rode the current, adrift on a golden sea that spread around her, sweet as honey.

Slowly, she set the pillow aside and found him watching her from where he knelt between her legs. "Good?" he asked knowingly.

"Better," she sighed blissfully once she could find her voice again.

He displayed his most evil grin. "Now it's my turn."

She waited, expecting him to rise up and angle himself over her.

Instead, he sat her up and placed her palms on the waistband of his drawers. "Undress me," he commanded. "I want to feel your hands on me."

She hesitated, her gaze dropping to the unmistakable bulge jutting insistently beneath the cloth. "So you don't want to—you know . . ." She let the words trail off, hoping her meaning was clear.

He arched a single golden brow. "Ready to surrender your innocence so soon, then?"

"Well," she said, glancing this time at her own naked body, "you seem to be doing quite a good job of corrupting me, so why not finish the task? Besides, after today, you can hardly say I'm innocent."

He laughed softly, then picked up a long skein of her hair and coiled it around his finger. "And yet you still are, in more ways than you can possibly realize. Be patient, my dear, and trust me in this. There are many paths to pleasure that don't require your complete ruin. Let's explore a few more of those before we go down a path from which there can be no return."

"But I've already told you I don't care if you ruin me." She ran a hand over his naked chest. "I'm ready. I want to know it all."

"Do you?" He took her hand again and pressed her fingers over his substantial erection. "Why don't we begin with this and see how it goes?"

Her heart jumped, pounding furiously as she touched him. His flesh was vibrantly warm and astonishingly hard, even through the material of his drawers. In spite of her bold assurances that she was ready, she made no move to unfasten the small ivory buttons.

He sighed indulgently. "Maybe I should do it."

"No, no, I will!"

"If you're uncomfortable, we can try this again later."

"Later? But you're . . . well, it doesn't seem like something that will keep for later."

A laugh escaped him, a reaction that caused his arousal to move against her hand. Without any conscious thought on her part, her fingers flexed.

He groaned. "Now you're trying to torture me, are you?"

"No." Her fingers flexed again, and she jumped slightly when his shaft flexed in response. "Oh!"

"Oh, indeed," he said on a low rumble. "Why don't I show you instead?"

Without waiting for her agreement, he laid his hand on top of hers and positioned her fingers so she was holding him. He felt even larger and more solid that way, his shaft throbbing through the thin cloth barrier. Slowly, he began sliding her hand up and down along his length.

To her surprise, he seemed to swell even more under her touch. She hazarded a glance up and became instantly mesmerized, his face rendered even more beautiful by the look of profound pleasure he wore. His eyes were half closed, his lips parted on a silent inhalation.

Suddenly her nerves melted away, empowered by the knowledge that it was her touch, her closeness, that had made him look that way. An all-over quiver ran through him, strong enough for her to feel it through their connection.

With her usual confidence restored, she slid her other palm over his firm, hair-roughened chest. "Why don't you lie down," she urged with an ineffectual little push that didn't budge him at all. "Let me take care of you."

His eyes opened fully again, their blue depths dark and hazy with passion. "Are you certain?"

"Absolutely. Actually I'm rather curious."

"Oh? About what?"

"Everything. I've never seen a man's naked member before, at least not in person."

His mouth twisted. "And you've seen one otherwise?"

"Only the artistic kind that haven't been covered up by strategically placed fig leaves. You've no idea how frustrating that is. Paintings and sculptures are rife with women's breasts, which I have no interest in seeing at all, but want to look at a man's . . . you know . . ."

"Cock?" he suggested helpfully, his own giving another flex under her palm.

Warmth spread through her. "Yes—*cock*—," she repeated, rather liking the impolite word, "and you'd think the world would cease to spin."

"Yet now, as luck would have it, you find yourself in the position of not only seeing one but of touching it too."

Her skin grew even warmer, especially her palms. "Exactly, Your Highness."

Determined not to lose her confidence, she stroked him again, relishing his quickly indrawn breath as she traced his rigid length.

This time, when she tried to push him back, he let her.

Chapter Fourteen

Stretching out across the sheets, Rupert waited, his heart booming like thunder in his chest, his shaft and balls pulsing with a vicious, unrelenting ache.

And to think she'd barely even touched him yet.

He forced himself not to move, determined to let her go at her own pace. Still, that didn't keep his mind from racing, his thoughts filled with the need to rip open his drawers and wrap her fingers around his naked shaft. He would make her pump him hard and fast and long until he released under her hot little hands, maybe more than once.

Actually, if he could do anything, he'd flip her on her back, spread her legs, and tup her until neither of them could remember how to speak. But he'd decided to leave her a virgin—at least that was his "honorable" plan—so manual stimulation would have to suffice instead. The worst part was knowing that he could take her, if he really wanted to. She'd given her consent and wouldn't stop him if he changed his mind.

Groaning inside his head, he curled his hands into fists at

his sides and held himself steady. He'd promised to teach her, to let her explore her sexuality, and he would keep his word, no matter how much he might suffer as a consequence.

If you could call this suffering, since he could hardly claim that he wasn't enjoying himself.

Mein Gott, she was passionate, taking pleasure in every act to which he introduced her. He'd relished watching her climax this afternoon at their picnic. And again tonight when she'd taken her release so forcefully she'd had to bury her face in a pillow to hide her cries.

He'd wondered beforehand how she would react to that last bit, when he'd buried his face between her creamy white thighs and surprised her with a far more intimate kiss than she could ever have imagined. But rather than shy away, she'd welcomed him, urging him on while he'd pleasured them both.

Even now he could taste her sweet honey on his lips. He smiled inwardly, promising himself that he would repeat that particular indulgence again soon. But for now he vowed to let her be the one to play.

She stroked him again through his drawers, exploring the contours of his straining erection. He shuddered yet again and fought to maintain strict control, wanting to make their encounter last as long as possible. But patience or no patience, if she didn't unfasten his buttons soon, his shaft would probably swell enough to pop them off for her.

Suddenly, she stopped her maddening exploration and reached for his buttons. He held his breath, watching her fingers hover over the fastenings. Tentatively, she touched the first one, moving a hesitant fingernail along the ivory.

"Do you need some help?" he offered, more gruffly than he intended.

Her gaze flew to his, her green eyes bright with nerves and excitement. "No, I'll do it. I w-want to."

He nodded and forced himself to lie still.

Slowly she freed the first button, then a second. He nearly reached down to rip the last one off himself, but held steady and let her finish. When she paused again, he decided she must be torturing him on purpose.

Then she folded down the cloth of his falls.

His erection sprang free, arcing boldly upward as if preening for her attention. He watched her widened eyes glaze over and her lips part, her breath coming in shallow draughts as she looked her fill.

"Oh, my," she said on a husky whisper. "Oh, my."

He couldn't keep from smiling. "Is that a good 'oh, my' or a bad 'oh, my'?"

Her gaze met his again. "Good. Definitely good. Though I must say you're not quite what I expected."

"How so?" He arched an eyebrow inquiringly.

"Well, it's just that in paintings and sculptures, the men aren't . . ."

"Yes?" he drawled, rather enjoying her naive discomfiture. He'd never lain with a virgin before; he was finding her reactions nothing short of delightful. "What aren't they, these other men?"

"So large," she admitted on a rush of honesty. "I mean, if they put your . . . cock . . . on a Greek sculpture, not only would it have caused an uproar, it would never have withstood the rigors of time. As soon as they tried to move the piece, someone would surely have knocked your . . ." She waved a hand. "Well, you know . . . off by accident."

He winced at the idea but laughed all the same. "A good thing, then, that I've never been tempted to commission a naked statue of myself."

An arrested expression crossed her face and then she grinned. "Mayhap you should. But only for your private chambers."

He laughed harder, then groaned as a fresh ache spread through his stiff shaft.

"So are all men as well endowed as you," she continued, "or have the artists been lying?"

"No and no. Size depends on the man, though I can't say that I've given the subject much thought since it's women's bodies that interest me. Then too there's the fact that I'm erect at the moment."

"Does that made a difference?"

He laughed again. "Quite a lot."

"Ah." She nodded again, studying his phallus as she considered. "And does it actually . . . fit?"

"Fit?"

A flush crept over her cheeks. "Inside. Would it fit me, for instance?"

His shaft flexed at the suggestion and he nearly groaned as an image took hold of lifting her over him and finding out exactly how pleasurable it would be to fit himself inside her. She would be exquisitely tight and warm and wet.

Perfectly right.

Perfectly wonderful.

"Yes, I'm certain I'd fit," he said.

She gave him a look as if she wasn't convinced.

"But for now," he said, ignoring the small visual byplay, "you're supposed to be undressing me, remember?"

She nodded.

"Then quit dawdling and remove my drawers."

"I'm not dawdling. I had questions."

"Which I've answered in spite of the fact that you are tormenting me."

"Am I?" she asked with a little smile.

"Yes, and you needn't look so pleased about it. If you're not careful, I'll torment you back."

"Promise?" she said impishly.

He laughed, then groaned again. "Ariadne," he warned through his clenched teeth.

"Yes, all right. Do I just slide them down?"

"That would be the general idea."

He watched as she took a moment to gather herself. Then she reached in. He shivered as her hands moved over his hips, her palms sliding along his thighs and briefly around to his buttocks before she worked the cloth lower. He angled his hips up to aid her, then lay back again as she tugged the drawers completely off. She tossed them in the direction of her nightgown, where they landed, already forgotten.

Then, once again, he let her look her fill, bending an arm beneath his head.

Breath came quickly from her lips as if taxed by her recent efforts. Her red-gold hair lay tousled becomingly around her flushed face and pale shoulders, her nipples peeping enticingly from behind the heavy silken locks that pooled over her pale thighs.

She looked like Eve must have looked in the Garden of Eden, tempted by the serpent and the apple. He had to confess he felt rather like a devil, leading her down the forbidden path. But she was halfway there already. What did a few more steps really matter?

"Shall I touch you?" she murmured.

"God, yes!"

She laughed a bit nervously. Then her little palms were on him again, moving over his calves and knees and thighs, learning the shape of his limbs before gliding along his hips again and up across the flat plane of his stomach and chest.

He sucked in his belly on a sharp inhalation. "You really are trying to torment me. I'll remember this."

She shivered visibly and smiled. "You're so warm. So hard."

Then her fingers wandered down his body once more and

finally curved around the one part that was literally aching for her touch. He arched involuntarily in her hand, sliding himself up, then down against her grasp before he forced himself to lie still.

"Y-you're hard here too, but smooth, almost like satin," she said with a sigh. She stroked him slowly from root to tip, clearly enthralled by the experience. "Am I doing this right? Do you like it?"

"More than you can imagine. Don't stop."

She repeated the movement, her next tortuous pass making him harden even more in her grasp.

"Faster," he ordered in a guttural voice.

"Like this?" she asked, increasing her speed.

"And harder. Grip me tighter."

She closed her fingers around him, but still it wasn't enough.

Reaching down, he enclosed her hand, manipulating her fingers to show her exactly how much pressure he wanted. Willingly, she obeyed, pumping him in her hand the way he'd instructed.

He closed his eyes, a long moan escaping his throat as she brought him closer to his peak, his seed swelling painfully in his balls. Then without any prompting from him, she moved her thumb over the ultra-sensitive head of his shaft, fingering the already wet slit with a skill that drove him straight to the edge.

Release claimed him, hard and fierce, his seed shooting over her hand and onto the sheets in thick, delicious, bliss-inducing jets. His body quaked from the exquisite pleasure, and for long moments he could find neither the breath nor the thoughts that would enable him to speak.

At length, he cracked open an eyelid.

She was kneeling beside him, an expression of rapt astonishment on her face.

"You're sure that was your first time?" he asked, his voice so low and rough it almost cracked.

"Of course. What do you mean?"

"Just that if you weren't blue-blooded, I'd suggest you consider a life as a courtesan. You're that good."

Her lips curved, eyes bright as if she were pleased by his reaction. "So, you liked it?"

He chuckled. "I believe you just had a very graphic demonstration of exactly how much. Yes," he said, reaching out to pull her into his arms. "I loved it."

Her smiled widened, a fresh flush spreading over her cheeks. "I did too. Does that make me very wicked?"

"Extremely," he said, running a palm over her bare bottom. He caressed her for a moment before giving her a playful little slap.

Her eyes widened and she wiggled against him.

"Tired?" he asked. "Should I go and let you get some rest?"

She shook her head. "Not unless you want to go."

Moving his hand lower, he slid his fingers between her thighs, then inside, where she was already slick again with need. "I'll stay a while longer. I don't think I'm quite done with tonight's lesson after all."

He claimed her lips in a dark, languid kiss and began to show her exactly what he meant.

Chapter Fifteen

Ariadne slept late the following morning and ate breakfast on a tray in her room. Luckily, she had being weary after last night's ball to offer as an excuse for why she had chosen not to eat with the others in the morning room. But the truth of the matter was that after spending the night in Rupert's arms, she just couldn't risk facing anyone, especially Emma. She didn't trust herself not to give away some hint of her secret, especially if she walked in and discovered Rupert already seated at the table.

She flushed to recall everything that had passed between them—each languid caress, every deep, delicious kiss still as vivid in her memory as the moment it had happened. She shifted against the bedsheets, her nipples peaking, as fresh need rose again between her thighs.

Merciful heaven, what has he done to me?

And when will he do it again?

She'd been very sleepy when he'd left not long before dawn. With the room still awash in darkness, he helped her back into her nightgown—for which she'd been extremely grateful when her maid arrived hours later—then he dressed in his drawers and robe.

"Be good," he whispered as he bent to give her a last kiss.

"Why?" she mumbled. "It's no fun being good."

He chuckled and kissed her again before tucking her under the coverlet and quietly letting himself out of the room.

She slept deeply after that, waking only when her maid pulled back the curtains to let the bright morning light stream in.

Nearly an hour and a half later, she finally emerged from her bedchamber, bathed and dressed in a pale lavender and ecru striped day dress. She walked down the main staircase, wondering with a flutter in her stomach how soon she would see Rupert again. How would it feel, after everything they had shared last night? Would she be able to keep her eyes off him now that she knew exactly how magnificent he looked both in and out of his clothes?

She smiled and suppressed a very un-Ariadne-like need to giggle. She couldn't remember the last time she'd given in to such foolishness—not even as a girl. But something about last night, about Rupert, left her feeling giddy. It was as if she'd drunk too much champagne and was floating on effervescent little bubbles. If there had been music, she was sure she would have danced.

Rather than give in to such undignified behavior, she contented herself by taking the rest of the stairs at a decidedly buoyant gait, her skirts billowing merrily around her ankles. She was just starting down the corridor toward the family drawing room when Emma appeared, the new baby cradled in her arms, young Friedrich walking at her side.

The toddler grinned up at Ariadne, cheeks dimpling, his rounded face a perfect blend of both his parents' features, though he quite definitely had his mother's striking blue eyes.

Ariadne grinned back and waggled her fingers.

The boy giggled.

Ariadne nearly joined him.

As for Peter, the infant appeared to be fast asleep, his dark eyelashes fanned in a beautiful arc against his milky cheeks, one tiny fist tucked securely beneath his chin.

"Good morning," Emma remarked with a smile of her own. "I was wondering if you were up and about yet. We missed you at breakfast, you know."

"Sorry, but I just couldn't seem to get myself out of bed. Late night and all."

Very late night, Ariadne thought. As for the "and all" . . . well, she would be careful not to mention anything about that.

"The extra sleep seems to have done you good," Emma continued. "You look quite refreshed. Your skin is positively glowing."

"Is it?"

Maybe the effervescent sensation she felt wasn't just on the inside. Could it be that all the good sex she'd had showed on the outside too? Perhaps she should make a study on the subject. After yesterday, she certainly wouldn't mind conducting additional research.

Emma gave her a curious look.

In the next second, Friedrich darted away from his mother's side and raced down the hall. Ariadne turned to see one of the family cats stroll into view at the end of the corridor.

"Kitty!" the boy squealed. "Come here, kitty."

The animal's head came up and he hurried faster, brown-and-black-striped paws flashing; clearly the cat was in no mood to be caught and held. Friedrich was usually quite gentle, as Ariadne had reason to know, but sometimes he got overly excited and squeezed a bit too hard.

"Friedrich, stop," Emma called. "Leave Mozart alone."

But the boy was too intent on his objective to listen.

"I'll get him," Ariadne offered, since Emma's arms were full of the baby.

Picking up her skirts, she gave chase. Friedrich was fast in a way only young children could be, and they were nearly to the end of the corridor before she managed to catch up. Gently but firmly, she took hold of his small hand and drew him to a halt.

"But I want to pet the kitty," he complained, straining to follow after the now vanished animal.

"You can see Mozart later. He doesn't want to be bothered just now."

"I won't bother him. I love him."

"I know you do, sweetie. What do you say we find Tuck instead? He's always ready for a good rub and a game of fetch."

Tuck was a King Charles spaniel that Nick had given Emma as a birthday gift during their first year of marriage. The dog was incredibly gentle, with bottomless wells of patience, and the ability to remain calm no matter how loud or rambunctious Friedrich—and now his baby brother— became.

Friedrich thrust out his lower lip in a moment of indecision, then smiled. "Okay. I'll play with Mozart later. Let's find Tuck!"

Ariadne sighed in quiet relief.

Emma strolled forward, the baby blinking sleepily as if he were on the verge of waking. "Are you sure?" she asked, addressing Ariadne. "We were all on our way up to the nursery."

"It's no trouble. I'll bring him up as soon as he's had a chance to enjoy himself with the dog. You don't know where Tuck is at the moment, by any chance?"

A fresh smile crossed Emma's face. "He's usually in

Nick's study this time of day. There's a chair near one window that he loves to sleep in. I'd try there first. Otherwise, just call his name and he'll come running."

She nodded and headed back toward the stairs, Friedrich's little hand held securely inside of hers.

"Don't play too long," Emma said. "Friedrich needs his nap, and you and I have to change. We're promised at the Rosedales' this afternoon, if you recall."

She stopped. No, actually she hadn't.

"I'm not sure I'll be able to make it," Ariadne said. "I think your brother is taking me for another driving lesson today."

Emma paused, a tiny frown moving over her brow. "Oh, I don't believe he is. I'm sorry, Aric, but he left the house an hour ago at least. He mentioned something about a meeting at the palace and not to expect him until after dinner tonight."

Disappointment washed through her like a small riptide, a reaction she instantly pushed aside. Obviously Rupert had meant what he said about not altering their usual habits and schedules in order to spend more time together. Then again, he was the one who'd dreamed up their driving lessons. She'd thought he might at least continue their new excursions longer than a single day. She supposed she would need to take nothing for granted and learn to count on *not* counting on him.

Putting on what she hoped was an airy smile, she shrugged. "Oh, well, my mistake. I'm sure the lessons will continue another day."

"He ought to have told you he was otherwise engaged," Emma said with concern, obviously seeing through Ariadne's false smile.

"Yes, he ought. But there's a prince for you. Arrogance at its finest."

Emma's frown deepened.

"Really, it's of no moment," Ariadne told her. "And this way I don't have to beg off the party with you. I love garden fetes. I hope they serve ices."

"As do I." Emma rocked the baby, who had dozed off again. "Arie, are you—"

"Ices! I want an ice!" Friedrich chimed, tugging on Ariadne's hand. "Mama, may I have an ice?"

Attention diverted, Emma looked at her son. "Not right now, sweetheart. Maybe later. I'll see if Cook can make some for you, but I can't promise. Now, if I'm not mistaken, you and Aunt Arie were off to find Tuck. He'll be wondering what's taking you so long."

Friedrich paused a moment to consider, then jumped excitedly in the air. "Tuck! Tuck! Let's find Tuck."

Ariadne laughed; it was impossible not to when one was around Friedrich. He was such a happy little boy.

"Yes, let's," she agreed, and together they set off, Ariadne determined to enjoy her day regardless of Rupert's defection.

He came to her that night, slipping between the sheets to kiss her awake. She woke drowsily, and without thinking kissed him back. It was only as her sleepiness gradually melted away that she remembered the day just past and the fact that this was the first time she had seen him without the gap of a ballroom in between.

"I shouldn't speak to you," she said, as he abandoned her lips and began kissing his way down her throat.

"Then don't," he murmured on a low rasp. "There's no need for conversation."

His fingers started opening the buttons on the front of her nightgown.

She made no effort to push them away.

"In future I shall have to remember to lock my door," she said. "One never knows what kind of—*oh*"—her breath caught as he cupped one breast—"intruders may sneak in without permission."

"But I am not an intruder." He licked the edge of her ear, then caught her earlobe between his teeth. "And I most certainly do not require permission."

She trembled as his thumb circled one peaked nipple.

"You aren't angry again, are you?" he asked, wetting her lower lip with the tip of his tongue before pressing his mouth to hers in quick, plucking kisses. "I told you how it would be."

"That doesn't mean I like it." She thrust her fingers into his hair and kissed him harder. "Next time we're at a ball, ask me to dance. You have done that before on occasion. It won't look out of character."

He smiled and pinched her nipple.

She arched and gave a mewling little cry.

"Then reserve a waltz and I'll take you flying across the floor." He reached for the hem of her nightgown and slid it up. "For now, what do you say if I take you flying another way?"

Breath burned in her lungs, her blood sizzling as he parted her thighs and slipped a finger deep inside.

"Wet already," he mused huskily. "Oh, Ariadne, you're a delight."

He began working inside her, bringing her quickly to the edge, but not quite over.

She skimmed her hands down his naked back and dug her nails into his skin, pleased when she felt his answering response.

"I think we should conduct a little experiment," he said in between kisses.

"Experiment?" Her voice was high and thin with passion.

"*Hmm.* I want to see how many times."

"Times?" she repeated dazedly. "For what?"

"For me to make you climax tonight." He pushed a second finger inside her folds and stroked deep, circling his thumb around another exquisitely sensitive nub of flesh in a way that drove her wild.

"Ah, here it comes, the first one," he said knowingly.

And he was right.

Crying out, she surrendered and let the rapture take her.

Chapter Sixteen

"Excuse me, Your Highness," Rupert said nearly two weeks later, "but are you promised for the next set?"

Ariadne turned at the sound of his murmured question, suppressing a delicious shiver at the husky tone of his voice. Luckily they stood in a far corner of the ballroom, the sheer volume of noise from their fellow partygoers loud enough to ensure they would not be overheard.

"I am now," she replied. "But are you certain we dare to be seen together? After all, we danced the waltz only the other evening, if you will recall."

He smiled softly. "I believe it's safe to risk it. As you quite rightly pointed out some days ago, our refusing to stand up together is far more likely to draw unwanted attention than not. Besides, this is just an ordinary set and not the supper dance."

No, of course not. They never shared the supper dance, just as they were careful never to engage in more than one dance on any given evening.

She sighed quietly. "I wish it *was* the supper dance. It

would be much more entertaining to dine with you than with my usual gentlemen escorts. Remember last Tuesday's picnic."

A dark gleam smoldered in his eyes. "I shall never forget last Tuesday's picnic."

Neither would she. Her breath caught just to recall what had happened at his friend's estate, alone once more in their secret garden.

The things he'd done to her.

The things she'd done back.

Technically she was still a virgin. Despite her continued efforts to convince him to make them lovers in all ways, he still refused to claim that final part of her innocence. The annoying thing was that she knew he was every bit as frustrated as she. Sometimes, when they made love, he had to stop and wrench himself away, his control near the breaking point.

If only he weren't so deuced stubborn.

Then again, so was she.

It would be interesting to see which one of them proved victorious in the end.

"Wipe that look off your face before someone sees," he warned softly, taking her elbow to angle her away from prying eyes.

"What look?"

"The one that makes me want to drag you off to the nearest private room so I can tumble your skirts up around your waist and kiss you until you're senseless with desire."

Tingles chased over her skin, her body heating at his suggestion.

I wouldn't mind that either.

"Which," he added in a chastening tone, "is the reason I don't dare take you in to supper. A few more of those looks and we'd be on the wagging tongues of every gossip maven from here to the Continent. Talking to you like this is temptation enough."

She arched a brow. "I'm not the one who mentioned kisses and tumbled skirts. But maybe we should find a room and skip the dancing. It would be a lot more fun."

He growled under his breath. "You've turned into a dangerous seductress, Your Highness."

"All thanks to your exceptional tutelage, Prince."

He laughed, the sound moving through her like a caress. Then he groaned. "I don't know if we should take to the dance floor now. I don't trust either one of us at the moment."

"Then let's not."

"Ariadne—"

"No one will notice if we slip away for a little while."

"What about my sister?"

"She's busy flirting with her husband at the moment, in case you hadn't noticed."

She watched him survey the room, his golden brows sweeping down when he located Emma and Nick. "They are far too familiar with each other in public," he complained. "Married people aren't supposed to behave like that."

"Oh, don't be so stodgy and conventional. I think it's romantic."

"You would. And I am neither stodgy nor conventional."

"Oh? Then why don't you prove it and sneak off with me?"

He locked eyes with hers, his own as deeply blue as the midnight sky outside. "I'll come to your room tonight."

She shook her head. "No, now. When I was returning from the ladies' withdrawing room earlier, I noticed an empty room at the end of the corridor near the ground-floor library. Why don't I meet you there in fifteen minutes? I'll leave first and you can follow."

He paused, his scowl deepening. "What about the set after this one? Are you not promised?"

"No, I refused offers from the two men who asked. They're both dreadful bores, so I decided I'd rather sit out than endure either one of them. Which means we've got an hour together at least."

Her heart pounded as she waited for his verdict, encouraged by his silent consideration.

"This breaks all the rules, you know," he said at length.

She barely hid her triumphant smile. "Fifteen minutes." Reaching out, she gave his hand a quick squeeze. "Don't be late."

His eyes smoldered again. "Don't worry. I won't."

Ten minutes later, Ariadne wandered idly through the small room in which she had agreed to meet Rupert, her nerves humming with anticipation. She'd lighted a single candle to dispel the darkness, and the flame provided just enough illumination to make the interior visible without attracting undue notice should someone happen by.

The room looked to be a study of sorts, complete with a pair of comfortable-looking old armchairs and a short but well-sprung sofa; she knew, because she'd tried it, bouncing on the cushions a couple of times experimentally. Shelved books lined the walls, the bindings smelling of leather and aging parchment. A narrow keyhole desk stood against one wall, with an equally narrow chair pushed beneath. The grate was bare and didn't look as if a fire had been lit for some while, giving her confidence that she and Rupert would remain undisturbed.

She walked the length of the room, then turned back, wondering how much longer he would be. Finally she heard a footfall at the door.

At last.

Smiling, she turned.

But her smile vanished when she realized it wasn't Rupert who had entered the room. "Lord Selkirk," she said with a frown.

He strolled farther inside. "Good evening, Your Highness. I saw you come this way and wondered at your being in this part of the house. I thought I would make sure everything was all right."

She made no reply, her mind racing as she considered a response. Selkirk had suspected Rupert's interest in her once before, and if Rupert showed up, the other man would realize he had stumbled upon an assignation. Then again, Rupert could be astonishingly intimidating when he chose. She was sure he would make it clear to Selkirk that nothing was to be said about their out-of-the-way meeting.

Besides, Selkirk hadn't caught her and Rupert doing anything, so it would be an easy matter for Rupert to claim that he had come in search of her in order to escort her back to the ballroom. If neither of them panicked, they could surely brazen out the situation regardless of initial appearances. In the meantime, she supposed she would have to speak to Selkirk, regardless of how much she wished he would take his leave.

"Of course all is well," she said with an unconcerned smile. "I was curious and a bit bored, if you must know. I thought I would sneak away from the ballroom for a few minutes and do a little exploring."

"Ah, I ought to have realized," he mused, moving closer to her. "Ever the adventuress, are you not, Princess?"

"Just so. You have caught me out."

"I must say it has been some time since we had an opportunity to talk like this."

She linked her hands. "You are right. It has been a while."

Actually they hadn't spoken since the night she had turned down his marriage proposal. Given that she'd begun her intimate relationship with Rupert that same night, she had to admit that she had barely given Lord Selkirk so much as a passing thought in the interim.

For his part, Selkirk hadn't seemed to mourn the loss of

her hand for long; from what she had heard, he'd begun dancing attendance on a wealthy squire's daughter. If she wasn't mistaken, bets were currently being laid as to whether he would propose.

She smiled, not wishing there to be any hard feelings between them. "So, how have you been, my lord? Enjoying the Season?"

His mouth twisted. "Not especially. It would seem I'm not having much luck with marriage proposals. I recently offered for another young lady, you see, and she turned me down as well. Or rather I should say she was willing enough, but her father forbade the union. Some concern about my lack of finances."

Her forehead drew tight.

Where is Rupert? He ought to be here by now.

"I am sorry to hear that," she offered.

"Are you? Were you warned off as well? Or did you truly think we would not suit?"

She studied him, seeing the lines of unhappiness on his attractive face. Whatever his demons, she didn't like knowing she had added to his woes. "Sadly, my lord, I think we would have made each other quite miserable as husband and wife. You are well quit of me."

An odd light flared in his eyes. "Then that is most unfortunate indeed." He held out an arm. "Come. Allow me to escort you back to the ballroom."

She shook her head. "I believe I shall remain here a while longer. Do go on. Don't trouble yourself over me."

"I am afraid I cannot do that. I must insist that you come with me."

A queer shiver chased over her spine, hearing something unsettling in his voice. "Thank you, but no."

Where is Rupert? she thought again. *He must be delayed.*

Selkirk sighed. "I didn't want to resort to such tactics, but you're not an easy kind of woman to convince."

"What?" she said, confused. "What is that supposed to mean?"

Suddenly he pulled something from his pocket—it was a knife. The blade glinted wickedly in the low light. He locked a firm hand around her arm. "Come with me now, and not so much as a word."

"And what do you intend to do with that? Put that thing away immediately and unhand me."

"I said not a word," he hissed. "Believe me, you don't want to test me, Princess."

"I am meeting someone here. He will wonder where I've gone."

He smirked. "Then we had best be on our way. I wouldn't want to hurt your companion."

"*He* is the one who will hurt *you*."

"Maybe. Maybe not. Now come, unless you want to start bleeding." He pressed the blade against her side just firmly enough to emphasize his threat.

Surely Rupert is somewhere in the corridor? The moment they were through the door, she would yell for him, knife or no knife.

But instead of forcing her toward the doorway, Selkirk hurried her toward the back of the room. Only then did she notice a false door in one wall, no doubt used by the servants. With a click, he opened it and pulled her through.

She began to struggle, opening her mouth to scream. Before she could make so much as a sound, he clasped his other hand over her mouth. She wrestled against him, but he was too strong. Before she knew what he meant to do, he shoved a handkerchief in her mouth, then bound it with another to hold it in place.

"Sorry, Princess, but it's the only way. Now, you can come with me easy or you can come with me hard. Your choice."

Screaming against the gag, she kicked him with as much force as she could muster. Sadly, her slippers did little damage.

He sighed. "Hard it shall be, then. Forgive me."

Putting away the knife, he pressed another handkerchief to her face, one that smelled of fumes. She tried not to breathe, but it was impossible. Her head swam as she was forced to draw the vile concoction into her lungs. Uncontrollable weakness stole through her limbs, along with the helpless dread of knowing she could not fight him. She made one last weak struggle anyway, refusing to give in. But the drug was too strong, darkness closing over her like the waters of an icy winter lake.

"Well, that is all most fascinating," Rupert said with barely concealed impatience, "but now you must excuse me."

"Oh, but I haven't told you the most interesting part of all," the other man insisted with a wave of his hands.

Rupert couldn't recall for certain, but he believed the chatty young man's name was Hodges. After Rupert had left the ballroom, he had been about three-quarters of the way to his destination when he happened upon Hodges standing at the turn to the last corridor. The other man asked him for the time; reluctantly Rupert withdrew his pocket watch from his waistcoat in order to reply.

Before he could walk on, Hodges asked him a second question—this one about the weather—then the man launched into a long story about his latest visit to Tattersalls and the team of horses he had purchased.

Ordinarily, Rupert would have shaken him off, but with the man showing no signs of returning to the ballroom, he had been reluctant to continue on to the room where Ariadne was waiting, knowing he was being observed. He was at least ten minutes late and realized that Ariadne must be wondering what was keeping him. He supposed if Hodges was still there when he reached the room where she was waiting, he and Ariadne would have to postpone their assignation until later that night. No matter how much he desired her—and his loins kept reminding him exactly how much that was—it wouldn't do to get caught, especially not by a blathering fool like Hodges.

Really, though, it was deuced annoying. Once Ariadne had put the idea of an illicit rendezvous in his head—and turned him randy as a green boy as a result—he'd been anticipating their secret interlude with rapt eagerness. Then, just when he was mere yards away from reaching her, he'd been waylaid by this puerile jackanapes.

By now he was more than done with being tolerant and polite.

Hodges smiled and gestured again in the direction from which Rupert had originally come. "Why don't we go to our host's study and have a drink? The Scotch here is quite excellent."

"So it is. Perhaps another time." Turning, Rupert started down the corridor again.

Before he'd taken more than three steps, however, Hodges sidestepped in front of him, blocking his path.

"Billiards, then?" Hodges suggested, his voice going high with what sounded like a hint of desperation. "Nothing like a good game of billiards to relax a man."

Rupert scowled. "I have no wish to be relaxed. Stand aside."

Hodges swallowed, his Adam's apple bobbing nervously. "T-there must be activity in which I can interest you, Your Royal Highness."

"I think not. Get out of my way."

But Hodges did not move.

Suddenly Rupert realized that he had been deliberately intercepted, deliberately delayed, and there could only be one reason.

Ariadne.

"Get out of my way," he ordered again harshly.

Shoving the other man aside, Rupert strode quickly down the corridor. Reaching the last room, he flung open the door without pause, not sure what he would discover inside.

But the room stood empty.

Where was she? She ought to have been here by now. Had he mistaken the room? But no, Hodges had not wanted him to come here, and he could think of no reason other than that the man wished to keep him from Ariadne.

Then he saw it, something that glimmered in the dull candlelight. Approaching, he leaned down and picked up an earbob.

Her earbob—a small pear-shaped drop made of sapphires and diamonds that he'd seen her wearing only half an hour since.

He'd just closed his fist around it when he noticed a servant's door in the far wall that had not been properly shut. Striding across the room, he opened the door and peered inside.

Empty as well.

This time, though, he caught a pair of scents—one familiar and one that sent a chill down his spine.

She'd been here.

He would recognize the light, honeyed fragrance of her perfume mixed with her own unique sweetness anywhere.

As for the other scent, it reminded him of a surgeon's office—or a chemist's shop.

Ether.

Aware he hadn't a moment to lose, he spun around and raced out of the room. The corridor was deserted.

Hodges. That bastard.

Where was Hodges—assuming that was even his name? Whoever he was, it was clear he was privy to whatever foul plot had befallen Ariadne.

Now he just had to find him.

Uncaring who might see, he broke into a sprint, heading back toward the ballroom and the main entrance. Pausing briefly, he scanned the milling guests, searching for the brown-haired head of his prey. But there were so many people, dancing and talking and laughing—their movements blocking his view.

Suddenly he caught a glimpse. He ran faster, knowing he couldn't give Hodges a chance to climb inside a coach or hackney and disappear.

Hodges was in the act of doing exactly that when Rupert caught up to him. Clamping a hard hand on the man's arm, Rupert spun him around. Hodges trembled and tried to pull away, his eyes as terrified as those of a cornered fox.

"Tell me everything," Rupert demanded, "or so help me God, I'll tear this arm I'm holding straight out of its socket."

Hodges whimpered and began to babble.

Chapter Seventeen

Ariadne glared at Selkirk, wishing it was possible for looks to actually kill. Her head ached, she was in a foul temper, and he was solely to blame.

About half an hour ago, they'd stopped at an inn somewhere along what she'd guessed must be the Great North Road. She wasn't sure of their precise location, having spent a large portion of the coach trip lying across the seat with her hands bound.

Earlier, he'd removed the gag when she'd awakened and become quite ill. The drug he'd used on her had made her horribly queasy; they'd had to stop more than once so she could vomit along the side of the road. Another black mark in the long list of black marks she was accumulating against him—kidnapping being first and foremost among them.

She'd been secretly pleased when she'd unintentionally splashed sick all over his shoes. He hadn't liked that much and had spent ten minutes cursing in a field while cleaning them off in some tall grass.

But that had been hours ago, the whole night and now most of the next day having passed. He'd finally decided they would stop to rest, then continue on in the morning to wherever it was he was taking her.

In the meantime, she had no intention of aiding him in any way.

"Try some of this ham," he urged from across the table of the private parlor in which they sat. "It's actually quite decent."

She glared harder, then crossed her arms and looked pointedly away.

He shrugged. "Suit yourself, but you're the one who'll suffer if you don't eat. You ought to drink something as well. It won't do to have you fainting because you aren't keeping down enough fluids, especially considering how ill you were earlier." He looked down at his plate. "Sorry about that, by the way."

"Which part?" she asked. "Drugging and making me sick, holding me at knife point, or turning criminal enough to kidnap me?"

He considered the question. "All of them, I suppose."

"If you feel so badly about it, why not let me go? Put me in a coach headed back to London and I promise I won't say anything about this unfortunate incident."

He smiled, his eyes twinkling as he raised his wineglass and took a drink. "You've got spirit, Your Highness. It's one of the qualities I've always admired most about you. But unfortunately I cannot afford to simply let you go."

"Why? Do you not trust me to keep my word?"

"You might, but somehow I don't think your friends would be so accommodating. They'd have the story out of you without a great deal of persuasion, then set every man they can command onto my trail. There's nowhere I'd be safe, either here or on the Continent."

"Then why risk any of this? My friends, who are closer to me than family, are certainly aware by now that I've disappeared. They will be searching for me and they will not stop until I am found."

"Nor do I expect them to. But so long as I stay two steps ahead, I'll be able to achieve my aims before anything can be done to stop me. Once that happens, it won't matter if they find us."

He slid a small basket of bread toward her. "Take a piece. I really must insist you eat. And drink some of that milk I ordered for you. It should help soothe your stomach."

She opened her mouth to refuse again, but something in his eyes made her stop. He might appear perfectly amiable on the surface, even reasonable, but he was still the man who had used force against her and spirited her away against her will. Would he use force again if she continued to refuse to eat and drink?

Taking a slice of bread, she laid it on her plate, then broke it in half. As he watched she put a small piece in her mouth and chewed. Her tongue still felt dry and too big for her mouth, her throat rebelling. She forced herself to swallow, waiting anxiously to see if it would come up again.

But mercifully the food stayed down and her lingering nausea eased slightly. She tried the milk next, even though she hadn't drunk a glass of milk since she was a child in leading strings. She didn't care for the tepid blandness, but after a long minute, her head began to clear a bit as well.

Resenting Selkirk all the while, she continued to eat and drink. He did the same.

Once she had eaten all she dared at present, she leaned back in her chair. "You said you only need to keep ahead of my friends until you achieve your aim, that afterward it won't matter. What is that aim? I presume it has something to do with money?"

He laid his knife and fork neatly across his empty plate, and patted his mouth clean with his napkin. Only then did he look at her. "You are far more intelligent than most people, a trait I've always liked, even if it isn't considered becoming in a female. Being that's the case, can you not hazard a guess at my plan?"

She could, but she didn't like any of the ideas that came to mind. "You need money and are going to hold me for ransom," she ventured, suggesting the least objectionable notion first.

"You're right about the money. I do need it. A great deal of it, as the case may be. But ransom? Really? And how would that solve anything?"

It wouldn't and she knew it. He obviously knew it as well.

"No. I plan to wed you. Everything would have been so much easier if you'd just agreed to marry me when I asked. But this is what things have come to."

"I thought you'd turned your attentions to that squire's daughter. Things appeared rather serious between the two of you."

His expression grew fierce. "They were. She's a comely little bird with a well-feathered nest. She would have made a tolerable wife, even if she has no more understanding of manners than your average goat. But sadly, just as all my plans were falling into place, her father started looking into my affairs. It seems he discovered a number of unsettled gaming debts and tradesmen's bills."

One of his hands tightened into a fist on the table. "He called me a fortune hunter and forbade me to see his daughter ever again. I might have convinced her to run off to Gretna Green with me, since she was in love, but he sent her away. To Italy, where she is utterly out of reach.

"Meanwhile, matters grew more serious, since I had by that point availed myself of the services of a moneylender, thinking at the time that I was soon to come into a great deal of wealth. When I did not, my thoughts turned once more to you."

She crossed her arms again. "So I presume *I* am now the one going to Gretna Green?"

His mouth curved upward. "Clever, Princess. I'm going to enjoy being married to you."

"Then it's a shame that I have to disappoint you yet again, since I have no intention of agreeing to be your wife."

He sighed with understanding. "I was afraid you might not be amenable at first and would need further convincing. You're quite ruined by now, you know. Even if your absence wasn't noticed by the *Ton* last night, it certainly will be by now. When next you are in Town, the rumors will be flying."

Leaning back in his chair, he drank more wine. "Once it becomes known that you spent several days alone in my company . . . Well, let's just say I can't fathom the number of doors you will find closed to you, regardless of your status as a royal. Your only salvation is to marry me. Some might sneer and point out that ours is an uneven union, but others will find it romantic that we eloped."

She sent him a fresh glare. "*Eloped?* Is that what you expect me to tell everyone? I think kidnapping and extortion will do far better."

"I only thought to put a positive light on our nuptials. But if you insist on the truth, then so be it. Don't say I didn't offer to spare you the extra talk."

She narrowed her eyes. "You want my money that badly."

"More like I need it that badly, but yes, I do."

"Well, that is a shame indeed."

"And just what do you mean by that?"

"Only that you have mistaken the situation. You see, I do not care overmuch about protecting my reputation. If you knew me better, you would have realized my views on the subject. Truth be known, I would much rather the world brand me a scarlet woman than be forced to tie myself for a lifetime to an unscrupulous rogue like you. There is not going to be a marriage."

He stared at her, his expression turning hard. "Ah, but there is. Believe me, Your Highness, you *will* marry me."

She gave a wry laugh and crossed her arms. "I will not. So you might as well take me back right now. The trip north would be an absolute waste of time for us both."

He contemplated her statement in silence and drank more wine. "I don't think so. You see, you are the one who is in error now. You seem to be under the impression that your consent is required for our union. I assure you it is not."

"Don't be absurd," she retorted with a huff. "I am a royal princess and if I choose not to align myself with you, I cannot be forced to do so."

"Were we remaining in England, that would indeed be true. But once we reach Scotland and Gretna Green, all I need do is find a willing minister and a pair of witnesses."

"All of whom I shall inform of my refusal to be your wife."

"Indeed, you may try," he told her with an unsettlingly smug assurance. "However, I have to warn you that once I inform the minister that I have been bedding you with great frequency over the course of our journey, he'll be only too happy to see us wed. After all, a child might be involved and as its father, I will wish to atone for such sinful behavior and make provision against its illegitimacy."

She curled her fingers around the dinner knife next to her plate. "So you are planning to add my violation to your list of crimes? I have to tell you now that I will never submit to you, not voluntarily and not without a fight."

He grimaced and held up a hand. "Here now, there's no need to be insulting. Most women enjoy coming to my bed."

"Not I."

And to think that at one time she'd toyed with the idea of taking this man as her lover. But now that she'd been with Rupert, she wanted no one else. Certainly not this black-hearted jackanapes who made such dreadful threats.

And Rupert? Where was he and why had he not arrived for their rendezvous in time to prevent her from being kidnapped? Surely nothing untoward had befallen him?

No, she assured herself. *He is well and will come for me.*

Until then, it was up to her to defend herself as best she could.

"Don't come near me." She clutched the knife harder.

He rolled his eyes. "Don't you be so dramatic. I've never forced my attentions on a woman and I don't plan to start now."

"But you said—"

"I said I would *tell* the minister that I'd deflowered you, not that I actually would. Although if you push me hard enough I might change my mind. For the time being, however, your virtue is safe. Once we're married, we can discuss the situation again."

"He won't believe you, the minister. I'll convince him you're lying in order to steal my fortune."

He sent her a look of cynical amusement. "You can try, but in the end it won't serve. If enough money exchanges hands at the time of the ceremony—and I'll make sure it does—the vicar won't care if I have to put that gag back in your mouth and drag you to the altar by your hair."

Blood drained out of her cheeks at hearing the utter sincerity of his words. If he managed to get her to Gretna Green, he would do whatever it took to achieve his aims. But they were still a long way from Scotland. She would think of some way out before then.

She hoped.

Chapter Eighteen

The next day, Ariadne gazed dully out the coach window, doing her best to ignore Selkirk. Seated opposite, he looked as if he were sleeping—his hands linked atop his stomach, his legs stretched out as far as the vehicle would allow.

But she didn't trust him. He was like a cat, apparently asleep one second, fully alert the next. She had good reason to know, since she had tried to escape last night and failed.

After dinner, he'd escorted her upstairs to a bedchamber that she'd been appalled to learn they would be sharing. But he'd kept his word about leaving her untouched, making a pallet for himself on the floor with the extra blankets and pillow he'd requested from the maid.

She'd refused to undress, lying underneath the coverlet on the bed, willing herself not to give in to her need for rest. She waited nearly two hours, listening until she heard the deep, even rhythm of his breathing, accompanied by an occasional light snore.

Careful to make no sound, she crept from the bed to the

door and silently turned the lock. She'd eased the door open barely an inch when with no warning at all, it was slammed shut.

And there stood Selkirk.

"Ah, ah, ah," he admonished. "You're a naughty girl, Your Highness, trying to escape, though where you thought you'd go, I have no idea."

Actually, she'd thought she would take a horse from the stables and ride as far and fast as she could manage. After all, if her friend Mercedes had been able to successfully elude a band of murderers a few years ago, then surely she herself could get away from a blackguard like Selkirk.

But to her great disgust, her plan had failed dismally.

"Back to bed, Your Highness, and get some sleep," he ordered. "We leave at first light."

Defeated, she'd trudged back to the bed and lay down again. To her further irritation, she'd had to watch as he moved his makeshift bed in front of the door, barring any further escape attempts, for that night at least.

So here she was, trapped with him in the coach again.

If she thought she could get away now, she would open the door and fling herself out. But the vehicle was traveling much too fast, and she knew the most she would do was cause herself a grave injury and be back in his clutches, even more effectively caged than before.

At least she had a fresh weapon—a fork she'd secreted in her napkin over the hasty breakfast she'd eaten. What she planned to do with it, she had no idea, but having it in her pocket made her feel better nonetheless.

As the day continued, the tedium wore on her nearly as much as her captivity. She tried to sleep, but the effort made her even more resentful, since every time she dozed off, the coach would hit a rut and jostle her awake.

In the past when she'd traveled, she had done so as befitted a princess, riding in an elegant equipage that glided over the highway with nary a bump. The interior had always been comfortably appointed, so much so that it had seemed almost like traveling atop a grandly padded chaise.

Selkirk's choice of conveyance left much to be desired, although she supposed most people would find little fault. At present though she was in no humor to be generous, finding fault with everything he said or did.

Narrowing her eyes, she sent him a black stare where he slept on in his own corner. She crossed her arms and added *poorly sprung coach* to the ever-increasing list of his crimes.

Still, she refused to complain. First, because it was beneath her dignity. Second, because she knew it would do her no good whatsoever.

As the minutes wore on, though, her stomach began to ache with a gnawing hunger that increased her discomfort tenfold. She was on the verge of breaking her resolve and protesting his insensitive treatment, when he finally roused from his slumber and rapped on the roof, ordering the driver to stop at the next inn.

She nearly wept with relief when he helped her out of the coach, her legs and back stiff from having been bent inside the vehicle for so long.

She let none of her emotions show, however, concentrating on maintaining an expression of calm disdain, even boredom. Inwardly, she might be exhausted, hungry, aching, angry, and even a little scared, but she would never reveal such weaknesses to a man of his stamp.

He tried to make polite conversation after they repaired to a private parlor, but soon ceased his efforts when she refused to reply. With a smirk of wry amusement on his face, he ordered a meal for the two of them, then leaned back in his chair, apparently content to sip a glass of wine and gaze out the window at the inn yard below.

Without meaning to, she found herself doing the same, watching the hostlers scurry to and fro, tending to the horses and coaches that disgorged the arriving passengers, then the departing ones as they packed back up and were driven away. The yard stayed busy as a beehive, people and animals and vehicles performing a bustling dance that never seemed to slow.

Once the food arrived, however, Ariadne forgot all about the rush of humanity below, concentrating instead on the helping of chicken pie and buttered peas that had been set before her.

The fare was far from what she usually ate, but it was surprisingly good, and her spirits lifted fractionally with each bite.

When the serving maid returned to clear away their empty plates, Selkirk downed the last of his wine, refusing her offer of dessert.

"No time, I'm afraid," he told the girl. "We need to be back on the road again."

"Surely we can take a few minutes more," Ariadne said. Anything but returning to that dreadful coach and the trip that brought her ever closer to a destination she had no desire to reach.

"Some cheese and fruit perhaps," she told the servant. "His lordship may not wish to have a sweet, but I cannot say the same."

Selkirk arched a dark brow. "Have something boxed for the lady. She can eat her dessert once we resume our journey."

After casting a glance between the two of them, the girl bobbed a curtsy, then scurried off to do as Selkirk had ordered.

Ariadne turned to him once the serving maid had gone. "Might I at least have a few minutes' privacy so that I may avail myself of the necessary?"

He studied her briefly, then nodded. "Of course, Your Highness. We have more long miles ahead of us today. I wish only for your comfort."

Hah! He's missed the mark on that one, she mused sourly. Then again, what could she expect of a man who would kidnap a woman so he could marry her and steal her inheritance?

As she made to leave, shouts and a great flood of voices sounded from the inn yard below. A glance showed that the mail coach had arrived, a knot of passengers disembarking from the heavily laden vehicle.

She still remembered Mercedes's tales of her brief adventures traveling by public conveyance. Apparently, the coach would stop long enough to deliver and collect the mail, unload baggage of those disembarking, and load any new passengers and their belongings. During the stop, travelers had only a few minutes to stretch their legs and eat a quick bite of food. The coaches stuck to a very strict timetable, arriving and departing without concern should anyone go astray.

She tapped a finger against her lips, her mind spinning with sudden possibilities.

Without another word, she made her way to the door and out into the hallway leading to the stairs.

Selkirk followed.

In the main entry, she turned to seek out the ladies' facilities. Selkirk continued walking behind her.

She stopped and rounded on him. "Your pardon, my lord, but where do you think you are going?"

"I shall accompany you."

She glowered, wondering how to rid herself of him for a few necessary minutes. "I think not. You may be forcing me to travel with you, but that does not give you leave to invade every aspect of my personal privacy. I shall rejoin you shortly."

"I prefer to keep you within my sights."

"And I prefer not to be spied upon." She crossed her arms. "Where would I go anyway? I have no coin and no means of transportation. You would notice that I was missing before I managed to get five feet away."

Lines creased his forehead as he considered what she'd said. "Very well, but one of the maids can accompany you. After that, you have ten minutes. Do not even think about trying to deceive me or I shall make you very sorry indeed."

"Of course," she agreed, deciding she wouldn't think about the sorts of retribution he might have in mind should she fail.

She did her best to look accepting, as if fully resigned to her present captive situation. But her mind was racing, weighing the risks and advantages of a dozen different scenarios.

The maid, of course, was a complication, but she would think of something. She had to, since she feared this might be her last and only chance to escape. They would reach Scotland in another day; she couldn't afford to wait for a better opportunity—assuming there would even be one.

The servant arrived, the girl listening obligingly as Selkirk issued his instructions.

"Ten minutes," he repeated before letting her continue on her way.

"The ladies' is just down here," the girl informed her, chatting pleasantly as they threaded their way through the patrons that crowded into the taproom and toward the back of the building.

A small room had been set aside for guests of quality who did not wish to use the common conveniences outside. Ariadne shut herself inside, wondering how much time remained before the coachman blew the horn to signal the departure of the mail coach. She couldn't afford to time matters incorrectly. If she went too soon, Selkirk would figure out her plan and have her back in his clutches before she could say boo. If she waited too long, the mail coach would depart and her chance of escape along with it.

Then, too, there was still the maid waiting for her just on the other side of the door.

She poured water into a small basin provided for that use and washed her hands, wanting to give at least the illusion that she was taking care of her personal needs. Hands dry again, she unlatched the door.

"All ready, your ladyship?" the girl piped.

Ariadne decided not to correct her error. "Yes, I am." She took a couple of steps into the hall, then stopped abruptly. "Oh, I just realized."

"What, ma'am?"

"Heavens, I forgot my fan upstairs in the parlor. Would you be a dear and run and fetch it for me?"

The girl frowned. "But his lordship said I weren't ter let ye out o' me sight."

"I know, but I do not want to be late returning to the coach and if we both go back upstairs, I fear I shall be. He'll be cross, wondering where I am. I don't like to make him cross." She met the young woman's gaze, her own eyes pleading for understanding. "*Please.* If you're quick, he'll never know."

The girl hesitated a few seconds more. "Ye go out ter the front and wait by the door. I'll be back in a tick."

And just like that, she was gone.

So was Ariadne.

The moment the girl was out of sight, she spun on her heel and raced for a nearby door that she prayed led outside. She planned to dash out and onto the mail coach at the very last instant and hope Selkirk didn't see her board. As for the fare, she would worry about that once she was under way. Surely, despite what she'd told Selkirk, she could convince the coachman or one of the passengers to help her. She had jewels. She couldn't believe there wouldn't be at least one person willing to make a lucrative trade.

She hurried around the side of the building, careful to avoid any patches of muddy grass. Her slippers weren't meant for travel and were nearing ruin as it was. Selkirk hadn't thought to bring her a change of attire—another black mark for him—and she was still wearing the ball gown she'd had on the night of her abduction. Indeed, she had received odd looks at a few of the inns where they'd stopped, but no one had asked if she needed help, including the maid she'd just sent upstairs. No, getting free of Selkirk was up to her, and so she needed to make this opportunity count.

Luckily, the inn's side yard was narrow and not much used, so she remained unnoticed. She slowed as she reached the front of the building, pressing herself close to the edge so she could peer around.

No sign of Selkirk, which was a relief. She needed a clear path to the coach, but it also left her wondering where he might be. Did he realize she had slipped the leash of her temporary jailer? Was he searching for her already?

Fear crawled in her belly, her heart thundering beneath her ribs. She stuck her hand in her pocket and curled her fingers around the fork she carried. It might not be much of a weapon, but at least it gave her an extra measure of courage.

As she watched, a few of the passengers she'd seen earlier began exiting the inn and climbing back into the coach. She scanned the inn yard, searching for some sign of Selkirk.

Moments later, the driver raised a hand to give some kind of signal, then went to slam shut the coach doors.

This was it.

Her chance.

Taking a deep breath, she left her place of concealment and ran as fast as her legs could carry her toward the coach.

The coachman was just closing the second door when she reached him. He looked up, startled.

"I am here and wish to board," she stated, a strained quaver in her voice. She darted a glance behind her, wondering again how close Selkirk might be. To her relief, she did not see him.

"We're just about to get under way, miss." He raked his gaze over her obviously fine attire. "This is the mail coach, ye know."

"I am aware of that fact and wish passage."

"We're full. There's only one spot left on the roof."

The roof?

She forced herself not to look horrified. "Any seat is acceptable. Now, please allow me to board."

"Have ye paid yer fare?"

She considered lying, since there was no time to waste. But the man would find out if she'd indeed paid her way and she had no desire to be tossed back off. "No, but I will as soon as we get under way."

He shook his head. "Sorry, but no one rides without paying. Why don't ye wait for the next coach? I've got to get going. We've a schedule to keep."

"Please," she pleaded. "You must allow me to travel with you. I am in grave peril and must leave here immediately. You can have this brooch." She pointed to the elegantly set cluster of diamonds and rubies pinned to her bodice. "It is worth far more than the fare."

He eyed the jewelry. "Is it real?"

"Of course it is real," she said indignantly. "Will you take it or not?"

"Well, it's not the usual thing, but all right."

She reached up and began to unfasten the brooch. She was just about to slide it free, when a hand clamped around her wrist.

No! she screamed in her head.

"Pin that back on, my dear," intoned Selkirk in a smooth voice. "There's no need for you to barter your jewels or to ride in this vehicle." From the corner of her eye, she saw him turn to address the coachman. "My wife and I had a small disagreement, you understand. She and I will work matters out between us as a married couple should."

"He is *not* my husband!"

The driver and everyone in the coach stared at them.

But Selkirk merely smiled with supposed understanding. "Now, dear, you're confused again, aren't you?" He looked over at the coachman and spoke in a lowered tone as if sharing a confidence. "She suffers from bouts of memory loss, forgets things from time to time, such as our marriage. It's the result of an unfortunate accident. I'm taking her home to the country, where we hope she will continue to heal."

"He's lying," she protested. "He abducted me and is forcing me to travel with him to Scotland. He wants to marry me so he can steal my fortune."

"As I've said, she's confused." Selkirk offered another smile, this one sadly resigned.

To her horror, Ariadne watched the expressions change on the faces of the coachman and the passengers, watched their interest turn to pity for her and belief in him.

"No! He only wants you to think that so you won't help me. He's lying. He's a fortune hunter. He drugged me at a ball in London two nights ago and kidnapped me. That's why I'm dressed the way I am. Please, all of you, you must believe me."

Doubt returned to a couple of faces, but she could see it was useless now. No one was going to get involved. No one was going to help her.

The coachman looked between them, his expression severe. "Maybe you should take this up with the constable.

Meanwhile, I've got a route to drive and I'm late. Sorry, missus . . . miss . . . whatever you may be."

"No, don't leave," she pleaded.

But he was already climbing onto the box and taking up the reins. Still caught in Selkirk's grip, she watched the mail coach drive away.

A small audience of hostlers and onlookers had gathered in the inn yard, having clearly been privy to the scene. She considered throwing herself on their mercy, but she knew there would be none to be had from them either.

Furious, she struggled to free herself from Selkirk's grip. "Let me go."

"I don't think so," he said in a low, harsh voice meant for her ears alone. "You've caused me enough trouble today as it is. Come along. We're late leaving too."

Tightening his grip even more, he began dragging her toward his coach.

But she dug her feet into the ground, struggling against his hold. She wasn't going with him. She refused. No matter what, she wasn't going to go quietly or without a fight.

Not even conscious of what she was about to do, she reached into her pocket and drew out the fork. Then, as hard as she could, she stabbed the tines into the top of his hand.

He yelled in pain and reared back, releasing his hold on her. "Damn and blast! What in Hades' name did you do that for?"

And she was running, to where she had no idea. All she could think was to get away, however she might manage, as fast as she was able.

She heard a commotion behind her, a rush of voices, and the pounding of a pair of booted male feet. She ran harder, her satin-covered feet slipping on the earth. Suddenly a hand closed around her arm and pulled her to a halt.

No! He was too fast. How had he caught up to her already?

She spun, fighting and struggling as she did, her other arm raised to defend herself. But as she moved to strike, she caught sight not of her dark nemesis but of a golden-haired angel instead.

She faltered, unable to believe what, or rather who, she was seeing.

It couldn't be.

Rupert.

He's found me.

He pulled her close, cradling her against his strong chest. "I'm here, Ariadne. You're safe."

And in that moment she knew she truly was.

Chapter Nineteen

As evening approached, Ariadne dozed, warm and comfortable inside the circle of Rupert's arms, his broad shoulder making a remarkably excellent pillow.

She was traveling by coach once again, but this time she didn't mind. The interior was luxuriously appointed, the ride smooth and seamless as the vehicle moved south along the highway with a quiet *shush* of the wheels and an occasional *clip-clop* of horses' hooves.

What a difference a few hours made.

To think that only this morning she had sat anxious and miserable inside Selkirk's coach, wondering how she could possibly extricate herself from his clutches.

Her escape attempt at the inn, such as it was, had proved a dismal failure. If not for Rupert's timely arrival, she would still be under Selkirk's control, riding in his wretched coach, with Scotland and an unwanted wedding just over the horizon.

At least she'd had the satisfaction of stabbing him with her stolen fork. Ordinarily she didn't hold with physical violence, but after everything he'd put her through, she thought he rather deserved a bit of misery.

Of course, she was sure he was currently suffering a great deal more misery, considering the punishment he'd received at Rupert's hands.

Once Rupert had determined that she was unharmed, he'd set her safely aside. Then he'd turned on Selkirk, literally chasing him down as the other man tried to climb into his carriage and escape. Rupert's fury was truly frightening to behold as he grabbed Selkirk and laid into him with vicious intent.

Selkirk—no weakling himself when it came to physical confrontations—did his best to defend himself. Well known for his boxing prowess, he landed a few brutal blows of his own to Rupert's stomach and jaw as the two men circled each other.

But Selkirk's efforts seemed only to inflame Rupert all the more as he rained blow after blow down upon the other man.

For a horrifying minute, she'd feared Rupert might kill Selkirk, but abruptly he'd regained possession of himself and stopped the attack. With a line of blood trickling from his lip, he let the other man collapse to the ground in a groaning heap.

But his punishment of Selkirk hadn't been fully complete. Leaning down, he smacked Selkirk's bruised and bleeding face to make sure he was conscious. Then he spoke, his voice full of chilling menace. "Don't ever come near her again, do you hear? If I find you within fifty feet of the princess, I won't stop with just a beating next time. I may not be sovereign of this land, but I can make you disappear easily enough should I wish to do so. Do you understand me?"

Selkirk, eyes already swelling shut, had nodded. "Y-yes. I understand."

"And if I hear of you kidnapping any other young women for their money, I'll come after you for that as well."

Rupert turned away, leaving Selkirk lying prostrate on the ground.

Ignoring the crowd of interested onlookers, Rupert had helped her into his coach—a plain black vehicle that bore no crest and gave no indication as to the identity of its occupant.

She hadn't thought much of it at the time, but now she was grateful. No one would know she had been at that inn. Many might remark on the extraordinary fight between two gentlemen over a lady, but no one would realize the identities of the participants, since she was very sure Selkirk wouldn't wish to be identified either.

She could almost feel sorry for him now.

Almost, but not quite, since he would have forced her to marry him had he managed to reach Gretna Green with her.

She shuddered at the thought.

"Did I wake you?" Rupert asked quietly. "I was hoping you would sleep."

"No, I'm fine. I've just been thinking about the past couple of days."

He rubbed a hand along her arm in a slow, soothing glide. "It's over. You don't have to think about it anymore. He won't bother you again."

"No, I heard what you said to him, so I'm sure he will not. I wonder if he'll even return to London."

His arm tightened briefly. "He won't if he knows what's good for him. And considering the financial straits he's landed himself in, it's doubtful on that score as well."

"*Hmm.* He mentioned something about moneylenders and being desperate for funds. He thought he could solve all his problems by marrying me."

"So I learned from his associate. That's why I was late meeting you the night of the ball. He set a man to detain me—or rather to detain anyone who decided to wander near while he was busy trying to spirit you out of the house."

He fisted a hand in obvious frustration. "If only I'd realized sooner and gotten past him in time to prevent this. Ariadne, I'm sorry. Sorry that I wasn't there to stop him from taking you."

"*Shh*. It wasn't your fault. You could not have predicted what he meant to do. Even I had no idea at first. Then he held me at knifepoint and drugged me . . . Well, it was easy for him after that."

"He threatened you with a weapon?" he said in outrage. "I knew I should have saved the beating and put a bullet between the blackguard's eyes instead."

"Well, I am glad you did not, for your sake more than his. I wouldn't want murder on your conscience."

"No, I suppose not." But he didn't sound entirely convinced.

She settled her head back on his shoulder again, everything silent except for the sounds of the coach moving down the road.

Beneath her, she could feel the tension in his body, a kind of coiled energy that he seemed to be holding in check.

"What is it?" she asked, laying a hand on his chest. "What's wrong?"

"Nothing. Just try to rest."

"I'm rested. At least as much as I'm going to be for now."

Angling her head back, she reached up and brushed a stray lock of hair off his forehead. She hid a wince at the bruise she saw darkening his cheekbone and another along his jaw.

He met her gaze, his own eyes intensely blue. "I keep thinking about the past two days, about you being forced to be alone with him. I know I asked before, but did he hurt you, Arie?"

Her eyebrows furrowed, suddenly understanding his meaning. Before she could reassure him, he continued on.

"Because whatever he may have done, you can tell me," he said. "No matter what it is, none of it is your fault. You are blameless in this. Absolutely without fault. If anyone is at fault, it is I. I should have been there. I should have found you sooner."

She made a dismissive noise. "Stop that. We've been over this already; you are not at fault. The only one who deserves blame is Selkirk, who at the moment is reaping some of his just deserts."

With careful fingers, she stroked his cheek. "But as to your question, he didn't touch me, not the way you mean. He made some threats in that regard, talking about consummating what he assumed would be our upcoming marriage, but he remained a gentleman for all that. Last night at the inn, he slept on the bedroom floor. He never came near me."

His arm muscles flexed. "You shared a room?" he said in a dangerous tone.

"Yes. He didn't want me escaping. And with good reason, as it happened, since I did try to escape. This afternoon was my second attempt, which failed as spectacularly as the first."

"I saw what you did to him with that fork." His mouth curved upward in a clearly satisfied smile. "Good for you."

"He was surprised, wasn't he?"

Rupert chuckled and met her gaze again. "Remind me never to get on your bad side if there's cutlery around."

"Duly noted. No arguments at the dinner table."

He barked out a quick laugh, then sobered again just as quickly. "It's good to have you back, Ariadne. I was . . . worried."

"I was worried too. Thank you for coming after me."

"Did you think I would not?"

"No." She laid her hand against his cheek. "I knew you would find me, but an expression of gratitude seems appropriate all the same."

Bending his head, he touched his mouth to hers. She closed her eyes and lost herself to their kiss.

Only then did she admit to herself how frightened she'd been during her ordeal.

Only then did she know how right it felt to be in his arms once again.

Burrowing closer, she encouraged him to deepen their embrace, parting her lips so she could taste his silken heat, explore his dark, heady flavor.

On a groan, he buried his face against her neck, kissing one of her most sensitive spots along her nape.

She trembled.

"We never did get to that rendezvous, did we?" he murmured, running his hand along her spine. Down, down he went until he splayed his fingers over the curve of her bottom. He gave her a little squeeze there, her flesh pliable beneath his touch, and pulled her closer still.

"We're alone now," she urged with an ardent sigh.

"So we are. But"—he claimed her mouth again, feasting on her with a relish that fired her blood—"we need to behave. For the time being at least."

"Maybe I don't want to behave." She threaded her fingers into his hair. "Maybe I just want to forget."

And she did, longing to put the past two days out of her mind, to pretend that nothing had happened between those last tantalizing moments at the ball when they'd agreed to meet in secret and this moment here in the confines of his coach.

But Rupert was nothing if not strong willed, taking her mouth again for another slow, sizzling kiss before easing away.

"This isn't the place," he told her, settling her comfortably, but less intimately, against his side. "Not this time at least. We'll be stopping for the night soon. After everything you've been through, you deserve an easy journey."

"Oh?" she said, her disappointment at their interrupted lovemaking lessening a bit at that news.

"We're too far from London to drive on tonight anyway." He folded her hand inside his. "Rest again for the last few miles."

Rest? How she possibly rest after the kisses they'd just shared?

But she could be patient if she must.

Leaning her head on his shoulder again, she listened to the quiet rhythm of the traveling coach. She wasn't exactly aware when her eyelids grew heavy, but suddenly she couldn't hold them open.

With a comfortable sigh, she snuggled closer and knew no more.

More than an hour later, Rupert added a last sentence to his note, then signed his name with a few quick scratches of his pen. Folding the paper, he dripped wax on the missive and sealed it.

"Take this to London without delay," he instructed the waiting messenger.

The man nodded his acknowledgment and hurried from the room.

Rupert leaned back in the chair at his makeshift desk—which in this case was a small table in the second-best bedchamber in the inn. Ordinarily he would have found the accommodations less than satisfactory, but for one night it would have to do. At least the place was clean and quiet and boasted what he'd been informed was "good, hearty English fare made by the finest cook in the county."

He would pass judgment on that last assertion as the evening wore on. Right now, he was merely thankful to have Ariadne safely under his protection again, the two of them assured a bed to sleep in and shelter from the rain that had begun to drizzle softly outside.

While Ariadne enjoyed a much-appreciated hot bath in the inn's best room, he'd decided to write to Emma and Dominic to put their minds at ease about Ariadne's welfare.

When he'd departed from the ball the other night to go after her, he'd taken only enough time to inform his brother-in-law that Ariadne had been abducted and that, according to Hodges, she was being taken north to Gretna Green. Dominic had offered to accompany him, but Rupert had assured him he could handle the situation on his own, reminding him that Emma would be beside herself with worry if they both took to the road.

He'd paid little attention at the time, but as he thought back now, he recalled the particularly shrewd look Dominic had given him. Did Dominic realize there was more to Rupert and Ariadne's relationship than simple friendship? But Dominic said nothing further, agreeing to stay and deal with Selkirk's accomplice, Hodges, as well as fend off the rumors that were certain to start concerning Ariadne's sudden disappearance.

For all the good that would likely do.

But such things were of no moment now. She was unharmed and back where she belonged.

A servant tapped, bringing in hot water and towels. He had the man set down the items, then leave, preferring to see to his own needs for the time being rather than endure the clumsy attempts of an untrained valet.

Before leaving London, he'd stopped at the town house only long enough to have a proper traveling coach made ready, secure a loaded weapon, and get money out of his safe. Much as he'd been loath to delay by even so much as a minute, he'd known it wouldn't be wise to race after Ariadne without a plan or any means of defense in place.

While he'd quickly traded his evening clothes for something more sensible to wear on the road, his valet had put another change of clothes and a few grooming items into a valise. Rupert had also ordered a dress, shoes, and some basic essentials packed for Ariadne, assuming rightly, as it happened, that she would be in want of them by the time he caught up with her somewhere on the road to Gretna Green.

He smiled now to recall her cry of delight when he'd knocked on her door here at the inn and presented her with the small satchel of her things. Laughing, she'd flung her arms around him and given him a rousing kiss in spite of the interested gaze of the maid who'd been busy preparing her bath.

"If you weren't a prince already, I would tell you that you truly are a prince among men, Your Royal Highness," she'd chimed happily.

Setting the case on her bed, she'd rooted through the contents. "A dress, stockings, shoes. *Huzzah*, I can get rid of these horrid slippers now. And look, there's soap and tooth powder and a hairbrush. Oh, and a nightgown too! How can I ever thank you? This is better than my birthday and Christmas all rolled into one."

In that moment, his chest had filled with an odd warmth as he'd stood enchanted, studying her luminous green eyes and rosy-skinned smile with a new appreciation. It was a curious sensation, and one on which he hadn't been certain he should dwell.

He turned away now, as he'd turned away then, putting such thoughts out of his mind to focus on other matters. After stripping off his shirt and tossing it on the bed, he opened his traveling valise and withdrew razor, strop, and shaving soap. He carried them to the stand, poured water into the basin, and began his ablutions in preparation for the dinner he and Ariadne planned to share this evening.

Chapter Twenty

"More wine?" Rupert asked nearly three hours later, the decanter held expectantly aloft above her glass. Ariadne tipped her head to one side, then smiled. "Maybe the tiniest little bit. Just a splash to brighten up the glass."

His mouth curved with amusement as he poured, stopping at the halfway point before moving on to replenish the contents of his own glass. Quietly, he set the decanter aside.

The Bordeaux—which was surprisingly palatable considering the circumstances—gleamed as lushly red as fully ripened cherries. Yet the color couldn't begin to compete with the exquisite flush that glowed on Ariadne's skin or the sultry hue of her lips that were full and begging for his kiss.

He'd barely been able to eat his dinner for watching them, her spoon or fork moving in and out, her tongue darting every once in a while to lick away a stray drop of water or wine.

As for the wine, he'd fed that to her with conscious intent, well aware of her low tolerance for alcohol. But he'd been careful to stop short of inebriation. He didn't want her drunk; he just wanted her relaxed and at her ease.

She'd been through an ordeal these past couple of days, even if she did her best to pretend it had had little effect on her. But he'd watched her tonight, and knew her well enough to realize that she was far more shaken than she wanted to let on.

And so he'd plied her with wine and food and pleasant conversation, determined that she should forget her difficulties for a few hours.

When she climbed between the sheets tonight, he wanted her to drift off without a care, and for her dreams to be easy ones without worry or fear.

He owed her that much for failing to protect her as he should have done. He owed her a great deal more for the trust she continued to place in his hands.

What if he hadn't caught up to her in time?

What if Selkirk had been a far less honorable man and had violated her in the cruelest of ways?

His fingers tightened around his wineglass, his bruised knuckles aching at the pressure.

At least he had the satisfaction of knowing that Selkirk would never come near her again; the beating he'd administered, as well as the warning, ought to assure that.

But Ariadne was still far too tempting a target for many men—and a vulnerable one, despite what she might otherwise believe. And now with her reputation damaged—as it most assuredly would be once they reached the city—she would be prey for even more unscrupulous sorts. Men who would seek to use and take advantage of her. Men who would try to seduce her for their own ends, then cast her aside with heartless disregard and potential humiliation, just as he'd warned her they might when the two of them had first begun their liaison.

Then too there were other fortune hunters who might make a play for her money. She believed her inheritance would give her freedom in the future, and in some regards she was right. But without the security of blood family, she presented a far more tempting target than other young women of means.

And as the past couple of days had so aptly demonstrated, her royal lineage was far from a deterrent to men who were already used to taking foolish risks. In fact, to many, her title was even more of a lure, an opportunity to align with royalty. The fact that her nation no longer existed would make no difference to them whatsoever.

So how to keep her safe?

Marriage was the simplest answer, of course.

But marriage to whom?

Eligible royals hadn't exactly been lining up before her abduction. Once this incident became known, there would be no possibility of an offer from such quarters, even if Ariadne could be convinced to accept one of them.

Such a stubborn girl she was.

A lesser noble might be convinced to wed her because of her lineage, even if she was considered damaged goods. An Italian—they weren't too fussy. Or an Englishman—several noble houses might consider such an alliance more than a fair trade.

Then there was the fact that she was very beautiful. Many men would take her for that single attribute alone. The chance to have her in their bed. The opportunity to possess her completcly, to claim all her sweet, hot passion and make it their own.

Ariadne might not notice the lustful male eyes that followed her wherever she went, but he did. She might be blind to the flirtatious overtures and hopeful looks that came her way, but he saw.

He knew and understood exactly what other men craved, because he craved it himself. But unlike them, he enjoyed her favors. She'd already let him into her bed.

And by God, he didn't want to give that up, to give her up. *Because she's mine.*

Rupert's hand tightened dangerously on his wineglass, sudden fury burning like acid in his gut. The idea of another man, any man, touching her made him half-crazed.

He thought again of Selkirk and the fact that he'd had her alone, had shared a bedroom with her. Ariadne said nothing had happened between them, but the idea enraged him all the same.

As for her taking a husband—he would want to kill the happy bastard before the priest had even finished reciting the vows.

He shook off the musings, wondering at the extreme thoughts suddenly possessing him. He wasn't acting like himself at all tonight. Usually he was coolly rational, practical, logical, taking the time to consider every angle, to weigh each decision for its merits and ultimate benefits. He tried his best to be a good monarch, his nation's welfare his only true concern. To that end, he did what was necessary, regardless of his personal wishes. His own happiness always came last on his list of considerations. But tonight he was tired of denying his own needs and desires. Tonight he wanted to do what felt right for himself—and for Ariadne.

Now he just had to decide precisely what that might be.

He took a long drink and set down his glass with a snap.

Ariadne sent him a curious look, her gaze languorous from too much wine and a lack of proper sleep over the past few days.

"It's late," he said. "You should get some rest."

"I'm not tired," she insisted. A yawn caught her seconds later, promptly ruining the effect.

"Ah, so I see."

"Not much anyway," she amended with a sheepish smile. "We haven't had dessert. Don't you want a sweet?"

"Not especially."

Not the kind she meant anyway. The only sweet he craved was her. His shaft swelled inside his trousers, his mind crowded with images of licking and kissing her, starting with her mouth and working his way down to her toes. Now that was a sweet treat both of them would enjoy.

But he'd promised himself he would let her sleep tonight, however much he would rather keep her otherwise occupied for the next several hours.

She yawned again, confirming his opinion as to her state of wakefulness. "I suppose I am rather tired after all," she admitted.

"Then, come," he said. "Let me walk you to your room."

He stood and offered his arm.

She took it, giving him a quiet smile that shot straight through his chest and down to his loins. He did his best to ignore both sensations.

At her door, they stopped.

"I'll say good night, then," he told her, reaching out to push the door wide.

"Oh, you're not coming in?"

"I wasn't. You need to rest."

Her fingers tightened on his arm. "But I assumed you'd stay. I know I would rest better if you did."

He laid his hand over hers. "There's no cause to be afraid. You're safe here. I spoke with the innkeeper and he assured me that no one comes inside without his knowledge and that he locks every door and window before he retires for the evening. We're the only guests tonight, so no one else is here to worry you."

"Of course, yes, you are right. I am just being foolish and shall be fine tonight on my own."

He scowled, hearing the anxiety in her voice. Suddenly he realized he was the one being ridiculous. She'd been kidnapped, for heaven's sake. Drugged and transported under threat of harm across half the English countryside by a black-hearted scoundrel who had terrorized her with the threat of an unwanted marriage. Of course she didn't want to spend the night alone. If he left, she probably wouldn't sleep a wink.

"On second thought, I shall ring and have the maid attend you; then I will return." He threaded his fingers through hers, lifting her hand to press a kiss to her palm. "You are not to worry, Ariadne. Not about anything."

A happy smile curved her mouth, her green eyes shining with pleased relief. "Don't be long."

"I won't. Lock the door after the maid leaves. I'll let myself back in with the key."

"I shall be waiting."

He kissed her palm again, then turned and strode away.

With her face washed, her hair brushed, and her teeth scrubbed and tasting pleasantly of the cinnamon and clove tooth powder she'd been thrilled to find in her valise, she sat on the bed, waiting for Rupert.

The maid had come and gone already, staying long enough to assist her out of her dress and into her fine lawn nightgown. The girl had left pitchers of hot and cold water and a small stack of new towels, then wished her good night.

As instructed by Rupert—though she most certainly would have done so on her own—she locked the door securely after the servant, then padded over to the bed.

The sheets were turned down neatly, the pillows plumped in invitation for a comfortable night's sleep. She smothered another yawn with a hand, eyeing the bed with interest.

But she didn't want to be asleep when Rupert arrived. She wanted to talk. And maybe if she managed matters right, he would make love to her. She wanted that closeness with him, needed to be held and kissed and swept away on a sea of pleasure, one that would make her forget all about the recent unpleasantness.

Rupert had started something between them in the coach and she wanted to continue it. She could sleep later. Right now, she wanted him.

But as she sat, her eyelids began to droop, weariness washing over her. She yawned again, blinking against the moisture that gathered in her eyes. Maybe she would lean back against a couple of the pillows for just a minute, and close her eyes as she listened for Rupert's key in the lock.

Unable to resist the idea, she scooted over and propped herself up against the plumped goose down.

Just a minute. Only one, then she would sit up again.

The room dulled around her, the rain that drummed idly outside creating a soporific effect. She listened to the pattering drops, even as she listened for the scrape of a key.

But one minute melted into two and despite her best efforts to rouse herself again, her eyelids refused to lift. Sighing, she turned her head and knew no more.

Rupert let himself into Ariadne's bedchamber, then closed and locked the door behind him. Night shadows obscured much of the interior, the darkness broken only by a solitary candle that had dripped down to a half stub inside its blue-and-white-glazed pottery holder.

Taking it in hand, he crossed to the bed, then stood gazing down at Ariadne where she lay deeply asleep. It was what he'd wanted for her—a peaceful night of uninterrupted slumber from which she would wake refreshed.

And yet he had to confess that he was disappointed.

Had he secretly been hoping he would find her awake and waiting for him? Had he wanted her to reach out a hand and draw him with her onto the sheets, where they could spend the night making love?

He shook his head at his own folly, ruefully considering all his so-called noble intentions to leave her alone tonight. But as it happened, the wine and her weariness had taken care of the matter for him.

He supposed he ought to return to his room; she would sleep far better if she had the full width of the bed to herself. Then again, he'd promised he would stay, had vowed that she would not have cause to wake and be alarmed in the night.

His shaft throbbed in complaint at the idea of lying next to her and doing nothing but sleep. He wasn't in the habit of sleeping with women. He coupled with them, then left to seek his own bed for rest. He'd kept to that same pattern with Ariadne over the course of their affair—coming to her bed to pleasure her, then going back to his own room to get a few hours of sleep.

Tonight will be a first.

Resigned, he set the candle on the bedside table, then bent and scooped her gently into his arms. She sighed and snuggled against him, but did not wake. Carefully, he moved her so he would have enough room to slide in next to her, pulling the sheets over her.

He removed his dressing gown, his erection straining insistently against his drawers. Ignoring it, he climbed in beside her, then leaned over to blow out the light.

Lying back, he closed his eyes and hoped for sleep.

Chapter Twenty-one

A loud clap of thunder brought Ariadne abruptly awake.
She lay for long seconds, listening to the drumming rain, unsure of her surroundings. Staring into the darkness, she was unable to see more than a few dim outlines of the furnishings in the room.

In the next moment, she became aware that she was not alone in the bed. Rather than fear, however, relief washed through her—and pleasure.

Rupert.

She would know him anywhere. The shape and sensation of his long, powerful body lying next to hers. The vital warmth of his skin, which always carried a trace of bayberry and lime and some unique something that was utterly masculine and utterly him.

She smiled and moved closer, resting her head next to his on the pillow and placing her hand on his bare arm. He didn't so much as twitch, clearly asleep, his breath moving slowly in and out.

She had no memory of his arrival, yet here he lay, exactly as he'd promised he would be.

Obviously he'd let himself in the room, only to find her asleep. He could have left. She was glad he had not, even if the emotion might make her seem weak.

She'd spent her life doing her utmost never to appear vulnerable, never to be anything but strong and resilient, as if nothing in life could bring her low. She was independent and self-reliant, knowing how to keep her head even when the world might seem to be crashing down around her ears. Not even the death of her parents and siblings had caused her to waver. However anguished and alone she had felt inside during those dark times, she'd made sure others couldn't glimpse her misery. And later, when Teodor, the cousin she'd loved as a young girl and with whom she had had an understanding, had tossed her over for a princess of greater wealth and position, she had smiled and sent him her best regards on his coming marriage.

Never had she allowed anyone to see her pain—or her fear.

Not even Emma and Mercedes, who knew and loved her better than anyone, truly saw beneath the resilient facade she wore like a shiny suit of armor.

So it was curious that she couldn't seem to hide her feelings, or herself, from Rupert. With him the pretenses fell away whether she wished them to or not. There were no secrets, no intimacies they could not share or which she would deny him.

She wasn't sure, even now, how she felt about him. He was her lover—and yes, she supposed, her friend. But there were times when he could still be Emma's annoying older brother. Infuriating, willful, and far too filled with the pride due his rank and lineage.

Yet he'd ridden after her without a moment's hesitation. He'd fought for her today and made sure she was safe. And he'd come here tonight because she'd needed him and he'd understood that she couldn't bear to be alone.

With a sigh, she stroked her hand over his warm, bare chest, threading her fingers through the short curls that grew there. She loved the feel of him, never tired of exploring, of running her hands over and along his exquisitely formed body.

Lower she went, trailing her fingertips across his firm pectorals, along the faint ridges of his rib cage to the taut plane of his stomach. She kissed his shoulder, then ducked under his arm so she could gain easier access, dotting his skin with random brushes of her mouth and tongue.

She found one of his flat nipples and nuzzled it, licking the tip with her tongue. It hardened, peaking as though eager for more of her touch. She hadn't kissed him like this before, but she'd thought about it. If her touch felt even half as good as his did when he used his mouth on her breasts and nipples, then he ought to find this quite stimulating. She raked her teeth over one small tip, then opened her lips wider and began to suckle.

A low moan slid from his throat.

Pausing, she listened to see if he had awakened. When he made no new movements or sounds, she went back to what she had been doing. Below, she continued to stroke his chest and stomach, gliding slowly back and forth, then back and forth again.

After a short while, she transferred her attentions to his other nipple, smiling when she found it as hard and ready as its brother. Tonguing him, she moved her palm lower, stopping only when she reached the edge of his drawers.

He was hard inside them, his shaft straining against the cloth in a way that threatened to pop the buttons off. With a few deft movements that he had taught her himself, she unfastened the buttons and let him spring free.

Still kissing his chest, she closed her hand around his rampant length, stroking him from base to tip in just the way he liked.

His hips arched and she looked up to see if she had roused him to wakefulness. But despite rolling his head on the pillow, he slept on, as if caught in some dream from which he could not seem to wake.

Does he imagine my caresses aren't real?

Then perhaps she ought to provide him with more reason to separate illusion from reality.

She hesitated, having done what she was thinking to do only one time before, and then for just a few moments. At the time, he'd pulled her up and away, ravishing her mouth as he pleasured her into a kind of drugged oblivion.

Maybe now it was her turn to do the same to him.

She liked the idea of him needing her as much as she did him.

Gathering her nerve, she slid down, caressing his stomach and his hair-roughened thighs before curving her fingers around his erection.

It pulsed inside her palm, the skin warm and velvety yet hard, with long veins that were engorged with blood. She ran a thumb over the tip and found it already moist, another bead of semen leaking out at her touch.

She wanted to taste him, wanted to find out if the experience was as satisfying as before. Hesitating only a few seconds more, she leaned down and took him in her mouth, shallowly at first, taking her time.

Learning.

He tasted better than she remembered—sweet and salty at the same time, rather like a marvelous treat. Closing her eyes, she swirled her tongue around, then gave a tentative pull.

His flesh throbbed against her lips and tongue, seeming to grow even harder and larger.

Caught up in the moment and filled with increasing confidence, she opened her mouth wider and took another inch. She suckled again, hard enough that her cheeks hollowed out around him.

A harsh moan filled the air, his hips bucking beneath her again as he arched upward. She leaned back slightly and might have pulled away, but suddenly his hands were on her head, fingers wrapped in her hair as he held her in place.

"Mein Gott," he cried. "Don't stop."

She waited, steadying herself again, deciding if she wanted to escape his grasp. But she didn't. She liked this, far more than she supposed any proper princess ought.

But then when have I ever been a proper princess?

Smiling, she drew on him again, loving the sensation as he shook beneath her with unrestrained need. Taking more of him, she circled her tongue and sucked on him as his hips moved gently back and forth.

Suddenly his hold loosened, his fingers slipping from her hair. "Ariadne?"

She didn't answer, not really able to form words at present. Then again he'd better assume she was the woman making love to him; otherwise he had some serious explaining to do.

His fingers curved around her head again, pulling her gently away. His shaft slid out of her mouth with a faint wet pop.

"I thought you were a dream." His voice was hoarse, rough from sleep and lust.

"Surprise," she murmured. "I'm not."

"So I see." He groaned again. "Or should I say, so I *feel*? Good Lord, Ariadne. You've half destroyed me."

"Don't you like it?" She frowned. She'd been enjoying herself, but maybe she'd done something wrong. Was that why he'd stopped her?

"Of course I like it! I'm hard as a pike and twice as thick. Isn't that proof enough?"

"Then what is the matter? I thought it was going rather well."

He stilled. "Did you?"

"Yes. I wasn't finished, but if you want me to stop—"

"No, no. It's only that some women . . . well, don't care for . . . that."

"Really?" She sat back on her haunches. "I find it . . . exhilarating."

In fact, she felt quite wanton and achingly aroused.

"As you ought to know by now," she told him, "I'm not *some* women." Taking his erection in her hand again, she gave him a long, firm stroke that made him shudder. "I am me. Ariadne."

He gazed at her, his eyes very blue even in the near dark. "Indeed you are. I shall be sure never to forget that again." Lying back, he fisted his hands at his sides. "Pray continue."

"Is that a command, Your Royal Highness? I could stop, if you prefer." She slid her hand down to the base of his shaft again and gave him another pair of hard, pumping strokes.

A guttural groan sang from his throat, his hips flexing upward. "I don't prefer, you teasing minx. Now take me between those sweet lips of yours or I'll have to punish you."

"Would I like your punishment?"

"Deny me and we'll find out."

A laugh trilled from her. "Perhaps another time." Bending down, she did as she was ordered.

Rupert's eyes rolled back in his head, as hot ripples of pleasure engulfed him. The warm, wet suction of her mouth was one of the most erotic sensations he'd ever known, and to think she was a novice at the act. Only imagine the miracles she might perform were she given more thorough training.

Clearly she was a natural.

He squeezed his fists tighter at his sides rather than reaching out to grip her head and force her to take him deeper. What pure bliss it would be to gently tup her mouth and show her how to bring him to completion that way.

But that was one lesson he would have to save for later. She needed more time and greater confidence before he introduced her to such intense intimacies. But, oh, my, how he was looking forward to expanding her education.

He trembled, the idea alone so arousing that he nearly released. Somehow he held back, wanting to prolong the encounter a while longer. Still, his shaft and balls ached with a fierce pain, his erection drawing even tighter when she slid her palms under his buttocks and flexed her nails into his flesh.

Hellfire, she's going to kill me.

Honestly, he didn't know how much longer he could hold on; it was just too good.

Abruptly she stopped.

Disbelief radiated through him. Without thinking, he reached out to bring her back.

But she eluded his grasp, leaning away.

He was reaching for her again, determined not to let her escape him this time, when she crawled up and draped herself over his body. Taking his face between her palms, she crushed her lips to his and kissed him with a wild and unbridled passion.

"Make love to me, Rupert," she whispered in his ear, as she scattered kisses over his face and neck.

"I thought that's what we were doing?" he rasped. "Making love."

She shook her head, her tousled hair brushing over his chest in a silky, shiver-inducing sweep. "No, I mean in all ways. I want you to take me, to make me yours completely."

Take her virginity, she meant. Lord knows he wanted that too, would give nearly anything to be able to sink his length into her sheath and ride her long and deep.

But he shouldn't. They shouldn't.

"It's too much of a risk." Wrapping her long hair around his wrist, he drew her down for a frenzied, openmouthed kiss in which he showed her how much he wished he could change his mind.

Clearly understanding that he needed additional convincing, she glided her palms over his chest, stopping to flick her nails over his tight, flat nipples.

His moaned, blood coursing through him at the temperature of an inferno.

Christ, he cursed. He should never have let her know how much he liked that. She had far too much power over him these days.

Dangerous levels of powerful and feminine persuasion.

"Please, Rupert," she pleaded softly. "I need you."

"You have me," he grated. "I'm right here."

"But I need you in me." She brushed her lips over his, again and again.

Softly.

Seductively.

"All I could think after Selkirk kidnapped me was 'What if he forces me? What if he steals my virginity when it ought to have been mine to give?'"

She caressed him with her hands as she scattered kisses over his skin, and they entwined their limbs like the lovers they already were.

"I want to give myself to the man of my choosing and I choose you. I want you to be my first. I understand the consequences and I'm ready. I don't want to wait anymore. Not another day. Not another minute."

He caught her in his arms and held her steady. "Do you?

Do you really understand what you're asking? I could get you with child, you know."

"Doubtful. I've been thinking about this for a while and taking herbs. I've been assured they should prevent conception."

"I won't ask how you acquired these herbs, but nothing is foolproof. There's always a risk."

"It's one I'll take. *Please*, Rupert, don't deny me. Don't deny yourself any longer."

When she put it that way, how could he refuse?

His throbbing, unsatisfied shaft agreed. *Take her,* his flesh urged. *Roll her over and thrust inside her. Do what you've been longing to do for weeks.*

Maybe even longer, if he were honest with himself. How long had he wanted Ariadne? Longer than he wanted to admit.

But always in the past his duty had gotten in the way.

Yet here she was, offering herself. Literally begging him to claim the last of her innocence.

He should say no.

Yet how could he, when she was everything he craved? Everything he wanted?

And really, wasn't it already too late? Hadn't they crossed a Rubicon of sorts a long time ago? Hadn't they been trying to deny their fate ever since? Perhaps this union between them was a kind of destiny, regardless of what might happen come the dawn.

She kissed him again and ran her hands through his hair, vulnerable and open, eager and trusting, curiously hesitant—almost like a bride.

He resisted her siren's call for a few moments more, then cast caution aside and kissed her. Pressing her mouth wide, he claimed her with ardent intensity, thrusting his tongue in and out in deep, relentless strokes that demonstrated exactly what he meant to do to her body.

She moaned and did her best to match his pace, quaking with undisguised need as he compelled her to take more, to take all.

Reaching down, he grasped the hem of her nightgown and, in a deft movement, yanked it over her head. She was naked underneath, her skin as smooth as silk, rubbing against his own.

He shucked off his drawers, kicked them to the floor, then turned back to her, his erection stiff as a steel truncheon.

Pulling her beneath him, he fit himself between her thighs.

"Tell me you want this, Ariadne. Tell me you understand what this means and that there will be no regrets."

"I want this," she vowed. "I want you, unequivocally and without hesitation. How could I possibly regret what is to come when I know it will be so very right?"

"Never say I didn't warn you."

Then he kissed her again, stealing her breath and in turn his own.

Chapter Twenty-two

Warn me? What is that supposed to mean?

But she didn't have time to ponder the question further, as his mouth and hands began making forays over her body that drove her nearly mad.

"Let's see how ready you are," he murmured in her ear, darting his tongue briefly inside the tiny canal before pulling back to catch her earlobe between his teeth. She trembled as he licked it too, giving another little nip that made her arch and moan.

Her moan increased as he placed his hand between her thighs and slid a finger inside her moist folds. Her hands tightened on his back as he lightly stroked.

"You're slick," he said, "but not as much as you need to be. I shall have to see what I can do to remedy that."

"Ah," she sighed. "Are you sure?" She shimmied against him. "I feel quite . . . moist."

He chuckled. "Trust me. You'll have a much better first time if you're literally dripping when I take you."

Her flesh contracted around his finger at that thought, her body dampening even more. But still apparently not enough.

"Offer your breasts to me," he said.

"What?"

"Your breasts. Cup them in your hands and push them together. You always like it when I suck your nipples. I want to try it this way tonight."

Ah, heavens, he was going to have her ready in no time at all if he kept talking like this.

Trembling slightly, she did as he urged, holding herself up for him—quite literally offering her flesh for his delectation.

And feast he did, burying his face between her plumped breasts with sinful purpose. While he rubbed the faint whiskered roughness of his cheek against one peak, he drew on the other, hard then soft, using his tongue to press her nipple against her teeth before catching the aching nub for a long, circling lick.

With a small movement of his head, he reversed the process, rubbing her wet nipple against his other cheek while he began suckling forcefully on the first.

Back and forth he went, steadily building her need until she felt as if her flesh were on fire. Her mind grew dim, her body throbbing everywhere.

Her hunger intensified even more as he slid his finger higher inside her and began rubbing a spot that made her squirm and shake and moan, as if she might fly apart.

She didn't know how much more she could take. She was teetering on a razor's edge, craving release with a need that approached desperation. Yet every time she came close to claiming her pleasure, he would ease off, as if he knew exactly how near she was and was determined to deny her.

He was a devil, increasing her torment with every lick and draw and stroke.

Hades above, I can't bear it!

"Please," she begged, too far gone to care about such petty matters as pride. "Please, let me. I need to take my release."

"Not yet," he told her, lifting his head briefly from her pleasure-swollen breasts. "Not until I've got you so wet and randy you'd promise me your very soul."

So he was purposely torturing her! She ought to have been angered by his arrogant admission, but she was too deep in his thrall to care, knowing he was the only means of putting an end to her suffering. The only way she would find her bliss.

"Spread your legs," he ordered roughly.

With blind obedience, she did as he commanded, giving him greater access to her most vulnerable feminine flesh. She nearly sobbed aloud when he pulled his finger out of her, insane with disbelief that he would stop. But before she could voice a protest, he slid gently in again, only this time using two fingers.

Her back arched, unintentionally forcing him deeper. Her hands fell away from her breasts, shaking so much she couldn't hold on any longer. Her arms fell to her sides on the bed.

A tiny slice of pain shot through her core as he delved higher, then withdrew again. He stroked in and out, then one time more before pausing in midstroke to scissor his fingers wide.

"Oh!" she cried, the pain sharper.

"Trust me," he whispered again. "This will make it easier."

Losing her maidenhead, did he mean?

Suddenly she remembered how large and stiff his shaft was, how thick he'd felt in her mouth earlier when she'd been pleasuring him. And now he was preparing her to accept him, to accept his hard, male flesh inside her.

Then she couldn't think again, his movements focusing all her attention to that one spot where he continued to spread his fingers open and closed. Then he rubbed her again in just the right way, reigniting her most profound pleasure.

He took her mouth with his again, leaning up to claim her

in rich, seductive draughts that she returned with dazed, heated fervor.

Truly, she would have let him do anything in that moment, her senses so heightened and on edge that he controlled her completely. And still he would not let her take her release, building her again until moisture gathered in her eyes.

Suddenly he pulled his hand away and settled his hips more fully between her thighs. Spreading her wider still with a hand, he positioned his shaft and thrust inside.

But he didn't get far, even she could tell that, only his tip lodged within her.

"God, you're tight," he said between clenched teeth. "I knew you would be, but you're even smaller than I thought."

"Is that bad?"

"No. It'll be fine, Ariadne." He kissed her mouth, though she feared he did it as a way to distract her.

Luckily it worked, leaving her dreamy and desirous again. At least until he rocked his hips and thrust into her again, his efforts gaining him another inch.

An inch that hurt—worse than his fingers.

She must have let out a whimper of pain, since he stilled and kissed her again. A sheen of perspiration damped his brow and he trembled, clearly striving to maintain his control.

She'd thought their joining would be so easy, so natural—but he was so big. "We're not going to fit, are we?" she whispered.

"Of course we are. But I think it might be better if we do this fast rather than slow."

Before she had time to debate the wisdom of that suggestion, he slid his hands under her bottom and locked her in place. Then he plunged, thrusting into her with one smooth, powerful stroke that forced his erection deep inside.

Too deep.

She cried out, bucking against him in an instinctive effort

to throw him off, but her move only succeeded in lodging him deeper, her tender flesh feeling as if it were stretched beyond its limits. She groaned and pressed her hands against his shoulders, but there was no budging him. He wasn't going anywhere he didn't want to go.

"Shh," he soothed, claiming her mouth in another long kiss. As he did, he slid one hand up to pet her breasts again in just the way she liked. Slowly the pain began to subside, her muscles somehow starting to accommodate his intrusion.

She gasped when he pulled back, nearly all the way out, then gasped again when he thrust firmly inside her once more. He did it again, pulling back, then plunging in, quietly establishing a rhythm.

Taking hold of one of her thighs, he urged her to wrap her legs around his waist. She obeyed, burying her face in his neck as she curled her arms and legs around him to hold on.

Once she did, she noticed that he added a new movement, circling his hips on each incoming thrust so that his shaft began to stroke her in the most delicious way.

A new sound, one of pleasure this time, soughed from between her lips. Her body responded without her express will, and she began to arch her hips in time to meet each of his thrusts.

"That's right, sweetheart," he said, encouraging her. "Just like that. Exactly like that. Do you want me deeper?"

And she did, her nails digging into his back as she pressed herself forward to take even more. "Yes! More, Rupert. Harder. Deeper."

He groaned and did precisely as she asked, increasing his pace so that he thrust into her with a kind of frenzy.

She repeated his name over and over, crying out with each fresh stroke, taking him into her body as fully as he could go.

And it was heaven and hell combined, every moment better than the one before, hunger lashing her until she thought she would surely die if it were not satisfied.

Then, without warning the world seemed to teeter, knocking her off the precipice and over into the void. She cried out as ecstasy burst within her like a golden sun, ripples of pleasure spreading through her until she shuddered from the sheer beauty and brilliance of it.

How could I have existed without this? she wondered. *How will I exist if I can't have it again?*

Above her Rupert continued to thrust, his skin hot and slick with his efforts. Abruptly he stiffened and shook, shouting out in pleasure against his fierce release.

Then he sank down upon her, pressing her tightly beneath him. She lay, feeling protected and happy, not the least bit crushed by his weight.

Hugging him closer, she fit her cheek against his and savored the moment, knowing it was one she would never want to forget, not even if she were to live forever.

Ariadne awakened the next morning with a smile on her face. She stretched her arms over her head, her muscles quietly protesting, along with a few other delicate internal parts. But she didn't mind the minor soreness; the night had been more than worth it.

"Good morning," Rupert greeted her in a whiskied baritone.

Her smile widened as she rolled toward him. "Good morning. Did you sleep well?"

"I did." He regarded her from where he lay with one arm bent behind his head. "For a couple of hours at least. As I recall, someone woke me up."

She trailed her hand over his chest. "*Hmm,* I wonder who that might have been." Leaning up, she kissed him, lingering for a span of several slow heartbeats.

He stroked a palm over her bare back, stopping to splay his fingers against the base of her spine. "Regrets?"

"No." Her pulse gave a sudden thud, a splinter of concern wedging itself inside her happiness. *Why would he ask such a question?* "You?"

The eyes that met hers were deeply blue and deeply introspective. Then he blinked the look away. "No. No regrets."

Spearing his fingers into her hair, he pulled her down for another kiss, taking her lips with a fervent, openmouthed intensity that left her mind adrift and her body aching to be joined with his once more.

Instead, he let her go. "It's late. We should be up and on the road."

"Oh." She blinked and sat up at his urging. "Yes, I suppose we ought."

Flipping back his side of the covers, he stood and went to retrieve his drawers.

Despite her dismay at his abrupt dismissal, she couldn't help but admire the view as he tugged them on, the muscles in his tight buttocks flexing with the movement. Next, he picked up his dressing gown and threaded his arms through the sleeves, then tied it closed with the belt.

"I'll ring for the maid to attend you." He thrust his feet into his slippers. "Shall I have breakfast sent in as well? It would be faster."

She pulled the sheets up over her bare breasts. "If that is what you prefer."

With a nod, he went to the door and let himself out.

She sat, unmoving, irritation gathering like a black cloud to smother her buoyant mood. Was he always so foul-tempered when he awakened, or had he decided to make this a special occasion? Since in the past, he'd always left her bed before dawn, she had no way of knowing.

She beat her fists on the sheets.

How dare he ruin my happy day.

But then she noticed the height of the sun in the sky, realizing that the hour was far more advanced than she had imagined. Maybe he was only concerned about the travel schedule and being able to reach London tonight. Men could be so annoyingly single-minded and dour about such things. Perhaps she shouldn't assume his grumpy humor had anything to do with her.

He did kiss me, after all.

Passionately and with obvious enjoyment.

Maybe he was tired and just needed a cup of strong coffee. She would be the first to admit that neither one of them had managed much sleep.

Her body tingled pleasurably at the reminder.

Yawning, she climbed out of bed, only then noticing the dried streaks of blood smeared on her inner thighs. When she glanced back, she saw that more blood stained the sheets, vivid proof of her lost virginity.

Is that what he'd meant about regrets? Had he worried that she minded giving herself to him after all?

Well, she didn't. Her innocence had been hers to give and she'd given it freely.

No, she thought again, *I have nothing to repine. I have no regrets.*

Rupert poured water into the basin, then wet a rag and used it to cleanse Ariadne's virgin blood from his shaft.

He scowled, realizing that just that simple act and the thought of her were enough to make him aroused again. He almost wished he'd taken advantage of her warm greeting while they'd been in bed and tupped her again. She wouldn't have refused him. Instead, she would have opened her arms and legs and welcomed him, letting him appease his lust while he roused her again to pleasure.

Still, he'd made a cock-up of all his plans—rather literally, as it happened. He'd been impulsive and unwise, allowing his animal appetites to rule his pragmatic head. Allowing himself to do what he wanted rather than what was best.

Even knowing all that, though, he could not regret their lovemaking.

Besides, it was done now and there was no point crying because the cow had kicked over the milk bucket. He had always been one to accept his responsibility and he would do so now.

What will Ariadne think?

Well, that no longer mattered either. She'd made her choices too. Now she would have to live with them.

A knock sounded at the door. Sorely in need of food and coffee, he went to retrieve his breakfast.

Chapter Twenty-three

"Oh, thank God, you're back!"

Ariadne had barely made it over the threshold of Lyndhurst House when Emma rushed forward to envelop her in a fierce hug.

"I've been so worried," Emma exclaimed. "Tell me you're well. Assure me you are all right."

Ariadne laughed and returned her friend's heartfelt embrace. "Yes, I'm fine. Scarcely the worse for wear, despite having traveled halfway across England and back."

Beside her, Rupert scowled at his sister. "You had my note, did you not?"

"We did, yes," Nick offered helpfully, stepping forward with a smile on his attractive features. "It came as a great relief, even if it did not keep Emma from continuing to fret."

"How could I do anything but worry when our dear Ariadne had been kidnapped, of all things?" Emma said. "Thank you, dear brother, for bringing her safely home."

"It was my pleasure." He met Ariadne's gaze over the top of his sister's blond head and sent her a faint smile.

Ariadne understood his secret message, her heart racing. It was the first time he'd smiled at her the whole day. Their journey home had been quiet and tediously uneventful. She'd hoped he might start something amorous in the coach on the way home, but after only one brief kiss around the halfway point, he'd set her aside and taken out a book.

She'd done her best not to be cross, deciding he must not want to begin something he couldn't finish, especially with the servants so nearby. And so she'd closed her eyes and surprised herself by falling asleep.

She'd been pleased to wake up in his arms, though, her face nestled into his wide shoulder. She couldn't remember having moved toward him, but somehow that was where she ended up.

Safe in his embrace, where I belong.

She frowned at that thought and was glad when Emma chose to hook her arm through one of Ariadne's and steer her toward the staircase.

"Come along to the family drawing room," Emma said. "You can tell me everything while you eat. I know you both must be famished and exhausted after such a long trip."

In tandem, they started up the stairs, the men following behind.

"Unless you'd like to wash and change beforehand," Emma continued. "Oh, but of course you would. Only listen to me—excess nerves are apparently making me prattle. If I'm not careful Nick will cast me aside for fear I am turning into his aunt Felicity. Not that she isn't a dear, but she does have a habit of rattling on and on."

Having reached the landing, the four of them stopped, Ariadne and Rupert deciding to repair to their separate rooms.

Nick strolled over and took his wife's hand. "I would never cast you aside, love, you know that—no matter how much you decide you wish to talk. Still, one Felicity in the family is unique. Two could be . . . a bit scary."

As Emma laughed, he leaned down and kissed her tenderly on the cheek. "Let's go arrange for that meal while your brother and Ariadne take a few minutes to refresh themselves."

"Yes, your maid and valet will already be waiting," Emma said. "Do not be too long."

Ariadne smiled, an odd suspicion forming. Surely Emma couldn't be expecting again already? But as soon as she thought the question, she realized it was very possible indeed. Nick was being extra gentle with her, and she'd been around Emma enough to recognize a pattern of sorts. Her friend tended to lose a bit of her usual steady aplomb in those first few weeks of pregnancy.

As Nick and Emma turned to stroll down the corridor, Ariadne saw Rupert's expression and could tell he was wondering the same thing.

Then his gaze met hers. This time he did not smile, a deadly serious look in his eyes.

Surely he doesn't imagine that I am with child? After only one time!

But from what she'd heard, sometimes one time was all it took.

She swallowed and fought the urge to squirm.

"Go change," he told her. "I shall see you shortly."

She nodded and moved off down the corridor to her room.

Two hours later, Rupert and Ariadne and Nick and Emma sat across from each other on cozy sofas in the family drawing room.

After retreating to her bedchamber, Ariadne had washed, then changed into a comfortable evening-at-home gown of sapphire silk and a pair of matching slippers.

In his own rooms, Rupert had bathed and shaved and allowed his valet to assist him into a fresh evening coat and black trousers.

By the time they rejoined Emma and Nick, a wonderful cold meal had been laid for them. Among the many selections were rabbit pie, chicken and beef sandwiches, tender summer lettuce with watercress, parsley, pickled radishes and ruby red beets, ice-chilled peeled shrimp and lobster claws with mayonnaise dill dressing, rose-hip jelly and lemon conserves, yeast rolls, cheeses, fresh blackberries, nuts, and for dessert a selection of tiny cakes and a spiced carrot pudding.

While they ate, the four of them confined the conversation to pleasant topics, even though Ariadne knew that Emma—and Nick, for that matter—were dying to hear all about Ariadne's abduction and the mad dash to rescue her.

Once the plates were cleared and the servants gone from the room, Emma demanded the tale. Over tea for Ariadne and a glass of wine for Rupert, they each gave their version of events.

"And you really stabbed Selkirk with a fork?" Emma repeated, her blue eyes wide with astonishment.

"I did! Though the fork I used wasn't nearly as well made as the ones the maids just cleared away."

"It more than did the job." Rupert spun his glass in a circle between his fingers. "He yelled and bled. What more do you want?"

"I wanted it to stop him. But he would have come after me again, if not for you. Rupert could not have arrived at a better moment."

"If I had timed it well, I would have arrived before he abducted you at all," he mused gruffly, taking another long drink of wine.

"That could not be helped," she countered. "You ex-

plained that you were purposely detained. Had you known
Selkirk's nefarious intentions, you would never have allowed
his man to interfere."

Ariadne sent Rupert an understanding smile.

He drank more wine.

"There's something I'm not clear about," Emma said, tap-
ping a finger against her lower lip. "How did you come to be
in such an isolated section of the house, away from the ballroom? How did Selkirk know to find you?"

Ariadne paused.

Yes, why was *I there?* Certainly she still had no plans to
tell Emma and Nick the truth—that she'd been on her way to
a secret tryst with Rupert.

What to say?

"Well, he followed me, you see, looking for an opportunity," Ariadne said, completely ignoring the first half of the
question. "Once he knew where I'd gone, he had his accomplice stand guard to waylay anyone who happened by."

Emma's fair eyebrows drew close. "But why was Rupert
on his way there too? It seems odd he would also be in that
part of the house at that time of evening."

"I needed some quiet time. Rupert obviously did as well."

"Yes, but—"

"Really, Emma," Ariadne interrupted, "what does all that
matter? I thought we were discussing how gallant your
brother was in rescuing me. He beat Selkirk to a bloody pulp,
you know. I feared for a time that he was actually going to
kill him."

"I had wondered if that's what happened to your knuckles," Nick observed quietly, his eyes fixing briefly on the
mottled bruises that colored Rupert's hands. "Fistfights are a
brutal business."

"Pistols or swords at dawn seemed too good for him,"

Rupert said. "And somehow I didn't think he would stick around long enough to honor a duel. A direct approach seemed most appropriate."

"I am glad he was punished," Emma stated. "Clearly it was well deserved. But it won't stem the tide of gossip that is sure to begin now that you are returned, Arie. Nick and I have done what we can to keep down the speculation about your sudden disappearance that night, but I fear it is having little effect. We've put out that you're ill, but I don't think anyone really believes it. Unfortunately you are almost never ill. And should Selkirk talk—"

"He won't." Rupert's expression turned grim.

Emma's eyes widened briefly before she continued. "Even if he says nothing, talk is bound to continue. Once it's known that you were abducted and forced to stay alone with Selkirk, you will be quite ruined."

"But nothing happened—"

"Society will not care. You know that as well as I."

Ariadne shrugged. "I've told you before, it is of no moment what English Society thinks. I care nothing for the opinions of toadies and narrow-minded sycophants."

"It won't just be them. It will be everyone. Doors will be closed to you, and not just here in England but everywhere."

"You exaggerate." Ariadne made a dismissive sound, then set her teacup aside. "No one of any consequence will care about a foiled kidnapping attempt and a partial journey to Scotland, particularly on the Continent. If the English prove troublesome, I shall find a house abroad and go on with my life quite happily. Italy is lovely in the autumn, I hear. An excellent time for an extended visit."

"I think you underestimate people's propensity to gossip, especially about a kidnapped royal princess who was going to be forced into an unwanted marriage to a fortune hunter.

The tale will spread like wildfire. But it's more than just Selkirk now—"

"What do you mean? Of course it's just Selkirk, since he is the one responsible."

"Don't you see? You have us, but we are not blood family, even if you are as dear as a sister. Your guardian is on the Continent and there was no one who could respectably have come to retrieve you. I would never for a moment have discouraged Rupert from doing so, though perhaps Nick and I would have been a better choice—"

"You're making no sense. What are you going on about, Emma?"

"I believe what she's saying," Rupert stated, reentering the conversation, "is that people will believe you every bit as compromised by *me* as you are by Selkirk."

She scowled, perfectly aware that she had been compromised by Rupert—and quite thoroughly, as it happened. But no one needed to know that.

"Rupert is a family friend," she defended.

"Yes, and we shall make certain to press home that point." Emma tapped a finger against her lip again in thought. "If we handle matters correctly, we ought to be able to think of some method for obscuring the most incriminating parts of the truth. We'll fudge the timing about how long you were with Selkirk, so it appears you were not alone with him overnight. And I'm sure we can find someone who will say they accompanied Rupert on the rescue mission in order to provide you with a suitable chaperone."

Ariadne linked her hands in her lap, deeply touched by her friend's unswerving loyalty. "That seems like rather a lot of bother just to salvage my reputation."

"Not at all." Emma sent her an encouraging smile. "After all, why should either you or Rupert be condemned for something that never happened? It isn't as if Rupert really has compromised you. It isn't as if the two of you are lovers."

Emma laughed, clearly amused by the sheer absurdity of the idea.

Ariadne knew she should join in, but the most she could manage was a pitiful half smile. She wanted to look at Rupert to gauge his reaction, but resisted, her fingers tightening even more in her lap.

In spite of the precaution, heat began to spread through her face, creeping like a rash up her neck and into her cheeks, where it lodged like an incriminating fever. She wanted to clap her hands over her cheeks, but what good would that do when the damage was already done?

She darted a helpless glance at Rupert and found him gazing back with resigned acceptance.

"Well, I'll be damned." Nick gave a quiet hoot. "So it *is* true."

"What's that? What is true?" Emma asked, looking questioningly at the three of them. Then her gaze settled on Ariadne. "Arie, your cheeks are as red as berries. Are you blushing? But why would you—"

Ariadne could almost see the inner workings of her friend's thought process as Emma's eyes moved quickly between her and Rupert. Back and forth, then back and forth again.

Suddenly Emma's cheeks turned red as well. "But you two—," she sputtered, searching for the words. "You . . . you . . . you don't even like each other!"

"I would say that has clearly changed," Nick observed. "Well, if this isn't a bold shot across the bow." He barked out a sharp laugh. "I wondered if there was something going on."

Emma's head whipped around, her gaze accusing. "And you didn't tell me?"

Nick visibly fought to wipe the smile off his face, without

much success. "It was just a passing suspicion. I didn't think it was my place to say anything."

"Of course it was your place to say. I am your wife." She stabbed a finger at him. "You and I will talk about this later."

Quick as a viper, she turned back to Ariadne and Rupert. "As for the pair of you. How long has this been going on? How far has it progressed? Are you really . . . have you actually . . . I mean . . ."

"Have we had sexual congress?" Rupert offered in a casual tone.

"Oh!"

"Please, Emmaline. Spare us the prudish affront." Rupert gave her a look of regal disapproval. "We are all adults in this room and as a married woman there is nothing Ariadne and I have done that you ought to find shocking. But in answer to your question, yes, she and I are lovers."

Ariadne's shoulders sank. Well, that cat was not only out of the bag, but its little feet had carried it all the way to the next county. Then again, she supposed confessing the truth had become inevitable the moment her blasted cheeks decided to turn hot as a forge.

Emma remained silent, bowing her head for a moment before looking up again. "What I find shocking is the fact that both of you have clearly concealed this relationship, and that you have lied to Nick and me about it while living under our roof."

Her gaze went to Ariadne, a wounded expression on her face. "As for you, Arie, how could you? He's my brother."

Ariadne drew back her shoulders. "He is, yes, which is one of the reasons I didn't tell you. I knew you'd fuss. The other is the fact that you never approved of my decision to take a lover."

"No, I did not. I still don't. Why can't you just find a husband like every other respectable young woman?"

"Why can't you let me live my life as I see fit? You certainly have some nerve castigating me for my behavior when you and Nick were intimate long before you got married."

"What's that about being intimate?" A thunderous scowl creased Rupert's forehead. "Lyndhurst, did you bed my sister before the vows? I should have known you couldn't keep your hands off—"

"Why is it you always say 'Lyndhurst' in that derogatory tone when you have some complaint to make rather than using that fancy title you insisted I take in order to marry Emma? Frankly I'd prefer Lyndhurst. It's a good English name and one I'm proud to bear." Nick crossed his arms.

Rupert's glare grew blacker. "If you don't appreciate the fancy *foreign* title, I can always give the order to take it back."

"He doesn't mean that," Emma interceded.

"Yes, I do, and he can take—"

"Enough!" Ariadne declared in a voice that cut through all the acrimony like a blade. "No more of this fighting. I don't want to hear another word from any of you." Shifting on the sofa, she turned toward her friend. "Emma, you have every right to be angry with me for lying to you. It was wrong and I apologize. But as for my decision to start a relationship with Rupert, that is my choice. Mine and his and none of your concern."

"But—," Emma began.

"*Phsst.*" Ariadne cut her off. "Not a sound. I am speaking."

She looked across at Nick. "Dominic, I understand your pride in your English heritage and would expect no less, but you do Rupert a great dishonor by throwing his gift in his face."

"I haven't—"

She waved her hand at him to be quiet as well.

He fell silent.

"By granting you the title of archduke, he elevated you far above any status he was required to give. He could have left you a simple peer, but he made you royal so that you would be fully part of his family. It was a generous, considerate gift, a true honor, and it is ungracious of you not to show proper appreciation."

Nick glared at Rupert. "Sorry."

Rupert regally inclined his head, looking a bit too pleased with himself.

Ariadne turned to him next. "As for you, you need to be nicer to Dominic. He and Emma have two children and if I am not mistaken, another on the way—"

"How did you know that?" Emma exclaimed.

Ariadne ignored her. "He's your brother-in-law, Emma loves him, and he isn't going anywhere, so you might as well find a way to like each other. You're men. Talk about horses, or sports, or world domination—anything you have in common."

Rupert arched his brow in amusement. "We manage satisfactorily already, but I shall remember those topics in future. World domination, in particular, I think."

Nick cracked a smile.

"As for telling our secrets tonight—"

"I do not see how they could have remained secret any longer, my dear," Rupert said softly. "It was time."

"Yes, maybe, but you didn't have to blurt it out like that. You should have let me know you were going to . . . tell. It was my secret to share too."

"So it was, but I'm afraid your pretty cheeks rather gave us away." Leaning over, he stroked a finger along one cheek that had turned annoying hot again.

"Next time—," she began.

"Are you planning on us keeping more secrets?"

Ariadne shrugged. "One never knows about these things."

Rupert tossed his head back and laughed.

When Ariadne glanced away, she found Emma staring at her, her expression surprised and oddly contemplative.

"Well, if we are finished, it has been a long day," Ariadne said, suddenly wanting nothing more than a few minutes alone. "I should like to retire."

"You may, of course. But there is still one matter left to resolve," Emma said.

"Oh, what is that?"

"The problem of your reputation. Whether or not you and Rupert are . . . lovers . . . it does not necessarily mean you must be publicly ruined. Clearly you've taken pains to keep your relationship a secret. We must think of a strategy to defuse the gossip and leave you—both of you—unscathed."

"Really, Emma, I am a grown woman and can handle whatever may come. Do not worry over it."

"But, Arie—"

"No, really, I—"

"Actually, there is no problem," Rupert stated in an emphatic tone.

Emma looked puzzled. "What do you mean? Of course there is a problem."

"But there is not. Ariadne and I shall be married. Once she is my wife, her reputation will be quite unblemished."

Chapter Twenty-four

"*M*arried?"
       "What?"

Ariadne wasn't sure which one of them spoke first, she or Emma. She wasn't sure who was the more astonished either, although on second thought it had to be herself.

What in Hades' name does he mean, we are getting married?

She turned incredulous eyes upon him. "I'm afraid I must have misheard you. I thought you said something about marriage, but it must be weariness from the journey clogging my ears."

There, I have given him an out. Now, God have mercy, he needs to take it.

The corners of his mouth turned up in a wry smile. "Your ears are working just fine. Beginning now, consider yourself engaged."

She shot to her feet. "You cannot be serious."

But his expression held not a trace of humor. "As a pair of sharpened bayonets. You should know me better by now than to think I would jest about something as irrevocable as marriage."

"But you don't want to marry me. You are being deliberately absurd."

"No, I am accepting the consequences of my actions." Rising from his chair, he crossed to the sideboard and poured a fresh glass of wine, taking his time as he replaced the stopper. "Marriage is the right thing to do, the only logical step to take."

"Logical?" Ariadne repeated, a faint note of hysteria in her voice. "That is the most *illogical* idea you've ever thought up."

"*Ahem*, perhaps Nick and I should give the two of you a bit of privacy." Emma got to her feet, quietly motioning for Nick to do the same.

"Sit down!" Ariadne ordered, barely sparing her friend a glance before turning back to Rupert.

Emma sat, Nick beside her, having never left the sofa.

As calmly as if they were discussing the weather, Rupert drank his wine.

"What do you think you're about, just deciding that we will wed?" Ariadne crossed her arms. "There is such a thing as needing my consent, you know."

"Which you more than gave last night, as I recall."

Her blush returned, incriminating as a scarlet *A*.

"Now, before my sister and brother-in-law are forced to listen to every lurid detail of our past dealings, why don't we let them go on their way? Emma is practically squirming. You can share the salient points of our discussion with her tomorrow."

"If I am to share, what difference does it make if she stays?" Ariadne demanded, flinging out an arm in Emma's direction. "And she'll just tell Nick later, so he might as well hear it all now too."

"That's unfair," Emma protested. "I am quite capable of keeping a confidence. I don't tell Nick everything."

"Really?" Nick mused, looking at his wife. "What is it you're keeping from me?"

"Nothing," she admitted. "I was just making a point—"

Rupert set his wineglass down with lethal care. "Emma. Dominic. If you would, please excuse Ariadne and me. As you can see, we need to . . . talk."

Ariadne balled her hands into fists. "This is their home and they should not be ordered out of their own drawing room. They'll go when they want to go and not a moment sooner."

"Really, we don't mind leaving," Emma murmured, making to rise again.

"We're not in Rosewald, you know," Ariadne continued, striding indignantly toward him. "You are not prince regent here, and you have no right to order them around. You've no right to order *me* around either, whatever you may think otherwise."

His jaw flexed, his eyes flashing like blue lightning. "Oh, don't I?"

"We'll just be on our way." Emma and Nick stood again, taking a few steps toward the door.

"No!" Ariadne said. "I am the one who will go. There is nothing I care to discuss with Prince Rupert. I believe everything has already been said, including my refusal of his offer."

"Ariadne," he said, his voice low and gruff with warning.

She ignored him. "I bid all of you good night. I shall see you in the morning." Turning on her heel, she started toward the door.

"Come back here, Princess. Now!"

Rupert's tone sent a tremor down her spine, but she refused to be cowed. He was not her husband or her lord and master. But even if he were, she did not take orders from any man. Not even Rupert.

Her back straight, she marched the rest of the way to the door, then turned the knob. She half expected him to stop her, but there was no rush of movement, no restraining hands or arms reaching out to bar her from leaving.

Behind her, in fact, there was nothing but silence.

Not daring to look back, she strode out into the corridor. It was only once she was well clear of the room that her nerve finally broke, and her quick walk turned into something that greatly resembled a run.

"Will there be anything else, Your Highness?" her maid asked more than an hour later, as she hung a last garment in the wardrobe.

Ariadne considered the question for a moment, part of her wishing she could act the coward and ask the girl to stay. Instead, she shook her head. "No, thank you, that will be all."

With a quick curtsy and a murmured good night, the servant let herself out of the room.

Ariadne waited half a minute, long enough for the maid to be out of earshot, then hurried to the door. She turned the key in the lock, daring to relax only once the door was firmly secured.

After returning to her room earlier, she'd kept expecting Rupert to arrive to continue their fight. But he hadn't. There'd been only a single interruption—which had nearly given her heart palpitations—when Emma had knocked on the door, wanting to see if she was all right.

"He's very angry, Arie," Emma warned after they settled themselves together in the sitting room, Ariadne's maid having departed to lay out her nightgown and robe. "I don't think you ought to have walked out."

No, it probably had been a rather suicidal decision. Then again, what was he really going to do about it?

"Well, I do not care how cross he is," Ariadne declared, tilting her chin up at a stubborn angle. "How dare he *inform* me that we are going to be married, as if I were one of his lackeys being ordered to black his shoes. Of all the arrogant, infuriating, condescending men, he is the worst."

"He's a prince, nearly a king. He is used to making decisions and acting on them."

"I am *not* a decision."

"No, I think you are a great deal more. I've never seen him so . . ."

"Pigheaded?" she suggested.

"Out of control," Emma said seriously. "Despite the fact that he can have a formidable temper on occasion, he always manages to keep it in under strict regulation. But tonight, with you . . . He broke his wineglass after you left. Snapped the stem right in two. He's very protective of you, you know."

"He's controlling and far too obsessed with matters of duty and honor. He just doesn't want a scandal that will sully his much-vaunted pride and reputation. I'm sure he's even now regretting the fact that he came after me to save me from Selkirk."

"You know he is not. But because of his pride and sense of duty to Rosewald, I also know he would not make an offer of marriage lightly. Are you sure—"

Ariadne leapt to her feet. "What I am sure of is that we would make each other quite miserable. We'd be at each other's throats within three months' time."

"Yesterday I might have thought so as well, but now I am not so sure." Emma leaned forward in her seat. "Oh, Arie, how ever did you and Rupert become lovers? I am still trying to fathom even the notion. I mean, you've always detested each other. What changed?"

She shrugged. "As you know, I decided to take a lover. He agreed."

"He *agreed*," Emma repeated in amazement. "I can tell there is a great deal more to this story than you are in the mood to share at present. You've also had a very long day—actually a few very long days—so rather than drag it out of you tonight, I shall make myself be patient a while longer. Why don't you try to get some sleep?"

Ariadne forced a smile. "Of course. A good rest is exactly what I need."

Particularly since I barely got any sleep last night. She'd been too busy giving away her virginity to Rupert. If she'd had any idea what he'd planned, she would never have let him near her.

Emma's brow wrinkled with anxiety. "You are certain you are all right? Nothing . . . untoward . . . happened between you and Selkirk? He didn't . . . ?"

"No. You may cease any worry on that score. Selkirk may be an unscrupulous fortune hunter, but he didn't force himself on me, not in the way you mean."

Emma studied her for another moment, then released a sigh of undisguised relief. "Good. Now I shall be able to sleep." She stood. "Well, I'm off to the nursery to check on the boys one last time, then to bed myself." Leaning down, she kissed Ariadne on the cheek. "It is good to have you home."

"It is good to be home."

And it was.

Yet, even as she said the words, she knew that some ineffable something had changed, understanding that this would never again truly be her home.

Now here she sat, alone, with the door locked, knowing she ought to do as Emma advised and go to bed. Lose herself in the comfort of sleep.

But would she be able to sleep?

And would Rupert attempt to seek her out?

He'd better not.

She crossed her arms.

Marry him indeed! When he hadn't even asked her. When he'd made no effort to deny the truth when she accused him of not wanting to marry her. When he'd said not one word about affection or love.

And to think she'd been so happy less than twenty-four hours ago, content to imagine that all he wanted was her body. If only they could go back to that. If only everything weren't so complicated.

On a sigh, she stood and went to the bed. The covers, already neatly turned down by the maid, were so much nicer than the ones she'd slept on last night.

Why did she almost wish those linens back?

Suddenly the doorknob rattled. Someone wanted inside, and she knew exactly who that someone was.

"Ariadne," Rupert said quietly through the door, "let me in."

She linked her hands in front of her, squeezing her fingers tight. "No."

A small silence fell.

"I have had time to calm down," he said. "I am not angry any longer. Open the door so I may come in."

"I'm tired and I want to go to bed."

"Of course, but we should talk first."

"We can talk later."

Much, much later—as in maybe never.

"I think we ought to discuss matters tonight."

"No, I'm sorry, not tonight. Go to bed, Rupert. I'll see you tomorrow."

She waited, expecting him to respond. But he said nothing and as she listened closely, she heard him move away from the door.

Was that it? Had he given up? And so easily too. Somehow it didn't seem like Rupert, but maybe he was weary as well. Maybe he realized it would be better to postpone things for another day when both of them weren't so on edge.

Unlocking her fingers, she slipped out of her robe, draping it at the foot of the bed. She climbed in the bed and pulled the covers over herself.

Rather than blowing out the candle, she left it to burn, needing its comfort.

Coward, she jeered at herself. *Since when are you afraid of the dark?*

But despite the inner recriminations, she closed her eyes and willed herself to sleep.

Five minutes passed.

Then ten, and still she was awake.

With a frustrated sigh, she opened her eyes. Perhaps she would read.

That was when she heard it, an odd scraping noise at the keyhole of her door.

She sat up.

Was he back? More to the point, what was he doing?

She got her answer seconds later, when the lock made a series of clicking sounds and the door swung open on silent, well-oiled hinges.

Rupert walked inside, then turned to shut and relock the door.

"What are you doing here?" she demanded, her earlier irritation returning. "I told you I didn't want to talk."

"Yes, you did," he agreed with equanimity.

"You have some nerve coming in here when I specifically said I didn't want to see you tonight. How did you get in anyway? Who gave you a key?"

He strode toward her. "No one. I let myself in. I picked the lock." With a smile, he held up a pair of slender metal implements.

"*You picked the lock?* Where in the world did you learn to do that?"

"Oh, I've been doing it since I was a boy. One of the palace footmen taught me. It's quite a handy skill to have when one wants to find out what's going on behind closed doors—or rather locked ones. Works on desks, writing secretaries, and liquor cabinets too."

He slipped one hand into his robe pocket and deposited the tools. By the time he withdrew his hand again, his smile had disappeared. "But don't ever think you can keep me out again. Do I make my meaning plain?"

She raised a hand and pointed toward the door. "Perfectly. Now let me make myself plain. *Get out!*"

Instead, he walked around to the opposite side of the bed. After untying his belt, he shrugged out of his robe and stood completely naked and almost fully erect before her—clearly unabashed about either state.

"I usually sleep in the nude," he explained, "but I've been wearing drawers for your benefit. After last night, I don't see the point any longer."

"The point is so that you do not give the maids a fright should you encounter one of them on the way back to your room. Put that robe back on and be good enough to leave."

He padded to the bed and climbed in.

"Rupert, you are the most mule-headed beast."

He laughed. "And you're lovely when you're angry. Come here and let's put all that hot blood to use."

She crossed her arms and turned her back to him in the bed. "I thought you wanted to talk."

"We can talk later." He smoothed a hand over her back, sending shivers rippling down her spine. "Take off your nightgown." He eased his hand up under her hair, massaging her neck. "In fact, as soon as we're married you might as well stop wearing night attire altogether. It'll only end up in a heap on the floor, or else get ruined when I tear it off you because undressing you is taking too long."

Her eyes slid shut, a tremor racing through her that she could not control. "There is not going to be a marriage."

"Of course there is." Leaning up, he pushed her hair to one side and began kissing her neck.

"No, there isn't." Her breath came faster—curse his wicked touch. "Your gallantry is appreciated but completely unnecessary. Whatever scandal may arise from my unexpected trip north will be forgotten as soon as the next Society cause célèbre rears its ugly head."

He slid his fingers under one of the straps on her nightgown and pushed it off her shoulder, then scattered leisurely kisses on her bared flesh.

"W-within the month," she continued, doing her best not to let her voice shake, "no one will give a rap about my story anymore. Besides, they'll all be too busy preparing to leave for their country estates where they can spend the autumn shooting birds and riding to hounds. I'll be the last thing on their minds."

He paused and raised his head. "I know that's what you'd like to believe, but even the English *Ton* have longer memories than that. The facts must be faced, Ariadne. You are ruined and I am the one responsible."

"Selkirk is responsible."

"No. He may have abducted you, but I did the compromising. I am the one who ravished you last night and sullied you long before that."

"But I wanted you to ravish and sully me. I practically begged you to do it."

He laughed softly. "And I could have said no on numerous occasions. But we've been caught now and it's time to pay the piper. A marriage between us will set matters to rights."

She pulled away, turning to meet his gaze. "I told you at

the start that this affair was just for fun. Truly, I don't care about my reputation. I mean it. I am not going to marry you, Rupert, so you may set your conscience at ease. You offered. I refused. That is the end of it."

"But it is not. In case you've forgotten, I took you last night, quite thoroughly. I spilled my seed in your womb. Even now, you could be carrying my child."

"That is highly unlikely." She shrugged and pushed her nightgown strap back up. "If that is your only concern, all we need do is wait a couple of weeks and see if my monthly arrives. Once it does, we'll know there is no child."

He tugged the strap back down, baring her breast with it. "But the scandal will be raging out of control in two weeks. We cannot afford to take that risk."

"I am willing to withstand any storm that may come."

"But I am not." Wrapping his hands around her shoulders, he urged her gently back onto the bed, then followed her down. "Your blood is as blue as mine, your pedigree as sound. You will make an admirable queen for me when the day comes."

"Maybe I don't want to be queen," she protested.

"Of course you do. You'll thrive on having all the ladies and gentlemen of the court at your beck and call. You love managing people."

"I do not *manage* people, not in the way you mean."

"Then let us say you steer them in a direction that is most in accordance with your wishes."

"As if you don't do the same thing yourself. You're always ordering someone about. Now you're trying to order me."

"I am a prince. Helping others follow the proper path is what I do best."

"Hah!" she retorted. "I believe I can decide the proper path for myself without your wise guidance."

"In this circumstance, my dear, I must disagree." He

threaded his fingers into her hair. "You will marry me, Ariadne. It is the only reasonable course."

Reason. Logic. Necessity. Those were the only points he had to make.

Where was affection?

Where was love?

"I don't care about being reasonable." She put her hands on his shoulders and tried to push him away. As always, she couldn't budge him an inch. "Let us wait and see if I am with child. Then we shall decide."

"No. You swore to me last night that you were willing to accept the consequences, so accept."

"B-but I didn't know that marriage was what you meant," she said on a note of desperation.

"Accept, Ariadne. You've taken me as your lover. You will agree to take me as your husband now too."

"But you don't want this. You know I'm not what you wished for in a bride."

He reached down and drew her nightgown up and off, baring her body to his hands and eyes. "I want you. That is enough."

"Rupert, we—"

But before she could say another word, he was kissing her, claiming her mouth in a way that demonstrated his possession and the endless depths of his demand.

She could have tried to push him away again, but it was no use. And deep inside, she didn't want to, no matter how much heartache might be waiting for her in the future.

Sliding her fingers into his hair, she kissed him back.

Chapter Twenty-five

As Ariadne sat down to breakfast the following morning, she realized, without entirely knowing how it had happened, that she was engaged to Rupert.

She had never actually accepted his proposal—as if anyone could call the royal edict he'd issued a proposal. She'd even refused him— more than once—and not only to his face, but in front of witnesses.

But even her chief witnesses, Emma and Nick, had apparently turned traitor overnight. She realized that only moments after taking her seat and laying her napkin across her lap when she looked up and found Emma grinning at her. Her friend's vivid eyes were alight with a jubilant twinkle—eyes that suddenly, uncomfortably, reminded her of Rupert.

Somehow, before the morning was out, she would have to find a way to put an end to this farce. Whatever Rupert thought—whatever they all assumed—she was not marrying him.

But right now she was just too tired to continue the battle. Rupert had kept her awake half the night making love, then roused her again near dawn to take her with a vigorous enthusiasm that had the power to send shivery tingles rippling over her skin even now.

She murmured a quiet "Good morning," then concentrated on stirring milk and sugar into the cup of strong black tea the footman had poured for her. Eyelashes lowered, she took a long, grateful sip and let the beverage's sweet heat sink into her system.

When she looked up again, she found Nick watching her over the top of his newspaper with an expression of amused sympathy. She could tell he thought the battle between her and Rupert already won—in Rupert's favor.

She supposed if anyone knew about the art of skirmishes with the Whyte siblings, it was Nick. The knowledge did not cheer her.

And then there was Rupert himself.

"Good morning, my dear," he said from his seat opposite her at the linen-covered table. He folded his newspaper in half and laid it aside. "I see you did not make a selection from the buffet. Allow me to have a plate prepared for you."

"I just want tea."

Ignoring her, he signaled one of the footmen. "A selection for the princess and more coffee for me."

"Of course, Your Royal Highness. Right away."

She scowled across at him. "I said I do not wish to eat."

"Have something regardless."

Grumbling under her breath, she drank more tea.

The servant returned shortly, bearing a plate laden with what looked to be a little of everything the cook had prepared.

"Try a few bites," Rupert encouraged once the footman had withdrawn. "You may find you have an appetite after all."

She glowered at him, but rather than argue, she picked up her fork. As she did, she noticed Emma looking on, an expression of happy bemusement on her face.

Resisting the urge to turn her scowl on her friend, she glumly ate some eggs. To her marked irritation, they proved delicious. She ate some more.

Five minutes passed while everyone continued the meal, the men opening their newspapers again to read. Emma sipped her tea and made a few pleasant observations about some of their mutual acquaintances.

Ariadne replied when appropriate and continued working her way around her plate. Yet every time she met Emma's gaze, it was to find that twinkling gleam in her eyes again.

Finally, she'd had enough. "What?" she demanded.

Emma seemed startled. "What do you mean, 'what'?"

"That look you keep giving me." Ariadne laid down her fork. "And the smile. What are you thinking?"

"Oh." Emma had the grace to look a little sheepish at having been so transparent. "I was only thinking how nice it is that we shall be able to have more mornings like this."

"You mean with Rupert tormenting me like some feudal tyrant about how much I eat?"

Nick guffawed and turned a page of his newspaper.

Rupert arched a single golden brow.

"No," Emma said, "I mean with the four of us being together."

"We've eaten in each other's company before. Why is this morning any different?"

"Because you are to be my sister in truth now." A beatific smile spread over her face. "Once you marry Rupert, we shall be sisters, bound not just by inclination but by blood. You truly will be part of my family, properly, for all the world to see."

Family.

For a long moment Ariadne could not speak, her throat growing tight. Family was something she no longer had, all of them having been taken from her by war and murder and illness. Part of her grew wistful, thinking what it might be like to have those kinds of ties again. To know herself to be part of a group whose links could not be divided or dissolved. What it would be like to truly belong again.

Yet as much as she would like to call Emma sister, this marriage to Rupert wasn't right. It was based on all the wrong things, and no matter how much she wanted him, how much she loved him, she couldn't allow it to proceed.

She froze, staring blindly down at the pretty pattern on the china.

What did I just think? Did I really hear myself say that I love him?

Yet as soon as the thought had gone racing through her mind, she'd known it to be true.

I do love him.

Probably had for far longer than she cared to admit.

No wonder she melted when he came to her bed. No wonder she couldn't resist his wheedling and cajoling, letting him bully her into eating breakfast and talk his way around any number of her protestations. If she weren't careful, she'd find herself bending to his will like a willow tree in a storm, begging for just a little more of his time, an extra measure of his attention.

But love him or not, that didn't make this marriage plan any less impossible. It didn't mean he loved her back.

What was it he had said last night?

I want you. That will be enough.

But it wouldn't and she wasn't naive enough to believe in faerie stories and tales of happily ever after.

"About that, Emma, I—," she began.

But Rupert interrupted, putting down his paper. "Yes, about that. I have made inquiries into obtaining a special license so that we may be married here in England. It should be ready in time for us to wed either tomorrow or the day

after. Of course, we will have to have an official state ceremony once we return to Rosewald, sanctioned by the church
and the government, but that will take some months and we
cannot afford to remain unwed until then. We'll do something small but official here, then have the real wedding once
we return home."

"Tomorrow?" Ariadne exclaimed.

"Or the next day?" Emma said at the same moment, both
of them talking over each other again.

Ariadne couldn't believe he was hurrying this marriage
idea along so quickly.

He must be insane. Tomorrow, or even the day following,
was entirely out of the question. Besides, as far as she was
concerned, it wasn't going to happen at all.

Before she could sputter out a refusal, Emma stepped into
the conversational breach. "But that is not enough time, Rupert. Ariadne has to have a dress."

*Of course, a wedding dress. What an excellent excuse to
postpone.*

"That's right," Ariadne chimed in agreement. "I cannot
possibly be wed without a proper gown."

Rupert's golden eyebrows drew close. "Surely you must
have something in your wardrobe that would be suitable."

But Ariadne shook her head vehemently. "Nothing in the
right color and style. It must be white and you know I never
wear white."

"No. Why would an unmarried young woman wear
white?"

She ignored his sarcasm. "A new gown must be commis-
sioned. With the selection of materials, sewing, and fittings,
I doubt anything can be made ready in less than three or four
weeks."

He shot her a narrow-eyed look. "You have one week.
Send for the dressmaker and tell her that price is no object.

She may hire as many seamstresses as necessary to complete the task on time."

"But a week still isn't—"

"*One week,*" he repeated firmly. "That is the most I will allow. Now, finish your breakfast. It's getting cold."

"I *am* finished." She'd had enough of his dictatorial ways for one morning. Folding her napkin, she laid it next to her plate.

He said nothing more, obviously aware she had reached her limit.

"I need to be off," Nick said, tossing back the last of his coffee before getting to his feet. "I'm meeting a man about some cargo I'm having brought in from the Americas. He's a hard-bargaining sort and I'd just as soon not be late."

Emma stood and accompanied him out into the corridor.

Ariadne got to her feet as well and started around the table. As she went past Rupert, he reached out and caught hold of her wrist.

His eyes were a sharp blue. "Don't think I don't know what you're doing."

"Oh? And what might that be?"

"You don't care a jot about that dress. I know you're just using it as a way to postpone the wedding ceremony."

How had he known? Double drat him.

"Don't think you're getting out of this wedding," he told her. "We've been through this and the decision is made."

"By you. I never have agreed to marry you."

"Yes, you have." His eyes darkened. "You did again last night. You do each time I touch you." He stroked his thumb along the inside of her wrist and made her tremble.

He smiled, clearly aware of her response. "Have your gown made, since it will please Emma. But know this, Ariadne. A week from now, you will be my bride."

Chapter Twenty-six

For the first time in her life, Ariadne feared that she had met a force that was truly stronger than she was—and his name was Prince Rupert of Rosewald.

While preparations were being made for the wedding—including numerous fittings for the bridal gown and small trousseau that were being painstakingly sewn by a virtual army of seamstresses—she found herself being swept along on a seemingly unstoppable current.

As each day passed, she came no closer to reaching a satisfactory resolution, no nearer to convincing Rupert—or even Emma or Nick—that the wedding should not take place.

Emma was living in some romantic fantasy, certain that her brother loved Ariadne and that Ariadne was just too stubborn to see the truth. But she knew Emma was wrong. Rupert might want her—of that she had no doubt—but love?

She knew what he thought of love—romantic love anyway. He had no time for such nonsense, as she'd heard him call it on any number of occasions over the years. In fact, she'd once accused him of having no heart, sure that his sole guiding principle was a dedication to honor and duty, with no room for emotions. It was his unswerving sense of honor on which he was acting now—that and a raging case of lust.

He came to her bedroom each night and despite her pleas that they exercise some caution, he took her with a fierce possession that she seemed utterly helpless to deny. In a strange way, it was almost as if he wanted to get her with child. But that made no sense, since she knew he assumed he'd already won the wedding battle.

And to be truthful, there wouldn't have been a battle at all if he had even once said those three little words. A single *I love you* from him and she would have given in.

Having finally admitted her own feelings, she found herself strangely unable to fight him toe to toe the way she had in the past.

Part of her desperately wanted to be his wife.

But part of her was horribly afraid.

There had to be more to a marriage than passion, even the all-consuming kind she and Rupert now shared. Flames like those burned fiery hot, but eventually such needs found a way of cooling. Without love as a foundation between them, what would possibly remain?

She couldn't bear the idea of someday waking to find herself in a one-sided marriage where she was the person with the broken heart. She couldn't bear to repeat the mistakes of her parents, with their endless fights and infidelities and bitter recriminations. They had married for duty and she didn't want that kind of life. She'd gone out of her way to avoid it.

Yet she did love him—too much, she sometimes thought.

But maybe, some tiny corner of her mind whispered, she might still have some chance of making him love her back. Not if she drove him away, though. Not if she fled and refused to go through with the wedding.

And so she drifted, caught in the grip of the most terrible

indecision of her life, each day speeding by faster than the last.

She wakened with only three days remaining and stretched against the sheets, her muscles pleasurably sore from the heated lovemaking they'd shared the night before.

God, the things that man can do. He might be a prince, but his true calling clearly lay in the bedroom arts.

Padding to her bathing chamber, she washed, then let her maid help her dress for the day.

Nick, Emma, and Rupert were at breakfast when she walked in, Rupert looking splendid in a coat of mallard green that set off both his golden hair and the vibrant color of his eyes.

He smiled at her and said good morning. She answered the same, with greetings to Emma and Nick as well, then went to the buffet.

She had just taken her usual seat at the table when Symms appeared at the door, a silver salver in hand.

"Excuse me, Your Royal Highness," the butler said, approaching Rupert. "This message just arrived for you. I am told it is of an urgent nature."

"Thank you, Symms." Taking the missive, which bore Rosewald's royal seal, Rupert broke the wax and opened the letter.

They all watched as he read, his mouth settling into a grim line.

"What is it?" she asked, her breakfast forgotten.

"Yes, Rupert," Emma said, her eyes wide with concern. "What has occurred?"

He looked at Ariadne for a moment, then at his sister. "Papa's health has taken a grave turn. His physicians say he is dying and ask that I return home at once."

"Oh!" Emma's lip trembled, her eyes filling with sudden tears. "Dying? But in his last letter, he said he was feeling so much better. Perhaps they are mistaken."

Nick reached across the table and took his wife's hand, giving it a reassuring squeeze.

"I hope that too," Rupert said, "but from this report, it does not look good."

"You must go without delay, of course," Nick said, his voice ringing with the calm authority of his former naval command. "We'll all follow you as soon as the necessary arrangements can be made to travel with the boys. I know Emma will want to see her father before he passes. We will make all due haste."

Emma nodded, looking distraught. "Yes, yes." She paused, her gaze going to Ariadne. "But what about the wedding? You were to be married in a couple of days."

"Obviously the wedding must be postponed," Ariadne said. "Rupert and I can be married once you know more about your father's condition."

Rupert turned his gaze on her. "I have the license. We could call for the minister to come to the house. I shouldn't think it would take above an hour or two."

"An hour or two could make the difference between seeing your father one last time and never seeing him again."

His forehead creased, hesitating.

"I lost my family," she said softly. "I know what it is not to have a chance to say good-bye. Go, Rupert. If you leave now, you may be able to make the coast and set sail by nightfall. I shall accompany Emma and Nick and the boys as soon as may be. We will all see you soon in Rosewald. Your nation and your father need you."

He gave her a hard look and for a moment she thought he was going to argue. Then he nodded. "Yes, you are right. I should not delay." Pushing back his chair, he stood and went to ring the bell.

Symms, who had discreetly retreated from the room while they discussed the letter, slipped quietly back in.

Rupert turned to him. "Send word to have my coach readied and inform my valet to have a change of clothes packed. I will leave as soon as possible."

"Of course, Your Royal Highness. Everything shall be made ready."

"We will be leaving too, Symms," Nick told the man. "Her Highness's father is gravely ill and we shall be closing up the house and traveling to Rosewald. Please advise the staff."

"I'll go to the nursery and begin making preparations for the boys." Emma wiped the corners of her eyes with a handkerchief. "Oh, I just remembered. We are promised at the Hoopers' and the Monmouths' later this week. I shall have to write and make our excuses."

"I'll do that," Ariadne offered helpfully. "Once I'm done with the notes, I'll see to the packing."

"Thank you, Arie. You're a dear." Emma sent her a tremulous smile.

"And I'll take care of our travel arrangements and see to anything else that needs doing." Nick went to his wife and wrapped an arm around her shoulders, then looked back at his brother-in-law. "Rupert, good journey. We shall see you again soon."

"Yes, soon."

With his arm still around her shoulders, Nick and Emma walked from the room.

Ariadne gazed at Rupert. "You had better go."

"I should, yes."

"We'll be no more than a day or two behind."

"I know."

"I'm so sorry about your father, Rupert."

He nodded. "I know that too."

Striding forward, he pulled her into his arms and fit his mouth over hers for a hard, swift kiss that made her heart pound like a wild thing.

As abruptly as it had begun, it ended, and he let her go. An ache of longing spread through her body, pain at his departure even though she knew she would see him again soon.

Foolish. Just like my love.

"Godspeed," she told him.

"Farewell."

Then he was gone.

They left Lyndhurst House the following morning, a train of three coaches loaded with Nick, Emma, Ariadne, and the children, along with nursemaids, maids, Nick's valet, footmen, and a virtual mountain of baggage.

Deciding that a largely overland journey would be too arduous for Emma and the boys, Nick had arranged for them to complete as much of the trip as possible by sea. He owned a well-appointed two-masted schooner that he had docked in Southampton. As a former naval captain, he knew all the routes and how to make the best time. He also had a crew who had been more than willing to make the trip on such short notice, including Goldfinch, a lively fellow who had once served as his bosun's mate.

Nick charted a course that would take them around the coast of Spain, through the Strait of Gibraltar, and across to Italy. From there, they would switch to coaches again and go overland through the mountains, then on north to Rosewald. He figured with the warm summer weather in their favor, and a good chance of steady winds, that the trip shouldn't take them much longer than proceeding the entire way by land.

Nick was in his element the instant they stepped aboard ship, a wide smile creasing his face as he gave orders that got them swiftly under way.

Once Ariadne and Emma got their "sea legs" under them, as Nick called it, they spent much of their time on deck, protected from the sun by large parasols, the moist, salt-scented wind tugging playfully at their hair.

Baby Peter and young Friedrich settled in immediately, taking to life aboard ship with an ease that caused Nick to remark that his sons were born sailors. "After all," he said, "they have the sea in their blood, on their father's side, at least."

The crew doted on the boys, and Ariadne and Emma had to smile indulgently when Nick took Friedrich up to the command deck and let the boy "steer" the ship—to both father's and son's immense delight.

But the specter of Emma's father and his failing health cast a bleak shadow over what would otherwise have been a grand journey. She and Nick did their best to cheer Emma, but signs of worry and sadness lay heavy in her friend's eyes. Unspoken was the question of whether he still lived and whether they would make it to Rosewald in time for Emma to say her good-byes.

And always in the back of Ariadne's thoughts was Rupert. Where was he? How was his own journey proceeding? Had he reached his home yet?

She didn't sleep well at night, telling herself it was due to the sway of the ship and the unfamiliar bed. But often she woke, stretching out a hand in search of Rupert before she realized she was alone.

Odd how quickly she had gotten used to having him next to her at night.

Unsettling how keenly she missed him, as if he had taken part of her heart with him when he'd gone away.

The voyage went as planned, and then it was back to the road, all of them bundled again inside several sturdy yet comfortable coaches.

Finally, after more than two weeks' travel, they arrived.

For years Ariadne had heard tales of Rosewald, but even

those descriptions had not prepared her for the beauty of the place.

Heavily forested mountains lay nestled beside lush green valleys and large fields of land planted with thriving crops. There were winding streams and deep, cold rivers, small, prosperous towns and bucolic villages. The villagers and townsfolk waved and smiled as their entourage drove past, children running alongside trying to catch a better glimpse of Archduchess Emmaline and her family. They welcomed Ariadne too, calling out happy greetings despite the fact that she was unknown to them.

Ariadne had grown up in a royal palace, but even she caught her breath at her first sight of Neuewaldstein Castle, the principal seat of the Whyte family for more than four hundred years.

The grand edifice was carved from a gleaming white stone that put her in mind of something from a faerie story. Corner towers with pointed turrets soared upward as if to touch the pristine blue sky above, while the massive structure itself stretched outward, majestic and imposing where it nestled inside its mountain stronghold. Capturing such a fortress would be next to impossible, but holding it for centuries as the Whytes had done served as a visible testament to their power and resilience.

She could see why Rupert spoke of his home with such pleasure and pride, understood his devotion to duty and how he would do anything to preserve and protect his heritage— not only for himself but for the generations yet to come.

The interior was even more opulent, she discovered, as their party arrived and alighted from the coaches to step over the threshold into the palace.

The floors were made of polished black-and-white marble, the walls paneled in beautiful watered silks, the moldings ornately carved and leafed in gold. The majestic ceilings were a masterpiece in and of themselves, each exquisitely wrought work depicting scenes of ancient myths or angels from on high. And everywhere there were glorious objets d'art—paintings, sculptures, urns, and armaments. There were even several suits of armor, no doubt worn into battle by Emma and Rupert's royal ancestors.

But there was no time to afford any of these splendors more than a cursory glance before they were led down one wide corridor after another to the family wing of the palace.

They didn't even stop to change out of their traveling clothes but went directly to see the ailing king. Knowing that the bedside of a dying man was no place for young children, Emma allowed the boys' nurse to take them off to the nursery, where they would be able to nap and have a meal.

Rupert came out to greet them. He did not smile, though the color of his midnight blue eyes did seem to intensify when he met her gaze.

Then he glanced away.

To most observers, she was sure, he looked as he always did—powerfully handsome, confident, and in command, as if he could take the weight of the world on his shoulders and not strain to carry it. But to her he looked tired and somber, already in a state of grief. She wanted to run to him and wrap him in her arms, kiss him and murmur words of comfort.

But she held her place and kept silent instead.

"Rupert, how is Papa?" Emma hurried forward, giving her brother a quick, fierce hug before letting go. "He's not—"

"No, but it won't be long. I am glad you are here. Sigrid and Otto are here. They are in with him now."

Sigrid was Emma and Rupert's older sister, and King Otto was her husband, a man who had at one time been promised to wed Emma. Thank heavens that had not come to pass and that Rupert had relented and given Emma permission to marry Nick, the man she loved.

Luckily neither Sigrid nor Otto harbored any hard feelings on the matter. In fact, from what she had last heard, Sigrid was quite content in her marriage, although, knowing Sigrid, she was even more content being a queen.

"He has been asking for you," Rupert said. "I'll warn you, though, that he is in and out of consciousness. I'm not sure what state he'll be in. He may not even know you are here."

Emma took a deep, bracing breath, then nodded, Nick at her side with an arm around her waist. Together they moved forward through a set of massive painted doors and into the room beyond.

Rupert did not follow, but turned and crossed to Ariadne instead. "How has she been?"

"Fine. Worried naturally, but bearing up well."

"And you?" He reached for her hand. "How was your journey?"

"Long, exhausting, but I am quite well."

He studied her more carefully, as if something further was on his mind. "You're certain? You are not . . ."

"Not what?" She considered for another moment before she suddenly realized what he must mean. "No! No, I am not"—she lowered her voice—"with child. I had my monthly last week."

An expression of immense relief came over his face, one that surprised, and oddly enough, displeased her. Not that she had wanted there to be a child, not now, with everything so uncertain and unsettled between them, but still, he didn't have to secm so happy about it.

Although perhaps she was being unfair. He had a great deal to contend with at the moment, not the least of which was the dreadful prospect of his father's approaching death. And when that occurred, he would become king, with all the attendant duties and responsibilities of that office. He was regent now, of course, but still, it was not the same. The weight of the nation would be his to bear alone.

"Ariadne, I—"

But he got no further, as a well-dressed man—one of his ministers perhaps—stepped forward to interrupt them.

"Pardon, Your Royal Highness, but a matter of some urgency has arisen. If I might perhaps have a word."

Rupert scowled and dropped her hand. "Yes, of course. Just a moment, if you would."

The man bowed. "Certainly." He stepped discreetly away.

"I am sorry," Rupert told her. "It seems there is always something to do since my return. I suppose I was away too long and must now suffer the consequences. I shall be back shortly. If you wish, you may join Emma and Nick."

"No, such times are for family. I would be out of place."

"Believe me, you would not. You are more family than many who attend my father. The room is crowded with physicians and clergy and friends come to pay their last respects. No one would complain of your presence."

She hated sickrooms, though she would never say so. "If you wish me there I shall go. Otherwise, perhaps I might be shown to my room. It has been a long journey."

"No, of course, you are tired. You must be allowed to change and rest." He strode across and pulled the bell. "Someone shall be here shortly to attend you. If you will excuse me."

She watched as he left, regretting as he disappeared down the long corridor that she had not found a moment to kiss him first.

Chapter Twenty-seven

"*The king is dead. Long live the king.*"

The solemn phrase that Ariadne had heard that fateful morning four days ago repeated itself now in her head. Friedrich IV, King of Rosewald, was dead and his son, Rupert II, had ascended to the throne in his place.

Yet to her Rupert was still just Rupert, even if he did rule a kingdom now.

Still, as she gazed at him from where she sat next to Emma in the palace's formal drawing room, there was no sign of the relaxed, playful man she had known as her lover. He was reserved and austere, his demeanor as stark as the black clothing he wore.

They were all attired in black, of course, now that the palace was officially in mourning. An elaborate state funeral had been held earlier that day, followed by a private graveside service attended by family only, which had included aunts, uncles, and myriad cousins, some whose connection was quite distant. She had been the sole outsider to be included, Emma insisting that she join them.

"Of course you must be there," Emma had told her before the service. "You and Rupert are engaged. That makes you family."

But other than the four of them, no one knew about the engagement. Rupert had made no mention of it since her arrival, and to her knowledge he had not discussed it with anyone else. For all intents and purposes, it appeared to be a secret.

Still, no one complained of her presence at the graveside. Nor had anyone complained when she held vigil with the family in the king's chambers while he breathed his last. Despite her aversion to such doleful matters, she'd sat on a sofa beside Emma and held her hand through the sorrowful ordeal. Nick had sat on his wife's other side and done the same.

Emma had wept on both their shoulders once her father finally passed away.

At least, Ariadne had whispered to her, she had gotten to see him again and he had gotten to see her and his grandsons. They had all been able to say their good-byes.

Rupert had stood across the curtain-darkened room, arms stiffly at his sides, clearly wishing for no sympathy. She'd tried afterward to offer him comfort, but he'd turned her gently away.

"Thank you for your concern," he'd said, "but I am entirely well. My father had been ill a very long time and this day was not unexpected. He is at peace now and what more can any of us wish for in the end?"

He had not shed so much as a single tear, though she knew he grieved. He had also not visited her bedchamber, an absence that made her all the sadder.

She sighed quietly to herself now and raised her teacup to her lips. Emma sat, her own cup full and untouched, forgotten. Gently, she took it from her friend and set it aside.

"Mayhap you ought to go upstairs and rest," Ariadne suggested. "You are expecting again, after all. I am sure no one would notice if you slipped away."

Emma sent her a wry smile, coming back from wherever it was she had been. "Then you do not know my family. Decorum is a must, and we are all expected to remain until the last of those wishing to pay their respects have gone on their way. Truly I am fine and thankfully Sigrid will make sure no one greatly outstays their welcome."

Yes, Ariadne decided, looking at the refined blond beauty accepting condolences across the room, that was a fact she could readily believe.

Mourners approached singly or in small groups to express their sorrow and share a remembrance or two about King Friedrich. Emma was gracious to each and every one, no matter how sad and weary she might be inside. Nick was there as well to buoy her up. Ariadne knew Emma relied on him, leaning into his strength when she needed an extra measure of support. And there were her children—currently safe in the nursery—who brought her joy and never failed to bring a smile to her face.

It was near the end of the reception when she left Emma and Nick and went in search of the refreshment table. She'd scarcely eaten more than a few bites of breakfast, and nothing since then, having refused a plate offered by one of the servants earlier in the day. But now she was ravenous and had no wish to wait until dinner to eat.

Picking up a beautifully patterned china plate, she began inspecting the selections on the buffet. As she did, she heard a pair of women conversing not far away.

"So which one do you think he will choose?" said the first woman. "They've all come here, you know, like merchants displaying their best silks, waving their prettiest wares under his nose."

"Estella, what a thing to say, and at a funeral no less. The old king is barely in his grave. I don't think the new one is thinking about a bride."

"He may not be thinking about it, but you can be sure his ministers are busy making plans, not to mention certain members of his family."

"Queen Sigrid, do you mean?"

"Certainly not the other one, married to that Englishman for love, no less, even if the fellow has been elevated into royal circles."

The second woman made noises of agreement; then the other continued.

"As for the parties in question and their lovely young daughters, they've all been playing up their expressions of sympathies, but have you noticed how careful they are to make sure the king gets a good look at the merchandise? He'll be in mourning for a few months, as required, but then it will be time to take a wife and start his nursery. After all, what king does not wish for sons to carry on his line?"

"True. Quite true. He'll pick a royal, of course."

"Undoubtedly. Princess Sophia of Lorraine must certainly be in the running. Now that the French monarchy has been reestablished, a connection there would only strengthen Rosewald's position, and I understand she has a dowry of twenty million francs. She has a lovely face, which cannot hurt either."

"Which one is she?"

"Over there near the window. The blonde seated to the left of the tall Grecian urn."

Ariadne looked across the room, locating a slender young woman with a demure cast to her fair-complexioned features.

"They would make beautiful babies together—do you not agree?" the first woman said.

If you like long noses and thin lips, Ariadne thought, gripping the serving spoon in her hand far too tightly. *That girl and Rupert will never have babies together.*

"Then there is Anna-Louisa of Carinthia," the woman named Estella continued. "She has Hapsburg blood, you know. Her father is one of the emperor's cousins. An alliance there would be quite advantageous to them both. He would gain a closer connection to the emperor, while she would be a queen. Were I one to wager, I would put my money on her."

"A shame she isn't a bit more personable, though."

"By which you mean she's a cold fish."

The other woman laughed. "As a Norwegian cod in February."

Ariadne tracked their gazes toward the far corner, where a dark, proud-looking girl sat next to an equally severe-looking older woman, who gave every indication of being her mother. Both women held their spines rigidly straight, as if they had steel rods in their corsets. And perhaps they did.

"If he chooses that one, he'll simply have to look for his pleasures elsewhere, as most men do. Then again, they all stray once they have an heir or two, and often long before that. No, compatibility in marriage is the last concern of any royal, and King Rupert will be no different."

A chill traced down Ariadne's spine and she turned away, not wanting to hear another word. Blankly, she stared at the plate in her hand, having forgotten that she even held it. She wasn't hungry anymore; the conversation had quite driven her appetite away. Though why that should be, she could not say.

Before leaving England, she'd been searching for the right way to end her engagement to Rupert, so what had changed, assuming there even was an engagement between them any longer?

She should be relieved if he was looking elsewhere.

Shouldn't she?

Yet the idea of him marrying one of those girls—it made her blood boil.

It made her sick.

But she could not afford to let any of those reactions show here, in front of so many inquisitive eyes. Taking a carefully measured breath, she composed her features, making sure they were quite blank.

Only then did she return to Emma's side.

From the opposite side of the room, Rupert watched Ariadne lean close and murmur something to Emma. A moment later she rose and left the room.

He wanted to follow, but forced himself not to go after her. Just as he'd forced himself not to seek her out at night these last few days.

Having her so near yet not touching her was killing him. But after she'd told him that she was not with child, he'd decided they shouldn't take the risk again. They'd been lucky before, although at the time he hadn't minded the idea. They'd been only days away from marrying and, more than anything else, he knew that a child would bind her to him, force her to realize that she belonged with him.

But nothing had been the same since his return to Rosewald.

First there had been attending to his father during his final days. At the same time he had been expected to resume the full weight of his duties as regent in preparation for becoming king.

Of course, he'd known this day would come, had had time to prepare himself for the loss of his father. Yet how could any man truly prepare himself for the enormity of such a situation? Dealing with the grief of losing a parent while at the same time assuming the mantle of his role as sovereign?

But he was king now; it was a role for which he'd been destined from birth. From his earliest days, he'd been trained to understand a king's duties, to know how he ought to behave and what was expected of him, not only in ruling the country but in his personal life as well.

His court and his nation were looking to him now for leadership and guidance during this time of transition. So however much he wished he could take Ariadne by the hand and lead her to the private family chapel to wed, he knew there were many who would view such haste with derision.

They would speculate that he was marrying her because she was with child. They would hear of the scandal in England and see her as a disgraced woman. There would always have been some murmurs to that effect, but they would be magnified tenfold were he to rush them into marriage so quickly after his father's death.

And so he had decided that he and Ariadne must wait.

The expected mourning period was at least a year, but waiting that long was absolutely out of the question—protocol be damned. A few months, he reasoned, first with an engagement, then with a wedding ceremony.

Six or eight months, that was the most he would wait. He supposed they would have to agree to some huge state wedding ceremony, but he would abide it if only Ariadne would consent to the union.

He scowled. He'd had her exactly where he wanted her back in London, hurrying her down the aisle before she had a chance to think of a way out. But now he would have to persuade her all over again, and for the first time in his life he wasn't entirely confident of receiving the answer he so strongly desired.

There was also another difficulty in selecting her as his bride. His ministers would not be in favor of the union. In fact, he knew more than one of them who would rail against what they would consider his imprudent choice and try to talk him out of it. Even his father had tried to do the same as he'd lain on his deathbed.

Rupert twisted the signet ring he now wore on his finger; it was the king's ring, wrought of ancient gold and a magnificent square-cut ruby that legend held had been part of a war prize won by the very first king of Rosewald. Rupert's scowl deepened as he recalled the conversation with his father.

"Rupert, I have but little time remaining." His father's voice had been thin and raspy, but with an underlying ring of strength and authority reminiscent of his prime. "You must remember your duty."

"My duty is always my primary concern. You know that, Papa."

"Then why have you not yet taken a wife?" The old king drew in a wheezing breath that rattled like a set of keys in his frail lungs. "Why have you not given me grandchildren to comfort me in such times? They should be playing here, my grandsons."

"You have grandsons. Emma and Sigrid's children. They visited you yesterday."

"But those boys cannot inherit. They cannot continue the line. Only you."

His father broke off, coughing long and hard. When it was over and the physician had withdrawn out of earshot again, his father's rheumy eyes locked on him with piercing intent. "Grandchildren. You must swear."

"I will marry and have children, Papa," Rupert assured him. "You are not to worry about my continuing the line."

"But I do worry." He took another thin breath. "Have worried but held my tongue."

Rupert refrained from lifting his eyes to the heavens. Over the years, his father had hardly held his tongue on the subject of Rupert's lack of a wife or his desire for grandchildren from such a union.

"You must swear to me that you will not continue to delay in selecting a bride," his father had said.

Rupert's thoughts had gone to Ariadne, and he'd found himself wishing suddenly that she was by his side. But giving his promise on this point no longer presented a problem. "I swear."

King Friedrich nodded against his pillow, his white hair hanging in lank wisps around his head. "She must be of excellent lineage, a virtuous woman of royal blood."

"Of course."

Again, Ariadne satisfied the requirements. As for the virtuous part, she had only been unvirtuous with him, so he didn't see how that could count against her.

"The alliance with her family must strengthen Rosewald, must help to make it invincible. You must do everything in your power to ensure that the kingdom not only survives but thrives. Select a bride with wealth and powerful political affiliations. One whose allies will become our allies and who will make our enemies, or any who would stand against us, quake at the thought of our very name."

Ah, now we have come to the impasse.

Rupert had fallen silent, considering his words. When he'd thought to marry Ariadne in England, he'd planned to return home and present their marriage as an irrevocable act that his father and everyone else would simply have to learn to accept.

But he had not married her, and since he had not, there would inevitably now be complications.

She had no family; not even her kingdom remained, as her ancestral lands had been divided up like scraps of meat tossed to a pack of hungry dogs. Nothing remained of Nordenbourg except its memory. She could bring no political ties to her marriage, for her former country had none. As for her dowry, it was adequate for her purposes but hardly sufficient to tempt a king.

She would bring nothing but herself to a marriage. Once,

he would have laughed to think of uniting himself with her, but no longer. He wanted her, in his bed and by his side as his bride, regardless what others might say.

Not that he had ever planned to get anyone's permission when it came to choosing his wife, not even that of his dying parent. But unlike earlier times when a royal could be an autocrat, this was the modern age. He could not simply act like some feudal prince and behead anyone who disapproved of his selection—however intriguing such an idea might be. Instead, he was obliged to consider other points of view—or at least appear to do so.

As he'd sat at his father's bedside, however, he'd realized that in his heart of hearts, he wanted his blessing on his choice of bride. Yet he'd hesitated to mention Ariadne. His father had remarked what a lovely young woman she seemed, but that didn't mean he would approve of her as a daughter-in-law.

"And what of compatibility in marriage?" Rupert ventured. "What of finding a woman who will be more than a good queen to our people but a good queen for me? A consort who will make me happy?"

"Happy?" his father retorted on another wheezing exhalation. "What does being happy have to do with marriage? That's why a man takes a mistress. Compatibility is for peasants, not kings. Why this sudden outpouring of sentimentality? You've always been so sensible about such matters."

The king's tired eyes narrowed. "You've spent too much time in England listening to that maudlin drivel of your sister's. It's all well and good for Emmaline to throw herself away on that English earl, but you—" He broke off, needing another long drink of water.

"I thought you liked Lyndhurst."

"He's a good man, but he's not the king she could have had. She threw Otto aside and let Sigrid claim him. Now there's a girl with a sensible head on her shoulders. Sigrid always has known how to keep her sights on what's important."

Yes, Sigrid had spent her life focused on status and riches, but she'd never struck him as being contented, certainly not as being happy. Sometimes he wondered if she regretted the choices she'd made in her life.

And what of himself?

Until a few weeks ago, his life had been set in a predictable path, one that included a marriage based solely on its benefits to Rosewald and the Whyte family line. But now he was no longer sure of that course.

And in those minutes when he'd sat talking to his father, he'd found himself questioning many long-held beliefs. For the first time in his life, he'd found himself wanting more than to satisfy the dictates of honor and duty.

Yet isn't that why he had offered to marry Ariadne? To satisfy honor? To keep her from ruin, since he had claimed her virginity? Or was it more? Was his insistence on a wedding between them just an excuse, a means of having what he really wanted—*her*?

Had Emma overheard him, she would have said he was in love.

But that really was nonsense. Even he hadn't changed that much.

No, he wanted Ariadne, craved her in his bed with an almost relentless desire. But she had many valuable qualities outside the bedchamber as well. She was a worthy companion, a woman who would make an excellent queen and consort. She wasn't intimidated by him and would never back down from a challenge. And she would amuse him too.

But that didn't mean he loved her.

It's just that he knew he wouldn't grow bored in her company, he wouldn't tire of her the way he would one of the other more eligible princesses on the list his ministers had prepared.

His father's final words to him had been to choose an advantageous bride. But he didn't see why he couldn't choose one who gave him pleasure instead.

He gazed around the drawing room again, taking in the black-clad royals and nobles who put him in mind of a murder of crows. Or perhaps vultures would be more apt, come to pick over the moldering bones of his father.

His lips curled cynically, fully aware that many of the young royal ladies here today were being paraded for his inspection. He wasn't naive; he knew they had come as much to catch his matrimonial interest as to pay their final respects.

But he wanted none of them.

His eyes drifted to the door through which Ariadne had gone, wishing again that he could follow her.

Instead, he lifted a glass of brandy to his lips and strove for patience.

Chapter Twenty-eight

The palace quieted once the funeral was over, most of the Whyte family relations and nearly all of the other mourners expressing their final condolences and their good-byes over the next few days.

Ariadne spent most of her time with Emma, who was already talking about returning to England. With another baby on the way, Emma didn't want to delay her return too long and find the journey more difficult. Sigrid and her children were still in residence, although her husband had left the day after the funeral, citing pressing business at home as the reason why he could not stay longer.

As for Rupert, Ariadne saw him at dinner each evening and then for cards, or some other entertainment, after the meal. But they never seemed to spend time alone and he still had not come to her room at night.

She thought about confronting him and demanding to know exactly where their relationship stood. Was their affair over? Had he decided he wished to end their engagement as well? But then she would remember that he had just lost his father and that he was in mourning.

In the end, she held her tongue and said nothing.

So she was surprised on the sixth evening when Rupert drew her momentarily aside, using the excuse of everyone arranging themselves into whist teams to have a private word.

"Meet me later tonight in the library," he said quietly, so that only she could hear. "I need to see you alone."

Her heart beat faster as she met his gaze, finding his eyes intensely blue. She gave a slight, almost imperceptible nod. "Yes," she whispered, her voice even quieter than his.

Usually she was quite adept at whist, but she let her partner down badly that night, playing one ill-chosen card after another. She just couldn't seem to make herself concentrate, her mind too focused on her upcoming rendezvous with Rupert.

What did he want? And why the library? Why not her bedchamber or his? Or did he mean to end things between them after all?

A lump settled in the pit of her stomach at the thought.

At the end of the game, her whist partner—one of the last Whyte cousins still staying in the palace—threw his cards down in disgust and stalked across to the liquor cabinet. Soon after, brandy glass in hand, he turned and glared at her.

She couldn't blame him. She didn't think she'd ever played so horribly in her entire life. But she would make their bruising loss up to him another time. Right now, she was thinking again about her upcoming meeting with Rupert.

Beside her, Emma concealed a yawn. "Mercy, I am done in," she said to Ariadne. "What about you? Tired?"

"*Hmm*, not quite yet, but do go on. I think I may drop by the library and see if there is anything to read."

"Well, if you cannot find a book in a library as expansive as this one, then you do not really wish to read. But I must admit we are all rather dull company these days. Do not stay up too late."

"I won't," Ariadne assured her. She sent Nick a smile as he joined his wife, watching with an uncharacteristic feeling of envy as he placed a loving hand at Emma's waist.

They all said their good nights, several others of their party doing the same, including Queen Sigrid. She and Ariadne shared a casual bit of small talk as they both strolled out into the hall, then parted at the main staircase, Sigrid going up while Ariadne continued on into the part of the palace that housed the library.

The room truly was as impressive as Emma had said, quite literally holding tens of thousands of volumes inside its floor-to-ceiling shelves. Woolen Turkey carpets in mellow shades of red and brown covered the floors, giving the library an intimacy that belied its size. A selection of plush sofas and chairs were arranged in easy groupings for the occupants' comfort, while on the air drifted the warm scents of polish, ink, and parchment.

All in all, it was an extremely inviting room—or so Ariadne would have thought had she been there under other circumstances. As it was, she paid little heed to her surroundings, her nerves on edge as she waited for Rupert to arrive.

She heard a footfall at the door, but it was only one of the servants.

"Is there anything with which I can assist you, Your Highness?" the man inquired.

She shook her head. "Nothing, thank you."

With a bow, he withdrew.

Ten minutes passed, then twenty, the time moving so slowly that she finally did go to peruse some of the selections on the shelves.

She had just opened a book of seventeenth-century French poetry when she heard movement at the door once again. This time it was Rupert who walked in.

She shoved the book back onto its shelf, then swung around to face him. "I was beginning to wonder if you'd changed your mind about meeting me."

"I was detained. My cousin Geoff never has learned to take a hint and know when an evening is over." He closed the double doors at his back, then walked farther into the room, his shoes silent against the thick carpet.

"I don't think His Grace was terribly happy with me at the card table tonight. I played dreadfully and we lost every hand."

Rupert smiled. "Defeat builds character. I am sure he will survive."

She moved closer, stopping when she was only a few inches away. Less than a month ago, she would have gone straight into his arms, would have kissed him without a moment's hesitation. Now she no longer knew if she should—or if he would want her to.

He made no move to embrace her either.

Rather than feeling her usual bravado, she felt her confidence shrink.

Loving him, she realized, made her unsure. It made her vulnerable. And she didn't like being vulnerable, especially when it all seemed so one-sided.

Raising her chin, she sent him an inquiring smile. "You wanted to meet privately, *Your Majesty*. What did you wish to discuss?"

He winced slightly. "I suppose I deserve that. I know we've seen very little of each other lately."

"We've seen almost nothing of each other lately." She linked her hands in front of her, against the skirt of her black silk evening gown. "I am aware that you have had a very great number of things with which to deal, now that you are king. I realize too that you have been mourning the passing of your father."

She took a quick breath, the words seeming to tumble out, almost against her will. "You might have come to me, you know. You might have let me at least attempt to offer you some comfort, some relief."

His golden brows drew close and he looked away. "Under the circumstances, it seemed better if I did not. We need to be more discreet here at the palace. I would not have your reputation blemished."

"It was already more than blemished before we left England. I hardly see how it can be damaged further."

"That is where you are mistaken, especially since you are to be my queen."

Am I?

Until that moment, she hadn't known if he still meant to go through with the wedding. But if he did, then why had he been so distant of late? Why had he not come to her bed at night when he'd refused to stay away before?

Of course, she had never actually planned to marry him, so she shouldn't care. Yet, to her dismay, she realized that she did.

Very much.

Too much.

"It's too soon yet after the funeral to make a formal announcement about our engagement," he continued, "but I wanted to reaffirm my promise to you. That's why I asked to meet alone here tonight."

Her heart gave a traitorous leap. "Oh?"

He reached into his pocket and withdrew a small box covered in black velvet. What he revealed inside stole her breath.

It was a ring, but not just any ring—the brilliantly cut emerald as rich and mysterious a green as the depths of a deep mountain pond. As for the size of the stone, it was huge, set into an elegantly cast gold band that looked at least a century old.

"I had my choice of the crown jewels," he said, taking the ring out of its silken bed. "This one reminds me of your eyes. I hope you approve."

How could she not? Without exaggeration, it was the most exquisite emerald she had ever seen.

"Yes," she told him. "It's beautiful."

"Shall we see if it fits?"

Without waiting for permission, he took her left hand and slid the ring onto her finger. She ought to have stopped him, ought to have found the will to protest, but somehow the words never came to her lips.

And then it was too late, the ring sparkling like some piece of treasure from an enchanted legend.

But as she gazed at it and thought about the reason why the ring now graced her hand, all of her old qualms suddenly rushed back. She still hadn't actually agreed to marry him.

Even now, he has not said he loves me.

"Rupert, I—"

But he spoke at the same time, his sentence overpowering her own. "So, the ring does fit." Satisfaction rang in his voice. "I thought it might. You have such delicate hands."

He lifted her palm and pressed a kiss onto her skin.

Her heart thundered beneath her ribs. *Maybe he does care for me, after all?* Maybe he assumed she knew how he felt and didn't think he needed to say the words?

Then he released her. "It is late and you must be tired. I should bid you good night."

"You don't have to, you know." She laid a hand against his cheek and gently stroked its length, relishing the sensation of warm male skin and the faint bristle of evening whiskers. "Come to my bed tonight. It's been so long."

His eyes darkened. "I know, but we cannot afford the risk."

"We found a way before. I'm sure we can manage again."

He covered her hand with his and pressed it close. Briefly, he closed his eyes, opening them again to gaze directly into hers. "Sadly, we cannot. This isn't my sister's house. There are far too many opportunities for us to be noticed."

He pulled her hand away from his face and lowered it to her side.

"But you are the king," she protested.

"Yes, and I will not have the palace whispering that I am keeping you as my mistress when you are to be my bride."

"Can I not be both?"

He smiled sardonically and bent to kiss her forehead. "No. Now go to bed, Ariadne. I shall see you tomorrow."

She wanted to argue, but could see there was no use. When he got into one of his stubborn moods, there was no shifting him from his course. There was nothing to say that she couldn't try again tomorrow night, though. She would be like water on rock, working to slowly erode his resolve.

"Very well, then. Good night." Reluctantly, she turned and made her way to the doors, opening one and passing through.

Once again, Rupert nearly stopped her.

Instead, he squeezed his fists tight at his sides and forced himself to turn away.

In need of a distraction, he stalked across the library's wide expanse to a small tulipwood cabinet and reached for the crystal brandy decanter on top. He poured a healthy draught into a glass, then raised it to his lips and took a long swallow; the alcohol slid down his throat in a warm burn.

He had just lifted the glass to his mouth again when he heard movement near the door.

Had Ariadne come back?

He swung around, his chest tightening in hopes she had returned.

But it was Sigrid who moved through the door on a sibilant swish of black satin. "I thought you had gone to bed," he remarked, then drank more brandy.

"I was on my way there," she said, walking deeper into the room, "but decided a bit of light reading might help lull me to sleep."

He arched one eyebrow skeptically. "Since when are you in the habit of reading?"

"Oh, I'm not. It bores me to tears. That's why I thought it would help me drift off tonight. I haven't been sleeping well since Papa died."

"I'm sure not." He finished his brandy and set down the glass. "So, why are you here, Sigrid? Or more to the point, how long you have been here, listening?"

She made a moue with her lips in a gesture that tacitly admitted she'd been caught spying. Then she shrugged. "Long enough to know you've somehow managed to entangle yourself with Ariadne of Nordenbourg and that you've given her an engagement ring."

Ariadne was halfway to her room when she decided that she ought to have taken a book from the library after all. Chances were good she would have trouble falling asleep tonight and a book might be just what she needed to distract her.

Of course she would rather Rupert distract her, but he had put a stop to that particular possibility. Then again, if he was still in the library when she returned, maybe she could change his mind. Really, when she thought about it, she'd given up far too easily. What could it hurt if she tried seducing him one last time? Assuming he hadn't already left the room by the time she got back, that was.

She heard the murmur of voices when she approached the partially open library door a couple of minutes later. Rupert was still inside; she recognized the smooth cadence of his rich baritone. A woman answered, her voice familiar as well.

Sigrid.

Ariadne hesitated, unsure whether to interrupt or not. Then she heard her name.

"It has nothing to do with liking Ariadne," Sigrid was saying. "I like Princess Ariadne very much. She is a charming, highly entertaining young woman, even if she does have a tendency toward rash imprudence. Her personality is not at issue. It is her pedigree that must be considered."

"Her pedigree is exceptional," Rupert retorted in a hard tone.

"Her pedigree is useless, of which you are very well aware. A marriage to her brings you nothing. You might as well take a milkmaid to wife for all the advantage Ariadne offers."

Outside in the hallway, Ariadne stood rooted to the spot, unable to move. She knew she should turn away, but she couldn't. Soundlessly, she pressed a fist against her chest, her heart beating fiercely beneath her knuckles.

"You are king of Rosewald," Sigrid went on. "You owe it to your country and your legacy to choose a bride who will not only increase your wealth but strengthen your position as monarch. A woman who will make you greater as king and Rosewald greater as a nation."

"I hardly need to be reminded of my duty," he said scathingly.

Sigrid did not back down. "Before tonight, I would have agreed. But the fact that you have chosen such an imprudent course—well, you must rethink matters before it is too late."

"There is nothing to rethink. I have given my word."

"Then retract it. Ariadne is a reasonable young woman. She will understand."

"I told you before that I am honor-bound to wed her. I will not withdraw my proposal."

"Yes, yes, some scandal that happened in England before your return home. But it will all blow over. There are always ways to smooth these things out."

Ariadne could almost see him grinding his teeth.

"Perhaps I do not wish to have it *smoothed out*," he said. "Believe me, Sigrid, if I did not listen to our father on this subject, I most certainly am not going to listen to you."

Ariadne barely stifled a gasp, pressing her fist against her lips.

"You spoke to Papa before he died," his sister repeated, "about marrying Ariadne?"

Rupert paused. "I did not specifically mention her by name, but I discussed the idea of taking a bride of my own choosing to wife."

"Clearly he did not agree."

"No. But this is my decision and my mind is made up."

"Then what are you saying, Rupert? I never thought I would live to see the day when you, of all people, would turn sentimental. Do you love her? Is that why you are insisting on this marriage?"

Ariadne's pulse sped faster, her breath shallow as she waited to hear his response. On tenterhooks, she closed her eyes.

"I've already told you my reasons," he said brusquely. "Do I look like the sort of man who would marry for love? I placed Ariadne in a compromising position and it is my responsibility to correct the damage. An honorable marriage is the only option. I have given her my pledge and I will abide by it, no matter the supposed wisdom of the decision."

"Even if your entire court objects?"

"Yes. Even then."

Ariadne leaned a trembling shoulder against the wall, a tear rolling in a damp slide over her cheek.

He does not love me. I am nothing but a duty. Just one more obligation in a very long list.

And a burden was something she had decided never to be, just as she had vowed not to marry where there wasn't love—on both sides.

Suddenly she straightened, fiercely wiping away the tear with the back of one hand.

She didn't want or need his pity. Obviously, she had sadly miscalculated the extent of his feelings for her, as well as his desire. He no longer wanted her—that much was clear. She'd wondered why he'd stopped coming to her bed, and now she knew. Knew as well why he'd turned her efforts at seduction aside tonight and sent her off to bed alone.

Apparently during their separation after leaving England, he'd had time to reconsider his actions. He'd had a chance to reflect and realize that he should not have been so hasty in offering her marriage. Of course when he'd offered his hand, he hadn't thought he would be king so soon. His father's death must have put everything back in perspective. But Rupert had given his word, and if there was one thing on which he could be counted, it was keeping his word, even if he regretted having given it.

In the next moment, she caught sight of the emerald engagement ring glittering on her finger. She shivered, unable to decide whether to wrench it off or flee upstairs to her bedchamber.

Instead, she did neither.

With her back rigidly straight, she gave a quick rap on the door and walked inside the library.

Chapter Twenty-nine

At the sight of Ariadne, Rupert's chest gave a sharp squeeze.

Bloody hell. How much did she hear?

One look at her face told him everything he needed to know.

"Excuse the interruption," she said, as she strode toward him and Sigrid. "I came downstairs again to get a book."

"*Och*, just like me," Sigrid said, clearly hoping Ariadne had only just arrived.

Ariadne fixed Sigrid with a hard glare. "Do me the courtesy of not dissembling, Your Majesty, and I shall offer the same."

"Perhaps I ought to leave," Sigrid said.

"Oh, do not go on my account. Obviously you are privy to far more of my personal affairs than I had realized," Ariadne said. "I must confess I had not expected to find you and Rupert discussing my relationship with him, but then as the old saying goes, one never hears well of oneself when eavesdropping. In my own defense, it was accidentally done."

With what could only be deemed a regal dismissal, she turned her back on Sigrid and moved to face Rupert.

"Ariadne, whatever you may have heard—," he began.

She cut him off. "Oh, I heard more than sufficient, enough to make me realize that a union between us would be a grave mistake. I told you from the start that you were under no obligation to marry me. I never asked you to do the honorable thing, but you would insist on acting the hero. The error in this is mine and I am to blame. I should never have let matters proceed so far between us. I certainly should never have allowed you to give me this."

Pausing, she twisted the ring off her finger and held it out to him.

"That is yours," he said roughly, an odd kind of panic twisting in his gut.

But she shook her head. "No, I cannot accept it, any more than I can accept your proposal—though you never did actually ask me to marry you, you know."

Inwardly, he cringed, knowing she was right.

"You'd made up your mind and wouldn't hear any answer but yes. Well, I'm giving you another answer now, the one I ought to have insisted upon from the beginning. I thank you for the great honor of your proposal, King Rupert, but I must decline. Find a bride who will be a credit to your nation and to you as a worthy consort."

"You are worthy and I do not release you," he said in a hard voice. He drew a breath, seeking patience. "You are tired and distraught tonight. We will talk more of this tomorrow, *without* an audience." He flashed Sigrid a quick glare, wishing her from the room. Wishing she had never come into the library tonight and that he had never spoken to her.

Looking remarkably shamefaced, Sigrid moved toward the door and out of the room.

He forgot her the second he looked back at Ariadne, but she would not meet his gaze.

"There is nothing to say," she told him. "I will not be married because you gave your word and feel you must do your duty."

"Arie—"

Reaching out, she grasped his hand and pressed the ring into it. "Rupert, I do not want to marry you. I cannot be plainer than that. We had an enjoyable time together and I thank you for the most . . . entertaining and instructive lessons, but now it's over. We are at an end. You owe me nothing."

He ground his teeth together, fighting the urge to drag her into his arms and shake her. Either that or kiss her, crush his mouth to hers until she took back every word she'd just said and begged his forgiveness.

She doesn't want to marry me, does she?

He should be glad, shouldn't he? He could make a far more advantageous marriage elsewhere. So why wasn't he relieved? Why did his ribs ache as if she'd just stuck a knife between them, then given it a twist?

But he didn't care what she wanted. He desired her and by God, he was going to have her. He'd decided to marry her and so they would marry, and damn whatever misery came after.

"It is unfortunate, Princess, that you feel as you do. The marriage will go forward regardless."

"But—," she gasped.

"And you will wear this, as my intended." Grabbing her hand, he pushed the ring back in place.

"It is late and we both need to get some rest," he said coldly. "Shall I escort you to your room or can you find your own way?"

She looked stricken, her eyes very green and filled with some emotion he couldn't quite fathom. "I shall return on my own," she said in a dull voice.

"Then I bid you good night."

With a nod, she turned and was gone.

Rupert strode into the breakfast room the following morning, hoping he would find Ariadne already seated at the table. Instead, there was only his cousin—the one who'd been so displeased with Ariadne's whist playing the night before—and his brother-in-law Dominic.

Emma apparently had chosen to remain abed, and Sigrid never left her room before noon. Obviously, Ariadne was taking a tray in her bedchamber this morning too.

Well, she could try avoiding him, but it wouldn't serve for long.

He would see to that.

He instructed his majordomo to send word to Princess Ariadne that she was to attend him in the family drawing room at half past eleven. He would not brook a refusal.

The servant gave a crisp bow and left to deliver the message.

That bit of business completed, Rupert went to the buffet, made his selections, then took a seat at the table. He and the other men made little conversation, content to read their newspapers and dwell on their own private thoughts. His were all for Ariadne and what had happened in the library last night.

It was pure bad luck she'd overheard him talking to Sigrid. If only his sister knew how to mind her own business. If only Ariadne had not come back downstairs to get a book.

But she had and she'd heard.

Then again, she'd always known he wanted to protect her and her reputation. What did it matter that he'd never made her a proper proposal of marriage? That first night together when he'd made her fully his own had been as good to him as sealing their vows. Besides, he hadn't wanted to give her a chance to refuse him.

And yet she still had.

I do not want to marry you . . .

Even now her words had the power to wound him. But he would find a way to change her mind and smooth over the rest. As for the supposed disapproval from members of his court, well, they could just learn to approve of their new queen or suffer his royal displeasure. Ministers and functionaries could always be replaced.

His cousin finished his meal, then excused himself, explaining that he planned to go for a ride through the royal woodland park, maybe hunt some game.

Dominic looked up as the younger man left the room, then folded his newspaper and laid it aside. "Rupert, there is something I feel I should tell you."

Rupert lifted an eyebrow and set his own paper aside. "Oh? And what is that?"

"Well, you see, this morning— "

A quiet knock sounded at the door and the butler stepped inside. "Pardon me. I am sorry to intrude, but I did not think this should wait."

"Yes? What is it, Mueller?" Rupert turned inquiringly toward the servant.

"I went to the princess's rooms to deliver your message, Your Majesty. I spoke with her maid."

"And?"

The older man straightened his already ramrod-straight spine. "And I was informed that Princess Ariadne departed the palace this morning."

"Departed? What do you mean by that? Where did she go? Did her maid say when she would return?"

"I was told that she does not plan to return. She ordered a coach early this morning and left word that she is returning to England."

"What?" Rupert shot to his feet, panic burning like acid in his veins. "Who gave permission for her to take a coach of any kind? And why was I not informed of this earlier?"

The butler's skin drained of color. "I did not realize she had gone or that you might wish to know immediately—"

"Well, I did. What in God's name were they thinking in the stables to let her leave like that? A woman cannot be permitted to make such a long and arduous journey on her own. Whoever it is who put her in that coach is to be found and escorted from the palace within the hour."

"Then I suppose I shall have to pack my bags," Dominic said from where he sat at the far side of the table.

Rupert's head shot around and he pinned him with a look. "What? What did you say?"

"I was about to tell you something, if you recall, when Mueller interrupted us. What I was going to say is that Ariadne left this morning."

"And you knew this how?"

"Because I am the one who put her in the coach. But she didn't go alone. I sent a man with her. Goldfinch. He's one of my former crew and not only able-bodied but highly trustworthy."

"Mueller, you may go," Rupert told the servant in a quiet aside.

The butler bowed, clearly relieved to be dismissed, and hurried from the room.

Rupert took a moment to collect himself before once again addressing his brother-in-law. "And why would you do this? Why would you let her leave?"

"Because she asked me to. Because she said she couldn't

bear to stay here another day and that if I didn't help her, she would go on her own. You know how she is. I thought it best to at least provide her with some protection."

Yes, I know exactly how she is. But how could she do it? How could she leave without so much as a word?

"I shall go after her," Rupert said, his voice sounding strained even to his own ears. "She can't have gotten too far."

Dominic had the grace to look regretful. "She knew you'd try to follow her and asked me to tell you not to. She said there's nothing further to talk about and that whatever you might have to say won't change her mind. She . . . um . . . also asked me to give you something."

"Did she?" he said dully.

A heaviness settled over Rupert's chest, a suffocating pressure that made him wonder if that was how it felt to drown, as if he'd been pushed into an icy lake and held under.

Dominic reached into his waistcoat pocket and withdrew something green and shiny.

The engagement ring.

She had returned it, this time for good it would seem.

The other man walked toward him and laid the jewelry on the table within his reach. "I am sorry. I did try to talk her out of going. She said to tell you good-bye and that she wishes you every happiness."

Every happiness?

He knew he would be many things in the years to come, but he was quite sure that happy would not be one of them. Wordlessly, he closed his hand over the ring, squeezing the stone and metal against his palm until it hurt.

"Will you go after her anyway?" Dominic asked after a long minute.

He could. He could drag her back and force her to do as he wished. He could bind her to him in all the ways the law would allow. But she would hate him for it. Without her willing consent, she would never truly be his. Without her love, his life would be meaningless.

Love?

How ironic that only now, when she'd deserted him, when he knew it was too late, did he realize what he'd lost.

Realize that he hadn't been honest with his sister last night.

That he loved Ariadne and would give anything, even his kingdom, to have her back.

"No," he said in an emotionless voice. "She told me last night she doesn't want to marry me. She wanted to go, so I shall let her." A wry smile curved his mouth. "She never was the sort who could live in a cage, not even a gilded one. I guess I shall have to let her go free."

Chapter Thirty

"**A**riadne! You're here!" Princess Mercedes of Alden, Lady MacKinnon, hurried across Castle MacKinnon's cozy family drawing room as quickly as her six-months-pregnant figure would allow. Arms stretched wide, she enveloped her friend in a fierce hug. "Oh, it's so good to see you. We had your letter, of course, but didn't know exactly when you would arrive."

"It's been a long journey," Ariadne said in a low voice. "I am so glad to be here in Skye at last."

And she was.

Despite Mr. Goldfinch's excellent care of her and the consideration he'd shown during the trip north to Scotland, she had still found the past few weeks grueling in a way she never had before.

From the moment she'd fled Neuewaldstein Castle on that final morning, a hollow emptiness had engulfed her, as if she'd left some vital piece of herself behind.

And she supposed she had.

After all, didn't one need a heart?

She ached during the day. As for the nights . . . oh, the nights were the very worst of all. She couldn't bear to even think of those.

But she was here with friends again in comforting, familiar surroundings, where there would be no reminders of him. He had never been to Daniel and Mercedes's home in Scotland, so she wouldn't have to worry about seeing him everywhere she went, remembering, as she would have done in any of Emma and Nick's homes.

Nick had been so kind to her when she'd told him she needed to leave. And Emma had understood, even as she'd begged her to stay.

But leaving had been the right thing to do—the only option under the circumstances.

Now that she was here, she would have to find the will to survive, the strength to heal. She just wasn't quite sure how to begin. She'd thought nothing could be worse than the death of her family, that she would never again know such total desolation. Yet without Rupert she felt utterly lost, adrift in a way that was nearly unbearable.

Some of her thoughts must have shown on her face.

Mercedes took her hand and led her to the sofa, where they sank down next to each other. "Tell me everything."

A hard lump swelled in her throat and she shook her head. "I can't."

"When you're ready, then. We have time," Mercedes said with infinite understanding. "Lots of it with winter approaching. It will be lovely having you here for the baby's birth."

Ariadne's gaze fell to her friend's rounded belly, swollen with child.

She wished suddenly, irrationally, that she had conceived. Then she would have something of Rupert, a living piece of him that would welcome her love. The love she knew he did not return, that he would never want.

Oh, God, how could their affair—something that was supposed to have been just a bit of lighthearted fun—have led to such bitter heartache? He'd been right from the start. She had been too naive to know what she was risking. She hadn't understood how high a price she would have to pay.

And suddenly, the tears she'd held back all these weeks, the tears that had refused to come even in the darkest night, burned hot and wet in her eyes.

On a muffled sob, she launched herself into Mercedes's arms and let them fall.

Rupert listened with half an ear to his private secretary as the man read out a list of business items requiring attention. His gaze wandered, watching the snow as it fell in blowing swirls outside his office window. By evening, the palace grounds would be draped in a thick blanket of winter white, just right for sleigh riding.

He would have loved to take Ariadne. He could imagine her pretty cheeks flushed pink, her green eyes flashing with excitement as the two of them sped across the snowy fields. But she would be warm and safe, bundled up in furs and soft blankets, laughing as he bent to—

Abruptly, he cut off the daydream.

What am I doing, thinking about her again? There would be no sleigh rides, just as there was no Ariadne. Four months had passed since that dreadful day when she'd left. Four months during which he'd had time to get used to the idea that she was gone from his life forever.

If only he could put her out of his thoughts once and for all. If only he could rid himself of his memories, when she came to him at night in dreams and left him reaching for her when he awakened alone in his bed.

What he ought to do was take a mistress and slake his frustrated passions on her. He'd even gone to the bother of setting up a flirtation with a receptive widow here in the court. But on the evening when matters should have progressed to his bed, he'd looked into the woman's plain brown eyes and wanted to see leaf green ones instead. And when he'd touched his mouth to her oh-so-willing one, he'd felt nothing.

No desire at all.

There was only one woman he wanted, and she had refused him in the most explicit manner possible.

She had given him back his ring and left.

Ariadne was in his past. He needed to remember that and move on. His ministers were quietly hinting at him again to select a bride, and he supposed he should. But he had no stomach for putting up with some simpering gaggle of girls, certainly none of the ones who had been paraded before him at his father's funeral last autumn.

Luckily he had the excuse of being in mourning to put them off. He would use it for a while longer.

In the meantime, he would work harder to extinguish the last of his emotions for Ariadne.

I shall banish her from my mind. And even more so, from my heart, once and for all.

"Do you not agree, Your Majesty?"

Rupert glanced at his private secretary, having heard not so much as a word the man had been saying. "What?"

"The arrangements for the coronation. Will you be wanting to personally review the guest list before the invitations are issued or shall we follow the traditional protocol?"

Rupert scowled.

The coronation again. It was months away yet, scheduled to take place in the coming summer, when dignitaries from all over Europe and beyond would be able to comfortably make the journey. He knew there was a great deal of planning to be done, but right now he could summon no interest in the matter.

"I have not yet decided," he stated.

"Yes, but the grand chamberlain said he—"

"I do not care what the grand chamberlain may have had to say on the subject," he snapped. "I will make a decision when I am ready and not a moment before. Is that understood?"

His secretary grew instantly silent, then nodded. "Of course, Your Majesty. Your pardon if I was too insistent. I clearly must have spoken out of turn."

But he had not, and Rupert knew that if anyone should apologize, it was he. His temper was unusually volatile of late, and his household had begun being especially cautious around him for fear he would lash out at them with the wrong side of his tongue or worse.

He'd dismissed one of his father's old retainers three weeks ago for bringing him shaving water that was too hot. He'd made amends later, giving the old man a generous pension, but the damage had been done.

He stifled a sigh and worked to moderate his tone. "Is there anything else this morning?"

"No. Only the correspondence. I have reviewed and organized it for your attention, everything except a letter from your sister, the archduchess, that is. I have it here."

The younger man passed him the stack of mail, along with a single unopened missive written on elegant cream-colored vellum.

So Emma had written him again.

She, Dominic, and the children were back in England, busy passing the winter at their country estate, Lynd Park. Last he'd heard, Ariadne was not with them but in Scotland with Princess Mercedes and her family, where she had been since the autumn.

But what did he care? He wasn't going to think about her anymore.

"Thank you," he told the other man. "That will be all for now."

His secretary bowed, gathered a few belongings, then left the room, closing the door behind him.

Rupert watched the snow for a long minute, then reached for the letter.

She spoke mostly of the Christmas celebration just past and how she wished he might have joined them, but understood that he could not get away easily. She relayed news of his nephews' latest antics, a boat race Dominic was organizing for late spring, and her good health concerning her pregnancy.

It was on this last score that he came to full attention.

I had a note only the other day from Mercedes, who was just recently delivered of a strapping baby boy. She had an easy time in childbed. One can only hope the same will hold true for Ariadne when that day comes for her.

When that day comes for her? What in the blazes was that supposed to mean?

Ariadne wasn't pregnant and she certainly wasn't about to give birth in the near future. So what could Emma possibly mean?

Unless she was trying to tell him something.

Unless . . .

He felt the color drain out of his face.

Unless she is pregnant, and with my child!

Chapter Thirty-one

Ariadne snuggled deeper into her chair and stretched her slippered toes toward the toasty fire that blazed in the drawing room's wide stone hearth.

Outside, the late February air was cold and damp, the winds that blew in off the Atlantic whistling around the castle walls in steady gusts that would have shaken a lesser building to its rafters. But they were all safe and warm and comfortable inside, the castle's formerly drafty interior pleasantly snug now due to Daniel MacKinnon's extensive, and most excellent, improvements to what had not long ago been a crumbling ruin.

Still, no matter how cozy she might be at the moment, tucked away with a book, a blanket across her lap, and a mug of hot cider, Ariadne knew she could not hide here with her friends forever. When spring arrived and the land turned green once more, she would have to make some decisions.

Maybe she would take a house in Italy or Greece for a few months. She'd been told the sunshine in such climes could chase away even the worst kinds of doldrums. If only the idea brought her some measure of excitement. But try as she might, nothing seemed to cheer her of late; not even Mercedes and Daniel's adorable children could rouse more than a wan smile.

Back at the end of September, her twenty-fifth birthday had arrived at long last, and with it possession of her full inheritance.

She was an independent woman now; she could do whatever she liked, go anywhere her fancy might take her.

Yet what had brought her such anticipatory joy only a few months earlier no longer had the power to excite her. Once she had dreamed of traveling the world and making her mark as a notorious adventuress, but the thrill over such plans had gone.

The whole notion bored her now.

As for finding a new lover, the idea left her ice-cold. She couldn't imagine inviting another man into her bed, not after Rupert. Anyone else would be a poor second, and she'd never been the sort of woman who was willing to settle for imitations. She'd given him her innocence and in turn he'd stolen her heart. She had nothing left to give anymore.

I wonder what he is doing?

Probably choosing a proper bride with lofty connections and a dowry that would line Rosewald's coffers with gold for the next millennium.

Scowling, she forced herself to return to her reading, pushing her spectacles higher onto her nose so she could clearly see the page.

A soft knock sounded at the door about ten minutes later. The butler came inside. "Excuse me, Your Highness, but a visitor has arrived."

Ariadne lowered her book. "A visitor? In this weather?"

Not to mention at this time of year. Daniel and Mercedes didn't receive many calls during the winter, not even from their neighbors, who had far too much sense to venture out on raw, blustery days like this one.

"Whoever it is must be here to see the major or Princess Mercedes. Did you put them in the drawing room?"

"I did. However, the gentleman asked specifically for you."

"For me?" she repeated, confused. "But who would call on me here?"

"I would," said a deep, silvery voice she had thought never to hear again. "Hello, Ariadne."

Her gaze flew to Rupert, her heart beating like a trapped bird as she drank in the sight of him.

He stood on the threshold, looking tall and magnificent and every inch a king. His golden hair was windblown, his cheeks ruddy from the elements through which he had so recently traveled. Had he come on horseback? The roads were notoriously slick this time of year; she wasn't sure a coach could even make the trip.

Without waiting for her permission, he strode deeper into the room.

She gave a nod to the servant, dismissing him. When she looked again at Rupert, he was staring at her, his eyes raking her body with curious intensity.

She crossed her arms. "What are you doing here? Did Mercedes or Daniel know you might be arriving? No one mentioned to me that you were expected."

Yes, why has he come? she wondered, her pulse racing as she considered the possibilities. She could think of only one reason that made any sense and yet it seemed much too good to be true.

Could it be that he had missed her?

Could it be that he had come here for her?

"They did not know I was en route," he told her. "I traveled quickly, sailing most of the way, and made the journey as fast, or faster, than a message could have been sent. But why waste our time exchanging useless niceties? You must know why I am here."

Again, his gaze fell to her lap and he stared hard at the blanket covering her, as if he were puzzling out some mystery he couldn't quite solve.

An answering frown settled across her forehead. "No, I am afraid I do not. You shall have to make it plainer."

Without warning, he stalked forward. "Do not dissemble with me, Ariadne. I had Emma's letter. I know that you lied to me."

"Lied? About what?"

"Remove that blanket and quit hiding."

"Hiding? You make no sense."

"Fine. I shall do it for you." Reaching out, he yanked the thick plaid up and away.

Rupert stared, prepared to find her belly round and heavy with his child. Instead, her figure was trim and slender, perhaps even a bit thinner than the last time he'd seen her.

Maybe she was one of those women who barely showed, even late in the pregnancy.

She rose from her chair and despite the new angle, he still couldn't find so much as a curve. Her stomach was as flat as ever.

"I thought there would be some visible sign of the child by now," he said.

"What child?" she demanded, her eyebrows arching.

He ignored her perplexed expression, reminding himself that she had deceived him. "The one you are carrying. Unless I miscalculated the date of conception, you ought to be about seven months along and displaying evidence of your impending maternity."

Though how he could have miscalculated he did not

know. They'd been fully intimate for only a short time late last summer; it narrowed the timing down considerably.

Her mouth fell open for a moment before she snapped it shut again. She crossed her arms over her chest. "So that is why you are here? Because you believe I am with child?"

"Clearly."

"And how does Emma factor into this?" she questioned. "You say she wrote to you?"

"As you ought to have done," he added, unable to keep the accusation from his voice. "How could you have lied to me like this? How could you have thought to keep my own son from me? My heir?"

All animation drained from her expression; then her chin came up at a dangerous tilt. "So that is what you think of me, is it? That I would be so low as to try to conceal a pregnancy and keep a baby from you?"

He raked his fingers through his hair. "What else am I to believe under the circumstances? Is that why you ran away? Because you thought I would not want our child?"

"I *ran away*, as you call it, because I refused to be forced to wed out of some misguided sense of honor. As for *your son*, assuming it would even be a son, I am afraid I must disappoint you on that score. There is no baby. I told you in Rosewald that I had not conceived and I have not. I am not with child."

His fingers clenched at his sides. "But Emma—"

"Said exactly what? Did she actually tell you I am enceinte?"

"Not in so many words."

"Then how, precisely?"

He cast his mind back, searching his memory for the wording. What had she said again? Something to the effect that she hoped Ariadne had an easy time in childbed when her time came. He supposed Ariadne was right; Emma had not come straight out and said Ariadne was pregnant. She'd simply insinuated, even though Emma wasn't generally the type to insinuate anything.

His gaze locked with Ariadne's.

Blazes! I've been duped! And by my little sister, no less.

"Exactly," Ariadne said, clearly reading on his face the conclusion he'd drawn.

"But why?"

"I can only presume that Emma wanted to play matchmaker. Even though I have told her our engagement was never real in a romantic sense, she has some misguided notion that we are in love. No doubt she thought if she got you to come chasing up here after me, we would talk and fall into each other's arms again, happy evermore."

She shrugged and looked away. "But all she has done is upset and inconvenience us both. You in particular. I am sorry that you traveled such a very long way for nothing. At least you can rest easy now that you know I am not with child."

His shoulders sank, an unmistakable sense of disappointment sweeping through him. Had he wanted Ariadne to be pregnant? He realized now that he had. He realized too that for all his anger over her supposed deception, he'd been exultant, knowing he would have a reason to bind her to him again.

But without a baby, there was nothing.

A dreadful bleakness spread through him, a sensation akin to death.

He'd come here prepared to take her home with him. Was he really going to leave without her? Was he truly about to let her go . . . forever?

Ariadne turned her back, unable to bear looking at him for another minute. It was killing her being so close yet knowing he had come only for the child he'd believed she carried. He didn't want her; he wanted his heir. He would have married her, of course, but out of duty again.

Always duty.

How could Emma have done this to her? And if she wasn't mistaken, Mercedes as well. She could well imagine the two of them conspiring behind her back, convinced that Rupert felt much more than he actually did. But they were mistaken, tragically so, their interference nothing more than wishful thinking.

"I cannot imagine what is keeping Mercedes, or Daniel either." To her consternation, her voice sounded high and oddly strained. "I'll ring for a servant to fetch them."

She started to move away, but he reached out and caught hold of her wrist.

"Don't," he said. "Not yet. We've barely had a chance to say hello."

Hello? He wants to be civil now, does he?

Still, she didn't pull away, her wrist lax within his grip. "I thought you didn't care to waste time on niceties," she said with undisguised sarcasm.

"Forgive me for that. My temper has been short of late."

"I imagine so, what with you thinking you had fathered an out-of-wedlock child with me. You must be greatly relieved."

He was silent for a long moment. "Actually, I am not."

Surprised, she turned and looked up at him.

He stepped closer. "I was angry, of course, when I believed you hadn't told me that you were expecting, but I never minded the idea of you carrying my baby."

"So you wouldn't have been upset having to bring home a bride you'd married over the anvil and a newborn baby who clearly had been conceived months before? Assuming, of course, that I had agreed to marry you at all."

His grip on her wrist tightened. "Oh, you would have married me."

"Would I? I am an independent woman now. I have plans. I am trying to decide between taking a villa in Italy or renting a whitewashed house by the Aegean Sea in Greece. They both sound delightful."

"And will that make you happy? Living in such hot climes?"

"I cannot see why it wouldn't," she said, hoping her lie sounded more convincing to him than it did to herself.

"You won't get lonely? Or are you planning to take a companion with you?"

She frowned. That was one part of her plan that had never set well with her. "I am sure I shall meet any number of interesting people. I won't have time to grow lonely."

"How about at night?" he drawled. "I know how restless you are without a man in your bed."

He was right. She was restless and hadn't enjoyed a truly good night's sleep since the last night she'd spent with him.

But why was he saying these things? What was his purpose?

"Maybe I will find someone new," she said, just to taunt him. "A swarthy Latin lover. They say such men have a streak of wild passion in them."

With a slight tug, he pulled her against him. "I think you are much more suited to blonds." He pressed a kiss against her jaw, making her skin tingle. "Besides, you already have a lover."

"No, I don't. You ceased being able to call yourself that months ago. You don't want me. You made that quite plain the last time we spoke."

"I don't recall saying anything of the sort."

"Then you have a faulty memory. I practically begged you to come to my room and yet you turned me away. You didn't want me then and you don't want me now. Cease this game, or whatever it may be."

"It's no game, and you are very much mistaken if you think I do not want you. Either then or now. I can see I handled matters badly before. Rather than worrying about your reputation, I should have tumbled you straight into bed the moment you arrived in Rosewald and bound you to me with a child. A real child."

As if to emphasize his point, he splayed his palm over her buttocks and pulled her flush against him, so tight that she felt his growing erection. "In fact, I think I'll use this time in Scotland to do just that. I can always claim I'm snowed in and cannot return home just yet."

He brushed his mouth over her cheek, then across her temple. "Once you're well and truly enceinte, then I'll take you back to Rosewald with me. Oh, and we'll get married here in Scotland. We don't even need the license I procured."

"Married? But you don't want to marry me—not really. This is just about your duty and your pride again. I won't be wed out of obligation!"

He looked her squarely in the eyes. "Then what *will* you be married for, Ariadne, since I cannot seem to do without you? I've been miserable since you left. Unbearable, if truth be told, terrorizing my court and making my servants turn pale every time I walk into a room. What do I need to do? What will it take for you to accept my pledge and promise to be mine from this day forward?"

She felt her heart skip a beat, then a second—unable to believe what she was hearing. "But I don't understand. You don't love me. I heard you say you didn't that night in the library with Sigrid."

He grimaced, his face awash with regret. "If only I could go back and erase that night, I would. But you're wrong, you know. I never said I didn't love you. If you'll recall, I asked her if I looked like the sort of man who would marry for love. You and Sigrid just assumed you knew the answer."

"But you *aren't* the sort of man to marry for love."

"You mean I *wasn't* the sort." He brushed his fingers tenderly over her cheek. "I didn't know what it was to love until I took the blinders off my eyes and truly saw you, Ariadne. Why else would I have sailed through dangerous, storm-tossed seas in the dead of winter? Why else would I have left my kingdom and raced halfway across Europe except for you?"

"The baby . . . the one you thought I was going to have."

"The one that gave me just the excuse I needed to come after you." He gave a half smile. "Emma may have gone beyond the bounds with that letter of hers, but she knew what I needed. She knew that I love you and that I'll never be happy unless I can make you my queen."

Something shattered inside her, as if her heart had been encased in stone and he'd just chiseled it free.

"Oh, Rupert." She took a gasping breath, tears streaming without warning down her cheeks.

"Oh, God, don't cry," he pleaded, his eyes tormented. "Please, darling, don't be sad. Maybe I shouldn't have spoken, but I had to try. I know you have your plans, that you want to travel. Can you trust me to find some way to make things work? I swear I will. Just don't push me away again. Please don't make me go away."

He pressed his mouth to hers and kissed her with an ardor and desperation she had never thought she'd feel from him again.

Is this real? Or am I dreaming?

Suddenly nothing made sense, but whatever fantasy it was that she'd fallen into, she didn't want it to end. And so she let him kiss her, let him take her mouth with one heady, feverish embrace after another.

"You wanted me once," he murmured breathlessly. "Give me another chance. I know I can make you want me again."

"I don't have to give you another chance," she said.

He stiffened under her hands, but she soothed him with a palm against his cheek. "I don't have to because I've never stopped wanting you. And I wasn't crying because I was sad. Don't you see? It's because I love you too. Have loved you for a long time now. I just never dreamed you might feel the same."

His arms tightened around her, his eyes turning a brilliant blue. "You love me?"

"Yes." She nodded, smiling. "More than you'll ever know." She twined her arms around his neck. "And I don't care about traveling. I only said that about Italy and Greece so you wouldn't know how miserable I've been. I still have some pride left, you know."

He laughed. "Well, you are destined to be a queen." He kissed her hard, sealing a vow. "*My queen.* Tell me now that you'll marry me."

"You're sure you don't want a more advantageous bride? Someone who will benefit your court and your country? Sigrid was right about that, you know. Objectively speaking, you could do far better than me."

"I was arrogant enough once to think that practical considerations were all that mattered, but sometimes the heart is wiser than the head. As for doing better, there is no one better for me than you. I choose you as my consort, and anyone who objects can go to blazes."

A weight seemed to lift from her shoulders as she realized that he truly did love her.

"Ask me properly, then," she said gently.

He studied her for a long moment, then released her and dropped to one knee. Solemnly, he took her hand and gazed up into her eyes. "Princess Ariadne of Nordenbourg, will you do me the very great honor of becoming my wife?"

A radiant smile spread across her face. "*Yes!* Yes, Rupert, my dearest love."

And suddenly he was standing and she was in his arms again, held tight as he crushed his mouth to hers. She closed her eyes and kissed him back, aglow in the knowledge that she would never have to leave his arms again.

He fit her closer still and was just starting to carry her across to a small sofa on the far side of the room, when a knock came at the door. Before either of them had time to draw apart, Mercedes came into the room, followed by her husband.

Mercedes was grinning, her eyes alight with obvious satisfaction. "See?" she said over her shoulder to Daniel. "I told you all that silence was a good sign."

Daniel's mouth twisted in a sardonic smile. "And I told you, love, that they had no wish tae be disturbed whatever might be transpirin' inside. A pardon to you both, but there was no restrainin' her."

Mercedes ignored the remark and looked at Ariadne, then at Rupert—who had tucked Ariadne against his side—then back to Ariadne again. "Well? Did it work? Are you engaged again?"

Ariadne nodded her head. "Yes, we are. For good this time. But you needn't look so smug about it."

Mercedes's brown eyes sparkled and she clapped her hands in delight.

"I knew I saw your hand in that letter of Emma's once Rupert told me about it," Ariadne scolded. "You two had no right to interfere, you know."

"But you interfered on our behalf when Emma and I both needed a push in the right direction," Mercedes returned. "We want you to be happy and so we thought it only fair that we return the favor. I could see how miserable you were without Rupert, and Emma knew he was sad and pining for you as well. So we thought we would give you both a little nudge."

"By telling him I was expecting his child?"

Daniel's auburn brows went skyward and he shot Mercedes a look. "Good God, woman, is that what you told him? No wonder King Rupert nearly froze himself to death racing up here. He probably near had heart failure tae boot!"

"It did the job, did it not?" Mercedes replied without an ounce of remorse. "Emma will be so pleased when she hears the news."

"When I see her, she'll hear a great deal more," Ariadne threatened.

Mercedes's smile diminished slightly. "You're not *really* angry, are you? You and Rupert have made up your differences, so all is well in the end."

And though she knew she ought to be cross, Ariadne couldn't muster even the slightest twinge of outrage.

"No, I'm not really angry," Ariadne admitted. She tipped her head back and gazed up into Rupert's eyes, seeing her own feelings of joy reflected back. "How can I be when I'm with the man I love once again?"

Rupert smiled. "And I can only express my gratitude, Mercedes. You and my sister have done what no one else could have. You got two proud, stubborn people to humble themselves and admit to what they could not live without— each other."

Then he bent and pressed his lips to Ariadne's, much to her great delight.

Almost instantly, she forgot about their audience, far too enraptured by the heady passion of Rupert's kiss to think of anything but him.

She was sliding her arms around his neck again when she became dimly aware of a pronounced bout of throat clearing coming from a short distance away.

"Shall we leave the two of you tae yerselves," Daniel remarked, his voice warm with laughter, "or would ye care to continue this in one of the bedchambers? We've several from which you can choose, and of course, Ariadne already has a bedroom of her own."

"Daniel, of all the things to say!" Mercedes admonished. "They aren't even yet married."

Unchastened, Daniel laughed. "That hasn't seemed to stop them so far."

Fairly caught, Rupert broke their kiss. His and Ariadne's eyes met and suddenly they were laughing too.

After a minute, Mercedes joined in.

Rupert kept Ariadne close inside his arms. "So what shall it be?" he asked her. "Shall we kick them out or go upstairs?"

"Or we could have luncheon," Mercedes suggested with a gentle smile. "The moment Cook heard that Rupert had arrived, she sent the kitchen maids into a frenzy. She'll be most put out if we refuse to eat her offerings."

"Luncheon?" Daniel remarked, his eyes alight at the idea. "I could do with a meal."

"You are always ready for a meal," Mercedes remarked indulgently.

Daniel patted his flat stomach. "'Tis what comes from years of soldiering. I ne'er knew when we'd get decent food, so I learned not to pass it up."

"Well, *liebling*?" Rupert gazed down at Ariadne. "What do you say? Which one first, luncheon or love?"

Ariadne sighed. "I suppose it will have to be luncheon, since I've met Mercedes's cook and I don't want to be on her bad side. If we're not careful, she'll serve us haggis."

The others laughed.

A slow smile curved Ariadne's mouth, her heart filled with so much happiness she felt as if it had swelled to twice its normal size. "Besides, what will a small delay hurt, when we have a lifetime ahead of us to love each other?"

"You're right, my dearest. This is only the start of our forever," Rupert said.

Then he leaned down and sealed their future with a kiss.

"**Y**ou no-good, low-down, scurvy dog!"

The door to Zack Douglas's office flew back on its hinges, striking the wall with explosive force. Madelyn Grayson stood framed in the entrance, hands on her hips, her blue eyes bright with rage.

Zack looked up from the storyboard he'd been making changes to and arched one dark eyebrow.

"You self-serving piece of scum!" she continued. "You underhanded bottom-feeder! You trough-dwelling, swill-eating pig!"

Zack leaned back casually in his leather executive chair and let her insults run off him, harmless as rain. "Good afternoon to you too, Maddie."

What a firecracker, he thought, watching her practically crackle with anger as she walked toward him shaking one well-manicured finger his way.

"Don't you dare *good afternoon* me, you lowlife. Not after the stunt you pulled today. You must think you're pretty clever, engineering things the way you did. And don't call me Maddie. The name is Madelyn or Ms. Grayson to you."

Holding back a grin, he took a moment to enjoy the sight of her. She was wearing a plain, pearl gray skirted suit that would have looked dowdy on anyone else, but seemed only to increase her attractiveness. Her breasts rose and fell beneath a long, tidy row of ivory-colored shirt buttons, the effect as sexy as a tight tee on a Hooters girl.

He lifted his eyes so he didn't get caught staring and noticed the wisps of red hair that had come loose from the librarian's bun she always kept it in. He pictured threading his fingers into the whole luxurious mass, popping and pulling at the pins until her hair came free around her shoulders. After that he'd go to work on those shirt buttons . . .

Careful, he warned himself, interrupting the thought. *Don't get distracted.*

"So, Madelyn, what terrible crime have I committed now?"

He was quite familiar with her less than glowing opinion of his character. She didn't approve of him or his reputation, the more titillating particulars of which had spread like a raging viral infection through the office grapevine within hours of his arrival at Fielding and Simmons, one of New York City's leading advertising agencies, some eight months before. Generally he found her reactions amusing. There was nothing quite like watching Madelyn Grayson—all neatly starched, five feet seven inches of her—get completely worked up.

Especially when it was over him.

She glared. "As if you don't know."

"Sorry." He shrugged. "I'm at a loss."

"Stop with the innocent act! What you did was sneaky and conniving, and I deserve an apology."

"I rarely give apologies, and certainly not for wrongs I didn't commit. You'll have to be more specific."

She planted her hands on the edge of his desk. "Specific? You want specific? *Specifically*, it's about your parading that overgrown jock through my fashion event, knowing he would monopolize everyone's attention. It was totally contemptible!"

"Karl Sweeney is a sports superstar. He can't help the way his fans behave."

"Exactly my point. You knew how people would react and deliberately chose that time of day to leave the building."

"If you mean I deliberately chose lunchtime to take a client to lunch, and deliberately decided to walk through the lobby on the way out of the building, then you're right. That's exactly what I did."

"Yes, but you set it up. You timed your exit from the building so you and your basketball star would just happen to meet up with Fielding at the perfect moment. A moment designed to get you an invitation to the executive level for lunch."

His eyes widened. "Is that what I did? Engineered lunch for myself in the executive dining room with our CEO? Whoa, that was genius!" He paused, his eyes moving beyond her for a moment. "You might want to close the door, by the way. We're starting to attract an audience."

Madelyn whirled around and saw one of the copywriters walking ever so slowly by in the corridor. She pinned him with a frosty glare, then shut the door. She turned back to Zack. "Now, you were saying?"

"I wasn't, actually, but look—the meeting with Sweeney ran a lot longer than expected, okay? He insists on providing his own creative input and his agent and I managed to work out an arrangement that keeps us all happy, especially Sweeney. We decided to conclude our discussion over lunch, and couldn't help but notice your fashion show in the lobby on our way out. It's only natural that Sweeney wanted to stop for a closer look."

"Oh, I see," she said sarcastically. "It was all Sweeney's idea."

"Once he got a look at the implants on some of those runway models, I couldn't pull him away."

She crossed her arms defensively over her own very real breasts. "While you, of course, shielded your eyes."

Madelyn was well aware of Zack's penchant for eyeing anything in a skirt, especially a tight one.

"A man can't help but look at what's put right in front of him," he said with a straight face. "Anyway, one thing led to another, Fielding showed up, and you know the rest. There was nothing calculated or premeditated about it. Nice job, by the by, on the campaign you put together for Evan. Very slick. It should double his sales."

"It'll triple his sales. I suppose you expect me to thank you for the compliment now, right?"

He stood, and came around the front of his desk to stand beside her. "Only if you want to. I'm not always the villain you make me out to be. The comment was honestly meant."

Sunlight streamed in through a modest side window, highlighting the strong lines of his jaw, and the beginnings of a five-o'clock shadow. He'd taken off his suit jacket, leaving him in a white shirt and a pair of tailored, charcoal gray pinstripe pants. At thirty-two, he was impossibly handsome, beautiful even, with a smile that could melt ice, and hearts. A woman would have to be dead to be immune to his charms. And Madelyn was very much a living, breathing female, though she did her best not to acknowledge it in his presence.

His kind words left her feeling churlish. She cleared her throat. "The fact remains that you took shameless advantage of the situation."

He leaned against his desk. "If you're talking about the invitation to dine upstairs, what would you have had me do? Refuse Fielding and drag away his favorite sports hero? Just between you and me, I'd like to keep my job.

"Look, Madelyn, you do great work, keep the clients happy, and earn the company a bundle. That's what's important and what everyone will remember. Not the fact that you missed out on lunch in the penthouse."

He lowered his voice as if to share a secret. "To be honest, you're better off. A meal up top is nothing but a lot of dry talk and heavy food." He tapped a fist on the center of his chest, mimicking heartburn. "A little of that French stuff goes a long way."

"Maybe so, but I deserved the chance to decide that for myself. I was entitled to that invitation."

Today was supposed to be my day, not yours. Why was it lately that he was the one receiving all the accolades?

"You're right," Zack agreed. "You were entitled. And likely you would have received it if Larry Roland didn't turn into a quivering puddle every time one of the top brass looks at him for more than two seconds in a row. But that's bosses for you. You'll get another chance; don't worry."

He smiled broadly, flashing her a glimpse of his perfect white teeth. "Are we square now?"

A weak, traitorous need to say yes ran through her. She choked it down.

Square? With Zack Douglas?

Her fiercest competition?

Her chief rival?

The only person who stood between her and the promotion that by rights would have been hers by now if he hadn't come along?

The man who'd been an aggravating thorn in her side from the instant he'd walked through the door?

The man who exuded charisma as if it were fine cologne and didn't mind taking advantage of the fact?

No, she'd never be square with him.

Still, the outrage that had propelled her into his office moments ago had largely evaporated. "I'll consider a truce; it's the best I can offer. A very short, very temporary truce."

"That'll do," he said. Then in a move that surprised them both, he reached out and gave the curl lying against her cheek a gentle tug, his fingers brushing her skin. "For now," he added.

Sensation burned like a line of fire where he'd touched.

"Wha . . . what was that?" she said, stepping quickly back and lifting a hand to tuck the loose hair behind her ear.

"Loose curl," he murmured, meeting her eyes.

"Oh." She took another step away. "Well, I should get back to work."

"We both should. Glad we had a chance to talk this out, Red."

Red? She blinked and opened her mouth to correct him but found herself at a loss for words. She turned and yanked open the door.

Once she'd gone, Zack returned to his chair. What had he been thinking, playing with her hair like that? Touching her? At least he hadn't given in to the impulse to kiss her, an idea that had definitely crossed his mind. But kissing a woman like Madelyn Grayson could have serious repercussions. The sort that might lead to long-term complications a man like him didn't need. God knows, the failure of his one and only marriage years ago had taught him that lesson well. Never let a woman get too close—that was his motto. Enjoy them, appreciate their beauty, then wave good-bye before they have a chance to curl their claws around your heart and squeeze.

But enough of that. He and Madelyn worked together, end of story. Besides, if the rumor mill was right, she was all but engaged to some rich international financier. He'd seen the guy's picture—tall and blond with a perfect toothpaste-ad smile—sitting on her office credenza. According to the other women in the office, blondie was as close to a knight in shining armor as any flesh-and-blood man could get.

He rolled his eyes at the ridiculous notion.

No, he'd done the right thing.

The wise thing.

Especially since he hadn't told her about the Takamuri account. Once Madelyn found out about that she'd be furious, leaving them both back at square one.

Shrugging off what he couldn't change, he picked up his pen and resumed work on his storyboard.

Read on for a sneak peek at the next
historical romance from Tracy Anne Warren,

The Bedding Proposal

Coming soon

London, England
October 1817

I should never have come here tonight, Lady Thalia Lennox
thought as she forced herself not to flinch beneath the
leering stare of Lord Teaksbury. She didn't believe he had
met her eyes once since they had begun conversing.

*Old lecher. How dare he stare at my breasts as if I'm some
doxy selling her wares.* Then again, after nearly six years of
enduring such crude behavior from men of her acquaintance,
one would think she would be well used to it by now.

As for the ladies of the *Ton*, they generally looked through
her as if she were some transparent ghost who had drifted
into their midst. Or, worse, they pointedly turned their backs.
She had grown inured to their snubs—for the most part, at
least.

Still, she had hoped tonight might prove different since her
host, the Marquess of Elmore, had known his own share of
personal pain and tended to acquire friends of a more liberal
and tolerant persuasion. But even here, people saw her not for
the person she was but for who they assumed her to be.

Ordinarily, she tossed aside invitations such as the one for tonight's supper party—not that she received all that many invitations these days. But she supposed the real reason she had come tonight was a simple enough one.

She was lonely.

Her two friends, Jane Frost and Mathilda Cathcart—the only ones out of all her acquaintances who had stuck by her after the divorce—were in the countryside. They had both invited her to join them at their separate estates, but she knew her attendance at the usual autumn house parties would put each woman in an awkward and difficult position. Plus, neither of their husbands approved of their continued association with her, so their friendship was limited to occasional quiet meals when they were in Town and the exchange of letters.

No, she was quite alone and quite lonely.

Ironic, she mused, considering the constant parade of lovers she supposedly entertained—at least according to the gossip mavens and scandal pages that still prattled on about her. Given their reports of her behavior, one would imagine her town house door scarcely ever closed for all the men going in and out—or perhaps it was only her bedroom door that was always in need of oil for the hinges?

Her fingers tightened against the glass of lemonade in her hand as she wondered why she was dwelling on such unpleasantness tonight. Better to put thoughts like those aside since they did nothing but leave the bitter taste of acrimony in her mouth.

A hot bath and a good book—those were what she needed this evening, she decided. Those and to tell the old reprobate still leering at her to take his eyes and his person somewhere else.

If only she hadn't given in to the temptation to wear this red gown, perhaps she wouldn't have ended up being ogled by a loathsome toad like Teaksbury. But she'd always loved the dress, which had been languishing in the back of her wardrobe for ages. And honestly, she was tired of being condemned no matter what she wore or how she behaved. *In for a penny, in for a pound,* she'd thought when she made the selection. Now, however, she wished she'd stuck to her usual somber dark blue or black, no matter how dreary those shades might seem.

Ah well, I shall be leaving shortly, so what does it really matter?

"Why, that's absolutely fascinating," Thalia said with false politeness as she cut Teaksbury off midsentence. "You'll have to excuse me now, my lord. After all, I wouldn't want to be accused of monopolizing your company tonight."

Teaksbury opened his mouth, no doubt to assure her that he didn't mind in the least, but she had already swung around on a flourish of crimson skirts and started walking in the opposite direction.

She'd made it about a quarter of the length of the room when a tall figure suddenly stepped into her path, blocking her exit. She gazed up, then up again, into a boldly masculine face and a pair of green-gold eyes that literally stole the breath from her lungs. The man sent her a dashing, straight-toothed smile, candlelight glinting off the burnished golden brown of his casually brushed hair in a way that only increased his appeal.

Saints above, she thought as her heart knocked hard inside her chest, her pulse leaping as it hadn't leapt in years—if it ever had at all.

Schooling her features so they revealed none of her inner turmoil, she gave him a polite nod. "Pardon me, sir." She waited, expecting him to step aside.

"You know, I don't believe I shall," the man drawled in a velvety rumble that sent tingles chasing over her skin.

Her eyes met his again. "Excuse me? What did you say?"

"That I'm not sure I shall pardon you, or let you go on your way. You're far too lovely not to detain." Smiling again, he executed an elegant bow. "Allow me to introduce myself. I am Lord Leopold Byron. My intimates, however, call me Leo."

Cocky, isn't he? Well, she'd met cocky men many times before.

She gave him a long, cool stare. "Do they? How nice for them. Now, I must insist you step aside. We haven't been properly introduced. As you ought to know, a gentleman never speaks directly to a lady with whom he is not acquainted. Pity one of your intimates isn't here to do the honors. Good evening, my lord."

She took a step to the right.

He matched her move, impeding her path once again. "Shall I go find our host, then?" he asked pleasantly. "I'm sure Elmore would be happy to effect an introduction. Frankly, though, it seems like a great lot of bother, particularly since we are conversing already."

Reaching toward the tray of a passing servant, he picked up two glasses. "Champagne?" he offered. Smiling that devastating smile again, he held out one of the crystal flutes with its golden liquid effervescing inside.

Audacious and arrogant—those were the two best words to describe him. That and handsome in a sinful way no man had a right to be.

Call me Leo indeed.

She didn't know whether to be annoyed or amused, particularly since she was sure part of his strategy in waylaying her was to provoke a strong reaction. Still, she found herself accepting one of the proffered glasses, if for no other reason than to give herself time to steady her nerves.

"As I doubt you'll volunteer your name, not without Elmore's aid at least," Lord Leo continued, "I suppose I must try guessing on my own. Lady Thalia Lennox, is it not? I confess I could not help but recognize you."

"Oh?" she said in a lowering tone, the wine suddenly sour on her tongue.

Of course, she realized, she ought to have known that he

was only playing games and knew her by reputation. Every-one in the *Ton* did, it seemed—even if they wouldn't associ-ate with her any longer. "Then you have me at even more of a disadvantage than I realized, my lord."

"Not at all, since we have only just met and need time to learn about each other."

"I am sure you've heard all you need to know about me. Divorce trials will do that for a woman. Now, if you'll—"

"If you're concerned that I mind a bit of scandal, I don't. I've weathered a few of them myself over the years, so such matters make no difference to me."

He'd been embroiled in scandals, had he? Vaguely she remembered mention of various members of the Byron fam-ily being involved in deeds that had shocked Society at one time or another. But none of their acts had made any of the Byrons outcasts. And being that Lord Leo was a man, the *Ton* was, of course, more apt to forgive, no matter how serious the trespasses might have been.

As for his *over the years* remark, he didn't look old enough to have weathered all that many scandals. In fact, just how old was he? Or maybe she should say *how young*?

Now that she looked more closely, she couldn't help but notice his youthfully lithe physique and unlined counte-nance. He was a man of confident maturity, of that there was no question, yet she sensed that the full height of his power, his male prime, as it were, still lay ahead of him.

Good heavens, is he even thirty?

Suddenly she knew he was not, a realization that was just this side of appalling, considering the fact that her thirty-second birthday was due to arrive next month.

She knew she needed to leave now more than ever. "It has been . . . interesting meeting you, Lord Leopold, but I really must be going."

"Why? The evening is early yet. Surely you can remain a while longer?"

"Truly, I cannot," she said.

He gave her a shrewd look, as if he saw right through her excuses. "Afraid you might enjoy yourself? Or are you worried I'm going to stare down your dress like Teaksbury?"

Her mouth dropped open before she could recall herself.

"It was rather hard to miss that crass display of his," Lord Leo remarked. "The man's a boor. It's a wonder he wasn't actually drooling on you. Not that I can entirely blame him, given your irresistible feminine charms. Still, were I to feast my eyes upon you, I promise it would leave you in no doubt of my sincere admiration."

Slowly his gaze dipped down, moving gradually over her body in way that felt almost like a caress.

She shivered inwardly.

When he met her eyes again, his own were alight with unrepentant desire. "You are the most exquisite woman I have ever beheld. Even a god would find himself tempted by you."

A hot flush burst over her skin, shocking her with its force. Only barely did she resist the urge to reach up and cover her hot cheeks with her hands. The sensation was truly singular, considering she hadn't blushed since her girlhood and her first London Season.

Experienced women did *not* blush.

Yet this outrageous young lord with his heart-stopping smile and velvety voice roused emotions in her that she hadn't realized she still possessed. He made her feel in ways she hadn't felt for years, stirring cravings she'd buried long ago and had no wish to resurrect.

"Now," he said, his voice husky, "why don't we go somewhere private so we can get even better acquainted? Your town house perhaps? Once we're alone, I want you to call me Leo. As I said before, all my intimates do."

All his bedmates, he meant, his intentions clear.

Without even knowing what she was doing, she flung the contents of her glass up into his face, causing champagne to splash everywhere.

He blinked wine out of his eyes, a surprised expression on his dripping face.

"You and I shall *never* be intimates. Good night, *my lord*."

Spinning around, she marched toward the door.

As she did so, she caught sight of a man standing across the room—a man she would have thought was Leopold Byron had she not known he was still dripping somewhere behind her. Her step wobbled slightly as her mind worked to figure out the unexpected anomaly.

Twins? Good God, are there two of him?

And his brother was laughing, making no effort at all to contain his amusement.

Well, let him laugh.

As for the rest of the guests whose stares pierced her from all directions, she was used to such scrutiny.

The entire incident would be in tomorrow's papers, of course. *But what do I care?* Tossing champagne into a man's face was nothing, not compared to what she'd been through already. For when you've known the worst, the rest is naught but a trifle.

Leo withdrew a silk handkerchief from his waistcoat pocket and dried his face as he watched Thalia Lennox disappear from view with a final flourish of her red skirts.

Lawrence appeared at his side moments later, his grin so wide it was a wonder it didn't split his cheeks.

"Well, that went swimmingly," Lawrence said with a hearty chuckle. "Had her eating right out of the palm of your hand, at least until she decided to give you a champagne bath!" He laughed again. "You owe me twenty quid. Pay up."

"I will when we get home." Leo wiped briefly at his sodden cravat before giving up.

"What on earth did you say to her anyway? I knew she'd rebuff you, but not with quite so much enthusiasm."

Somewhat begrudgingly, Leo provided him with a brief recounting.

Lawrence erupted into fresh gales of laughter, so loudly that the outburst drew every eye.

"Oh, do shut up, won't you?" Leo told his brother. "I think there might be one scullery maid in the kitchen who hasn't heard you."

Rubbing moisture from the corners of his eyes, Lawrence did his best to silence his mirth, though his lips continued to twitch. "My condolences for your loss." He laid a consoling hand on Leo's shoulder. "You know what your trouble is?"

Leo sent him a baleful look. "I'm certain you shall be happy to illuminate me."

"You're too used to being fawned over by women. When was the last time one of them turned you down? You were, what? Fifteen?"

"Thirteen," Leo countered, unable to repress a grin. "Remember that gorgeous little chambermaid at Braebourne? She never did let me steal more than a kiss."

Lawrence's eyes twinkled with clear recollection. "She let me steal two."

Leo shot him a fresh glare.

"Never say you weren't warned," Lawrence continued. "I told you the ex–Lady K would knock you down and kick you into a convenient corner. From now on, stick to more accessible, and appreciative, females."

Leo considered his twin's remark. "I do not believe I shall."

"*What?* But surely you've had enough."

"No," he said, his gut tightening with the knowledge that he wanted Thalia Lennox, now more than ever. She'd said they would never be intimate; he was going to prove her wrong.

"She may have eluded me tonight, but she will be mine," Leo promised. A smile curved his mouth slowly. "Let the games begin."

ALSO AVAILABLE FROM
NEW YORK TIMES BESTSELLING AUTHOR

Tracy Anne Warren

HER HIGHNESS AND
THE HIGHLANDER
A Princess Brides Romance

While journeying home from Scotland, Princess Mercedes
of Alden's coach is set upon and her personal guard killed.
Barely escaping, she finds protection with the dispossessed
Laird Daniel MacKinnon, who is home after years
of warfare.

At first she only needs his sword, and he her open purse.
But Mercedes's life is still threatened, and as the dangers
increase, so does the desire she and Daniel feel for each
other, until the two of them must face the greatest danger
of all—falling in love.

"Tracy Anne Warren is brilliant."
—*New York Times* bestselling author
Cathy Maxwell

Available wherever books are sold or at
penguin.com

facebook.com/LoveAlwaysBooks